D0191407

Also by
Caitlin Crews

A TRUE COWBOY CHRISTMAS

Cold Heart, Warm Cowboy

CAITLIN CREWS

St. Martin's Paperbacks

This is a work of fiction. All of the characters, organizations, and events portrayed in this novel are either products of the author's imagination or are used fictitiously.

First published in the United States by St. Martin's Paperbacks, an imprint of St. Martin's Publishing Group.

COLD HEART, WARM COWBOY

Copyright © 2019 by Caitlin Crews.

For information, address St. Martin's Publishing Group, 120 Broadway, New York, NY 10271.

www.stmartins.com

ISBN: 978-1-250-29525-5

Our books may be purchased in bulk for promotional, educational, or business use. Please contact your local bookseller or the Macmillan Corporate and Premium Sales Department at 1-800-221-7945, ext. 5442, or by e-mail at MacmillanSpecialMarkets@macmillan.com.

Printed in the United States of America

St. Martin's Paperbacks edition / August 2019

10 9 8 7 6 5 4 3 2 1

To Jane, who took me to Clovis, introduced me to bull riding, and made me wish I was a cowgirl.

Acknowledgments

Thanks to Monique Patterson, Mara Delgado-Sanchez, the wildly talented art department, and everyone else at St. Martin's for being part of the great team that makes these books happen!

My eternal gratitude to copy editor extraordinaire Christa Soulé Désir, who performs the rare magic of improving my sentences without ever taking away from my voice.

This was a wild ride of a book, and I couldn't have made it to the finish without the encouragement, kind words, all-caps reactions, and general enthusiasm of Nicole Helm, Maisey Yates, and Jane Porter.

None of this would be possible without my marvelous agent Holly Root, who I can never thank enough.

I also want to thank all the bull riders, rodeo queens, and everyone out there on the bull-riding and rodeo circuits for the many, many hours of entertainment.

And most of all, I thank you, wonderful reader, for letting me tell you a story. Happy reading!

1

Hannah Leigh Monroe—which wasn't her actual, legal married name because she didn't quite know if she was actually, legally married any longer—had been driving up and down the same county road in the Longhorn Valley outside of Cold River, Colorado, this pretty summer morning for going on two straight hours.

It had been easy enough to keep up her courage all the way from her tiny little hometown in rural Georgia, hurtling along the highways with Miranda Lambert turned up loud for support and inspiration. It had been easy to sing along and pretend the singing was the same as grit. Or the working backbone she wished she'd had more than a year and half ago, though that was spilled and spoiled milk. *Wishbones weren't backbones,* as her mother liked to say.

Hannah had opened her eyes this bright July morning in a roadside motel room, indistinguishable from any other, right down to the scratchy coverlet that left a rough pattern on her cheek. She'd woken up buzzing with that curious combination of stubbornness and bone-deep hurt that had been the bulk of her life for so long now, she was convinced she probably wore it all like jagged scars across her skin. Like that motel bedspread pattern on her face, only worse.

She wondered if the scars she wore these days—the ones the man she'd loved so much and so recklessly had put there over a handful of terrible March days almost eighteen months ago—would be visible to him when she found him. If he would notice them.

If he would care.

But then, if the rumors were true, there could be a reason for everything that had happened. A reason that wasn't simply that he'd never been the man she'd imagined he was. A reason that wasn't the unpleasant one she'd been living with since she'd last seen him—that men lied to get what they wanted and then threw it away when things got complicated, the way her mother had always warned her they did.

Maybe the last eighteen months were a mistake. And not what Hannah deserved for imagining she was different when she should have known better. Not what she'd brought upon herself for daring to imagine she could somehow outrun fate.

The rumors were why Hannah had gone looking for the husband who had discarded her so cruelly after all this time. Or more precisely, the ad campaigns she'd been unable to ignore or avoid in the rodeo magazines she should have canceled her subscriptions to, all breathlessly touting his one-night-only return to glory in the rodeo's bullriding ring. Plus, one throwaway comment about him that she'd let take over her mind. Until it was all she could think about.

Until she had to know for sure, one way or another.

Because stubbornness was an engine and righteous

indignation was its fuel, and Hannah had been running flat out on both for a good long while. She was pretty sure she could keep going like that forever. But hope . . . Hope was a killer.

Hope stopped her dead. Hope made her silly. Stupid. As foolish as she'd been from the start where one particular no-good man was concerned, no matter how she despaired of herself. No matter how she wished she could make herself immune.

There's no point hunting a man down and begging him to take what he doesn't want, her mother had said, her mouth tight and her gaze glittering hard, the way it did when she was talking as much about herself as to Hannah. *You know better than that.*

Hannah did know better. Mama had raised Hannah well aware of the lengths she'd personally gone to try to make Hannah's father accept his paternal role. This, after her own parents had tossed her out for getting knocked up before she graduated high school. But preppy Bradford Macon Collingsworth III hadn't wanted any part of Luanne Monroe or the mess he'd left behind him on his way to Duke. That mess being Hannah.

His slick, rich parents had paid off Luanne while relocating to their other house in Virginia. Everyone had washed their hands of "the situation," and Mama had raised Hannah herself. With her iron force of will, sheer determination, and the enduring kindness of her older sister, the only relative who would talk to her following her fall from grace. Hannah had nothing but fond memories about the back room she'd shared with Mama in Aunt Bit's house in sleepy, judgy Sweet Myrtle, Georgia.

Maybe someday Hannah would find it funny—or at

least ironic—how dedicated Luanne had been to making sure that Hannah didn't end up in the same situation. All those lectures about men and sex and how to avoid the pitfalls of each, until Hannah was half-convinced that so much as a sideways glance at the wrong boy could get her pregnant. She'd been so studious, so committed, and so determined not to end up like her mother. She'd been the town warning, and she'd made herself a rodeo queen.

Then she'd ended up right back where she'd started, as disgraced as her mama had been and then some. Because unlike Luanne, Hannah had actually made it out of Sweet Myrtle with a crown, a dream, and the grudging backing of all the locals who'd been so sure she was destined for a bad end. The fact she'd come back, crown tarnished and her reputation in shreds as her belly expanded, made it all worse.

It wasn't every girl who could go from rodeo queen to the punchline of a joke at the roaring speed of a single bad decision, but Hannah had always liked to distinguish herself. That bad decision's name was Ty Everett, bull rider and all around rodeo star, whose easy swagger and lazy, lopsided smile had made all the girls swoon for as long as he'd been on the tour.

Hannah had never dreamed she'd be one of those girls. She'd been certain she was too smart, too ambitious, too *her* to fall for a man like Ty.

How the mighty always fall, her mama had said, her arms crossed there in Aunt Bit's kitchen the night Hannah had come home for good, *especially when they think they have wings.*

Hannah no longer had anything like wings. These days, she counted herself lucky if she made it through to another bedtime. Wings were for other, smarter girls. Girls with shiny, gleaming futures that still belonged to them. Not Hannah, who had traded hers in for an adorable, red-faced tyrant of a baby boy who she hadn't meant to have on her own, but loved beyond reason, no matter the circumstances of his birth.

And she had driven all this way, up into the towering Rockies and out to the ranch that had been in his family forever, to tell Ty the truths he hadn't wanted to hear the last time she'd seen him. To see what he had to say for himself now that a good chunk of time had passed since the brutal fall that had put him out of commission for so long—and had broken her heart in the bargain. Though maybe the chronology wasn't quite so cut and dried. He'd already crushed her heart into pieces before that bull had done the same to him.

Either way, Hannah was here to untangle herself once and for all from the cowboy who had brought so much misery into her life.

Don't forget the joy, something in her piped up, right on cue. The way it always did.

Because there was always that *thing* in her that wanted to defend him. From herself, if necessary. Even after he'd proved beyond a shadow of a doubt that the man she'd fallen in love with had been a figment of her imagination right from the start. That she should never have trusted him. That she should have listened to her mama and her own intuition and steered clear.

The trouble was, all her stubbornness and righteous indignation had drained right out of her when she'd driven into the town of Cold River where—or so Ty had said back when she'd believed in him and had hoarded every detail he'd shared about himself like treasure—his family had lived since the pioneer days. She'd wound her way through the beautiful mountains from Aspen, carpeted in deep summer green and exuberant wildflowers. She'd had to order herself not to gasp and sigh as one spectacular view outdid the one before it. She'd come in on a meandering road from the south, following the narrow two-lane highway that cut through impressive rock faces, circled around soaring mountain peaks, and eventually deposited her in a perfect postcard of a western town.

There was a gleaming river, blue in the sunlight. Sturdy brick buildings stood proud on both sides of a tidy Main Street with flower boxes in the shop windows and lampposts hung with baskets of more bright, cheerful blooms. Cold River didn't look real. It looked like an Old West daydream Hannah hadn't realized she'd been longing for all her life.

She wanted to cry, but decided what she needed was a decent cup of coffee. It was clearly the lack of caffeine that was making her feel hollowed out and raw, nothing else. She drove past a diner packed full of hardy-looking working men hunched over huge platters of food, but parked her pickup outside an old western brick building with a sign that read Cold River Coffeehouse in fancy lettering.

She was dawdling. Because it was one thing to leap into a car and charge off to right wrongs, on fire with all the slights and injuries she'd been nursing. It was something else entirely to be *here*. In the town where Ty had grown up.

She could step through the coffee shop door and see him, right there in front of her, kicked back at a table without a care in the world. The possibility that she might made her chest hurt. It made her cheeks start to burn and sent her stomach into knots.

She honestly didn't know if that was her temper, her enduring pain and heartbreak—or something far more shameful. Like anticipation.

As if he'd never abandoned her in the first place.

Hating herself hadn't done a single thing so far except make things worse, but Hannah didn't let that stop her as she pushed the coffee shop door open—maybe a little aggressively, she could admit—and looked around as if she expected Ty Everett to materialize right there in front of her.

He didn't.

A quick glance proved he wasn't one of the men in cowboy hats lounging at the tables or waiting in line at the counter.

She assured herself she was thankful for that small mercy. Not the least bit let down or deflated.

Cold River Coffee was cozy and inviting, with distressed brick walls and battered wood floors. There was a fireplace on one wall and an old bookcase stuffed full with paperbacks, fat and bright and beckoning. There were cozy-looking leather couches tossed here and there, like a home away from home. Hannah bought a dramatic coffee drink, then picked a table near the door, wishing she had the time—or the life—to sink into an oversize couch and daydream the day away.

But she'd squandered her right to daydreams on a lazy smile. She didn't get to indulge in them any longer. That was what her mother had told her, there by her bedside in the hospital when they'd placed newborn, squalling Jack in Hannah's arms.

Your life is over, Mama had intoned, dark and dire, one hand on Jack's back and her eyes boring into Hannah's after ten hours of labor. *This is* his *life now.*

Because that was how Luanne Monroe greeted the birth of her first and likely only grandchild. An endless grim march of painful sacrifice. That Hannah knew that was how Luanne expressed love didn't make it any better.

I appreciate the pep talk, Mama, Hannah had muttered. *That should really help me figure out how to get a good latch.*

Hannah had taken her point. And she was in Colorado now to clean up her messy life, not dream it away. She drank her coffee, enjoying the punch of sugar and caffeine more than she should have, given the price. Meanwhile, all around her, people who lived in this place and very likely knew Ty Everett carried on with their lives. Their conversations and laughter washed over her, while the pretty woman making the drinks delivered each order with a ready smile and a quiet efficiency, as if she were in no way uncomfortable with her big, pregnant belly.

Hannah sat there longer than she should have, conjuring up happy-ever-afters for the smiling, pregnant woman, because somebody deserved them. Hannah would have liked one herself.

When she was finished, and could reasonably delay it no longer, she took herself outside again. She climbed back into her pickup, punched the name of the Everett family ranch into her phone's GPS—another one of the eight million details about Ty she'd filed away and couldn't make herself forget, no matter how she tried—and did what she'd come all this way to do.

She'd driven out of downtown Cold River, which was

nothing but another small town, no different from any other aside from its spectacular mountain setting. It wasn't a postcard. It wasn't a daydream. It was in no way magical, no matter all the dizzy summer sunshine spilling over the mountains as she drove. She followed a different road over yet another impressive mountain with even better views stretching out toward forever, then down into a wide valley that was all rolling fields with adorable farmhouses tucked between them.

Until she reached that blunt, matter-of-fact sign at the end of a dirt road that read COLD RIVER RANCH that she'd already driven past more times than she could count.

Back and forth. Back and forth. Because maybe Hannah didn't want the answers she would find here. Or not find here. Maybe she didn't want to know if it was really, truly as over as it had seemed in that hospital room in Kentucky.

You need to know what you want out of this, Mama had told her when she'd announced what she wanted to do. Where she wanted to go. *And what you plan to do if you don't get it.*

But that had been the trouble all along, hadn't it? Hannah didn't know what she wanted. An explanation, if possible. A different ending to their story, whatever that looked like. Everything and nothing.

You already know he lies to your face, her mother had said. *A wise woman wouldn't give him another opportunity.*

Luckily, Hannah had never pretended to be wise.

She cranked up the music in the pickup, wishing she felt half as dangerous as a Miranda Lambert song, and turned onto that dirt road at last. She bumped along as it cut its way into the land, her windows rolled down to let in the sweet summer air.

After a while, she found the sprawling ranch house at the end of the dirt road. It was timber and glass, built big and rambling to hold its place against the mountains all around, and its different parts cobbled together suggested the sweep of history. Yet for all that it was big and old, it struck her as unpretentious. The outbuildings were tidy and looked practical. There were cottonwoods everywhere, horses in the corral, and a bright, leafy vegetable garden to the side of the house on a bit of grass beneath lofty maple trees.

Her throat was so dry, it hurt. And the knots in her stomach were so tight, she was afraid they'd never come out.

She pulled up in the yard outside the ranch house and forced herself to open the truck's door when really, she wanted to spin around and drive back to Georgia. Right now.

"Breathe," she ordered herself.

Hannah had once been known for her calm under pressure. She could remember that version of herself from not so long ago, young and heedless. And so reckless because she hadn't known then how much there was to lose.

She wasn't the least bit calm today, but it didn't matter if her heart was kicking at her or her palms felt damp, as long as it didn't show. And it shouldn't. Hannah had taken care with her appearance today of all days. She'd treated it like a competition. And she'd always been good at those.

Her cowboy boots hit the dirt. She slammed the pickup door shut behind her and ran her hands over hips that were wider than she'd like, now. But no matter the size, she knew how to wear a pair of jeans and a pretty western shirt as neat and sparkly as her blond hair was hairsprayed into place.

Perfect curls and waterproof mascara and Hannah was good to go.

She rounded the back of the pickup truck and stood there for a moment, trying to breathe. Trying not to bend in half because her belly was so knotted up. Trying to access that part of her that had loved queening so much. Nailing her interview, barrel racing, and then riding whatever new horse she was assigned to at each local rodeo, learning their personalities and habits on the fly. The part of her that had even loved falling right if she were going to fall, so she could get up with an even bigger smile on her face to win over the crowds.

It was all about the smile. And she fixed hers on her face like the armor it was as she looked around.

Cold River Ranch spread out on all sides, as pretty as it was vast. She found herself moving toward the barn and the paddock where a pair of horses watched, their clever gazes and quiet muttering making her feel lighter than she had in a long while. Because she recognized these horses. She'd gotten to know them on the sly as she and Ty had toured the country together. Together, but always in secret—like everything else. Hannah moved to the fence and stood there a minute, murmuring nonsense words as she stroked her palms down familiar silken muzzles, breathing in the rich scent of earth and these horses who were part of the life she'd left behind.

It was worth it. Jack was worth it.

But that didn't mean she didn't miss what she'd lost.

After a while, the heaviness in her chest shifted a bit and turned into something less raw and more . . . nostalgic.

Eventually she turned around again, because she wasn't here for the horses. That Ty's horses were here meant she'd been right to come. He was here. Or he'd been here. But hard as she looked, there didn't appear to be a soul around the place or any sign of activity. Not in the big house and not in the collection of outbuildings dotted around this part of the property.

Hannah hadn't really thought past getting here.

She blew out a breath, shakier than she'd like.

And that was when she saw him.

He came out through the screen door of one of the buildings set back from the barn and started toward her, all slow swagger and summer heat.

It was like the first time. It was like every time. All Ty Everett ever needed to do was laze his way onto the scene, and her heart stopped. The world stopped.

And this time, the punch of it—of him, even from a distance—nearly took Hannah to her knees.

Hannah had imagined this moment over and over. She'd plotted. Prayed and planned, then prayed some more. She'd revised what she would say time and time again. She'd cried. Lord help her, how she'd cried, until her pillows were damp and her cheeks hurt and her eyes felt welded shut.

Her eyes were wide open today. Up above, the sky was blue and the sun was warm, dancing on the breeze that smelled rich like livestock and sweet like the mountains in the distance. The last time she'd seen this man he'd been a dark, wounded fury strapped to a hospital bed. Tubes and bandages and beeping machines and that terrible blankness when he'd stared straight at her.

When he'd told her to leave and never come back.

Though not that nicely.

Today, he stood upright. And she couldn't keep herself from letting her gaze move all over him, looking for remnants of that hospital room. Looking for signs that he really had survived what that angry bull had done to him. That he was somehow in one piece.

And was actually planning to get back up on that same ornery bull next month and do it all over again.

He's walking, she snapped at herself. *And he's clearly still ambitious. He's fine.*

Fine enough to man up to his responsibilities if he'd wanted to. If he knew he had responsibilities, that was.

She expected him to say her name, which would have been its own torture, but he didn't. He kept coming toward her.

His hair was dark and thick beneath his cowboy hat, his gaze that same guarded, mysterious dark green. He was tall, especially for a man who'd made his living riding bucking creatures that wanted him off. He looked lanky and careless, but she knew that he was all sinew and grace, hardpacked muscle and astonishing control, especially when he seemed the laziest.

He walked toward her like he'd always been heading for the same fence, and everything about him screamed *languid*. Slow and unhurried in his Wranglers and boots, when the truth of him was a seething, earthy intensity. Darker and infinitely more dangerous than he pretended.

Her treacherous heart kicked at her, and worse still, her body shivered into that same, alarming awareness that had gotten her into all this trouble in the first place.

Hannah couldn't speak. She felt frozen solid. Trapped out here in this yard with the horses looking on, staring down her past.

Ty appeared to have no such trouble.

He came to a stop when he was still a few feet away from her. The corner of his mouth kicked up as if he was about to drawl something at her. In that way he did, with that voice she remembered too well sounded like whiskey and a long, hard night, no matter what time of day it was. Rough like velvet, bright with sin, and the memory of his voice in her ear made her shudder, deep inside.

And she hated herself for that too.

But there was only one reason she'd come all the way here to put herself through this. Jack. And that snapped her out from under his spell—

Well. It reminded her what happened when that spell wore off, anyway. And how he'd left her, broken and ashamed, when he was done.

She waited for him to speak, but he didn't. He shifted, an arrested expression playing over a face that was almost too beautiful, save for that decidedly masculine jaw that he often—like today—didn't bother to shave.

He was looking at her as if he'd seen a ghost.

Hannah would very much like to haunt him. Poltergeist his butt and leave him screaming for mercy. For starters.

"Hello, Ty," she said, because the sudden spike of fury loosened her tongue once again. And it was much better than that raw ache. "It's been a long time."

He shook his head as if he couldn't quite make sense of this. Of her. Or of the way his favorite horses acted like they recognized her when he looked very much as if he didn't.

"You know me," he said, and then his head tilted to one side, his dark green gaze warier than before. "And my horses, apparently."

"Don't worry if you can't return the favor," she drawled, long and loose, because Hannah was a Georgia girl and she'd never met a vowel she couldn't make into its own alphabet. Or two. Especially when she wanted to cry. "The last time you saw me, you were sure you'd never laid eyes on me before in all your life."

"That doesn't sound like me." He was smiling again, that easy, public smile of his that was as empty as he'd turned out to be. Hannah had never hit another person in her life, but she wanted to punch him. "I've never met a pretty girl I didn't *want* to recognize."

"I'm flattered." She wasn't. "You finding me pretty is quite an upgrade. Last time you were convinced I was a lunatic."

She might have been frozen in place, but he wasn't. He ambled in her direction, and Hannah remembered too well the particular grace of his saunter. The way he'd gotten up from each and every fall except that last one and walked out of the ring under his own power. She hadn't expected she'd ever see it again.

He favored his left leg. It had been over a year now, and all that was left of that fall of his was the suggestion of a limp that he'd turned into more of the same saunter that had always defined him. Devil may care, laid-back, and like everything about Ty Everett, a lie.

He stopped a foot or so in front of her and tucked his thumbs into the pockets of his jeans.

This close, his dark green gaze was . . . careful. So was his expression, but what she really noticed was that beautiful jaw of his, because she could still remember what it was like to wake up with him and press kisses there, both of them smiling in a way she hadn't before or since.

"Did you come and see me after that bull finished with me?" he asked.

"Don't you remember?"

Hannah held her breath. And she studied him while she waited for his answer.

Over and over on the long drive across the country, she'd told herself that she would be able to read the truth on him. That this time, armed with the rumor she'd heard from one of her overly chatty former friends and no longer hopped up on pregnancy hormones, she would know what to look for.

She saw a blankness in his gaze, followed by something sharper. And the way he smiled in the next instant, as if he wanted to cover it up.

"I don't know a man alive who dares have too good a memory, darlin'. That's asking for trouble."

"That's real folksy, Ty. I see you're putting your charm to good use. But I want to know. Can you remember me or not?"

"You're breaking my heart," he said, and that smile of his was brighter than before. Lazier, if possible.

Empty, she reminded herself.

On the list of ways she'd betrayed herself with this man, she would add this. That even when he was putting on an act, it didn't matter. She could still feel that heat and wonder inside of her. There was the hurt, the anger, and the grief, but she couldn't deny that beneath it all, she still melted.

Like she was nothing but a country song, some done-wrong woman who didn't have enough sense to pick herself up, brush herself off, and find herself a better man. Or live out her life the way her mother had, pointedly and defiantly and on her own.

Hannah was a terrible cliché. She was her mother's worst nightmare come true. She was everything she had been raised to reject.

None of that changed the fact that Ty Everett's patented, practiced grin danced around inside her like summer, encouraging her to forget every single thing he'd done to her. And not only to her.

That sobered her, instantly.

"Funny," she said, and she didn't bother to smile this time. "I would have sworn you didn't have a heart."

"That sounds perilously close to bitter." Ty shook his head. "And if I caused it, I'm truly sorry. If it makes you feel any better, I'm a changed man."

"Changed into what?"

"I used to be a rodeo cowboy. Now I'm a ranch hand."

"A ranch hand." Hannah sighed. "You mean, a ranch hand who's going to jump back up on the bull that wrecked him. In a matter of weeks, right here at the rodeo in the great state of Colorado. That kind of ranch hand? The kind who isn't really a ranch hand at all?"

His eyes flashed. "The backbreaking work feels about the same."

"From where I'm standing, your back looks fine." She looked around the empty yard. "It's the middle of the afternoon. Shouldn't you be out somewhere? Breaking that back?"

"I'm sorry I can't help you," Ty said, as if she'd asked

him to. As if she'd arrived with a list of demands and a
court order, the way she could have. "But if I were you,
I'd climb back up into that pickup and drive on out of here
before I'm tempted to lose my grip on my gentlemanly
manners."

Hannah laughed. "Wow. That bull really did stomp the
sense right out of you. I'm not afraid of your temper, Ty.
I've already survived it, haven't I? At least it's real."

He stiffened, though he didn't lose that grin. "I don't
know what you're talking about."

"All this time, I thought you sent me away. Me, personally. But you didn't, did you? You don't remember me at
all, do you?"

Ty didn't move, but he . . . changed. One moment he
was standing there, that lazy grin on his face and that suggestion that his actual spine might be made of molasses,
and the next . . . this.

The truth of him, electric and vivid. A storm about
to break, hectic enough to put her hair on end, and that
gleaming intensity in his gaze.

She remembered this too. She remembered him all too
well.

"What I remember or don't remember is no concern of
yours," he said, and there was no laziness in his voice anymore either.

A whole lot like she'd done more than simply state the
truth. More like she'd hit a nerve.

Oh, you know Ty, Laura, another former rodeo queen
contestant, had said when she'd visited last week. She'd sat
there on Aunt Bit's wide front porch, her untouched glass
of sweet tea sweating on the side table. Laura been the one
to bring up all those glossy ads heralding Ty's "rematch"

with the bull that had thrown him, like it was a heavy-weight boxing fight instead of a professional rodeo event. Hannah had pretended she hadn't seen them. And Laura had smiled the way she always had at the rodeo, all teeth and the slightest hint of malice. *More ego than sense. Could he ever resist an ad campaign? I swear, that bull must've stomped the memory straight out of him.*

Hannah had laughed along. But after the other girl had left in a cloud of hairspray and bad intentions, she couldn't stop thinking about Ty and his memory. With that same mix of hope and fury that had been her constant companion over the last year.

Because Hannah had looked up that fateful day in a dusty ring in Bozeman, Montana, and there he'd been, staring right back at her with that curve to his mouth and a gleam in his gaze she'd felt everywhere.

Nothing had been the same since.

She wanted to throw it all in his face. The way he'd worked his way through her resistance, slow and steady. Their secret wedding. Her unexpected pregnancy. Her sweet, perfect Jack, who'd never met his daddy.

She didn't know why she didn't. Why she stood there face-to-face with Ty at last and *didn't* move in for the kill, the way she'd dreamed all this time.

Almost as if she wanted to protect him too, despite everything. When she should have wanted to kill him. When she *did* want to kill him—but not if it would hurt him.

You're pathetic, she told herself. But that wasn't exactly news.

"I don't know how to break this to you, *darlin'*," she drawled instead. "But you and I are complicated, whether you remember it or not."

2

Ty Everett wasn't afraid of curvy blondes packed into denim with blue eyes like weapons. He wasn't afraid of "complicated."

He wasn't afraid of anything, as he planned to prove next month when he returned to the rodeo, dominated, and went out on top. Instead of on a stretcher.

He was fine.

Fine.

And so what if he'd spent more time than he'd like this past year dealing with things he couldn't quite remember? He'd learned, through careful reconstruction and entirely too much time spent googling himself, that he'd been on the rodeo circuit during the time he couldn't remember. He'd watched himself in hundreds of videos roping, wrestling, riding bulls and broncs, winning more than his share of prizes, and occasionally ending up facedown in the dirt too.

There was even footage of the fall almost eighteen months ago that had changed everything. Entirely too much footage, given it was his body getting trampled on-screen. And from every wince-inducing angle.

Ty was perfectly happy to continue not remembering *that*.

Especially when it didn't matter what he remembered, because next month he was going flip the story of his career-ending fall on its head. And own it.

"I'm not all that worried about 'complicated,'" he told the blonde before him, who looked wholly unimpressed with him. Not a reaction he often got. It made him . . . restless. "Even if it does come in the form of Western Barbie."

"'Western Barbie'?" she repeated, and that sweet-as-peaches drawl of hers couldn't disguise the snap in her voice. Or how her hands found her hips, drawing his attention to the way her shirt stretched over her curves. "Is that supposed to be me?"

"All that blond hair. And that sweet—"

Ty checked himself. He hadn't felt the slightest need to flirt with anyone since he'd come back to town, angry and bitter, for the funeral of a father he would have happily raised up from the dead—so he could give Amos Everett the fight the bitter old man had always been spoiling for. And no matter how many nights Ty had warmed a stool at the more disreputable of the two bars in town, he'd never gone home with anyone. He'd never even made some time in the parking lot. Come to think of it, he couldn't recall the last time he'd allowed himself so much as an eyeful of a woman.

Then this one turned up out of nowhere, talking about his memory. And he turned into . . . someone else.

"—pair of cowboy boots," he finished.

Her blue eyes glinted. "Because you really appreciate a fine pair. Of cowboy boots."

He grinned, because he was good at that. But she unsettled him.

He'd come in after a long morning playing rancher out in the fields, because his bad leg hadn't been behaving and he had a long afternoon ahead of him. Buck Stapleton, the president of the Rodeo Forever Association, had decided to make Ty a main event again and didn't care which way it went, but Ty had every intention of riding the bull that had trashed him again for all eight seconds and a high score. This time, he planned to leave the ring and the rodeo on his own feet and his own terms. He'd iced his leg, alternated the ice with heat, and had been contemplating cutting it off for approximately the nine hundredth time that week when he'd heard a truck pull up outside.

Ty wasn't exactly the Everett family welcome wagon, so he'd ignored it. Neighbors tended to drop off whatever it was they had, then leave. Smaller ranch deliveries were usually the same deal. Bigger ranch deliveries weren't random, and Ty was never left to handle those on his own.

But when he glanced out the window of the small bunkhouse he'd claimed when he'd decided to stay on the ranch, he'd seen a woman he didn't recognize standing over by the barn. Making time with his horses.

He still didn't know why he'd gone outside. One of his brothers would turn up, the way one of them always did. Responsible eldest son Gray had been in charge of the ranch most of his life, in and around Amos and his drunken benders. And Brady, the youngest of the three of them, had committed himself to the ranch for the time being and was always overplaying his helpfulness. Likely so that when the year he'd promised Gray was up and a discussion about selling the ranch was back on the table, Brady could remind their older brother that he'd really given this his all.

Gray's wife, Abby, was usually around to deal with the domestic side of ranch life when Gray was out in the fields. Or Gray's daughter, Becca, who was sixteen and often seemed to be competing with her father for the title of Most Responsible Everett Ever.

Whoever the blonde with rodeo curls was, it wasn't any of his business.

But the next thing he knew, Ty was out the door and walking toward her anyway.

There was something about this particular blonde. There was something about the way she stood there, watching him approach. There was tension all over her body and her chin was tipped up like she was bracing herself.

And looking at her made him feel haunted.

But as far as Ty was aware, the only thing haunting him these days was himself.

He grinned wider, because that was easier than worrying about ghosts that tried to come at him in broad daylight. "Seems to me if you're going to stand out here and claim there's some complication we ought to discuss, you owe me your name."

She let out a laugh that struck him as a little too harsh. A little too dark. And no matter that she smiled when she was done.

"Yes, let's absolutely talk about what it is you think I owe you."

"My name is Ty Henry Everett." Though he figured she knew that already. "Fun fact. Ty isn't short for anything. No Tyson. No Tyler. No Titus. Just straight up Ty."

"Congratulations." The word was like a slap. "You were clearly born to be a cowboy."

Ty figured he was missing about two solid years of his

life. There were gaps here and there before that, and what he did remember was curiously absent any feeling one way or another, but those two years were gone. When he'd woken up in the hospital and had dragged himself out of the confusion, the pain, and those loopy painkillers, he'd decided no one needed to know that he was missing time.

The doctors told him there was no medical reason he couldn't remember those years. That sometimes the mind blocked out things it couldn't handle. Ty had braced himself, waiting to discover what it was he couldn't handle. But as the months passed, he'd begun to believe that there was nothing lurking in those years. Nothing but a bad fall, a long recovery, and the unpleasant parts of his life that he only *wished* he could forget. Like his father.

Until this moment, he would have said that he'd never given any woman reason to stare at him with hostility simmering all over her.

"I'm Hannah," she said after an unduly long while. A lot like she didn't want him to know her name. And when she shifted, it drew his attention to the curve of her hip.

He had the strongest urge to wrap his arm around her and pull her close, and not only because he liked all her curves—*no.*

You can't touch her, something inside him said. *Not where someone could see.*

He blinked at that pop of weirdness and eased himself back on his heels.

"Hannah," he repeated. His grin felt forced. "If that's supposed to ring a bell, I hate to break it to you. But it doesn't."

"How convenient."

"You think I should recognize you, clearly. Want to tell me why?"

It wasn't that he didn't *want* to claim he knew her. He did. She was pretty in that extra-feminine way he could admit he liked. More than liked. Brady had been ranting about the appeal of *natural beauty* over too many beers earlier in the summer, and Ty had nodded sagely while drinking along, but he was a rodeo cowboy down into his bones. He liked big hair, too much eye makeup, and big, sugary smiles. Rhinestones everywhere and athletic thighs that could grip a horse and make a man cry tears of joy.

Hannah had all of that going on and more. He suspected she was well aware of it. Just as he suspected she wouldn't appreciate it much if he mentioned it.

"Here's what I'd really like to know," she said, and she might have been smiling, but the look in her eyes was flinty. "If you *can't* remember me or you don't *want* to remember me. Because they're not the same thing."

He didn't know why he didn't open his mouth and tell her the truth. Maybe she could fill in those missing years. But he didn't do it.

He hadn't told his brothers. Or anyone at all, except the doctor in the hospital in deep, dark Kentucky where he'd recovered from his injuries and spent long, frustrating months doing physical therapy.

It wasn't like he was hiding what had happened to him, Ty reasoned. Anyone who looked at him could see his scars and his limp. And when people told stories he was expected to know already, he played along. Most times, all he had to do was grin and wait, and they filled in the blanks for him.

He'd spent his first couple of months back in Colorado as drunk as it was possible to get and remain upright. Or occasionally not so upright, but he'd contained that to the privacy of his cabin. Because whiskey filled the gaps. It gave him something to do. It provided order to his days: wake up with a killer hangover, tend to it, throw down a little hair of the dog, and start all over again. The best part of being drunk was that he couldn't tell the difference between what he couldn't remember and what he didn't want to face.

But come the new year, that had changed. Buck from the rodeo had called to float an idea past him. Assuming he was up to the physical challenge, would Ty—always a big fan favorite—like to make a limited comeback? Would he like to take another ride on the bull that had broken him and, fingers crossed, walk away this time?

Sign me up, he'd said.

Immediately.

Which meant it had been time to put down the whiskey bottle and get himself back in shape, so that was what Ty had done. Day after bitterly cold winter day, straight on into spring. By the time the year anniversary of his accident rolled around, Ty was starting to recognize himself in his mirror again. More scarred and weaker than he liked, but the same tough and capable rodeo cowboy he remembered. If slightly more gimpy.

Neither of his brothers appeared to notice his transformation. Out here on Cold River Ranch, the four hundred-plus acres his forebears had hacked out of the unforgiving Colorado Rockies and claimed as their own, Everetts ran cattle and tended the land they'd claimed, one tough winter after the next. Everetts also tended to drink themselves dark and mean when the mood took them, but it didn't matter what nonsense a man spouted from the depths of a bottle when he still had to wake up before dawn to tend to the family legacy. The ranch was what mattered. As long as Ty showed up to do his part of the work and otherwise kept a low profile—meaning, didn't flip tables and start fights like their late, unlamented father—his brothers left him to do his thing.

Ty told himself he liked it, but he sometimes had the notion that if there really was a ghost flitting around, it wasn't one of his ancestors. It was him.

Maybe that was why this woman was getting to him.

She was looking at him as if she could see straight through him. As if she knew him, inside and out. Not his name, or the popular story concerning Ty Everett, rodeo star—but the real truth about him.

That no matter what Ty saw in his mirror, there was nothing there.

"Am I supposed to guess at this complication of yours?" he asked her, his voice low and gritty, but he didn't do a thing to remedy it. "It's always the same thing when a pretty girl turns up, isn't it?"

"Does this happen to you a lot?"

There was a warning in the way she asked that, but he was too busy giving in to a foolhardy, suicidal urge inside of him to take notice of it the way he probably should have.

He stepped closer. And compounded that grave error by reaching over and cupping his hand over the curve of her cheek. His hand knew exactly where it was going. And knew it would fit. And Ty had the clear notion he *needed* to touch her when that didn't make any sense.

Because touching her was a mistake.

A big mistake.

It was like a bolt of lightning, searing and terrifying at once. Ty wanted to jerk his hand away like he would have if he'd accidentally slapped it down on the wood stove in his cabin—but he didn't want her to know she got to him. He didn't want her to see any more than she already did.

"It's always about sex," he said, his voice too gruff. Too dark. "You either want to complain about it or you want more. Which is it?"

He'd miscalculated. Badly. He should have stuck to grinning like a fool. He shouldn't have put his hand on her.

She was too soft, for one thing. But that wasn't the worst of it. Her skin was so warm that he felt like she was *filling him* with her heat. When all he was doing was touching her face.

He hadn't even realized until now how cold and empty he really was inside.

His heart skipped a beat in his chest. His ribs felt too tight. And that voice deep in his head kept saying: *No. You can't touch* her. *Not here.*

When he was pretty sure he'd do almost anything to keep his hand right where it was.

"Let me make sure I'm understanding you." Hannah was smiling, but he was close enough to see the murder in her pretty blue eyes. "This is something that happens to you. All the time. Your discarded sexual partners turn up here on the ranch for . . . What? A fight? A round or two of making up?"

"You tell me."

"I'm not marching along in your tawdry romantic parade, Ty," she said, and he could have sworn there was something else in her voice then. Some kind of pain that thickened it.

She reached her hand up to his, and for a moment—the slightest, scant moment—covered his hand with hers.

But in the next second, she pushed him away.

"If you can't remember me, that's fine," she said, though her eyes were suspiciously bright. It made his ribs ache. "I only want to know if it's because I'm that unmemorable, which says more about you than me, or if it might be a medical condition."

How did she know to ask him that?

"Does it make a difference?"

"Of course it makes a difference. One makes you an amnesiac. The other makes you a garden-variety ass."

If she'd wrapped her hands around his throat and squeezed tight, Ty couldn't have been more surprised. Something swelled in him, a dark and terrible wave, and he wasn't sure he could keep his feet beneath him while it crested over him.

But he blinked that away. Because he could hear his brother's truck in the distance.

An ill-timed interruption—or his salvation. He couldn't tell which.

"My brother Gray is coming in from the fields for lunch," he heard himself say, as if from far up on one of the watching, waiting mountains. As if he was as distant as the far-off peaks. That removed. "You're welcome to hang around and exchange cryptic remarks with him. It's one of his favorite things to do. Does that sound like fun?"

"The only one having fun is you."

That hit him like a blow, and it shouldn't have. Because he didn't know her. He didn't *want* to know her. If he'd gone to all the trouble of closing off all those doors inside him, he was sure he had a reason.

He was positive there had to be a good reason.

"What do you want from me, Hannah?"

She looked away then. "What I want isn't going to be served up with lunch in a ranch kitchen."

"Your call."

He didn't know what that thing inside him was then, clawing and harsh. He only knew that there wasn't a single part of him that wanted to let her walk away. And that shocked him most of all.

He didn't want anyone. He didn't need anything, except another shot at that bull.

"Where are you staying?" he heard himself ask gruffly. "In town?"

She didn't say yes or no. She only turned back, fixing that steady blue look of hers on him again.

And Ty didn't know if he wanted to cup her face in his hands, then tilt her mouth to meet his—or if he remembered doing it. He couldn't tell the difference.

"Meet me tonight," he urged her, because he was a stranger to himself anyway, and nothing he did made sense. He'd never wanted to drown himself in a bottle of whiskey more. "At the Broken Wheel. It's a bar."

"You want to meet me in a bar?"

He didn't understand that note in her voice, then. It was almost . . . Weary. Resigned, maybe. "Why not a bar?"

"A bar sounds great," she replied, and that wasn't the right answer. Or it wasn't true, anyway.

But Gray's truck was drawing closer and Ty felt a certainty deep in his gut that he needed to keep this woman away from his older brother. From his entire family. From everyone and everything on this ranch, because they not only didn't know he couldn't remember years of his life, he still hadn't exactly gotten around to telling them he planned to take a break from the ranch next month to redeem himself.

He didn't think Gray would be all that into Ty's redemption tour. And he *knew* Gray couldn't be around Hannah, in a way he'd known very little since he'd woken up to the exciting news that a two-thousand-pound bull named Tough Luck had vented its considerable spleen all over him, ending his life as he'd known it, whether he remembered every detail of that life or not.

"Eight o'clock," he said.

Hannah swallowed, but then her eyes narrowed before he was tempted to imagine that had been a flash of vulnerability on her part. "Because I have nothing better to do than hang around in bars, waiting for cowboys who think I'm after them for sexcapades."

"If you have anything better to do than that, Hannah, I truly feel sorry for you."

Her gaze was much too blue. But she didn't throw any kind of clever retort back at him, and he felt something unpleasant and familiar turn over inside him. Shame.

She turned away then, swift and sure like she was used to walking away from him. He couldn't say he liked that notion. Or the fact he couldn't manage to keep his eyes off of her as she headed toward the driver's side of her pickup. A lot like he was used to watching her walk away.

This was all wrong.

But Ty had to stand there, unsettled straight through, as she climbed in the pickup, turned it around, and drove away.

He was still standing there when his older brother pulled up from his morning in the upper fields.

Gray unfolded himself from his truck, frowning back

toward the road where Hannah had driven away in a cloud of summer dust. "Georgia plates? Who was that?"

Ty shrugged. "A tourist who got lost," he lied. With such ease it gave him pause. Because surely it shouldn't have been *quite* so easy to lie to his own brother, and no matter if it was Gray. Grave, certain Gray, who often seemed indistinguishable from the mountains that had loomed over the land Ty's entire life. That enduring. That annoying. Gray, who had always known his place was right here. Gray, who had never bothered to fight their father when he could tend to the land instead.

Of course, Ty had been lying to his brother since he'd come back. He usually did it by omission.

Gray slammed his truck door shut, that relentlessly stern gaze of his moving over Ty the way it always did. Ty didn't even know what he was looking for. Evidence of intoxication? Proof that Ty was as useless here as Amos had always claimed he was? Maybe he was looking for something Ty couldn't remember, and therefore couldn't ask about without showing how little he knew. Or did Gray know more about what was going on with Ty than he let on?

Gray nodded toward Ty's left side. "Your leg okay?"

"I'm fine," Ty said gruffly. *Perfectly fine.*

"Glad to hear it. You planning to work this afternoon?"

"I'm always *planning* to work," Ty said with a grin, the way he usually did.

Gray studied him for another tense moment.

Possibly only Ty was tense. He couldn't tell anymore if there was *stuff* in these silences, or if his guilty conscience put it there.

"Abby left us lunch," Gray said after a moment, and started toward the house. "Come eat something."

Ty didn't know why the slightest expression of kindness from his brother—or, really, anyone at all, including his new sister-in-law Abby who acted like she *wanted* to cook for Gray's surly brothers—hit him like this. It made him feel . . . raw. Open in ways he knew, in the strange, out-of-body way that he knew anything these days, was no good. Not for him.

But there was nothing he could do about it unless he wanted to have a conversation about all the things he didn't remember, didn't understand, and didn't want to learn. Not to mention the plans he'd made for next month when he'd promised Gray the ranch would have his full focus for a year.

Gray wouldn't understand because he couldn't understand. Gray was a part of this ranch, always had been. He had those Everett roots that sank down deep into this soil and anchored him here. Ty was like their mother in more than the looks his father had sneered at and called *much too pretty for a man.* Bettina had gotten out of Colorado; she hadn't looked back, and she'd been floating around out there ever since. No connections. No generations of land, land, and more land. Bettina did as she liked, rootless and easy.

Some people weren't meant to stay put. It was as simple as that.

Ty was giving the ranch thing a year because he'd promised. But a promise wasn't roots. And unlike his older brother, this land had never wanted anything to do with him. As far as he could tell, it still didn't.

He tried to shove the mysterious Hannah out of his head as he dutifully followed Gray into the kitchen of the ranch house.

Home, something in him said, but that, too, didn't land.

Because home was one more thing Ty couldn't quite remember.

3

One of the indignities about getting older, Ty thought as he pushed his way through the doors of the Broken Wheel Saloon before eight that evening, was that the hometown bar he'd tried so hard to talk his way into when he'd been underage didn't bother to card him anymore. Or even inquire.

Not only that, but the supposed den of iniquity right there on Main Street served tasty burgers and truffle fries, not exactly sin and vice on a toasted bun. There was live music from local bands on the weekends, not fistfights and intrigue. And the saloon itself, with its rough-hewn walls covered in old pictures of Cold River when it had been little more than a pioneer outpost inhabited by Ty's far-hardier ancestors, was significantly friendlier and more family-oriented than it had been in his imagination when he was eighteen and certain he was a man grown.

He lifted his chin in the direction of the usual familiar faces as he walked inside. The Kittredge boys—who would be called boys until the day they died, and were certainly not *boys* now as they were mostly in their thirties, same as Ty—sat around one of the scratched and scarred wood tables with a few beers and some friends. He and Jensen Kittredge had been in the same high school class, so Ty gave the man an extra head nod to acknowledge that he remembered and yet indicate that he didn't really want to revisit old times.

Without stopping to engage, he made his way to the wide, polished bar where one of Doc Winthrop's girls—though Tessa Winthrop was about as much of a girl as Ty and the Kittredges were boys—was slinging drinks under the direction of newcomer Jackson Hale, who had bought the place some years back. Jackson had found Cold River after some time out on the West Coast, or so Ty had been told, at length, by Brady. He certainly hadn't asked. Jackson liked to rattle on about local microbrews and IPA flights in a way that made Brady and his investment portfolio excited, which Ty knew entirely too much about for someone who didn't care about any of those things.

Tessa slid Ty his usual drink—a regular local beer on this side of his romance with a whiskey bottle last year—without him having to ask. Ty smiled his thanks because he was a nice, friendly guy as long as he didn't have to talk to anyone who knew his family or had once interacted with him in elementary school. Then he turned, so he could look out at what passed for Cold River's rocking nightlife.

It was a weekday, so the lights were on, the music from the jukebox was there for background instead of as a soundtrack to regrettable Saturday night decisions, and most folks were engaged in conversation at their tables over burgers and fries.

Ty should have suggested that Hannah meet him at the other bar within Cold River city limits. The Coyote catered to more disreputable types. Bikers. Committed drunks. Folks out looking more for a fight or the bottom of their bottle of choice. Ty had almost suggested it, because the benefit of the Coyote was that it wouldn't be chock-full of Ty's old friends and nosy neighbors. And no one in the Coyote tended to talk too much about what they might have seen there any given evening. Shame by association was its built-in insurance policy. He'd opened his mouth to tell Hannah to meet him there and somehow had told her to come to the Broken Wheel instead.

He had no idea why.

Maybe the problem wasn't that he'd been stomped on the head by a bull. Maybe the trouble was there hadn't been much there to worry about stomping on in the first place.

He took a swig of his beer and settled in. And at eight o'clock on the dot, the door to the bar swung open in his peripheral vision. By that point Ty was busy watching Matias Trujillo, back home after a stint in the marines, hit the bull's-eye on the dartboard. Again and again, with unnerving accuracy, like he was quietly announcing his competence. It got Ty thinking about things he usually preferred to repress or drink away, like what a man was supposed to do when the dreams that had taken him out of Cold River ran their course. He had his one shot next month, but it was a one-night kind of deal. Then what?

Small towns like this one were filled with dusty old heroes of bright and shining former lives only they remembered. Ty couldn't decide if it was a comfort or a tragedy that they all ended up back in the same bar on the same street in the same town where they'd first vowed they would be bigger and better—and had been, for a while. Just a little while.

He heard the door open. And then it didn't matter what he was doing or what he was brooding about.

Because he could *feel* her.

That strange electricity seared through him all over again. He felt it settle at the base of his spine, hot and insistent, then reverberate out through his body like a summer storm. It lit him up, everywhere. It made him wonder why, exactly, he'd lived through his injuries, was whole in all the ways that mattered and stronger by the day, yet hadn't celebrated his continued existence the way a man should.

He took his time turning his head, because he already knew who he was going to see. And while he was lollygagging, he got to witness the table full of Kittredges and assorted other reprobates get an eyeful of the new arrival. It was like a ripple effect, rolling through the bar like a wave, and Ty had the simultaneous urge to laugh out loud at the dumbstruck expressions he saw everywhere and start kicking the butt of every man who was looking at her that way.

He shook it off. Then turned his head all the way.

And there she was. Hannah.

Mine, a greedy voice inside him insisted. He ignored it. Or tried.

Her blond hair spilled past her shoulders in careful curls, highlighting that she was both delicate and strong at once. She had that delectable cowgirl physique he loved, as lean as she was curvy. She wore a shiny belt buckle to emphasize her slimness and yet was packed into those jeans that cupped her butt and made him heat right up. Like more of the same electricity, turned up high.

She looked around the bar, and he knew she hadn't seen

him yet because she didn't have that guarded expression on her face. Without it, he couldn't stop staring at the softness of her lips. Or the odd, almost wistful look in her blue eyes.

Then she found him, and he watched her face change. Like a wall came down, shifting her from wistful to wary in a heartbeat.

Ty should have been concentrating on the error in judgment he'd made by inviting her here, where every person he knew—or worse, knew him, whether he could recognize them or not—made no attempt to do anything but stare as she headed straight for him.

But all he could concentrate on was Hannah.

There was a roll to her gait that made him wonder what it would be like to roll with her. It was impossible not to focus on those hips of hers, lush and sweet, and paint himself pretty pictures of the things he could do with his hands. His mouth. Her lips curved politely enough as she approached, but he'd seen how soft and vulnerable she'd looked before she caught sight of him. And all he wanted to do was taste her.

God, what he'd do to taste her, there and then.

You can't, that same strange voice from earlier warned him. *Not with everyone watching.*

He flashed his easy grin at her instead of investigating all that noise inside him. "Evening."

"You can spare me the courtly cowboy nonsense," she replied, her voice so sweet that it took him a beat to process what she was saying. "I already know it's a lie."

"That sounds a lot like vicious slander."

"But you don't know, do you." It wasn't a question. She slid in next to him at the bar, leaning against her barstool instead of sitting on it, so she could face him. And despite the sweet voice and the smile she aimed at him, he wouldn't describe the energy she gave off as particularly friendly. "You can't remember your own character, can you?"

Ty's grin got edgy. "Character isn't something a man remembers, darlin'. He either has it or he doesn't."

"Noted. I'm assuming you think you have it. But how can you know for sure? Have you tested it?"

"What can I get you to drink?"

Ty supposed he ought to have been grateful to Tessa Winthrop, then, and yet another interruption. Tessa tossed down a coaster in front of Hannah with her usual efficiency, and managed to keep her expression impassive. Instead of greedy and speculative like every other person in the bar.

"What he's having, thank you," Hannah said, gifting Tessa with a far warmer version of her megawatt smile than she'd so far shared with Ty.

Tessa moved to fetch a beer, and they stood there in a silence that Ty figured Hannah probably found awkward, since she was the one who claimed she knew him. While he was . . . disquieted by her presence. And he was going to chalk up his odd reaction to her to his lack of female companionship ever since he'd gotten hurt. He was obviously so out of practice he didn't know up from down.

Tessa slid the bottle of beer in front of Hannah.

"You can put that on my tab," Ty told her.

"No, thank you," Hannah said stiffly. "I'll pay for my own beer."

"By all means," Ty drawled, shifting his attention back to Hannah as she busily set a few bills on the bar. "Let's argue about that too."

Tessa left them to it.

"I don't need you to buy things for me," Hannah told him, through a smile that looked like steel.

"Why not? It's a beer, not a diamond ring."

She went still at that. Too still, and Ty didn't know why the back of his neck . . . itched.

Hannah frowned at him, lifting a hand to toy with the chain around her neck. "A diamond ring? You like to throw those around?"

"It's a figure of speech."

"Most men don't wander about mentioning diamonds left and right. Or at all. They're careful not to give a girl the wrong impression. Careful to a fault, in fact. But not you."

"You tell me." He was still grinning, like this was all a joke. "You're the one who seems to know so much about me. Maybe I hand out diamond rings like a gumball machine."

She toyed with that chain, though whatever pendant hung from it was concealed by her shirt. And she was looking at him like he was a specimen under a microscope. "You don't remember anything, do you?"

His neck itched again. More. That same weight that had been there since he'd woken up in the hospital, weird and heavy and dragging down on his solar plexus, shifted and sunk deeper. His head wasn't right. And he was used to all of that. It had been this way for over a year.

But Hannah made it worse.

"That sounds like a loaded question," he said after a minute, doing his best not to let any of the weirdness into his tone.

"You don't know if it's loaded or not because you won't answer it."

"I don't know how to answer it," he said, more gruffly than he'd intended. So gruffly it made his throat hurt. "I was under the impression admitting you might not recall a woman who clearly recalls you was impolite."

"*Impolite.*" Her eyes were too sharp, too bright, as she repeated that word. She made it roll on forever with that drawl of hers until it almost sounded like a song. "Heaven forbid you be *impolite.*"

"I appreciate the sarcasm. I do. But that's circling right back around to character, isn't it? Maybe there are men in this world who enjoy stomping all over a woman's feelings, but I'm not one of them."

"You're sure of that?"

He couldn't be, of course, which made him feel that same . . . disquiet. Only stronger. But all he did was shrug, then make an opera out of tossing back his drink and setting the bottle down on the bar. Without allowing the complicated sensations inside him to bleed through. He hoped.

"Here's what I know," he said, leaning in. Which maybe wasn't his smartest move. She smelled fresh, new. As if she'd bathed herself in sunlight, then added sweet-smelling flowers to lock it all in place. Which registered like a kick to his gut. "You hunted me down out on the ranch."

"I didn't so much hunt you down as drive down a dirt road, sit there, and wait for you to appear."

"You keep wanting me to answer questions. Why don't you return the favor and tell me what *you* want?"

"What I want is what I already asked you. Do you remember me or not?"

"I don't really—"

There was something in her blue gaze that made his

lungs constrict. "It's a yes or no question, Ty. Yes, you remember me. Or no, you don't. The end."

Was he afraid that if he answered the question truthfully, she would go away? Or was he worried that she wouldn't?

He could remember the feel of her soft, warm cheek beneath his palm. And the strangest sensation that he'd held her like that before. And more.

Or maybe that was wishful thinking. He'd gotten used to blank spaces. But why couldn't he tell the difference between a *wish* and a *want*?

"No," he forced himself to admit, and his voice shouldn't have sounded like that. Gritty and rough. As if this were hard for him. "I don't remember you."

He was too close to her. Ty could see the way her pulse beat in her throat. He could tell that she'd been holding her breath as she'd waited for him to answer. And he could feel it when she let it go.

Hannah nodded, once. Then blinked, as if she was trying to keep him from noticing the too-bright sheen in her gaze.

"To clarify, what is it you don't remember? That I visited you in the hospital? Or . . . anything?"

"If you were in the hospital, you shouldn't have been," he bit out, because his temples throbbed and that itch on the back of his neck was irritating him. He missed the oblivion that only whiskey could bring, smooth and sure like a hammer with a kick. He didn't really want to poke at those first days strapped to a hospital bed, when he'd been lost in a haze of painkillers and broken bones. He didn't like to think about it now that he'd not only survived it, but planned to redeem the situation. "It was family only while I was in the ICU, and none of my family were in Kentucky. And by the time they moved me to a regular room, the tour had left the city. Then there was nothing but month after month of excruciating physical therapy. I'm glad there were no witnesses."

That wasn't entirely true, but then, Ty didn't count Amos as a witness. More like a grave misfortune.

"You were in a lot of pain," Hannah said. Not as if she was projecting so she could empathize with him. As if she *knew*. "It's not surprising that you don't remember."

Ty rubbed at the nape of his neck. "I keep waiting for someone to invent a painless way to get thrown from the back of a bucking bull. Or, better yet, a painless way to survive it when a bull decides to kick you around on your way down. But as far as I know, there's only the one way. Not dying. And yes, there's a lot of pain." He flashed his grin at her because it was a reflex. And because he wasn't going to ask Tessa for the bottle of Jack he could see right there on the shelf behind her. "I'm living the dream, darlin'."

But Hannah didn't smile back at him. "So, what you remember from the hospital is pain and physical therapy. Is that it?"

Ty had no intention of sharing the rest of it with her, or with anyone. Ever. His fury at his own fragile body. The reality of the wear and tear of the years he'd spent chasing the rodeo around. All the old broken bones, bruises, pulled muscles, and whatever else he'd stitched together and ignored since he was eighteen, all come back to make him weaker.

And then Amos in the middle of it, making it worse. The way he always had.

In the hospital, even the parts of Ty that hadn't been

crushed and torn apart ached. He didn't have to remember every detail of the past couple of years to know that was a constant for a man in his profession. The doctors had told him he'd been in excellent shape, all things considered, for an aged bull rider. They'd used that word. *Aged.*

Ty had spent months trying to figure out what the hell he was supposed to do with his life now. Or drinking his way around the fact he had no idea what came next. He wasn't destined to work the land like his brother. He'd never belonged here, as his father had gone to such lengths to remind him last summer. But he had no idea what else he was good for if he was really too old for the rodeo.

A one-night stand with a bull was the perfect stop-gap.

But he wasn't about to tell Hannah that.

Why did you come and meet her if you didn't want to tell her . . . something?

Ty ignored that voice inside of him the same way he was ignoring the siren call of the whiskey across from him. Meaning, they both irritated him. Or she did. And he was still trying to make that freaking itch go away. "If there's something you think I ought to remember, you should tell me what it is."

"Why?" Her blue gaze was uncomfortably direct. "Let's say I knew something about your life. And I told you, but you don't remember anything. What's the point of that? My telling you isn't going to make you suddenly recall it."

"It might."

"Why would I want you to pretend to remember something you've forgotten? It's entirely possible you want it that way."

There's no medical reason for your amnesia, the doc-

tor had said, her expression entirely too kind and understanding.

Ty didn't understand the wave that washed over him
then, but he leaned into it.

"That sounds philosophical, Hannah. But mostly I want
to know if we got naked."

He was sure he hadn't meant to say that. Not so . . .
baldly. He felt surly. Misshapen with it. But if he expected
Hannah to curl in on herself, or run away, he was in for
a surprise.

Because all she did was laugh at him.

"Explain to me again how concerned you are with being *impolite*," she dared him, but he was focused on that
laughter. The way it wove around her like another scent,
rich and seductive. The way it danced in the space between
them, making Ty . . . yearn. For things he didn't know how
to name.

He would have given anything to keep her from stopping, the way she did after a moment. She shook her head
as if she didn't know why she'd been laughing in the first
place. Then she picked up her beer and took a healthy pull.

And if Ty had ever wanted anything more than to reach
over and touch the column of her throat as she drank, well,
he certainly couldn't recall it.

"I'm assuming you're from Georgia, like the plates
on your pickup," he heard himself say, too darkly. *Desperate,* that voice inside needled him. "Are you passing
through? Or did you come to Cold River specifically?"

She set her bottle of beer back down on the bar and took
her time looking at him. He could see her shift into that
state of wariness he was pretty sure was all for him. The
expression on her face turned . . . careful.

"I was looking for you," she said after a moment. "But I'm still only passing through. I mean, I certainly don't plan to stay. So . . . both."

That wasn't quite an answer, was it?

"And are you getting what you wanted?" He'd meant that to come out lazy. Teasing, almost. But somehow, between his intention and his tongue, it didn't come out that way at all. Ty leaned forward instead, feeling something grip him, hard. "Am I everything you hoped and dreamed, Hannah? Poke and prod a man long enough, and congratulations, you can find each and every hole he's convinced himself wasn't there in the first place."

"Some people might be grateful to lose their memories," Hannah said, and he hated the note he could hear in her voice, then. And the look in her eyes that made everything inside him tighten. Viciously. "Maybe you should view this as an opportunity, Ty. You have a clean slate. You can be anything and anyone you want."

"You say that like I need a clean slate."

"The past is messy. Dirty. It's tangled up and used. There are those who would pay to walk away from the messes they made."

"If you're accusing me of something, make the accusation already."

"All I'm saying is that the mind is a delicate thing. Sometimes it goes to great lengths to protect you from things you don't want to know. Maybe you should listen to what your brain is telling you. Maybe you should keep right on doing whatever it is you're doing, hiding away on a ranch in the middle of nowhere."

Why did she keep echoing secrets he hadn't told anyone? Who *was* she?

"I'm not hiding."

That was all he could manage to get out, his head spinning like she'd sucker punched him.

She had.

Her expression was thoughtful and something like sad. She tipped her head to one side, and those curls of hers bounced. The sight made that weight on him press down deep. Even harder than before. Until he was surprised his solar plexus didn't give way, right there at the bar.

"Really?" Hannah asked, that gaze of hers never wavering and Ty went cold at the notion of what, exactly, she might see. What she might have already seen that he couldn't remember. What she knew about him that she shouldn't. "Are you sure?"

4

Hannah's *shoulda, coulda, woulda* list grew longer by the second.

She should have kept right on going when she left Cold River Ranch earlier. Instead of turning down into town and heading across the river, she could have driven right back over the mountains that separated Cold River from Colorado's famous ski resorts. She could have made it halfway to St. Louis by now. Because there was no need to stay here. She already had her answer.

Ty didn't remember her.

That meant he clearly also didn't remember anything that had happened between them. She couldn't decide if that was a great relief, because it meant he wasn't ignoring his own son deliberately. Or if it made everything that much worse.

These are things you can worry over to your heart's content back home in Georgia, she'd lectured herself. Sternly.

She absolutely had not looked in her rearview mirror as she'd driven herself away from him. But she went ahead and turned her truck toward cute little Cold River, not toward the interstate when she had the chance.

There was a Grand Hotel standing proud and pretty on one of the corners along Main Street, but it looked much too rich for Hannah's blood. She kept driving until she found a cute, small bed-and-breakfast. It was tucked between a darling bookstore and a boutique gift shop that sold a selection of bold, big necklaces Hannah hadn't known she'd wanted desperately her whole life, if the window display was anything to go by.

Not that she was here to shop in boutiques.

She told herself that if the bed-and-breakfast had a room, she would stay. And if it was full up, that was a sign that she needed to get out of here immediately. What she certainly didn't need to do was meet Ty Everett for drinks in a bar.

If she knew anything in this life, it was the danger inherent in meeting Ty Everett anywhere.

But the bubbly woman behind the desk introduced herself as Katrina, and assured her that they did, indeed, have vacancies. And she led Hannah to a room set up over Main Street with a lovely bay window, so Hannah could look up, down, and all around the pretty postcard town and pretend the place wasn't a wedge in her heart.

"Well?" Mama had asked when she'd called home. "Did you find him?"

Like the father of her child was a lost sock, hidden at the back of a very large dryer the size of Colorado.

"I found him."

"I hope that's not emotion I hear in your voice, Hannah Leigh. You're not on a date. That's the man who left you pregnant by the side of the road. Just about literally. If it's not too much trouble, I'd ask you to remember that why you're out there, hopefully not compounding the error."

"I'm meeting him tonight," Hannah had blurted out, because she had almost always been constitutionally incapable of holding back information from her mother, even when doing so would make her life easier.

Was she a glutton for punishment? Or an idiot?

How could she be a grown woman, a mother far removed from her rodeo queen days when Mama had acted as her chaperone, and still not know the answers to those questions?

"I'm not going to tell you what to do," Mama had said, which was never true. Ever. "But I will tell you this. I've spent your entire life so far waiting for your daddy to wake up and do the right thing no matter the hush money his parents paid us. And guess what? It never happened. It's never going to happen. Do you want to know why?"

Hannah had sighed. "Because you can't trust a man."

"Because you can't trust a man," Mama had agreed, like it was a hallelujah. "Men always lie. They're no good and they're simply made that way. I don't even blame you, baby girl. But you need to be smart. You lost your crown because of that man. You lost your reputation because of that man. You lost respect, decency, and your good name. What else are you going to lose?"

Then she'd put down the phone so that Hannah would have to sit with that question instead of making cooing noises at Jack and making sure he was okay without her, which was why she'd called in the first place. Hannah had accepted that as the punishment she was due. Because the only thing Luanne had ever raised Hannah to do was not repeat her own mistakes.

Yet here they were.

Hannah liked to argue—in her own head, obviously,

because there was no arguing with Mama when she'd
worked up a head of steam, or really at all—that at least
she was married. And not a teenager the way Luanne had
been. But what good was a husband if he denied the marriage? Then went ahead and forgot about it either way?
Was it better to be single than discarded when it all ended
up the same, living in Aunt Bit's back room, the talk of
Sweet Myrtle all over again?

More questions Hannah should surely have been able
to answer, yet couldn't.

Instead, she'd sat there on the edge of the bed in her
tidy room that smelled of gardenias, glaring at the cheerful blue-and-white bedspread, missing that familiar back
room. And missing her baby so much it hurt. She scowled
down at the bedspread rather than surrendering to the tears
that threatened. It looked as if it had been quilted with
love and skill by the sorts of women Hannah imagined
lived in a place like this.

Women who were never fooled by smooth-talking cowboys who hid lies and temptation behind all that flirta-
tious patter. Women who held fast to their values, were
clear on what they stood for, and never, ever squandered
their good reputations on well-known bad boys who lived
for nothing more than one more notch in their belts.

The kind of woman Hannah had been *so certain* she
was. Because she'd always believed in her own virtue as
if it was as much a part of her as, say, her leg. She'd never
imagined that it was as fragile as a single choice. As delicate as a *yes*.

Cold River looked like the sort of too-perfect town that
was populated entirely by good, solid, decent people who
knew their worth, never said *yes* when they should have

shouted *no*, and definitely never threw away everything they'd ever worked for because of some guy.

There was a part of Hannah that wanted to blow it up.

But that was hugely unproductive and wouldn't help her any, even if she knew how to operate explosives, which she didn't. So instead of getting her gunpowder and lead on, she'd gone back downstairs and out onto Main Street. Then she'd succumbed to the siren call of Capricorn Books next door. For hours.

She'd patted the huffy tabby cat who lived there, fat and outraged with its tail twitching. Then she'd lost herself in books, the way she hadn't been able to do in a long while. Not since Jack was born. And not for a long time before that, with all her commitments to the rodeo. It reminded her of being sixteen in Sweet Myrtle and spending any free time when she wasn't on a horse, in the library. She'd read anything and everything she could, and had dreamed of all the glorious, magical things she was going to do with her marvelous life.

She'd spent a handful of sweet hours in the used section of Capricorn Books, leafing through old comfort reads to make herself feel better. Then, when she was ready to go, she'd picked up a worthy-looking book on the opioid epidemic because she, by God, did not need to loll around in self-pity a moment more. She needed to remember that her life, though not quite what she'd expected it to be when she'd been sixteen with too many oversize daydreams in her head, was fine. Good, even. Especially in comparison to people with real problems.

"Now, tell me something," the woman behind the counter said, with a big, warm, conspiratorial smile that instantly made Hannah feel happier than she was. As if the woman were her friend. "Why does someone who sat here reading all the good parts of three different Jane Austen novels want to walk out of here with this? Not that it's a bad book. It's terrific. But it's not exactly the same mood."

"I need a different mood."

"If you're looking for hopeful," the woman said mildly, "a treatise on the evils of pharmaceutical companies is probably not your read."

"I don't believe in hope," Hannah replied. "I believe in cold, hard facts."

"Are they mutually exclusive?" the woman asked as she rang up the purchase, still smiling. "What I like about hope is that it takes the cold and the hard out of facts and lets them simply be . . . factual."

Which, for some reason, felt like another sucker punch in a day full of them.

Hannah had found herself back in her cheerful room in the lovely bed-and-breakfast in this pretty, happy town, staring at the depressing book she didn't want to read. She felt as out of place as the freaking book was. As obviously wrong, surrounded on all sides by all the curated *rightness*. The carefully preserved brick buildings. The tidy streets. The flowers everywhere.

Even the drive out to Ty's family ranch and back had been like something out of a western movie. Those rolling fields beneath the summer sun with the impossible mountains soaring all around. Hannah's own small town featured far more boarded-up windows, questionable convenience stores with grown men on small bikes milling about outside, and abandoned cars with plants growing out of them behind chain-link fences.

Here in Cold River, she was clearly the wrong sort of

small-town girl. And worse, she was sure it showed. She might as well be an unkempt yard full of discarded engines and rusted farm implements staring out through the chain link.

Which was how she'd always felt growing up as *that Luanne Monroe's little girl with no daddy.*

Putting on her rodeo queen face and acting the part had convinced her she could be someone else, all done up in curls and a smile. The kind of someone else who deserved a marvelous, big life and all those pretty daydreams no matter how scandalous her birth had been. Ty Everett had proved otherwise.

You can't trust a man, a voice inside her chimed in, right on cue. And Hannah couldn't tell anymore if it was Luanne in there, deep, or if it was her. If she'd become her mother in all the ways she'd always promised herself she wouldn't. Ever.

She changed into something nicer, then changed back, because she didn't want to send the wrong message. She certainly didn't want Ty to imagine she'd dressed up for him, like the empty-headed groupie he clearly believed she was, something that would likely lay her out with breathless rage if she let it.

She didn't let it. She poured her fury into her curling iron and her mascara instead. And she reminded herself that homicide would mean Jack was down two parents instead of one. She had no intention of abandoning her baby the way Ty had.

Hannah considered getting something to eat once it started to grow late, but she wasn't hungry, because it turned out that all the times she'd eaten her feelings before, they had been the minor, inconsequential sort that were easily soothed with a pint of ice cream and three bags of chips.

Real heartbreak—true grief—made her crave nothing but more time to try to forget it.

Now she was standing in a bar with Ty when she, of all people, knew better. He was a clear path to sin and perdition. It was written right there on his beautiful face and sadly backed up by her own traitorous response to him. Even now.

And throwing back beer on an empty stomach—no matter how twisted up it was—was not the smartest thing Hannah ever done. But it was that or give in to the fury that charged around in her veins like fire. And burned dark enough to hint that maybe it was despair dressed up in those flames. She'd chosen the beer.

"I'm not hiding from anything," Ty was saying now, and there was something stark on his face that got to her. When nothing about him should get to her. She couldn't help being attracted to him, apparently, but was it really necessary that she *feel* for him? "My father died last fall. My brothers and I run the ranch now. More or less together."

"I'm sorry to hear about your father."

Ty shrugged, his gaze shuttered. "I should miss him more than I do, probably."

Hannah could have said a whole lot of things on the subject of disappointing fathers, but she restrained herself. "You always said you would retire here."

His dark green gaze sharpened. "Did I? We sat around talking about my retirement?"

She smiled faintly, because that would indeed be weird . . . if she were one of his groupies. She didn't get the impression the cowboys did too much talking with the girls who chased them from town to town.

She would never know how she managed not to throw her beer at him for suggesting, however indirectly, that she was one of them. When she had been so good. So proper. So uptight when it was always clear everyone else was having more fun. And when she had only ever let her guard down once.

Ty had promised her he was worth it.

They all promised that, her mother would say. That was why there were so many painful songs about unreliable cowboys.

"You're on the wrong side of thirty, Ty," she said with admirable calm, not that she expected him to appreciate it. "You didn't have much time left riding bulls. Not well, anyway."

"You know a lot about riding bulls, do you?"

"Nothing personally, because I'm not suicidal. I've watched *you* ride a bull, if that's what you mean. And experience goes a long way, but at a certain point, the risk of permanent injury outweighs the possibility of a win. You know that."

"Didn't we spend a whole lot of time establishing that I suffered a pretty big wallop to the head? Could be I think I'm invincible."

"Do you?"

"You appear to know everything about me already. Including my retirement plans. Are you going to tell me why or are we going to keep playing these cute little guessing games?"

"I don't have to know anything about you to know that your age was always going to be a factor in whether or not you get to stay in the ring. How are you supposed to compete against eighteen-year-olds?" Hannah shrugged as if the way he glowered at her didn't register. "You can't."

"I appreciate the vote of confidence."

"You're not the first person in the world who got aged out of the thing they loved. You're unlikely to be the last. You should count yourself lucky that you have a family ranch as plan B. Not everyone can say the same."

His green gaze glittered, dark and dangerous. "Are you talking about yourself now? Or are we still pretending you're talking about me?"

Hannah hadn't realized how close they'd gotten, standing there tucked up at the bar. She'd forgotten they were even at a bar. She'd been much too wrapped up in him, which was vying for the phrase most likely to end up on her tombstone.

"You definitely don't know the first thing about *me*, Ty," she said after a moment, fighting hard to make her pulse behave. And failing. "You said so yourself."

"Well, darlin', I don't have to know you personally to figure out all kinds of things about you."

"Have you suddenly become insightful about other people?" Her drawl was heavy and her tone was dry, and she wasn't particularly inclined to change either. "That would sure be an exciting development."

"You came looking for me, not the other way around."

"I told you I was passing through. I thought I'd drop in on an old friend. See if you survived that bull after all."

"All my old friends are sitting around the same tables right here in this saloon, still talking about what we wish we did in high school, but didn't. That means I know you from the rodeo."

"Everybody knows you from the rodeo. That's the price of fame."

"You're sketchy on the details, Hannah, and it's beginning to feel deliberate. Still, it's clear you know me personally. Possibly biblically. And look at you."

She didn't know where he was going with this. She hated that she didn't have the confidence she'd come to take for granted during her rodeo queen years. Before her body had changed so much, that was. Before she'd learned, in the most profound and beautiful way possible, what it could do—and had also had to face the fact that it would never look the way it had before.

Hannah did the best she could with what was left of that girl she'd been, but she hadn't had the opportunity to test it.

Especially not where this man was concerned.

"You've got those curls," Ty was saying, looking and sounding lazy again. "Rhinestones on the pockets of your jeans. Fancy patterns on your cowboy boots and that perfectly made-up face. All you're missing is a cowboy hat with a shiny crown slapped on the front of it."

"I keep that in the truck."

"Amen." He didn't actually grin, but she could see the hint of it in his dark green gaze, and that was far more dangerous. "I can identify a rodeo queen when I see one."

"Past tense," Hannah drawled, as if it didn't hurt. As if it wouldn't always hurt. "My crown got a bit tarnished."

"I'm sorry to hear that. I bet you look good in a glittery crown."

And nothing else, he'd used to tell her. The words hung there between them, as if he was thinking them now. She certainly was.

Because she was that ridiculous. That pathetic and sad.

Except . . . did it count as abandonment if he couldn't remember what he'd left behind?

"Here's what I know about rodeo queens," Ty said, and he reached between them to pull one of her long, careful curls between his fingers, the way he'd done so many times. Hannah should have batted his hand away. But she didn't. "Driven. Ambitious. Sweet at a glance and sharp to touch."

"You shouldn't go around touching rodeo queens. They're not out there busting their butts for your entertainment."

Everything about him was as lazy as that grin. "Are you sure about that?"

"A rodeo queen is an ambassador," she told him primly, and pretended her heart wasn't stuttering in her chest. "For the western way of life. They deserve respect, not cheap come-ons from drunken cowboys who are afraid to be alone because they might have to take a hard look at themselves in the mirror."

"Now, darlin'," Ty said, finally sounding outraged. Until he grinned again. "I like what I see in the mirror just fine."

Hannah laughed before she could catch herself, and worse, leaned toward him, angling herself closer to that grin. It was instinctive. Natural, even.

And she hated herself for it.

What on earth was she *doing* here?

He was a flashback come to life, standing there before her as if nothing had happened. And that was the kicker, wasn't it? None of it *had* happened. Not to him.

She was the one who should know better. She *did* know better. Hadn't she already seen what happened when she let this man flirt with her? It had been bad enough when she was a rodeo queen finishing out one term and starting another. She'd had Luanne as a fierce and usually harsh chaperone and gatekeeper, but that hadn't stopped Ty. More important, it hadn't stopped her from sneaking out to see him and lying to her mother for the first time in her life.

It hadn't stopped her from making every dire prediction her mother had ever uttered come true, because she'd been so sure that she was smarter and Ty was better and they were in love.

And now she had his baby. She *missed* his baby so much it was like a hollow behind her ribs. But he had no idea who she was.

He had no idea Jack existed.

Her response to seeing him again was to stand in a bar, like a moth to the same old flame, and make it that much worse.

She *hated* herself for this.

"I have to go," she said. Abruptly.

Hannah turned in a rush, and didn't realize that more people had come out to fill up the bar while she'd been entirely focused on Ty. The world could have ended and she wouldn't have noticed, not when she had all of that dark green attention focused on her again.

Selfish, stupid girl. Her mother's voice rang in her head, the way it had when she'd broken down and confessed everything after Ty's bad fall and the scene in his hospital room. *All you had to do was keep your legs closed.*

Hannah felt bile, thick and acrid, at the back of her throat. She almost stumbled as she dodged around clumps of people with too much speculation all over their faces—and the only saving grace she could come up with was the fact she didn't know a single one of them.

Though, had everything gone the way it had been supposed to when she'd married Ty, she might have. These people would have been her neighbors. They might even have become her friends.

She shoved her way out the heavy saloon doors and onto the street. The summer evening was burning itself out, hot and red. It felt like an omen.

Her phone buzzed in her pocket, but she didn't check it. Because she knew who it was. Who it always was. Luanne, who had never quite relinquished her role as Hannah's chaperone, even after it was clear she'd failed in her primary mission. She was checking in. And more likely checking to see if Hannah had her clothes on.

If it was an emergency with the baby, she would call back instantly. Hannah took a breath while she waited. Then another breath, deeper than the one before.

But her mother didn't call back. Likely because she was already imagining the worst. And Hannah might not have tossed her clothes off—yet—but that didn't mean the worst hadn't happened.

Ty didn't remember her. Yet she was still in love with him.

There was nothing to do but stand there on a quiet, perfect street as the summer shadows grew into full dark and ask herself what she hoped to gain from flinging herself, face-first, into the irrevocable weight of what she'd lost and couldn't have.

"You came all this way to see me and you're running off without a goodbye?"

Ty's drawl was a low insinuation against the night, but Hannah didn't turn around to face him. Her eyes closed, and she wrapped her arms around her middle, though she couldn't have said if she was trying to keep herself from swinging at him—or from doing something far more unforgivable.

Like burying her head in the crook of his neck.

"You don't remember me either way," she managed to say, evenly enough. "What does it matter to you if I say goodbye?"

"It matters."

His voice was rougher than it should have been. And she couldn't help herself. She turned, though her heart kicked at her and her stomach twisted into that knot she'd given up trying to unravel.

She should never have come here. This man was her weakness, and she couldn't believe she'd imagined that that could change. She couldn't believe she'd actually thought she'd grown up.

Because even now, even after everything he'd done and said that terrible night he got hurt, she looked at him and she melted.

The only difference was that now, that melting sensation came with a side helping of deep shame. Hannah wanted to kick herself. Or him. She wanted to knock their heads together, but she knew better. Touching him had only ever led to one place.

And then, eventually, straight on to right here.

"You look at me like I'm a ghost," he said, closing the distance between them.

His dark green gaze was troubled. And God help her, but she wanted that to mean things it didn't. It couldn't.

"Maybe I'm the ghost," she said quietly. "A hilariously ineffective one, if so."

"I wouldn't call you ineffective."

"I shouldn't have come here," she said, and some of the distress she was feeling must have shown on her face, because his expression changed.

She recognized the way he looked at her, then. Hannah recognized it, and it made her want to cry, right there in front of him.

Because it turned out that there was something a lot worse than Ty Everett looking at her like he'd never seen her before. And that was him looking at her the way he used to. Like he cared when he didn't.

"I need to go," she said carefully. Because that wasn't what she wanted. That was never what she'd wanted.

"I'm guessing you came to Cold River for a reason. You've done a good job of talking in circles all night. But you should probably tell me why you're here."

"I honestly don't know if I should. You don't remember me. So what good is calling on your memory?"

"Are you some buckle bunny, Hannah?"

"Of course not," she retorted before she could help herself. Before she could think better of it. "I wouldn't know where to start."

She expected him to do what he usually did. Hide the darker thing in his gaze behind that lazy grin of his, then say something provoking, so no one would see the real him lurking there behind all the flash.

But he didn't. He looked . . . uncomfortable.

"It's not you, personally, that I can't remember." His voice was stiff. Gruff. "I . . . I'm missing some time."

She didn't know why that struck her as hard as it did. When surely the way he'd looked at her with no recognition on the ranch should have hurt the most. Or the fact he could make jokes about buckle bunnies with her, when she'd given him her innocence. When he'd promised her he would cherish it, and her, forever. Surely those things should have flattened her.

But instead, it was this. Ty standing before her out here in the dark, proud, scowling, and stiff with discomfort. Talking about *missing some time*.

This was what made tears prick the back of her eyes, while something unwieldy lodged in her chest and made her throat ache. As if she was already lost in a sob.

"What do you mean by *some time*?" she asked.

"Near as I can figure, two years. Give or take."

Two years. Meaning, the entire time he'd known her. All . . . gone. It was one thing to suspect it. It was something else to hear him confirm it, and Hannah wanted to *do* something. Scream. Cry. Beat on him a while. Hold him, maybe.

Rewind to the terrible night that March and . . . not tell him she was pregnant. Not have that horrible fight when he'd turned into someone she barely recognized. Not watch him storm out into the ring and get thrown the way he had.

But he couldn't remember any of that. He didn't know who she was.

Hannah had to swallow down the sob that threatened to pour out of her. Or become her. She had to keep it to herself.

She didn't know how she managed it. "What does your doctor say? Are you going to get those years back?"

Ty aimed for that grin of his and didn't quite make it. "I was lucky to walk again. Asking for perfect recall is pushing it."

"Head injuries are tricky," Hannah said slowly. "Or so I've read."

"Sometimes the memories come back and sometimes

they don't. I know who I am. I know my family. I get up every morning and I can walk. I'm going to get back on that bull and things are going to end differently this time. I'm good."

"I'm happy for you," she made herself say, and she almost meant it. She really, truly, *almost* meant it. "You're very lucky—"

"Hannah. Tell me."

He took a step toward her and made as if to put his hand on her again. But he stopped. She didn't know if that was because he could feel it too. That same electric spark that had always been there between them. Every time they looked at each other in those dusty, crowded rings. *Every time.* She'd been so sure she disliked him, at first.

She'd wanted so badly to dislike him.

But she hadn't then. And, though it made her deeply ashamed, she didn't now either.

It had never occurred to her that she might feel sorry for him. All that hurt and betrayal inside of her had nowhere to go. She felt swollen with it.

"This is a terrible idea," she muttered, and she stepped back the way she should have done back then. The way she had, day after day, until that night she hadn't.

"Please," he said, a different kind of grittiness in his voice. "Tell me. What did I do to you?"

It had been one thing to imagine herself yelling at him. She'd wanted to yell at him. She'd staged confrontations in her mirror a thousand times, practicing for this moment.

You have a son, she would shout, bristling with self-righteousness. *He's adorable, he's perfect, his name is Jack, and he deserves a father—even if it's you.*

She'd yelled it. She'd said it quietly, with great dignity or ringing condemnation. Every way there was to say it, she'd tried it out. But she'd never expected . . . this. Could she yell the truth at him when he didn't remember anything about her? Could she use it as a weapon when he didn't remember injuring her in the first place?

Was it even okay to tell him? She was sure she'd read something, somewhere, that confronting someone with memory problems was a bad idea. Possibly even damaging.

If it was a precarious medical situation, should she have come barreling in like this? She wasn't sure he counted as a deadbeat dad when he didn't know he had a child. And she could ask him for a divorce here and now, but he probably didn't know he was married. He could have broken their marriage vows a thousand times already, a notion that made her ill, except . . . Did it count as breaking a vow if he couldn't remember making any promises in the first place?

Hannah needed to regroup. She needed to think, and maybe cry some more. She had to consult a better medical authority than a Google search, and figure out what was best for everyone involved. And yes, she should have thought this all through before she'd kissed her baby goodbye, jumped in her truck, and come all the way out here. Much less confronted Ty.

But the real truth was, she hadn't really expected him not to remember her.

His potential memory issues had been an excuse. On the off chance he couldn't remember her, she'd driven for two days straight so she could put herself in front of him again. Because she'd expected that *of course* he would know her. And all she'd really wanted was a good excuse to turn up again all this time later.

To see if he'd really meant it when he'd told her to leave him the hell alone.

Now she had no idea what to do. It was easier to hate him from afar.

Jack comes first, she told herself now, past the ache and the confusion. *Jack has to come first.*

"You didn't do anything to me," she forced herself to say, though the words came out wrong. They sounded too plaintive. Too much like the lie they were. "Not on purpose. After all, a famous bull rider can't be expected to remember every groupie who comes along, can he?"

She didn't know why she said that. The real problem was that she didn't know what she was doing, but at least that was familiar ground. With Ty, she never had.

"The thing about groupies and buckle bunnies, Hannah, is that they're mostly in it for the buckle. They don't show up a year later, no rodeo in sight, no cheering crowds, and no prize money. They follow the rodeo, not the rider."

"It's late," she said, her voice still much too . . . wispy. "I have to go."

"It's not even ten o'clock."

"Good night, Ty," she said, and then she turned around again because looking at him was too hard. She started down the sidewalk because her bed-and-breakfast was on the next block. She wanted to barricade herself in her pretty bedroom, curl up in a ball, and sob until she felt like herself again.

If that were even possible.

"Hannah," he said. As if her name made him ache. "No one knows."

5

Hannah stopped walking.

It felt more like she'd slammed into a wall in the middle of the sidewalk and might have the bruises to prove it, but she didn't turn back around. She didn't want him to see her face. She had no idea what might be written all over it.

"No one knows about my memory," Ty said, as if the words were torn from him. Maybe that was why they felt like bullets, each one slamming into her flesh. "Not really."

She heard the door to the bar open behind them, spilling out laughter and music into the dark street. When it closed again, the quiet was that much more treacherous. She wasn't surprised when Ty came up beside her, his hands shoved into his pockets and that hunted, dark look on his face that made her poor, battered heart flip over inside her chest.

"I haven't told anyone," he said gruffly. "I keep hoping I won't have to."

"Because you think you'll wake up one day and remember?"

"Why not? I woke up one day and forgot."

Her throat ached with the tears she hadn't shed in front

of him. The words she'd barely managed to keep from saying to him. The memories only she had of what had happened between them, clamoring to get out. She curled her hands into fists to keep from reaching out to him. "Why did you tell me?"

Hannah hated the part of her that wanted so desperately for that to mean something. That he knew her, maybe, on some level. Deep inside of him.

Stupid girl, that voice inside her scolded her. *Always so deeply stupid.*

"I don't know why I told you."

"I'm not going to tell anyone else, if that's what you're worried about." She said it as much to the summer night as to him. "Since one of the things you can't remember is me."

He was standing too close to her, which made her want to lean into him. To touch him, even if it was only briefly, and feel that heat he generated like he was his own furnace. She wanted to bury her face against him to see if he still smelled the way he should, the crisp scent of the no-nonsense soap he used and that rich, indefinable thing that was only him. But then what?

She forced herself to put some distance between them. And she faced him, because at least if she was looking at him, she couldn't *accidentally* slump against him and lose herself in him. Better to see it coming if she was going to betray herself completely.

Something about the way he watched her, braced as if he expected her to take a swing at him, undid her. Made her want to swallow down all the harsh things on the tip of her tongue and tell him whatever sweet lies he needed to hear that would make this better.

When he didn't know what *this* was.

"I didn't come here to make things harder for you," she said, when the moment stretched out from tense into something very nearly painful. Again.

"Then why did you come here?"

"I don't know," she said, and it wasn't as much of a lie as it should have been. "But I'm not going to figure it out on the street. Late at night. When decent people are tucked up in their beds, getting ready for a new day."

It wasn't that late, and she wasn't that decent anymore thanks to him, but she didn't say that. The Ty she'd known would have grinned lazily at her and encouraged her to sin her way into the nearest scandal. Preferably starring him. This Ty only frowned.

"It hasn't escaped my attention that you haven't given me your whole name, Hannah. You keep waiting for me to do or say something, but I haven't. And now . . . what? You're running away?"

She let out a laugh that felt like one more bruise tonight. "What's really funny is you don't know how hilarious that is."

"Tell me something." His voice was more urgent then, his gaze darker. And Hannah wanted so desperately to believe he could feel the enormity of the things he didn't know. She wanted so badly to imagine that somewhere inside him, he remembered *something*. That she'd left some part of herself behind in him. *Stupid girl.* "Tell me one thing that proves I know you."

"Is this a test?"

"Call it what you want."

Hannah waited for him to back down, but this was Ty

Everett. He was as bullheaded as the great beasts he rode, and twice as stubborn.

"You have a scar on your left side," she said quietly.

"I have a lot of scars. And a lot of them on my left side."

"This one isn't from a bull. It isn't from getting thrown off a horse when you were a kid on the ranch either. You sometimes tell people that it's one or both of those things, but it's not."

His expression tightened into a kind of alertness that surged through Hannah like a new heat. But she had always been good at tests. She'd passed every test she'd ever taken. She'd had big plans and even bigger dreams before she'd met this man.

Maybe someday that would stop hurting, but she doubted it.

"You were playing hide-and-seek with your brothers," she told him, repeating the story he'd told her himself. "You were about ten. There was an old barn on the property that was off limits, so naturally that's where you went to hide. You were in such a hurry, you tripped and fell, ripping a chunk out of your side. And you'd get in trouble if you admitted where you'd been and how you'd hurt yourself. So you had to sneak back out, creep into the other barn, and pretend to hurt yourself on something inside it. But the thing you chose was rusty, and before you knew it, you were being whisked off to get stitched up. With a bonus tetanus shot. And what you're really mad about to this day is that you lost the game."

She didn't tell him how or when he'd told her that story. They'd been stretched out in a beautiful meadow in Montana with nothing to entertain them but the crowded night sky above. So many stars it hurt to look at them, but that was okay. They'd only had eyes for each other. Hannah had been propping herself up on one elbow, gazing down at him, and somehow managing to keep her hands to herself. Even when he'd wrenched up his T-shirt to show her the scar in question, that lazy grin of his making her smile despite herself and acres of his mouthwatering torso on display.

He'd been infectious. That had been the word that kept boomeranging around inside of her then. *Infectious.*

She had tried so hard not to fall in love with him. Maybe that was the test she should have worried about acing. Instead, she'd been so certain she would pass it with flying colors that she hadn't even seen her own failure coming straight at her. Like a train. Not until it was too late.

That was the sort of thing she liked to turn over and over in her head when she was awake in the middle of night, pretending she heard the baby when really, it was her conscience clamoring. And her eternal shame.

But here and now, on this street in the Colorado summer dark, Ty looked stricken straight through, the way she'd always imagined she wanted. She wanted it less, now. Because she'd neglected to factor in how little she actually enjoyed seeing him in pain.

"You told me you never admitted the truth of how you got that scar to anyone, not even your brothers," she managed to say. She could feel how heavy her eyes were. Too full of emotion she didn't dare show in front of him. Not when she had no idea what to do with it any longer.

"But I told you."

"Yes."

"Why?"

And what was she supposed to say? How was she supposed to answer that?

*We were falling in love, you see, and you wanted me to
know everything about you. That was the night you would
tell me that you hadn't been the same since you clapped
eyes on me. I would pretend not to believe you, but I did,
because it was the same for me.*

*We were falling in love, and then we fell, and when you
proposed to me, you told me it would be forever.*

How could she say any of that?

Or was the truth that she didn't *want* to say it? Because
how could you tell someone they were in love with you
when they didn't feel it? When they couldn't even remember your name on their own? She would sooner bash her
head against the nearest brick wall. It would feel about the
same.

"Maybe you only pretended you never told anyone
about it so you'd seem mysterious," she suggested, though
she knew better. "Maybe you actually told everybody
whenever possible. Maybe there were billboards."

"Did I have a particular reason for telling you a story
like that?" He sounded baffled.

Because the man standing before her would no more
tell a random woman that story—or any story about
himself—than he would strip off all his clothes, run naked down the center of Main Street, and give his neighbors a show. She understood that.

She didn't know whether to congratulate herself
because she truly had been special to him, or grieve the
loss all over again.

Neither option did a thing for her fatherless child.

"This is the problem with this entire situation," she

said, and there was a different kind of electricity shooting through her then. A restlessness. Because she was tired of holding it all together. She wanted to go scream into her pillow for an hour or two. Or a year. "I can't give you an emotional context for these things you don't feel. I might as well be talking to you in a different language. There's no point to it."

"I want to know."

"You don't want to know it, you want to feel it. And my telling you stories about people who don't make any sense to you now isn't going to make you feel anything. Except maybe confused."

"For God's sake," he gritted out. "Tell me what the hell I did to you."

"I'm sorry, Ty, but I can't."

Because she couldn't. Of course she couldn't. What would she do? Show him one of the approximately twenty thousand pictures of Jack she had on her phone—so he could stare at them blankly?

This is the baby we made together, she could say. *The one you weren't too excited to hear about in the first place.*

And then maybe, if she was lucky, they could relive the terrible fight they'd had the night he'd gone out and taken his last ride.

"*I can't,*" she said again, more fiercely this time.

Because she could break her own heart. And had. But she would protect Jack's no matter what.

She could no longer control her tears, then. They spilled over, humiliating her. Horrifying her.

Telling Ty too much, too quickly.

She didn't wait to see how he planned to handle that.

If he planned to do anything. She turned on her heel, accepted that she had no dignity left to lose where Ty Everett was concerned—whether he could remember it or not—and ran.

Ty spent the drive home from Cold River . . . unsettled.

Disquieted straight on through, making that scar Hannah had mentioned begin to throb in time with his heart, until they were both kicking at him.

He was missing things, sure. Two years and change.

But that game of hide-and-seek he could remember down to the moment after he'd hurt himself in the decrepit old barn he definitely wasn't supposed to play in. He remembered staring down at the hunk missing from his side in sick fascination, waiting for the pain and the blood to follow the injury. And the dizzying wallop when they did.

He remembered that as completely as he'd forgotten those critical two years. And yet he still felt certain—the way he was about his name, the fact he dressed to the left, and the soapy evil that was cilantro—that he didn't usually make women cry.

Not *at* him and *because* of him. Not like Hannah had.

Or, even worse, turn and run away from him. Literally. Down the street like she was being chased, so she could fling herself through the front door of the bed-and-breakfast on Main Street, and leave him standing out there like . . . He didn't even know what.

His own father, maybe, who had excelled in nothing so much as chasing the women in his life away from him. And everyone else while he was at it.

A comparison that made Ty want to break things.

Which, of course, would make him even more like the old man.

Ty had wanted nothing so much as he'd wanted to turn back around once Hannah was inside the B and B, take himself back to the bar, and reacquaint himself with the whiskey he hadn't touched since he'd decided he was going back to the rodeo. At least for one night.

Instead, he'd headed back to the ranch, which still didn't feel like home to him, but was as close as he was going to get. Because what was a man supposed to do when he'd forgotten how to feel much of anything? Whiskey had picked up that slack for a while, but it made him maudlin. He was pretty sure that if he kept at it long enough, it would turn him mean like Amos.

The only other thing that had gotten under his skin since he'd dragged himself back to the ranch last fall was Hannah. And Ty had no earthly idea what that meant or what to do about it.

The drive over the hill and out into the fields was long and dark, and left him with nothing to do except rack his brain for any stray bit of memory lurking around in there.

There was nothing. But something about Hannah called to him.

At one point, out there on the street, he'd wanted to haul her into his arms and . . . hold her, or something. What was *that*?

She'd told him that he should view his missing years as an opportunity. And maybe he should. Who was he really? Who did he *want* to be?

He didn't particularly want to be the guy who had to paste a smile on his face when he got back to the ranch because his brother Brady was pulling in at the same time, back from a few days tending to his former life down in Denver.

But whatever else Ty might have lost along with his memory, he still had his grin. He could still turn it on and off at will. He could still flash it around until people mistook that for actually saying something.

"Where have you been?" Brady asked as he swung a duffel bag over his shoulder.

"Didn't realize I had to check in with my den mother," Ty drawled. Still grinning. "Don't worry, Denver. Look at your watch. I made curfew and all."

Brady made a genial anatomical suggestion that was, happily, biologically impossible. "Glad to see you're as charming as ever. Every time I go away for a few days, I tell myself that I must be imagining it. That both my brothers can't be this much of a pain in the butt. And yet every time I come back, here you are to prove me wrong."

"I'm the charming, disreputable drunk, Brady," Ty chastised him. And it didn't escape him that Brady didn't argue with that description. Meaning he thought Ty was still as drunk as he'd been after Amos's funeral. Which was to say, constantly. "Come on now. Gray's the grumpy, overbearing pain in the butt."

"Not since he married Abby, he's not." Brady eyed him. "Luckily we have you to carry that torch."

"Because you're so personable."

Brady grinned. "I'm a freaking delight."

"As long as your right hand agrees, little brother, you're good to go."

He headed toward his bunkhouse, waving off Brady's raised middle finger. Brady headed into the ranch house itself and the room downstairs where he'd been staying since he'd moved up here after Christmas.

Ty liked being out in the dark. Alone. It was the only time his lack of memory was less obvious. He could see the flickering light on up the second floor that told him his niece, Becca, was home from her summer job at the Trujillo family's florist shop in town. Gray and Abby were likely home too, but responsible, dependable Gray had always liked an earlier bedtime, given the hour at which he had to get up in the morning to tend to the ranch. When they'd been kids, Gray had never complained about morning chores, even if it meant shivering half to death out in the barn on winter mornings before school.

Ty had always complained. With a grin, of course, to try to avoid getting a whack from their father. Brady, ever the political operative in the family, had timed his complaints better and avoided Amos's heavy hand. But Gray had actually *enjoyed* all that crap.

Ty eyed his older brother's window, high up on the second floor of the ranch house. Gray had always been irritating like that.

But then Gray had gotten married over Thanksgiving weekend to their long-time neighbor, Abby Douglas, uniting two of the original families that had settled this valley and stayed here ever after. And Abby actually made stern, too-serious, always-grumpy Gray . . . happy.

Ty might have called it a holiday miracle, if he were that kind of person. As far as he knew, he wasn't.

It wasn't that Everetts were destined for unhappiness, necessarily, no matter what Ty's mother liked to say to the contrary. And Bettina Crowther—because she'd dropped the Everett from her name on the way out the ranch house door, long before the divorce went through—always had a lot to say on that topic. Ty had caught up with her in a variety of different places over the years. San Luis Obispo. Walla Walla. Scottsdale. Santa Fe. Baton Rouge. She never stayed any one place for long. The only constant in her life was her continued bitterness over her marriage to Amos.

Ty figured she wasn't one to talk about the general unhappiness of the Everett family, since she'd helped make Amos Everett into who he was when she'd run off and left him with her three boys to raise. Something he imagined he must have had feelings about, back when he could feel things.

Ty hadn't ever *really* believed that they were all cursed to follow in Amos's footsteps straight on into a life of misery that ended alone, angry, and ungrieved, but it had sure been shaking out that way. Before Abby.

Abby, who made Gray laugh when he had previously displayed precious little of anything resembling a sense of humor. Abby, who'd gotten her Christmas-phobic new husband to celebrate the holiday anyway when he'd declared it banned, had thrown her brand-new stepdaughter a sweet sixteen party and invited the parents of Gray's long-dead first wife to build a bridge with them, and had quietly insisted on family dinners on Sundays all through the winter. Abby, who treated Ty like her own brother and made him imagine he could be one when he couldn't remember what that was supposed to feel like.

But while he was standing out in the dark thinking about his sister-in-law and all the surprising changes she'd brought to this family, he kept seeing Hannah's face instead.

When Ty got to his bunkhouse, he wasn't in the mood

to crack open a book or work on his push-ups. He didn't feel like watching anything, and he felt too wired and weird to go to bed.

The next thing he knew, he was outside again, walking away from the ranch house toward the cool, blue river that tumbled down from the mountains and through the fields and gave the ranch—and the town—its name. It was a mile or so, out there beneath the stars, and he told himself it was good to get out. To walk as much as possible on that bum leg of his. Loosen it up and get it ready for next month's ride.

That was true enough, but he didn't really know what he was doing until he found himself at the family's plot of graves that sat beneath the willow trees out this way. In the dark, the trees were little more than shadows, and the starlight made the graves themselves inky. Mysterious.

When they weren't. They were just graves. A pretty, tidy end to messy, complicated lives.

The idea that he could live out his life and end up here, stuck beneath this land that had defined every member of his family going back generations, when he wasn't like them and didn't deserve to be a part of the land the way they were, made Ty . . . restless.

When he'd been a kid, he'd hated this place. He'd hated his father, certainly, because Amos had never been a kind man. Or much of a good one, by any measure, even before Bettina left him. He'd loved nothing more than to come down hard on his sons. Ty could remember the fights the old man would pick. The number of times Amos had flipped the kitchen table, sending everything on it flying, because he liked the commotion.

I don't know how you put up with that man for all those

years, his mother had said when he'd seen her in Santa Fe after the rodeo spent a weekend out that way. She'd even given one of her theatrical shudders.

I didn't have the option of divorcing him like you did, Ty had replied. With a grin, of course. Always with the grin. *And you left us with him. So he couldn't have been too bad, right?*

But he'd always understood Bettina. When push had come to shove, literally, she'd left and she hadn't looked back. The same way Ty had on the morning of his eighteenth birthday, with the black eye his father had given him the night before and Amos's birthday encouragement ringing in his ears.

You're good for nothing, you little punk, Amos had slurred at him. *Never have been, never will be, just like your mother.*

Ty had figured he might as well be a famous good-for-nothing, then.

But that was the funny thing about his memories. Everything before those lost two years remained curiously dim. He could remember what had happened, but like there was a film over it. He could remember that he'd been angry. Or he could assume that he'd been angry, based on the memory. But he couldn't really feel it.

He might have been tempted to assume he was a happy-go-lucky kind of a guy. But the whiskey had taught him better than that, repeatedly. And now there was Hannah.

Hannah, who tugged at parts of him that were anything but happy-go-lucky, whether he could identify those parts to his satisfaction or not. And if he'd had any doubts left on that score, he was standing in a freaking graveyard in the middle of the night.

The Colorado winter had pounded down his father's grave, so it was as flat as any of the others. Some of the headstones were cracked and crumbling, but not Amos's. It was too dark to read, but Ty knew what it said.

It was not *good riddance*, as Ty himself had suggested the night after the funeral, whiskey bottle dangling from his fingers. It was Amos's name and dates, no more and no less. Terse and to the point.

Tonight, it hit Ty that a name and a couple of dates were a piss-poor monument to a life. Or maybe what was hitting him was the fact that if he died tomorrow, he would never know what had happened to him in those years he couldn't remember.

But he was pretty sure Hannah could.

And he acknowledged, out here where there was nothing between the river and the sky but the bones of the men who had made him, that there was a huge part of him that didn't want to know the secrets she had to tell. Because he'd almost gotten used to what he knew about himself now, gaps and all.

But if he wanted to fill in those gaps, he needed Hannah to do it.

He walked back to the ranch house and climbed into his truck, then headed back toward town before he could talk himself out of it. The land out this side of Cold River had been farmed and ranched by the same handful of families forever. He passed the farmhouse where Abby's grandmother still lived off the same county road and knew the lights in the distance when he started up the side of the hill belonged to the Kittredge spread.

Some people—Gray, for example—liked those deep,

eternal roots. They liked feeling connected, as if they were a part of the land already. Ty had always worried his roots might strangle him, the way Amos had tried to do before Ty got too big and too unpredictable.

He drove back into town, past the turn toward the Coyote where he could find trouble if he wanted it, and around to the small parking lot in back of the bed-and-breakfast where Hannah was staying.

Where his headlights picked her up as she threw a bag into the back seat of her pickup.

Ty pulled up next to her and climbed out.

The town was quiet. The stars were out up above. And Hannah looked as unsurprised to see him as he was to see her.

She'd changed into a plain T-shirt. Her face was washed clean of the makeup she'd been wearing earlier, and her blond hair was braided and tossed over one shoulder. That made something in him click, then hum. He found himself rubbing at his chest almost absently.

"I'm not running," she told him, frowning. And she tipped up her chin like she wanted to fight him. "I'm leaving. It's not the same thing."

"I don't want you to go."

He didn't know where that came from, exactly. But the words rushed out anyway, and there they were, cluttering up the night like noise.

Hannah sighed as if he'd hurt her.

"You know things about me I don't," he said. He wanted to touch her, but he didn't dare. He was afraid he wouldn't let go. He was afraid his body remembered things he didn't, maybe. "I want to know them. All this time I've been back I've been waiting. To remember. To feel something. Whatever you don't want to tell me is as good a place to start as any."

"Ty . . ." She shook her head. "I don't want to *make you* do anything."

He took a step toward her and thought better of it, and angled himself back against his truck instead. It was as close to surrender as he had in him.

"I can't force you to tell me," he said, his voice low. "But I wish you knew what it's like to stand in front of a person knowing they could start filling in a big, blank space in your life, but . . . won't."

She looked away for a moment, while the night breeze played over the curls she'd braided.

And Ty . . . *felt.*

There was that pressure in him, like a weight, that he worried might crush him. And he couldn't tell if he wanted it to or not. There was that restlessness that had always been in him, but this was different. This was more focused. It wasn't scratching at him to get out, get away, get himself lost out there in the world again. It was aimed squarely at Hannah.

He wanted to touch her. He wanted to taste her, sure, but it was more than that. He wanted to sink his hands in her hair. For some reason he wanted her to smell like rosemary, and he wanted to get close enough to find out if that was a memory or a wish.

He *wanted* her and that was like a revolution inside him.

Because the only things he could remember wanting until now were revenge, redemption, or oblivion.

Hannah crossed her arms, and Ty couldn't tell if she was trying to ward him off or hold herself in. Off in the distance, on the other side of the line of buildings where Main Street lay, he heard a burst of laughter from the Broken Wheel. It reminded him that they weren't the only people out in Cold River in the dark tonight.

But all he could see was Hannah and the way the starlight made her blue eyes look even deeper. Fathomless.

"I don't know how to do this gently or make it okay," she said, and he would have said she was being matter-of-fact if it weren't for the faint tremor he could see run through her.

"Just do it, Hannah. Please."

Even though that weight on him felt a lot more like foreboding, suddenly.

"Remember you said that," she said softly, and her lips curved, but it wasn't a smile. "I'm not a groupie, Ty. I'm not a buckle bunny, though more power to them, and I never was. I'm your wife."

6

Of all the things Ty expected her to say, it wasn't that.

Wife.

The word echoed inside of him. Too loud, though she'd said it quietly enough. Too . . . sharp. It was impossible, if not outright laughable—and yet he wasn't laughing.

He was pretty sure he'd never felt less like laughing in his life.

Ty had absolutely no idea what to do next. What he remembered stretched back to last March, but during that time, he'd always had a plan. Get off the painkillers. Stop hurting everywhere, so bad he wanted to pass out every time he breathed. Learn to use his busted-up leg again. Walk. Head back home to the ranch. Stay at the ranch and work it with his brothers. Then start training to take back his pride and his reputation from the bull that had stomped it out of him.

In retrospect, all of that was easy.

"My wife," he said. Flatly. Like it would make sense if he said it too. Or maybe prompt her into laughing and admitting that this was all a big joke at his expense.

But Hannah didn't laugh either. The night seemed

thicker than before, but she didn't appear surprised by Ty's reaction. Or his lack of a reaction. She already had her arms crossed and her chin up, and he could only describe the look she aimed his way as belligerent.

"I'm afraid so." But her accent made that a whole thing. A symphony or two, soft and sweet and yet decidedly not here for his nonsense.

"I mean . . . We actually . . ."

"We sure did. That's why I used the word 'wife.' Not girlfriend. Not fiancée. *Wife*. Because yeah. *We actually*."

"I got married. To you. In a big . . . church thing with the matching dresses and people throwing rice and God and everything else."

He was no longer leaning against his truck. Or languid in any way. It was like his body was betraying him all over again, except this time there was no bull to blame it on.

"You look unwell, Ty. A little intense." By contrast, she looked almost entertained. "There was no big church. It was you and me and our own, personal officiant."

Something in him . . . flatlined. Too much noise, and then one continuous roar, blocking everything else out. He'd never panicked in his life, but he was pretty sure that this was it. This was panic.

All the panic in the world, and then some. "I have to go."

He didn't realize he'd said that out loud until she shook her head, her eyes glinting dangerously out there in the dark.

"What a tremendous shock."

"Just for a while," he said, maybe fiercer than he intended. Not that he had any idea what he intended with all that roaring inside of him and his heart beating so loud, he was half-afraid it would kick its way through his chest. "To clear my head."

She looked as if she expected him to break into a jog and head for the foothills. As if it was possible he already had. "If you say so."

He could barely make his jaw operate. "I have to think, Hannah. And I have chores I need to do on the ranch in the morning."

"You do chores?"

The fact she looked as baffled by that as she did amused made that roaring thing in him rock, darkening at the edges.

"It's a working cattle ranch. Of course I do chores. But then—"

"Oh, sure, the mythical *then*." Hannah shook her head as if he'd already let her down. Right here and now. "So, whenever *then* is, when you're finished thinking and working and whatever else you come up with to put this off, we'll . . . what? Come up with new ways for you to disappoint me?"

It was one blow after another, and that one nearly took him down. Ty felt off balance. Like he didn't know up from down, and the only clear thought he had in his head was that he needed to get away from her.

Just for a minute. Just to regroup. Just to remember what little he knew about himself, and do something about the throbbing thing in his temples, like a pulse.

"Give me your phone number," he bit out, too gruffly. "I'll call you. And we can . . ."

But he didn't know how to finish that sentence.

"Talk about our marriage?" Hannah asked brightly. "Won't that be a treat. Because as you can guess, what with me standing out here in the middle of the night loading up my truck and you having no idea who I am, it's been pretty stellar so far."

"Fantastic. More things for us to talk about. But not now."

"And you already have my phone number, Ty."

It was that, more than anything else she'd said to him so far, that . . . wrecked him. If she'd produced a baseball bat from the back of her pickup and whacked him one, he doubted he would have felt any less beaten up.

She held out her hand, and Ty found himself digging into his pocket and pulling out his phone. Then handing it over wordlessly, with the dizzying sensation that he'd done this before. Maybe a lot.

She swiped a few times, scrolled down, and then handed it back to him.

He stared down at the entry on his screen. "This says *Ball* as a first name. And *Chain* as a last name."

"You're a funny guy."

Ball and chain. Wife. Ty was sure that the earth was leaping and buckling beneath his feet, but when he looked around, there was no damage. His truck stayed put. The buildings remained standing.

There was no earthquake, there was only Hannah. And the way she stared back at him, implacable and certain, that only made that buckling sensation worse.

"We thought that was funny?"

"You thought that was funny," she corrected him. "But I can see you don't want to believe me. Go ahead. Call the number."

If it was a test, he failed it, because he hit the call button. Then they both stood there as the phone she clearly had stuck in her back pocket started playing Johnny Cash's "I Walk the Line" into the night.

"Yes, we know each other," Hannah said when the ring tone died away, her voice as even as her gaze was steady. "Yes, you not only have my phone number, but you kept it. Under a cute little nickname. And yes, I really am your wife. I'm sorry if that upsets you."

He almost laughed at the notion that he was *upset*. As if this was *upsetting*, instead of, to pick a word at random, *catastrophic*.

"You were leaving," he managed to say, trying to gather himself when all he wanted to do was hit himself on the head repeatedly to make his memory work again.

"Yes, I was leaving," she said in the same distressingly even tone. "Because you can't remember, and I don't know that I have it in me to argue with you about the life we lost at the same time you lost your memory."

The hits kept coming.

"Okay." Ty shoved his phone back into his pocket. Then he rubbed his hands over his face. Neither made him feel particularly better, but he stopped wishing something would fall down from the mountains and crush him where he stood. "Go back inside your hotel. Let me . . . take this in. Can you do that?" And when she only stared back at him, another word was torn out of him. "Please?"

There was something so stark on her face, then. Heart-breaking, even.

"I can do that," she said softly. "For now."

Ty was entirely too aware of her as he backed away. Then he rounded his truck, climbed into it, and drove out of the small lot.

Before . . . whatever was coming at him transformed into a train and flattened him.

He had no idea how he got himself back to the ranch. Or into his bunkhouse. All he could focus on was that buckling feeling, out there in the dark behind the B and B. That shaking, as if he were being turned inside out, over and over, without end.

Like a ride on a rank bull that went on and on, long past the usual eight seconds.

Ty had no memory of going to sleep, but he woke up with a jolt when his alarm went off at four thirty. It was still dark outside. But that was morning on the ranch, every day at *you must be kidding* o'clock. The four-thirty alarm was part of the deal.

He launched himself up. He staggered into his shower, feeling as wasted and hungover as if he really had drowned himself in whiskey last night the way he'd wanted to.

Whatever Hannah had done to him, whoever she was to him, she was far more potent.

He fixed himself coffee in his efficiency kitchen, grimacing at the kick of it, and when he felt fortified enough, he headed out to the barn. He had horses to tend to, his own and the ranch's. He and Brady handled the stalls, feed, and water while Gray went out to do the initial check of the pasture and the herd.

Then it was into the ranch kitchen for a quick bite and more coffee before heading back out into the fields to get down to business. The fences always needed checking. The animals always needed feeding and care. The paid hands were working on the irrigation system, so once feed and water was handled, the brothers rode the fences. Repairing them as needed, which was exactly the kind of physical labor Ty craved.

Maybe if he beat down his body enough, his memory would catch up with him.

"You're a lot less cranky than I expected," Brady said at one point, as they set to work on a downed stretch of fence in one of the upper pastures. "Since you apparently went back out last night."

"You must not know how to hold your liquor, baby brother," Ty replied, keeping his hat tilted down low over his face so Brady couldn't really see his expression. "If you think I'd show it one way or the other the next day."

"Do you actually handle your liquor?" Brady asked with a laugh. A genuine laugh, as if Ty were telling jokes. "Or do you drink so much all the time that you're always more drunk than not?"

Brady had said something similar last night. Everyone believed Ty was constantly wasted, and up until last night, Ty had been fine with that. His father had been the egregious drunk of the family, staggering around kicking up violence and making a mess out of everything he swayed near. Ty didn't know why he'd taken up that torch every time he came home. Amos had always told him how worthless he was, so Ty had belly flopped right on down to meet those low expectations, maybe. Or had Ty wanted to try to meet his father on his own level?

Whatever the reason, he'd been drunk at every family event he could recall before January, and he'd never made any announcements when he'd stopped getting quietly wasted, so it had been amusing to watch his brothers tiptoe around his supposed problem. Also, if he were drunk all the time, he certainly couldn't be training for anything like a redemptive bull ride. He'd figured it was a good camouflage.

But that was before Hannah held his gaze and talked about him disappointing her. And suddenly Ty didn't find it all that entertaining that Gray and Brady basically thought he was the reincarnation of Amos.

"I'm wasted right now," he told Brady, his voice too dark. "Who knows? I might pound you into the ground instead of this fence post. Anything could happen."

Brady wiped at his face, and then eyed Ty much too closely.

"You don't actually have to fill Dad's shoes, you know," he said. Quietly. "Just because he was a lousy drunk, it doesn't mean we need another one around like some kind of monument to him."

Ty wanted to make a monument out of Brady's face, but restrained himself. And when he pulled out his grin, it didn't quite fit the way it used to.

"I'm a charming drunk," Ty drawled, as if there were nothing dark in him at all. "And if you don't know the difference, Brady, I really don't know what all that fancy education of yours was for."

Which changed the subject for a while, because Brady's college years were a sore spot between him and Gray, who'd never been shy about pointing out that Brady could have used his education to help the family enterprise. And hadn't.

But in case Ty had forgotten that he was now living in the midst of his family like he was a teenager all over again, Gray weighed in after he and Ty had finished wrestling with another stretch of fencing some time later.

"How many times did you come and go last night?"

Gray tilted his own cowboy hat back on his head, the better to pin Ty with one of those stern looks of his. Ty would rather die on the spot than admit that he, a grown man, was reacting to his older brother's *sternness*. "If I didn't know any better, I'd think this was still high school and you were sneaking out to see that girl. What was her name?"

"I can't rightly say," Ty drawled. He squinted at his big brother. "What was your high school girlfriend's name again?"

Gray's mouth curved at that. "Now it feels even more like high school. And you wish."

"You and Brady must lead deeply depressing lives if you're this interested in mine," Ty pointed out. "You're like a couple of mother hens."

He even made a clucking noise.

"I'm not a hen. I don't cluck." Gray shook his head. "But I do pay attention to trucks coming and going in the middle of the night. Right outside my house. Where my sixteen-year-old daughter sleeps when she's not walking around entirely too pretty for my peace of mind."

"It wasn't Becca. It was me."

Gray shot him a darkly amused look. "Believe me, I know who it was."

Ty had absolutely no doubt that unlike Amos, who'd spent his nights passed out and snoring, Gray knew every single thing that happened in that ranch house. The same way he had when he'd felt it was his business to monitor his younger brothers way back when.

"Unlike your teenage daughter, or even teenage me, I don't need to give you an accounting of my whereabouts last night. Pleased as I am that you're so obsessed with my social life."

That curve in the corner of Gray's mouth deepened. "You can do whatever you want. But it sure does make me wonder why you want to keep secrets."

It wasn't the first time Ty had noticed that his normally forbiddingly laconic older brother had gotten downright chatty, relatively speaking, since he'd married Abby. But he was still Gray, so when Ty didn't take his bait, the conversation turned to the usual ranch concerns, like water rights and hay, or blessed silence, until they trooped back in for lunch.

Abby was there in the kitchen, cutting slabs of freshly baked bread, while Becca stood next to her, piling the slabs high with roast beef and cheese from their own cows. There were vegetables from the summer garden, tomatoes sliced thick and dark green lettuce. There were jars of tangy homemade pickles, and the airy mayonnaise Becca had been experimenting with making this summer.

"You need to try this version," she told Ty with her daddy's air of command, and the smile that Ty knew was for him. He was her favorite. "It's lemony."

"Do I want lemony mayo? My gut reaction is no."

"You want *my* lemony mayo, Uncle Ty. Obviously."

Ty accepted the plate his niece handed him and ruffled her hair a bit, to make her grin. He liked this lighter, happier version of Becca. Abby had been good for her too. Becca was far less brittle than she'd been back in the fall. These days, she worried about perfecting her mayonnaise, not whether her dad was going to be okay.

Ty chose not to share with her that if pickup trucks ever started showing up at the ranch for her—in the middle of the night, or at all—her dad's reaction would be the least of her concerns. Gray was the good man in the Everett family.

Ty went and sat at the oversize table that took up almost all the available space in the eat-in part of the kitchen. It had been fashioned from a barn door, taken from the very same barn that had made Ty bleed a million years ago—a secret only he and *his wife* knew.

His wife. Ty couldn't let himself go there. To her. Not here, in front of his family, when they were all watching him and waiting to see if he'd keel over into an alcoholic blackout at any moment. He focused on the old table instead. The door they'd started using because Amos, who had enjoyed actual alcoholic blackouts with regularity, had broken every other table that had ever sat here.

This table was hardy and sturdy. It could take all kinds of abuse. Amos could flip it as he pleased, and he had. It went over, but it never splintered into pieces. There were scratches worn into the surface, where the old man had used to sit there with his ever-changing will, muttering darkly as he scratched out names, entered in new, angry directions, and generally used the thing to make threats and force compliance.

Or at least, Ty assumed Gray had been compliant. Ty had been gone.

It had been right here at this kitchen table that Amos had given Ty that black eye, after a scuffle over yet another ruined dinner.

With such great memories, Ty couldn't help but wonder if it was for the best he had all those blanks. And better still that he couldn't really feel any of the things he could remember. It was all very clinical inside of him. If asked, he could have told the story well enough. He'd turned eighteen three days after graduating high school.

He'd told Amos he was joining the rodeo, and Amos didn't like it.

Because Amos really didn't like it when the people he was used to controlling and beating on took off. It wasn't personal.

Still, it had felt personal when the old man leaned in and called Ty names.

You've never been anything but a disappointment, he'd sneered. *If you didn't have your grandfather's build, I'd swear there wasn't a drop of Everett blood in you. You have your mother's face, boy, but pretty fades. You think you have some bright future out there? Wake up. You've never had a talent for anything but causing trouble.*

Sounds like a rodeo champion to me, Ty had snapped back.

Working in the rodeo takes respect. That stock could kill you as soon as look at you. You have no respect.

I give respect when it's due, Ty had thrown at him with a sneer.

You're a useless waste of space, Ty, Amos had growled right back. *You're not dependable like Gray. You're not bright like Brady. You're nothing but a joke. You really do take after your mother, don't you?*

Ty had swung on him and gotten a shiner for his trouble. He remembered it all. He could even make the story funny in the retelling, if he wanted. That Amos, always so predictably nasty, ha ha. But whatever way he told the story, he didn't feel a thing. Not what it was like to have his father whale on him. Then kick him out, which had stung even though he'd already planned to go.

And he couldn't have said why, when he remembered

these things, he thought about Hannah. Had he told her that story? Had he made her laugh?

But even as he wondered it, he knew better. Hannah wouldn't have laughed at a story like that. Her big, beautiful blue eyes would have filled up with tears instead, for the angry, essentially fatherless eighteen-year-old kid he'd been. She would have looked crushed. *For* him. She would have reached out, taken his hand, and—

Ty blinked. Was that a memory? Or a daydream?

Either way, he was unsettled when Brady swung into the seat next to him. Abby lowered herself down into the chair across the table, one hand rubbing her enormous belly as she went. Only when Abby was settled and Becca sat down next to her did Gray take his seat, and only then did they all start eating.

As if they were marginally civilized after all.

Obviously that was more of Abby's influence. If Ty remembered those drunken holidays when Amos was alive correctly, when they'd been left to their own devices, they'd all choked their food down like they were in jail.

As they ate, Abby asked Gray direct questions about the state of the ranch and how he'd spent his morning. Gray answered her, in detail, and not for the first time, Ty was struck by how much of an actual partnership the two of them had hammered out. Abby was invested. She was genuinely interested. She also did all of the ranch's paperwork, which was much different than what Ty remembered from watching his mother interact with his father right here in this same kitchen.

All Bettina had ever done at the ranch was complain. Ty couldn't recall a single instance of her helping Amos with anything. There had been other women around after

Bettina, but none of them had pitched in either. And Ty hadn't spent a whole lot of time here after he'd started up with the rodeo, but his memories of Gray's first wife, Cristina, had put her firmly in the unhelpful camp.

Ty could remember sitting at this very table years back, listening to Gray and Amos argue about calving season. When he'd looked up, Cristina had been angrily spearing green beans on her plate while rolling her eyes.

Cows, cows, and more cows, she said, supposedly to Ty. But loud enough so there was no doubt Gray could hear her too. *Some days I wake up and ask myself, what was life like when I talked about something else?* Anything *else?*

Cattle pays for the roof over your head, girl, Amos had growled.

Gray had said nothing, which had been normal. Ty didn't remember him smiling much back then either.

Abby, by contrast, was a farm girl, born and bred. She didn't complain about the livestock. She'd grown up five miles down the same road on the old Douglas farm, here in these fields where her own ancestors had eked out their living over the course of generations. Her grandmother came from a long line of dairy farmers. She could talk about cows forever, and did.

But it wasn't the conversation about the latest issue with this or that buyer that fascinated Ty today. It was the way Gray tilted his head toward his wife as they talked. He leaned into her as they spoke.

She reached out and toyed with the hand he lay on the table, almost absently. And in the middle of their conversation about the latest speculation about beef prices, without missing a beat, Abby shifted Gray's hand from the table to her belly. Then held it there.

"Is he kicking?" Becca asked excitedly from her place at Abby's side.

"Like it's his job." Abby smiled. "And we don't know that he's a boy."

"He could as easily be a boy as a girl," Becca countered.

Ty watched his brother and the way he focused on his wife's belly. On whatever he felt beneath his hands. And the way that made his face change into pure delight. And love, if Ty wasn't mistaken.

He had to look away. It was all too . . . vulnerable.

"My money's on another girl," Brady chimed in. "So far, I've done well with nieces. I want to continue the trend."

"You have one niece, Uncle Brady," Becca said, grinning. "That doesn't count as a trend."

"It will when there's a second one."

"I'm personally rooting for a baby," Abby said, her eyes on Gray. "As healthy as possible. That's all."

Gray still had his hand on his wife's belly. "What Abby said."

"Come on, Dad," Becca teased him. "You must have a preference. You have a preference about everything else, including Christmas."

Gray eyed his daughter. "I love Christmas, Becca, if that's what you mean."

"Sure you do. But if you and Abby have a boy, you'll have one of each. Isn't that what everybody wants? A set?"

Gray's hand rested on Abby's belly, though there was that curve to his stern mouth. And something warm, and maybe approving, as he looked at his family. Becca, Abby, and the baby on the way.

It took Ty a minute, but then he got it. Gray looked *content*.

And that was like another earthquake, rocking Ty where he sat, his sandwich demolished before him.

Gray had always been a mountain. The rock of the family. He'd basically raised Ty and Brady after their mother left, because Amos certainly wasn't up for the job. He was grim and determined. He made the ranch work. His first wife had died in a car accident on her way to cheat on him—not for the first time—and he'd soldiered on. Ty had seen Gray at ease. He'd even seen him riled up on occasion. He'd seen him . . . okay, always, one way or another.

But he never would have imagined that a man like his older brother—or any man in his family—could be *content*.

Ty knew about surviving. If the last year had taught him anything, it was that he had an endless capacity for holding on against all the odds. And he could remember other parts of his life too. The rodeo tour that had been eight seconds of glory here and there, recovering from those few seconds, and a whole lot of grueling travel in between. City after city. Highway after highway. All for the dubious pleasure of a belt buckle and the prize money that went with it. And the knowledge that he could do a thing, repeatedly, a wise man never tried.

Ty had been doing that thing his entire adult life. He was going to do it again. But he couldn't *feel* it.

And that was what hit him, like another full-size bull landing on his head.

Hannah made him feel things. She didn't have to do anything. She showed up, and earthquakes took him over. He didn't know what that was, but it was better than . . . this. Surviving on a mix of bullheadedness and whiskey, ranch work and dreams of redemption next month, sitting at the same table where his father had taught Ty everything he needed to know about drunk and mean.

He'd had over a year of pure survival, two missing years before his bad fall, and then the dry, clinical sweep of the life that had come before that. So many stories he could tell and not care at all about any of them. Like he didn't really exist.

Hannah's number was programmed into his phone. She'd known exactly how to find it.

She'd known exactly how to find him too.

There was nothing in all the years he could remember that suggested Ty was the marrying kind. He would have sworn up and down he wasn't. And yet he still wanted to touch Hannah more than he wanted to drink himself quiet inside. Even when he knew it was foolish, he wanted to talk to her, touch her, be near her. He'd gone running after her last night, twice, though he would have said that wasn't something he did.

He never had, according to his grayed out memories.

Hannah rocked him, straight through, and his initial re-action to that was to deny it. To push her away. To return to the ranch and act like everything was normal.

But what was normal?

He had a wife. Ty let that settle into him. He let it sink in deep, like it was finding its way into his bones and set-tling there.

He had a wife.

That probably meant a lot of things he didn't want to face, but it was possible it also meant that she could re-mind him how to live. How to feel.

How to be something more than an angry miracle after a run-in with a bull, a bottomless bottle of whiskey, or a one-night comeback story to pack the stands so people like Buck Stapleton made money.

It was only when his entire family was staring at him that Ty realized he'd pushed back from the table and stood.

"You doing all right over there, Amos Junior?" Brady asked mildly. He would need to pay for *Amos Junior*, obviously. Later. When Ty had sorted a few things out.

Gray only studied Ty like he knew something, when Ty doubted very much he did. Given he didn't know much himself.

"I have to go into town," Ty said gruffly. And too loudly. "I'll be back later."

He didn't wait to see how that announcement landed, especially since that clearly meant he was shrugging off the afternoon's workload.

He didn't really care.

Ty had a wife. And he needed to find her. Now.

7

Hannah was positive she would be up the rest of the night, heart and head racing, going over and over every word she'd said and every expression that she'd seen on Ty's beautiful face. Expressions she'd once known so well, she'd been sure she could tell what was in his head at a glance.

When she woke up the next morning, groggy and well-rested despite herself, she was shocked. When was the last time she'd slept so deeply?

You know when, that irritating voice inside her jumped right in.

But she didn't want to remember those stolen nights in her secret marriage. Not when Ty's reaction to learning she was his wife had been to shut down. Then leave.

Then again, hadn't that been his response to everything he didn't like, as long as she'd known him? Why should anything change now?

Hannah sat up in her bed and scrubbed her hands over her face as if that could reset . . . everything. She tried to let the glorious colors of the rising sun outside her windows soothe her. When that failed, she went to the bathroom to make sure she looked pulled together, calm, and confident. Reasonable inside and out. And then she went back, settled on her bed, and called her mother. On video, so she could see her baby and soothe that hollow feeling inside her.

Because there was nothing on this earth that did her heart better than her baby boy's face. And better yet, his delighted laughter when he saw her.

Jack was her reset. Jack was what mattered. He was the reason she'd come here, and too bad if that felt more complicated than it should in Ty's presence.

Her broken heart would heal or not. Her child trumped her pain, every time.

When Mama finally swung the phone around so she could study Hannah's face while Jack amused himself with his squishy blocks, Hannah may or may not have "accidentally" switched the angle on her own phone, so she could make it clear without saying a word that she was all alone in her room.

"How long are you planning to stay out there?" Luanne asked coolly, when Hannah held her phone steady again.

"I don't know yet. As long as it takes."

"Until what?" Luanne asked. And managed to keep from rolling her eyes. Hannah chose to view that as encouragement. "Until his convenient memory loss reverses itself?"

"Your feelings on this topic have been noted, Mama. Repeatedly."

"I don't understand your approach to this at all," Luanne said with a sniff. "It doesn't matter what he pretends he can't remember."

"He was crushed by a two-thousand-pound bull and is lucky he's upright and walking. He's not faking."

Luanne sighed. And lost her battle—well, Hannah was assuming it was a battle on her part—with her dramatic eye rolls.

"You have a marriage license. His name is on Jack's birth certificate. He can remember or not remember as he pleases. The facts remain." She shook her head, as if Hannah didn't know all that. "He needs to step up."

"I've been in Cold River for less than a day," Hannah pointed out, reminding herself that she needed to remain calm. If only because if she succumbed to emotion, Luanne would claim it was Ty's bad influence on her. "I don't know what I could have done in that time that I haven't done already."

"It doesn't take more than a moment to say, 'Congratulations, you're a daddy. And by the way, here's the bill for the child support you owe me.' Do you want me to time it?"

Hannah's head ached, and she only wished it was from the one beer she'd had at the bar. And her jaw hurt from the fake smile she had welded to her lips.

"Will you please let me do this? My way?"

"I don't have a choice, do I?" Mama retorted.

But she didn't hang up in a huff, the way she normally would. Hannah asked after Aunt Bit, the only person alive who found Luanne's controlling nature entertaining, probably because she was the older sister and could ignore it. Hannah cooed at her baby more, trying not to cry, because this was her first separation from him. And it turned out, it hurt her heart even more than she'd expected it would.

This time, her mother actually said goodbye before she hung up.

"Progress," Hannah muttered out loud.

The way her voice hung in the room only reminded her that she was all alone, again, which was another thing she hadn't been for any extended period of time in a long, long while. Not since she was a kid, really. Before she'd started down the rodeo queen path, there had been Aunt Bit while Mama was working. Librarians. The people at the stables where she worked mucking out stalls and whatever else needed doing to help pay for her riding lessons.

Once she'd started doing rodeos regularly, her mother had become her chaperone. And Luanne hadn't taken her eyes off of Hannah for years. Not until Hannah had found a way to deceive her—another one of Luanne's favorite topics. She liked to trot that out when Hannah least expected it, the better to use it like a hammer.

But Luanne wasn't here. Besides, Hannah had found herself significantly more sympathetic to her mother in the ten months since she'd had Jack. She'd had no idea it was possible to love anything or anyone that much. She'd had no clue how *ferocious* that love was. How deep and primal.

If Luanne needed to express something that huge and unwieldy through her relentless nitpicking, Hannah could live with it.

Right after she let herself sob because she was away from her baby, and no one had explained to her what that would feel like. How did people . . . let them grow up? Move out? Make terrible decisions about their own lives the way Hannah had?

She rubbed at her eyes, laughing at her own sentimentality.

When she swung her legs over the side of her bed, she was as alone as she'd been when she'd gotten off the phone.

In this lovely B and B she probably couldn't afford. In Cold River, Colorado, where her husband lived and continued not to know her or want her.

Hannah glared at the book on her bedside table that she'd imagined could make her feel better about her own life. The trouble was, she could read about other lives, but she still had to live *this* one. Things could be worse. Things could always be worse. But that didn't make the things that were less than great right now feel any better.

She took her time getting up. Then dragged her feet as she got herself ready for another day that might potentially include run-ins with Ty. To add insult to injury, she kept checking her phone like some kind of overwrought teen to see if he'd called. When of course, he hadn't.

"And won't," she told herself. "Because men can't be trusted."

By the time she pushed her way back out onto Main Street, she felt, if not exactly ready to face another round of memory games with her errant husband, at least sufficiently armored to handle the day. The morning was cool, and she'd taken her outfit down to a more casual level, like that might help her blend. For Hannah that meant jeans, a T-shirt, her hair pulled into a side ponytail, and enough mascara that she could be seen from space.

Because a girl needed her face on to tackle the day.

She walked down the street to Cold River Coffee, and ordered herself an espresso drink and some breakfast to go with it. She found a seat in the back near the overstuffed bookshelf and helped herself to the nearest romance novel as she ate.

Hannah couldn't remember when she'd finished eating, or the last time she'd checked her silent phone, but she was well into chapter six when a shadow fell over her table. She looked up, trying to hide her annoyance at being jolted out of the world of a brooding pirate hero and the heroine who was more than a match for his antics.

It was the woman from the bookstore, holding a to-go cup in her hand.

"Look at that," she said, grinning. "Looks like you couldn't help but find yourself a better mood."

"Guilty as charged," Hannah replied. When she smiled back, her smile felt real. Not the one she trotted out for awkward social occasions and liked to hide behind everywhere else. That struck her as significant. "I guess I was looking for hope after all."

"As a matter of fact, my name is Hope, so you've already found it," the woman said with a laugh. She stuck out her hand. Hannah shook it, murmuring her own name as she did. "It's nice to meet you, Hannah. When you're ready to come exchange that book you bought, I'll be waiting."

Long after she left, Hannah was still grinning. Until it occurred to her the way it had in the saloon last night that if everything had gone according to plan, she might have come to this town with Ty when their time with the rodeo was through. Hadn't that been one of the plans they'd talked about on those long, stolen nights? If they'd moved here, maybe she would have already befriended Hope from Capricorn Books.

Maybe it wasn't the fact that Cold River looked like such a pretty postcard that kept digging beneath her skin, an itch she couldn't quite scratch. Maybe it was that she was visiting a phantom version of her life. She was peering down the road not taken, and sure enough, it was filled with ghosts of what could have been.

Her phone was still silent.

Hannah made herself concentrate on her book, not any ghosts-of-lost-futures that might have been hovering around. After a while, she moved over to the comfortable couch. She ordered herself more coffee, and then she lost herself in a novel the way she hadn't done since Jack was born.

When she went up to get her third coffee drink, because she could, the coffeehouse—crowded and busy when she'd walked in this morning—was quiet. The doors were propped open to let the summer breeze in, and overhead fans circled it around lazily. Hannah could hear her boots against the hardwood floor, a richly satisfying sound.

The girl behind the counter had her hair tossed back in the kind of messy bun that Hannah always admired, but could never do herself. Hannah had been raised on curling irons, endless amounts of hairspray, and the sure knowledge that messy buns were for other sorts of girls. The truly effortless girls, unlike rodeo queens, who had to put time in to appear that way. Easy, carefree girls who didn't have to work so hard to be beautiful.

"Didn't I see you in the Broken Wheel last night?" the girl behind the counter asked, tilting her head slightly to one side.

Hannah studied the girl—the easy, effortless, carefree girl who was much too pretty in that laid-back, woke-up-like-this way Hannah coveted and maybe hated a little—more intently. She read the name on the tag on her chest. *Amanda.*

The only thing Hannah had been aware of in the Broken Wheel Saloon last night had been Ty. The husband who didn't know he was a husband. The husband who didn't know he'd made vows.

It was a lot easier to ponder all the ways he could have broken those vows, and how it wouldn't really be his fault if he couldn't remember he was married, when she wasn't staring straight at the sort of girl he might very well have done his vow-breaking with.

Her stomach heaved.

"Did you?" she asked, as noncommittally as she could, and hoped none of her turmoil showed on her face.

Because maybe it wasn't Ty's fault if he'd broken his wedding vows. But it wasn't Hannah's either.

"You and Ty Everett," Amanda said, with exactly the sort of blissful confidence that a girl like that *would* embody, from her head to her toes. It wasn't her fault Hannah felt numb with horror everywhere except her knotted-up stomach. Nothing was anybody's fault, yet Hannah still wanted to scream. "You must know him from the rodeo."

"Must I?"

The girl grinned as if Hannah hadn't sounded like she was chewing nails.

"I'm Amanda Kittredge," the girl said as she handed back a few bills. She shut the register and leveled a look on Hannah. Then held it. "Kittredges and Everetts have been neighbors out there over the hill since the dawn of time. Or the 1800s, anyway, which is basically the same thing. And Ty has always treated me like the bratty kid sister he never had."

A surge of relief washed over her, so intense it made her knees tremble, and Hannah wanted to hate herself for it. But what she knew about her husband was that he had very, very healthy appetites. Was she really going to try to convince herself that he'd ignored them all this time? When, from his perspective, he had no reason not to indulge as he pleased?

"Everyone in this town treats me like a bratty kid sister, as a matter of fact," Amanda was saying, which at least kept Hannah from really exploring how ill she was making herself. "I guess I should count myself lucky. It's not every girl who gets to stay sixteen years old forever in the eyes of every single person she knows. Even when she actually hasn't been sixteen in six years."

Hannah leaned into the counter. As much because she was suddenly *in love* with this girl Ty treated like a kid sister as for emphasis. "Funny you should say that. I grew up in a small town myself. Every person in it treated me like a stick of dynamite about to go off from the day I was born. An immature stick of dynamite, I should say, no matter how old I was."

Even when some Sweet Myrtle residents had pitched in to help with her queening, they'd made it clear they always remembered where she'd come from. And therefore where she'd end up. And look at that, they'd all been right.

"I wish anyone worried about my potential for mayhem." Amanda sounded rueful as she moved from behind the cashier over to the big, sleek espresso machine. "I could actually strap myself in dynamite and explode right there in the middle of Main Street. No one would think it was dynamite. They would think, 'What's that Kittredge girl doing out in the street by herself? Does her mother know where she is?'"

"Unless you actually blew something up. I find that often cures condescension. What with the exploding."

Amanda looked thoughtful. "What an excellent idea."

"I feel I should clarify that you probably shouldn't blow anything up that you can't put back together. And there are worse things than condescension. I'm really talking metaphors here."

Amanda scoffed at that. "This is the Wild, Wild West. We prefer directness over metaphor, every time. We used to have shoot-outs in the street."

"Here?"

"Not *here*. But in the west in general."

Amanda quickly fixed the drink Hannah had already forgotten she'd ordered and slid it onto the countertop between them.

Hannah stared at the drink. She reached out and ran her finger down the Cold River Coffeehouse logo. And reminded herself that she'd already lost all her dignity, and then some. What was a little pride?

"So, what are the Everetts like?" she asked. Innocently. So very innocently. "Out of idle curiosity."

Amanda's eyes gleamed. "The Everetts helped found Cold River," she said, leaning into the counter that separated them. "They're basically a part of the scenery. Amos Everett died last fall, making pretty much nobody sad, and left the ranch to his three sons. The oldest, Gray, married Abby Douglas, whose family has also been around forever and who happens to manage this coffeehouse. They're about to have a baby."

It occurred to Hannah that the pregnant woman she'd seen here yesterday was Abby. Her sister-in-law, who she didn't know. Who she'd stared at, making up a life for, because she'd had no idea the woman was married to Ty's brother. It made her feel . . . hollow. One more road not taken.

"The youngest is Brady. He's . . ." Amanda stopped. Her cheeks heated, then she rolled her eyes. "Annoying. But the middle one. Ty."

"Yes. That one."

"He came back last fall for the funeral. And he's been here ever since."

"At the Broken Wheel Saloon?"

"Sure. Sometimes he hangs out with—or I should say, near—my older brothers. But you know. He was badly hurt. Folks say he's not quite the same since that bull trampled all over him." Amanda made a big show of wiping the already clean counter. "I wouldn't know because I'm everybody's little sister and apparently my ears are too tender for the truth. Still. My impression is that Ty was never short of company. Back when he was a rodeo star."

"But not since he's been back here?"

Hannah should really have despised herself for asking that question. And maybe she did. It was hard to tell, mixed in as it was with all the rest of the strange, outsized emotions knocking around inside of her.

"That's why I asked you about him in the first place," Amanda said, with understanding in her voice and that level gaze. "Because it was such a novelty."

And Hannah was horrified to find she was *this close* to breaking down and crying. Right there at a coffee counter with a perfect stranger.

"Thank you," she managed to say. "I shouldn't have asked."

"Don't thank me for sharing simple facts," Amanda replied. She grinned. "But should you see me blowing something up out in the middle of Main Street, non-metaphorically, definitely don't ask me what I'm doing out there unsupervised."

If Hannah pretended her throat wasn't tight, her voice had to sound normal. "I wouldn't dream of it."

A group of people swept in, then, laughing their way up to the counter, and Hannah honestly couldn't tell if she was grateful or frustrated that her conversation with Amanda was interrupted. She took it as her cue, carrying her coffee back to her couch. Her book.

Her unexpected morning of peace and quiet, with sugary-sweet coffee drinks.

But it was different now. Her heart felt swollen. With shame and embarrassment for asking, on the one hand, because she'd revealed far too much. And with relief and gladness, on the other hand, because maybe he hadn't broken his vows after all.

Sure, she wanted a divorce, but she would prefer not to have been cheated on in addition to having been left pregnant by the side of the road. Or in a Kentucky hospital, to be more precise.

That was why, when she looked up again to see someone walking toward her with purpose and intent, she forgot to mask her natural reaction. She forgot to be wary.

Because Ty was coming toward her, all cowboy saunter and his mouth in a harsh line, and there was no way she managed to conceal her simple, involuntary joy at the sight of him.

Because he was hard and lean and as dangerous as he was beautiful. She didn't know how everyone around them didn't see it. And today he wasn't aiming that lazy grin of his all around, hiding himself in the process.

He was focused on her, his dark green gaze intent.

It made her heart clutch at her. It made her stomach flip over.

It made her remember.

Her body too. Because there were parts of her that didn't care what he'd done or what he might have done. Parts of her that ran soft and sweet for him, now and forever, and when he was this close to her, Hannah forgot to feel ashamed about that.

He stopped in front of her, his gaze moving over her as if this were the first time. As if she was new, or he was, and Hannah supposed she should take offense at that. But he'd always looked at her that way. As if he couldn't believe she was real. And for a moment, she forgot to let it hurt.

"I thought you left again." He didn't sound accusing. He sounded . . . *intent*. "You weren't in the bed-and-breakfast."

"I told you I wouldn't leave. Though if you took a few days to do all that thinking, I can't promise I wouldn't have revisited the idea."

Something moved over his face, and she couldn't read him anymore. That she'd lost that, too, made her chest tight.

Hannah glanced away, because she was afraid he could still read her too well. She blinked, bringing the front of the coffee shop into focus, where Amanda was making another round of drinks. The other girl caught her eye and nodded once. In support.

It was the funniest thing. Hannah had considered the

other girls in the rodeo queen program friends, but they had also been competitors. They traveled around together in packs, but girls were always coming and going, depending on how they handled themselves and the demands of the program.

There were girls who were too overwhelmed to handle the rodeo schedule. There were girls who thrived on it. There were girls who seemed aloof and snobby when they were really shy. There were always girls like Laura, who would be the first to call Hannah sister, particularly while she gossiped about her to everyone else. Hannah had loved her time with them. But she'd missed the sense of camaraderie more than she'd missed anyone in particular.

Yet here was Hannah feeling a sudden kinship for Amanda that she'd never felt for the girls she'd toured with. Because she'd never dared tell *them* the things she'd revealed to Amanda over a coffee drink.

She jerked her attention back to Ty and found him studying her, a storm she didn't understand brewing in his gaze.

"I told you I need to think. I've done that," he said. Almost formally.

Hannah got to her feet, clutching her romance novel to her chest like it was her Bible. "And what have you decided?"

Ty's gaze moved over her, as if he was trying to slot her into place. Fit her into a bigger puzzle to make the image come into focus. Then he reached out his hand, over all that distance between them, which was about a foot. And a very long eighteen months.

He didn't speak. He only held out his hand, and waited.

Hannah stopped breathing.

There were a thousand reasons to slap his hand away. Slap him, while she was at it. There were a thousand reasons for bitterness. Anger. Tears. A thousand reasons to try to hurt him, so he would know how it felt.

There were a thousand reasons, but she loved him.

As angry and hurt as she'd been, as she still was, she had never stopped loving him. She had fallen in love one time in her whole life, and she wasn't sure she was capable of falling out of it again. Even if that made her a bigger fool than she already was.

That was the only reason she could think of as she slid her hand into his.

His hand was as big and hard as she remembered it. Callused and warm.

Right.

Like a key into a lock, he'd told her once, and she was sure she could feel that same old deadbolt in her heart slide home.

"We need to have a conversation," Ty said, and Hannah was sure she could hear the same sensation she felt, everywhere, in his low voice. "But not here."

He waited for Hannah to nod her agreement, and then he started for the door, her hand still swallowed up in his.

She felt ripped apart, yet sewn back together at the same time. Did he feel what she did? How easily they fell into their usual pace. How natural it was to walk like this, hand in hand. How they were clearly meant to lace their fingers together and walk side-by-side.

Hannah was sure that people were watching them go, and not only Amanda. She tried to tell herself that she was anonymous. That even if she wasn't, they didn't have to hide anything anymore, the way they had while Hannah was finishing up her last year as a rodeo queen and had to pretend she was married to the rodeo, not a man. But her cheeks reddened anyway, because old habits die hard.

Ty led her out onto the street and over to where he'd parked his truck. He opened the passenger door for her, then waited. She wanted to say something. Anything. Make a joke, or say something silly enough to break the strange, fragile and yet fraught tension that grew between them more and more with every moment.

But all she did was climb into his truck and keep her eyes straight ahead as he shut the door. She stayed like that when he climbed in, put the truck in gear, and started driving.

There was country music on the radio, the summer sun pouring in from above, and Hannah laced her fingers together in her lap and tried to breathe.

Ty drove out of town, crossing the bright blue river and the aspen trees that lined its banks before heading up the side of the steep hill—she would call it a mountain— that led out to the Everett ranch. But he didn't stay on the main road. As they neared the crest of the hill, he veered off and followed a dirt road into the woods. They bumped along, while Cam sang about a burning house and made Hannah break out in goose bumps, like foreboding. There were cool shadows and the smell of sunlight on pine, and then they were out of the woods again. Then he was parking, there at the edge of a sharp cliff with a sweeping view back over Cold River and out across the Longhorn Valley.

When he turned off the engine, the silence was so intense that it made Hannah jump. Or maybe that was her heart.

He undid his seat belt and then turned, draping one

arm over the steering wheel. He tossed his hat off onto the dashboard, raked his hand through his dark hair, and then fixed that stormy green gaze on her.

"You say we're married. I don't imagine you'd turn up to drop that bomb unless you could prove it."

"I have the marriage certificate," Hannah said quietly, trying not to take the word *bomb* to heart. Speaking of metaphors. "Right here in my bag, if you want to inspect it."

He nodded, though it was more a jerk of his head than a request to see documentation. "Tell me the story."

"The story?"

He didn't move, and yet she was convinced that he grew. Until he took up all the room inside the cab of the pickup. The air was seething with all the things between them, remembered or not. Or maybe he was seething, and stealing all the oxygen while he did, and Hannah's heart catapulted around inside her chest. Until she was almost too dizzy to sit up straight.

But she didn't dream of looking away from him. She couldn't.

"Tell me how we met," Ty said, his voice a dark command. "Tell me how we're married, but no one knows about it. No one mentioned a wife to me. And while you're at it, Hannah—tell me where the hell you've been all this time."

8

Every time he saw her, she was prettier. Or it hit him harder.

Ty didn't know what kind of black magic that was, but it worked on him. She worked for him and through him, laying down tracks of fire and need, a whole lot like she was the kind of whiskey he'd used to reserve for the nights he either won big money or nothing at all.

He didn't know what to think about the possibility that he'd been applying whiskey to his problems since he'd left the hospital when maybe, without knowing it, he'd been substituting whiskey for everything he couldn't remember about Hannah. One of his physical therapists had gone on and on about what was stored in the body. Trauma. Pain. Memory.

Why not a whole marriage?

He'd driven her up to the lookout point on the hill, which in his time had always been pretty crowded after dark. But at this time of day, it was deserted. For once, Ty wanted to avoid an audience.

Because he didn't know what to think about any of this.

That pulse in his temples didn't hurt, exactly, but it didn't go away either. He couldn't imagine what look he had on his face. He could see the expression Hannah had on hers, and that was painful enough.

"I don't know why you want me to tell you something when you're not going to remember any of it," she was saying again, and his finger itched to touch her. But he didn't. "I could make up a complete fairy tale. I could tell you anything at all, and you wouldn't know the difference."

"Tell me anyway." He had liked holding her hand back there in town. More than he was comfortable admitting to himself. Was that muscle memory? Or did he want it to be, because it was better than not remembering? Because he was getting sick and tired of the things he couldn't remember. "You can start by telling me why, if we've been married this whole time, it took you more than a year after my accident to come clue me in."

Her eyes went cool. "I was unavoidably detained."

"What does that mean? Prison?"

She let out a short laugh. "Not the way you mean."

There was something about the way she held herself, then, too still and too ready, as if she expected him to push her to answer. It made him stop. Because he wasn't sure he wanted to know whatever it was he could see lurking there in her blue gaze. Maybe he needed to get his head around the fact he was married—*married*, for the love of all that was holy—before he focused on why she'd abandoned it. Him.

"We can circle back on that," he said when all she did was wait to see what he would do. And he couldn't tell if that had been a test, much less if he'd passed it. "Start at the beginning."

Something had changed. Ty had left the ranch, driving too fast on his way back into town, the way he always did. *Relentlessly reckless,* the high school principal had called him back in the day, and Ty couldn't argue with that assessment. Back then, he'd seen it as a badge of honor. He'd basically made recklessness his own personal brand.

But he hadn't liked not finding Hannah where he expected her to be, and he was sure the girl at the front desk of the bed-and-breakfast was going to spread that tidbit of gossip far and wide. He didn't care. Because when Ty had found Hannah in the coffeehouse, everything inside him . . . crystallized.

He'd been fuzzy and out of focus for eighteen months, but looking at Hannah sitting on a couch in the coffee shop Gray's wife Abby managed—surrounded by his past and hints of those roots he'd always hated so much—suddenly everything was clear again.

A truth he'd kept to himself was that Ty had been coming back home to Cold River even before he'd gotten the news that Amos had died. He'd been in a bad way. The only thing he'd ever known how to do was the rodeo, and sure, he'd known he was too old and pushing his limits when he'd hit thirty a few years back. But he hadn't had anything resembling a back-up plan. Getting stomped the way he had ended the debate. He was out.

He'd put off the decision to return to the ranch as long as he could, especially after Amos's unsolicited appearance in the hospital had reminded him exactly what sort of tender encouragement he could expect from his dear old dad. But then Amos had thoughtfully kicked the bucket, almost literally, and there Ty was. Stuck on the ranch again, where he'd never belonged.

And for the first time in his life, without Amos to fight against.

Ty was pretty sure that Gray and Brady grieved their father on some level. Or the father Amos had never been and now never would be, maybe. But not Ty. He didn't miss his father at all. What he missed was the constant antagonism. The sure knowledge he'd always had that whatever he did, however reckless he got, Amos would always be the worst-behaved Everett around.

Amos had alienated the entire valley. He'd chased away every woman who had ever been foolish enough to take a chance on him. He'd done the same with his own sons, except Gray—but then, Gray was good at disappearing right there in plain sight. He carried on doing what needed to get done, no matter what storms were raging on Cold River Ranch.

Ty had been fighting against his father his whole life. But now Amos was gone.

And Ty had become him. His brothers certainly thought so. Because he'd encouraged them to think it, sure. But hearing it from Brady today had stung a lot worse than it used to.

Because Hannah said she was his. And it was like a switch was thrown inside him when Ty had walked into Cold River Coffee and seen her sitting there.

Mine, that greedy thing in him had asserted. Again.

Maybe it didn't make sense. Maybe he would never remember what had happened between them. But she said she was married to him, and the one thing Amos had never managed to do—famously—was hold on to a wife.

Ty could start proving he was nothing like the man right here, right now.

He wanted to flash his usual grin at her, high up above the land he'd been trying to escape for most of his life, but he couldn't quite get there. "I'd help you out, darlin'. But I don't know the story."

She flushed. And even that was pretty. "You met me at the rodeo."

"I figured that part out already, Hannah."

"You had quite a reputation. I heard about you a long time before I actually met you. I was warned off repeatedly, in fact. By pretty much everybody, their mothers, and three-quarters of the livestock too."

That sounded about right to Ty. What he could remember about the women he'd known was enjoying them. Thoroughly.

"Where did we meet?"

Hannah settled back against the passenger seat, turning her body to face his. He mirrored her. "Bozeman, Montana. Two years ago in May. I was competing for the Miss Rodeo Forever crown, and I wanted nothing to do with you."

"Why not? I'm sure I was charming. I'm always charming."

He didn't question how he knew that was true.

"Rodeo queens don't date. And even if we did, I wouldn't date you. You took entirely too much pride in your bad reputation."

Ty shrugged. "No point having a bad reputation otherwise."

"So you made sure to tell me."

He felt his mouth curve in one corner. "Glad to know I'm still me, no matter what I can remember."

Hannah made a sound that was somewhere between a

sigh and a laugh. Or maybe the idea she might laugh about any of this was wishful thinking on his part.

"I can only tell you what I remember. And what you told me. You said that everything changed." And he could see the vulnerability in her eyes, then. "You said you looked up from your life, there I was, and nothing was ever the same."

Ty couldn't speak. He felt as if the wind had been knocked out of him. He felt greedy and guilty, and there was too much *stuff* inside of him, like dirt kicked up in a rodeo ring. He was afraid he might choke on it.

"It was the same for me," she said quietly. "But I didn't know what was happening at first. I told myself I disliked you. I wanted to, anyway. You would try to talk to me and I hated it. But you were in my head way too much when I didn't see you for a while. And when I won Miss Rodeo Forever and traveled around with the rodeo the way you did, I looked forward to you trying."

"How exactly did I try?"

She shifted her shoulder against the back of her seat, curling into it. "First, you would stop me and say hello. Then comment on how I replied."

"Did your replies need commentary? Maybe I thought we had a collaborative situation going on."

"You sure wanted it to be. And there was always a critique. Though you usually couched it as more of a suggestion for the future. Not that *you* minded that I was ever-so-slightly abrupt, but you wouldn't want me to find myself in a situation down the line where someone less open-minded than you was tempted to take offense."

Ty blinked. Not at what she said, but the way she said it in a spot-on imitation of his laziest drawl.

She smiled. Faintly. "You were generally more positive about my horseback-riding skills."

"I do admire a woman with skills."

"When you say things like that, it's hard to believe that you really can't remember all the other times you said the same thing. The *exact same* thing."

"That must be weird," Ty allowed. "But I bet it's a whole lot weirder to have somebody sit and tell you what you said and what you did. To them. Like they're talking about someone else."

"We don't have to talk about this at all. We can stop right now."

"I'm not the one who's reluctant to hear this story." He considered her as she sat there, one knee pulled up on the bench seat. "You ready to tell me why?"

The color in her cheeks deepened. But she didn't answer his question.

"I didn't think so," Ty said.

Hannah swallowed and kept going. "You talked to me a little here, a little there. I tried to make it clear that I wanted nothing to do with you. But that was a lie. I did. And pretty soon I stopped pretending I found you irritating. And you started asking me for a date."

"You keep telling me rodeo queens don't date."

He knew they didn't. At least, not out in the open. There was no actual rule Ty was aware of that decreed the girls couldn't date, or have boyfriends when everyone knew they did, but any outward, visible signs of attachment were frowned upon.

Suddenly he wondered if that was why that voice in him had told him he couldn't touch her—not in public. Not her.

Not rodeo royalty who belonged to the sport while she wore her crown, never to a man.

That pulse in his temples hurt. His heart walloped him. Did that count as a memory?

He studied her, blond and pretty and obviously something to him, or why would he keep having these reactions? Maybe the memories didn't matter. He focused on her story instead. "You made an exception for me?"

"It was my last year of queening. And my reputation was absolutely spotless. I took a lot of pride in that. Winning Miss Rodeo Forever once was an unbelievable honor to me. It was what I'd worked for since I was small. But I was the first girl to ever win the crown two years running. I was grateful. I was proud. I was humbled."

"Hannah." Ty's voice was low in the scant space between them. And probably more amused than it should have been. "Are you trying to tell me I came along and compromised your virtue? Or your crown?"

Her cheeks flushed brighter, fascinating him. "We had to keep it a secret. Not only from everyone involved with the rodeo, but specifically from my mother. She traveled with me as my chaperone. And she didn't waffle about whether or not she disliked you. She straight up hated the sight of you."

Ty took that in. "I'm not surprised to hear I have that effect on mothers. I'll take that as a compliment."

"I'm not sure you should. I'd never lied to my mother before in my whole life. About anything. But I did for you."

"For me?" He didn't know where the question from. Maybe the same place those memories that weren't quite memories swirled around inside of him and made his head hurt enough to keep him on edge. "Or for you?"

She didn't respond immediately. Ty could hear the breeze rustling through evergreens outside the windows. The far-off sound of the falls that poured out of the side of the mountain and tumbled toward the valley floor. But it was the steady kick of his heart that was deafening him.

He waited for her to answer him, but she was too busy frowning down at her jeans. "Did I make you lie, Hannah?"

She took her time lifting that fathomless blue gaze to his.

"No," she said after a moment, as if it was a hard confession. "You didn't make me lie. I did that all by myself."

If that was a victory, it landed wrong. Ty ran a hand over his jaw, because he couldn't shift that heavy weight off his chest, and pushed on.

"What you're telling me is we snuck off when we could. Made our own trouble and pretended we didn't know each other when we were in public again." He shrugged. "That doesn't strike me as anything too unusual."

"We didn't make as much trouble as you might imagine." That flush on her cheeks changed shades again. He wanted to touch it, and had no idea how he managed to keep his hands to himself. "It took me a long time to let you kiss me."

He'd been kidding when he'd mentioned her virtue before. Because what did Ty know about virtue? He doubted he'd encountered any. But the pieces suddenly slammed together.

"Hannah." Every time he said her name, it tasted better. Especially this time. "Was I your first?"

"My mother raised me to believe that if I so much as looked too long at a boy on the street, it would be the end of me. I believed her." Hannah let out a shuddery sort of breath that charged the air between them, but then straightened. "I'd never looked at another man. I'd certainly never kissed one. And you kind of liked that."

Any doubts Ty might have had that he'd touched this woman, intimately, disappeared at that moment. Because the way she looked at him held too much heat. Depth. Knowledge. And more, he could feel his own body's deep, enthusiastic response to the notion that he'd been the only one to do it.

He still liked that idea, it turned out. More than *kind of* liked it.

And the certainty felt good.

"There was no possible way I was ever going to have sex before marriage," she told him, and he didn't need to touch her face to see how bright she was burning. But he did anyway. The faintest brush of the back of his fingers against one cheek.

She was hot like fire and soft like satin, and the feel of her sank deep into him.

Like another dose of certainty.

It was as if he was waking up.

"You said you could respect that," she said, but her voice was softer. Shakier. "But you had no intention of marrying anybody. You'd sworn your whole life you'd never marry anyone. I figured that was the end of the conversation."

"And the end of us . . . not making trouble?"

"No. We still did our thing. But it got . . . frustrating."

Ty wished he could reach over and pull her memories straight from her head as easily as he'd touched her face. He wished she could project them in front of her like some kind of movie screen. Because he had the feeling he would give almost anything to rewind through what she called frustration and linger there a while.

And the hotter her cheeks got, the more sure of that he became.

"You went home for Christmas that year." Hannah looked out the front window. "You came here. And I was sure you would probably let things fade away. Because we talked and we talked, but it never went anywhere. We didn't want the same things." She pulled in a breath. "Or we didn't want them in the same way, at the same time. You talked a lot about *someday*. But I didn't want to gamble everything on *someday*. I was already risking my reputation as it was."

"You sure wouldn't want to throw more than a reputation after a rodeo cowboy," Ty drawled. With more darkness than he'd known was in him. And barely managed to keep from calling her *darlin'*. "That never ends well."

She took a breath. Then she shocked him by reaching over and putting her hand on his leg. He felt the heat. That same kick of certainty.

Mine, that voice belted out, and this time, without any further instructions about when and how.

He didn't care if it was memory or not. It felt right.

"My reputation was my job," Hannah said, her voice quiet and her gaze direct. "And I had to fund-raise to get that job in the first place. I went to UGA on a full academic scholarship, and that certainly didn't include appropriate rodeo outfits. Or travel costs. When I talk about losing my reputation—and my crown—I'm not talking about my ideals. I'm talking about letting down good people who believed in me and gave me their hard-earned money to represent them in a sport they love. That mattered to me. It still matters to me."

But all Ty could really focus on was how easily she kept her hand on him. There was nothing awkward about it. Nothing new. It was intimate, not necessarily sexual, as if she'd put her hand on him a thousand times before. It underscored everything she'd told him, because Ty's mind might have decided to play tricks on him, but his body was the same instrument it had always been. He knew every inch of it, what it could do, and where it was weak.

He also knew his own physical familiarity with another person. He didn't have to remember her when his body was doing it for him. He didn't need the ache in his head to kick at him again.

Hannah was still talking to him, her hand on his leg and her gaze locked to his. "But when it came to that Christmas, and why it seemed over, it was because we'd been going around and around in circles. I couldn't give you what you wanted. You couldn't give me what I needed. No matter how much we loved each other."

That was like a detonation. Ty's ears rang from the blast of it. "We loved each other?"

Her smile about broke his heart. "Of course we loved each other. Or it wouldn't have been so hard. And it wouldn't have hurt the way it did."

9

Ty didn't know what to do with that. The concept of loving anything or anyone was hard enough to get his head around. He hardly understood it when it was his brother, *content* in a way Ty had never believed in. Not for any truthful, real people outside of Hollywood.

Real people weren't happy, if they were honest. People wanted to be happy so they declared they were in love. But love was nothing but a claim trotted out so no one could see the darkness inside them. The demons, the despair. They posted carefully perfect pictures all over the internet and wrote glowing stories about their own wisdom and resilience. Growth and perseverance. They made a lot of noise about faith. They practiced their public faces and they learned how to get along. They went through the motions and they numbed themselves out however they could, in sacrament or in sin, whatever worked.

Anything to feel, but not too much. Anything to pretend it all mattered. Anything to connect with the darkness inside them, through piety or shame, and call it a journey.

But none of it was *real*. None of it was honest. And it had never been him.

"It was hard?" he asked. "It . . . *hurt*?"

Hannah's gaze was steady. "You can love someone with everything you have and still not be right for them. That's where we were, then. That's what you told me."

The pressure inside him doubled. Tripled, maybe. It felt like a kick to the gut with a concrete block.

Ty had never believed in love. Why would he? He'd never seen it.

Yet Hannah told him he'd loved her so much it had hurt. So much he'd decided it would be better to part than to hurt *more*. And it was clear she didn't mean the kind of hurt he knew best. Not the loud, ugly, drunkenness Amos had used to batter them with. At the kitchen table and everywhere else. Day and night.

All in the name of Everett family tradition.

He tried to shake that off. "I told you I loved you but I wasn't right for you." The words felt weighted. Barbed. "I actually said that."

"The last time I saw you that December. It was at an event after the last rodeo of the year in Nevada, and yes, that's what you said. And we both very sensibly agreed we should take a break, get our heads on straight, move on." Hannah's mouth curved. "But that didn't work."

Somewhere between what might have been a memory and the growing certainty that their relationship was what she'd said it was—that he'd married her, and not at gunpoint or otherwise under duress—Ty realized he'd started to care far too much about where this story was going. Especially when he already knew the ending.

"You were going to be in Vegas for New Year's Eve

because you had a bunch of sponsorship events there," she said. "And you asked me to meet you."

"I thought we broke up."

Hannah made a sound that he might have optimistically called a laugh, however small. Then she sat back, taking her hand away, and Ty wanted it back with a ferocious burst of need that should have knocked him over. Instead, he sat there and let it roar in him until his leg started to ache.

Not because it hurt, like the other one. But because he wanted her to touch him again.

"We weren't any good at breaking up," she said, and there was a softer note in her voice that . . . did things to him. He tried to ignore those things and concentrate on her. "We agreed to take some time, and then we talked anyway."

Ty tried to imagine any part of the complicated relationship she was talking about. Love, for one thing. Then nobly deciding that love wasn't enough, only to ignore all of that and keep right on going. He couldn't reconcile anything she was saying with what he knew about how he behaved.

But then, he didn't react to her the way he did to anyone else. He was messed up listening to this story, which should have been as relevant to him, personally, as any other story she could have told. About anyone. Even if he'd wanted to protest and claim this wasn't him, that certainty in him, stronger by the moment, told him it was.

Or he wouldn't care about this story or anyone in it, and he did.

"I told my mother I was going on a New Year's trip with college friends," Hannah said. "It wasn't anything to do with my reign as Miss Rodeo Forever, so her presence wasn't needed. There were no cowboys to ward off and no reputation to keep pristine with friends I'd studied agricultural communications with. She didn't believe me, but what could she say?" She made a rueful noise. "By which I mean, she said a whole lot, but I went anyway."

"You have a degree?"

"Rodeo queens have to have some education to win a crown, formal or otherwise. You know that. We have to answer any questions that come our way, whether it's why we exist or whether we approve of the latest headline news. Or why the barrel-racing course is set up the way it is. Why steer wrestling is called bulldogging. Or if the animals are sad, which is an actual question I've been asked more than once."

"Bulls are generally mad, not sad. And happy to let you know it."

Hannah smiled. But she didn't let the easy moment roll on too long. Her expression changed, and she continued her story. "You picked me up at the airport and took me back to your hotel room."

Ty knew how much he'd changed already in the course of this conversation, because he didn't make any kind of suggestive remark at that. He didn't try to joke this away or make it matter less. He was too busy watching her, as tense as if he expected her to swing at him.

And she did.

"When we got there, you got down on one knee," she said softly. "You told me you loved me and asked me to marry you. Right there and then."

Ty added that to the list of things he shouldn't have been

able to imagine. And yet, it was somehow easier to picture than it had been before she'd come to town. He didn't know if that made it better or worse.

"So." He had to clear his throat. "We eloped?"

"Rodeo queens are single, never married," Hannah replied in that same soft, quiet voice that he still marveled hadn't knocked him flat. "But you'd thought it all through. You said we'd keep it to ourselves for the rest of my term. People might suspect, but suspicion wasn't the same as an announcement, so we'd be fine. A lot of girls wander around with awfully close 'cousins' or 'friends' while they're doing their thing, who magically turn into boyfriends when they're done."

"Please tell me I didn't offer to be your cousin."

Hannah's eyes gleamed. "You said we could keep doing what we'd been doing. And then when we found moments to be together, we could be husband and wife instead of not enough of one thing, too much of another, and frustrated all the time. You knelt there before me, with a big smile on your face that doesn't look a single thing like that grin you flash at the slightest provocation. And you told me that you could give me your mother's ring, but it was likely cursed. So you bought me one instead."

That went through Ty like a chill. Because he had his mother's ring. Bettina had handed it to him with great drama one of the times he'd caught up to her in some far-flung city. *I'll never allow it to touch my flesh again,* she'd said. *But maybe you'll get some use out of it.* As if the diamond solitaire was a tool he could carry around with him and hang on a utility belt, instead of the emblem of a relationship he wouldn't wish on his worst enemy.

"That sounds like me," he heard himself say.

"So we did it," Hannah told him, her eyes suspiciously bright. As if these were happy memories she was sharing with him. Good memories of this love story he'd starred in, that she'd held onto all this time.

It was another sucker punch.

"We got married in a chapel right there in Vegas. And the ceremony was sweet. Beautiful, if you want to know the truth. There were no expectations or eyes on us. There was no speculation or commentary. There was only you and me and this thing we had together, plus a minister who made us laugh. It was perfect."

There was something humming in him, more powerful than any earthquake. He could feel it in that pulse in his temples. He could feel it in the weight that he couldn't shift from his chest.

Because it didn't matter how perfect it was. Not when it led here, to a truck on a mountain, a man who couldn't remember, and a woman who'd been "detained" for a year and a half.

"And then what?" he managed to ask. "We kept it hidden?"

"For three months or so."

Ty opened his mouth to ask *why three months,* and then got it. It was three months from New Year's to March. And that fall he didn't get up from.

"I expected it to be frustrating in a whole new way," Hannah said, and there was that heat on her cheeks again. "And it was. It really was. But it was fun too, because we didn't have a dirty secret anymore. We had the best secret. For a while, it was the best of both worlds. Like marriage with training wheels. We could try it on in bursts here and there. Ease into it and see how it fit before anyone knew about it. While it was still ours."

"This is a pretty story," Ty gritted out, aware that his voice was too thick.

He was giving himself away. He was messed up and he knew it. He could *feel* it, the way he'd wanted to feel something, anything—but this wasn't compartmentalized or locked away.

He couldn't control it.

Like your memory, something in him chimed in.

But that made it worse.

Ty focused on Hannah. "It can't have been as magical as you're making it sound. Or you wouldn't be sitting here telling me about it, because I'd know."

If his rough tone got to her, she didn't show it.

"I didn't say it was magical. It was a honeymoon."

"Tell me what happened eighteen months ago that brought the honeymoon to a screeching halt," he said. Even rougher.

She looked away, then, out toward the view and the world and all the things she knew about him that he didn't. "We had a fight. A bad one. Then you lost your memory, and here we are."

"Here we are?" Ty echoed. He let out a gruff sound that even he wouldn't call a laugh. "I don't know a lot about marriage. Until recently, I would've told you I'd never seen a good one. But I'm pretty sure that the sickness and health part is a key component to the whole deal. And getting trampled by a pissed-off bull falls pretty squarely into that category. Or am I missing something?"

Hannah was trembling slightly, but the look she leveled on him reminded him that she really was a rodeo queen.

Pretty as a picture, but tough as nails beneath. Capable of mucking out stalls, riding someone else's horse but never blaming it if it balked, explaining the history and relevance of the rodeo to anyone who inquired, handling more livestock, and doing it all looking as perfect as she did right now.

Capable of sauntering back into his life when he didn't know she'd left it, and sitting right here while he digested the news.

"I can't imagine the confusion you're feeling right now, Ty," she said, and she didn't raise her voice. But it wasn't all that soft anymore either. "And I feel for you. But I would strongly caution you to tread carefully here. Because I remember what happened."

"Like you said earlier, I have only your word for it. A perfect honeymoon. And then you're gone." He snapped his fingers. "Like it never happened."

Hannah muttered something he didn't catch, and then turned away.

"What's that?" he asked, and he was too edgy. He was jacked up on too much adrenaline and all these weird emotions he couldn't control or identify.

"I need some air," she said, cool and precise, which only made him edgier.

She pushed her way out of the truck, jumping down and then walking out toward the fat boulder that marked the edge of the cliff.

Ty took his time following her. Not only because of the picture she made, standing there while the summer breeze picked up stray curls here and there and made them dance. When he got out of the truck, his bum leg felt stiff—

as stiff as if he'd been overtraining, when he hadn't been. *Great.* Maybe it would act up now, like he really was a four-hundred-year-old *aged bull rider.* Maybe his bones would alert him to every stray drop of rain.

Or, apparently, every emotionally intense moment.

He rubbed at his hip, then leaned back against the front of his truck. He let the breeze and the blue sky work on him a moment or two. Then a moment or two more, when it didn't take.

"I'm not trying to give you a hard time," he said when the edginess had smoothed out some. "I want to know what happened. That's all."

"Are you absolutely sure you want to push on something when you don't know what's waiting there on the other side?"

Maybe he hadn't smoothed anything out after all, no matter how clear it was today.

"You keep asking me that, Hannah. And my answer is consistently the same. Yes, I want to know. Yes, I'm standing here, asking you to tell me all the gory details you think I can't handle."

"Maybe I'm the one who can't handle it, Ty," she bit out. She wiped angrily at her cheeks, but when she turned back around to face him, he couldn't see any trace of tears. "Maybe you're lucky that you can't remember what happened. Because it was ugly. Obviously. Or you're right, I would've been sitting next to your hospital bed, showing you pictures to remind you who I am. But I didn't realize there was a problem with your memory until about a week ago."

He let that sink in, and couldn't tell what was rocking

him anymore. At this point, an actual tectonic shift would feel like a gift. "What are you telling me? That you'd already left me before I went into the hospital?"

"I had no intention of leaving you," Hannah said fiercely. And there was nothing quiet or cool about her voice now. She sounded as ragged as he did. "You told me to go. You demanded it. And I didn't know you didn't know who I was—or who you were—so when you said it, I assumed you meant what you said."

"What could I possibly have said that could wipe out this whole big story?" he demanded, not particularly calm himself.

Hannah's lips flattened. She crossed her arms, like she was holding herself. And when she opened her mouth again, it was to let out a string of profanity-laden curses and a series of nasty observations that Ty was fairly sure would make a convict blush.

It made something inside him curl up and die.

"My father was good for pretty much nothing." His voice was barely audible to his own ears, but he couldn't tell if that was because his head was pounding too loud, or if he could barely speak. "But while my grandfather was around, he took the time to pick up my father's slack. You could say he dedicated himself to it. And if he taught me anything, it was how to speak respectfully to a lady."

"Yeah. I wasn't too happy about it either."

Ty couldn't take what she was saying and make it track. He couldn't make it *him*. "I've never talked like that to a woman in my life."

"Except you did."

"This was in the hospital?" He raked a hand through his hair. "When I was out of my mind on painkillers?"

"I don't know if you were out of your mind," Hannah retorted, her voice hitching. "I don't know what you went through because you didn't tell me. You told me to leave. And I did. I figured when you felt better, you would call me, but you didn't."

"Because I didn't know I should."

But she didn't seem to hear that, gritted out from between his teeth. "You find it easier to believe you could have a marriage you forgot about than that you could have sworn up a blue streak? I really don't know how to take that."

"Believe me, I know my way around a curse word. But I've never been the kind of man who could take a strip out of a woman. Or would." Ty shook his head again. "Whether I was married to her or not."

But he knew a man who could. And had.

He'd watched it play out in front of him every night of his childhood. He'd heard the things Amos had said to Ty's mother, to his second wife, to any other woman who'd been foolish enough to try to get close to him. He'd said the same and worse to his own children. When it came to nastiness, Amos Everett knew no boundaries.

He had always, always found a lower place to go.

It made Ty physically sick to imagine he could have acted like that. Like the man he'd always hated most.

"Show me our marriage certificate," he said, surprised on some level that he could still speak.

That sick feeling was so thick inside him he was uneasy with it. He couldn't tell if it would take him out at the knees, or send him heaving into the bushes. Or worse, continue to sit there where it was, polluting him.

Reminding him that he was no better than the worst man he knew.

"Because now you want proof. Now that you made me tell you all my happy memories, but you don't like the bad ones."

"I believe you," Ty said, and it was only when she released a breath with a big sound that he realized he hadn't told her that. Not yet. He hadn't clued her in to that certainty in him—or how it kept growing.

"Well," Hannah said unevenly. "I'm happy to hear that, I guess."

He rubbed his hands over his face, but that couldn't rub the Amos stink off of him. Could anything? Or was he stuck with it forever, whether he wanted it or not?

He focused on her, aware that his own gaze was hard. And he couldn't make his mouth curve any longer. But he focused on that certainty in him, because none of the things he'd ever been sure about—his horses, his abilities, his talent for sticking on a bull—had anything to do with Amos. Ty had only ever been sure about the things he'd learned and become *despite* Amos.

"I can't imagine falling in love. And I always vowed I would never get married. But when I make a decision, I stick to it. Always have. If I looked up one day, saw you, and my life changed forever . . ." He shrugged, never taking his eyes from her. "I'd act on it. That's who I am."

She ran her tongue over her teeth, her arms still crossed. "So this is a game of trust, but verify."

"I said I believed you, Hannah. I didn't say I trusted you."

"Of course not. Because why would anything with you be easy?"

"Because it's not lost on me that you're leaving out a critical part of this story. Are you going to lie to me about that? Are you going to look me in the face and pretend that's not exactly what you're doing?"

She swallowed again, and he could see the way her throat worked. Then she moved back toward the truck stiffly, telling him more about how she'd been gripping herself tight than he needed to know. Because it didn't do him any good.

Ty kept his eyes trained on the view while she opened the passenger door. The sweet summer day made the valley so bright, he almost forgot he was staring down into his past. His roots, whether he liked it or not. Generations of Everetts before him, mixed in with the fields and the cattle. He heard Hannah rummage around inside the truck, then slam the door shut.

When she appeared in front of him again, she was holding a thick piece of paper in one hand.

"When we move from belief to trust, I'll decide if I can trust you with the rest of the story," she told him, her eyes dark and glittering. "*If* that ever happens."

She offered him the paper in her hand. Ty took it.

And it was right there before him. Las Vegas. A chapel on the strip. His name and hers.

"Hannah Monroe," he said. As if it were a prayer he'd memorized when he was a child, and he could recognize the sound. But he still didn't know the words.

She searched his face. "Monroe isn't my married name."

Ty reeled at that. And understood that she'd known he would—that was why she'd only told him her first name.

"Everett," he said, as if he'd never heard the name before. "You're Hannah Everett."

"That's what you liked to call me. I was in the process

of switching it all over legally. But we were taking our time, waiting for my reign to end."

Ty handed her back the certificate, too carefully. He raked his hands through his hair again, but that didn't help. He wasn't sure anything would.

Hannah stood there before him, too pretty to have eyes so sad. There was all that fight in the way she raised her chin. And nothing but steel in the way she stood there before him. The way she'd walked him through the memories he'd lost.

The way she had yet to ask a single thing of him.

She was his wife. He had married her, loved her, and lost her, but she'd come back.

He couldn't say the same about any of his father's women. His mother in particular, who enjoyed nothing more than having a few cocktails and sharing the things Amos had said to her during their marriage. The things Ty had heard himself as a kid were bad enough. But Bettina liked to marinate in the specifically nasty things Amos had said to her in private.

It horrified Ty in ways he couldn't articulate, down into his gut and his bones and his battered old soul, that he had ever said such things himself. Much less to Hannah.

For the first time, he understood what that doctor had been trying to tell him. There were some things it was better to forget. And sometimes the mind made that determination all on its own. He might not like it, but he got it.

"This fight you don't want to talk about. How bad was it?"

Hannah's chin inched higher. "It was bad."

"You're going to have to give me more than that," Ty growled. "I would have sworn to you on a stack of Bibles that I wasn't the kind of man who would say those things to a woman, but you tell me I did."

"I'm sorry."

That made it worse.

"I can also stand here and tell you that I also know, beyond any shadow of a doubt, that I would never lift my hand to a woman. But I have to accept the possibility that I'm wrong about that too." His stomach was a painful knot. "Is that what I did?"

The sickness in him threatened to burst out of him, but Ty swallowed it down. Because he couldn't make sense of who he'd been, but he knew who he was.

The very least he could do while facing up to the damage he'd done was look the woman who'd suffered it in the eye.

"No," Hannah burst out immediately. She looked appalled. "No, Ty, of course not. You didn't *hit* me. That's not who you are."

"I'd like to agree with you," he gritted out. "But I can't."

"A fight can be ugly without it being violent," she said, her voice fierce again. "There's a darkness in you. You know that. You never let it tip over into something worse."

Her gaze searched his and she must not have liked what she saw, because she moved closer. And then, stunning him, she took his hands in hers.

"Hannah." But he was touching her again, and it was better than he remembered. It was better than remembering. "I want to apologize for whatever I did that made you stay away for year and a half. But how can that mean anything when I don't remember what it was?"

She smiled, even though he could see her tears now, tracking down her cheeks. "And I want to tell you it's okay."

But she didn't.

Everything felt poised on the edge of shattering, or maybe that was only Ty. He couldn't tell if the noise and riot inside him were trying to destroy him—or if this was what he needed to bring him back to himself.

Ty wanted to be whole. He wanted to be *him*. Even if that meant he had to reconcile himself to these things he couldn't imagine himself saying or doing.

"Were you tired of keeping us a secret?" he asked.

Hannah looked startled, but she didn't pull her hands away. "I wouldn't say I was tired of it, because I knew why we were doing it and I knew it only had to go on like that through the summer. But it wasn't ideal."

"What did you do with that ring I gave you?"

Her gaze locked to his. She pulled one hand away and wiped at her face. When she met his gaze again, she smiled.

Ty watched, transfixed, as she dug beneath her T-shirt, and pulled a chain out from beneath. He'd seen the chain around her neck last night, but hadn't paid attention to the fact he couldn't see what was hanging from it.

He saw it now. A diamond ring.

His diamond ring. He didn't have to remember giving it to her the first time to feel the rightness of it.

He'd spent so much of his life trying so hard not to be his father, but it turned out he'd become Amos anyway. In the most horrible of ways. But unlike Amos, Ty had a second chance. Maybe the bull kicking him to pieces was what he deserved. What he'd earned for giving into the darkness inside of him.

Whatever he couldn't remember, he couldn't care about that, because it had brought him Hannah.

She made him *feel*. She messed him up. He'd taken one look at her by the fence, making nice with his horses, and nothing had been the same.

Ty intended to make the most of his second chances.

He pulled her close. He felt the way she trembled, but she melted into him, and that heat in him tripled, like a hard kick. He let his greed and desire roll through him as he reached behind her to work the clasp of the chain, his hands a good deal less steady than he'd like.

She bent her head, giving him better access to her neck, and he almost felt like a kid again. Undone by the heat of her and the scent of her shampoo. There was something about the combination of that and whatever she rubbed into her skin that got to him. She smelled like rosemary, the way he'd wanted her to in the Broken Wheel last night. And that told him more about the kind of intimacy they'd shared than her story could have.

Because on some level, he recognized it. The scent shot through him—*she* blossomed her way into him—making him feel outsized things that had nothing to do with the simple undoing of the clasp of a necklace.

He let it all sink into him, through him, like memory. Then he let the ring fall off the end of the chain and into his palm.

Ty tucked the length of chain into his pocket, then he took her hand. He watched her eyes get even bluer than the sky.

"I can't remember being your husband, Hannah. But I want you to be my wife."

"That sounds like a good start," she whispered.

But it felt like more than a good start to Ty. It felt something like profound as he slid that diamond ring onto her left hand and stood there a moment, admiring the way it caught the sun. And enjoying the way she did too.

"Ty . . ."

She was going to tell him more things he didn't want to hear. And he resolved to listen, no matter what. It was the least of what he owed her.

But instead, her smile changed. "I believe that in moments like this, it's traditional to kiss the bride."

"I didn't realize there was any part of this that was traditional."

"That's a good point." She swayed closer, bracing herself against his chest. "I've got you covered, cowboy."

Then she surged up onto her toes and kissed him.

10

He tasted like fire. Like love and memory.

And best of all, like him.

Hannah hadn't meant to do more than give him a quick peck. If that. Because he was here in front of her after all this time, and she'd given up believing that could ever happen. Because for the first time in a long while, there was hope.

She had told him their story, and he hadn't laughed in her face. He hadn't turned his back on her and walked away. Or any of the things she'd been afraid he would do.

He believed her.

And if she wasn't mistaken, if it wasn't simply wishful thinking on her part, there was a part of him that remembered her too.

But she'd forgotten how potent he was. How demanding.

Because the kiss didn't stay soft or sweet.

There was that kick when her lips brushed his, flame and longing, loss and hope—and then he angled his head, took the kiss deeper, and everything went . . . volcanic.

It was always this way.

His hands in her hair. Her body melting, yearning.

Her hands were on his chest, and it was like a dream, getting to *feel* him again. Hard muscles, honed to perfection. Whipcord strength, leashed power, and all that delicious heat.

She had been the one to start this. But he took control, the way he always did. The way he always had.

Hannah felt safe once again. Beautiful and effortless. Wild and greedy for every sensation she'd believed was lost.

His lips against hers. The scrape of his tongue. His taste and the torment of it, winding through the whole of her body. The way he gathered her to him, held her against him, and she was never in the slightest bit of doubt how much he wanted her.

And in return, how very much she wanted him.

Every kiss made it hotter.

It had always been like this. It would always be like this. This was why Hannah had risked everything she had for him. This was why she'd lost it.

This was everything. He was everything. And even knowing the whole of the story she'd told him, and the rest of it besides, she couldn't keep herself from losing herself in him.

Again and again and again.

When he pulled his mouth from hers, then set her away from him, she didn't understand. There was too much sensation storming through her. Reacquainting her with parts of herself she'd assumed were out of commission forever.

It occurred to her that for a few brief seconds she hadn't

worried about Jack. Not while Ty kissed her. She hadn't thought about anything except him. Them. This.

And instead of filling her with the typical guilt and shame, it made her . . . oddly grateful. Because she hadn't believed she would ever feel like this again. Beautiful and sexy. Desirable. Made of fire and magic, alive beneath his hands. Instead of a collection of practical body parts there to house and care for a tiny, dependent human.

Hannah felt tears prick the back of her eyes, and she almost told him then. It almost spilled out of her on its own. That they had a baby. A little boy. That he was the best thing that had ever happened to her, that being without him made her ache, and that Ty was his father whether he wanted to take on that role or not.

That in this moment—high up on this hill where she'd done nothing but break her own heart all over again—Ty, who'd made her a mother, reminded her that she was first and foremost a woman.

It was a gift. But she couldn't thank him for it without telling him everything.

Men love sex, not babies, Luanne had always told her. *Never forget that.*

Hannah bit back the words. The truth and the ache and *Jack.* Even though it hurt.

Ty was holding her away from him, those big hands of his wrapped around her shoulders, firm and gentle at once.

The look on his face made everything in her stutter, then glow.

She remembered the first time she'd seen that expression. How stunned she had been to discover that she could do that to him. This worldly, beautiful man, who could have anyone and likely had, if all those rumors were true. But she was the one who made him look . . . undone. Wild with all that fire and desire, passion and longing, and something like astonishment.

"Okay," he said now, something decidedly male in his dark green gaze and no trace of his easy, lazy grin. "I guess that explains a few things."

Hannah didn't understand why they were talking when there were so many other things they could be doing. Sure, there was a lot of noise inside of her, much of it sounding a lot like her mother in high dudgeon. But did it matter if it was smart to touch him like this? Did it matter what happened next?

The liberating thing about the worst having already happened was that she wasn't afraid of it anymore. Her life had already come apart at the seams, and she was still here, with a beautiful, sweet boy in the bargain. There were no more monsters under her bed, lurking around, ready to claim her if she made the slightest misstep.

She'd survived her worst nightmares. Each and every one.

Ty had taught her things about her body she'd never known. Before or since. Hannah had been on a horse almost before she could walk. Aunt Bit had a friend outside of town with stables and a kind heart, who had taught Hannah how to ride. Riding had been her escape. Her pleasure. Her sport.

Hannah had been using her body athletically as long as she could remember. Ty had taught her how to use it passionately. Joyfully.

He'd made her brand new.

And God, had she missed that.

"We can't," he said now.

The words took a moment to land. Especially because he was very clearly not joking.

Hannah blinked. "I can honestly say that's a sentence I never expected to hear come from your mouth."

The mouth in question curved. His thumbs moved on her shoulders, stroking up, then down, and it might have destroyed her, if she let it. She didn't let it.

"This is some intense chemistry," he said in that low, almost-careful voice. "It would be tempting to jump in headfirst. See how it played out."

"Why do you say that like it's a bad thing?"

The irony wasn't lost on her that their positions were reversed, for once. That she was the one who wanted and needed and was prepared to argue for it. And he was the one holding back. It was almost poetic, really.

Hannah had always hated poetry.

"I believe you," Ty said with that same quiet intent. "But I hurt you. And I can't remember why or how. The only thing I do know is that I don't intend to do it again."

"That sounds very noble. Really it does. But—"

"I can't promise you that I'll get my memory back. I can't tell you that I'll figure out how to be the man I was, because I don't know if that will ever happen. Or if that's even a good thing. But I can promise you this." His hands tightened around her shoulders. His dark green gaze was serious. "I will be a man you can trust, Hannah. I will honor you, and the vows we made. Until trusting me feels as easy as that kiss did."

Hannah could hardly speak. She wasn't sure she'd have been able to keep her balance if he hadn't been holding her up.

"Ty . . ."

"And about those vows." He sounded almost grim, then. "I didn't know I was married."

"Oh God," she said, her stomach knotting up. "Please don't feel you need to confess anything to me. I don't want to know."

Mama would say that was vintage Hannah. Sticking her head in the sand. Plugging up her ears and singing *la la la* while the world burned. As if any good could come of watching an inferno as it swallowed you whole.

"I have nothing to confess," Ty told her, his dark gaze clear and his voice perfectly even. Steady. "You are the first woman I've even looked at since the accident."

It matched with what Amanda had told her in the coffee shop. And it made Hannah's heart warm. She shifted back onto her heels, breathing better as the knots in her belly loosened.

"I'm glad to hear that." But she studied him a moment. "Though I don't really understand how that's possible. You told me that waiting as long as you did from the time we started talking to the night we got married was the longest dry spell of your life."

The crook in the corner of his mouth deepened. "I can't say I've ever been happier to be fully unable to comment on that."

He reached out and ran a hand over her hair, the gesture as sweet as it was familiar.

She was so afraid to hope. But she loved him. Everything else was a work in progress. She had to believe that.

Not least because this was the man she had married. The character he played at the rodeo, happy-go-lucky Ty

Everett, with that easy smile and an occasional dangerous edge to his drawl, was for strangers.

Here, with her, he had always been simply Ty. He had always been hers.

Tell him, something inside urged her. *Now, before it turns into another terrible lie. And this time, making you the liar.*

She couldn't. It all felt too fragile. How many bombs could she drop on the man before he shattered completely?

But Hannah wasn't trying to protect him.

The darker truth was that she could handle it if he didn't believe her. She could handle it if he sent her away. She already had.

But if he did the same to Jack . . . If she told him he was a father and he reacted the way her own father had, refusing to see her, severing his parental rights, and disappearing without so much as a backward glance . . .

There was no coming back from that. She would never forgive it.

Not now that Jack was here, a little person in his own right, and a whole lot more to her than a positive pregnancy test and a series of missed periods.

Not again.

"We're not at the rodeo anymore," Ty said. "No one's watching. No one needs me to be your cousin. So. Hannah Monroe Everett. How do you feel about trying this marriage on for size?"

"I don't understand what that means," Luanne said coolly, and Hannah could hear her frown through the phone. "It all sounds heartwarming, baby girl, it really does. But how exactly does trying it on for size equal a man living up to his responsibilities?"

"This is him doing that." The more Hannah defended Ty to her mother, the more certain she felt about the whole thing. She was tempted to say so, but thought better of it, because Luanne would only come up with a new tactic. "He can't man up to responsibilities he doesn't know about. I told him we were married, and he believed me, even though he can't remember any of it. And he instantly stepped up."

She looked down at her hand and the ring that sparkled there. The ring she'd never gotten the chance to wear in public. The weight of it on her finger now felt a bit like she was tempting fate. Another tidbit she opted not to share with her mother.

"You're not exactly hard on the eyes," Luanne said. "What red-blooded man wouldn't leap at the opportunity if you appeared out of nowhere, claiming you were his wife?"

"I appreciate the vote of confidence, Mama."

But Hannah couldn't work up a head of steam the way she might have before. She understood her mother too well these days. Before Ty, before Jack, she'd viewed her mother's laser focus on her every move as her personal cross to bear. And she hadn't always borne it with good grace.

Now, she understood. She heard the fear in it. More than that, the resolve. Her mother couldn't change the world to keep Hannah safe. She couldn't protect Hannah from the things she'd suffered. So Luanne had done her best to change Hannah so that she'd stay safe no matter what the world threw her way.

Hannah got it. She really did.

"You think I don't understand, but I do," Mama was saying. "You're not the first woman alive to fall in love. And it's no small thing that he can't remember marrying you, but wants to hold onto his wedding vows anyway. But what is playing house with him going to accomplish?"

Hannah looked out the window of the bed-and-breakfast there on Main Street. The summer afternoon was bright and golden, warming up the brick buildings and making the flowers fairly burst with color. And Ty waited for her down there, leaning against the side of his truck like a cowboy fantasy come to life. The sun danced over him, making love to his jeans and boots, the T-shirt that showed off every inch of the lean, mouthwatering torso she'd finally touched again, and his swoon-worthy square jaw beneath his tipped down cowboy hat.

He looked lazy. At his ease. Perfectly content to while away a summer afternoon down there.

But Hannah knew he was waiting. For her. And no matter how languidly he thumbed his hat to the folks who passed by and greeted him, he was coiled tight.

Because the real Ty was all that wild intensity hidden right there beneath the picture of laziness incarnate. Hannah had always gotten a thrill out of getting to be the one who saw the truth behind his mask. Today was no different.

"I wouldn't call it playing house, exactly," she told her mother, hoping she sounded thoughtful and pious instead of muddled up with lust and longing. "And obviously, it can't go on for too long. I don't actually like being away from Jack, you know."

"I never said you did."

"Not in so many words, no."

"Hannah Leigh, I am not going to argue with you about what you *think* I said. I have no doubt at all that you love this baby boy. But you wouldn't be the first woman in the world who let a man confuse her some on that issue."

"I'm not confused."

"Then why didn't you tell him he has a son? If he's the man you want to believe he is, ready and willing to jump feet first into every responsibility you lay before him, he's not going to thank you for keeping that to yourself."

As usual, Luanne managed to stick her fingers directly into the tender, painful center of Hannah's worst fears.

"I'm not going to tell you what I'm doing is right, because I don't know if it is," she said after a moment, when she was sure she could keep her voice steady. "I can only do what I think is right under the circumstances."

"I can't bring myself to understand—"

"Mama. Stop."

Hannah wasn't sure she'd ever used that tone with her mother before. A stark command with no pleading in it at all. She hardly knew where it came from. Even more astonishing, it worked. Luanne actually fell silent.

It was such a shock, Hannah almost apologized.

"You never got a second chance," she said quietly instead. "And I'm so sorry for that. But I need to take the one I've been given."

She hated herself, deeply, when she heard the small sound her mother made, then. A tiny, hurt sort of gasp. Hannah squeezed her eyes shut and made herself keep going.

"You're not saying anything to me that I haven't already said to myself, believe me. But there wasn't a single moment in my relationship with Ty when we weren't sneaking around. And maybe that's all we ever were to each other. A dirty little secret. I don't want to believe that, but I need to know. Because I can't bear the idea of throwing Jack into something that's only going to fall apart. And badly." She took a deep breath. "Can you let me do that? Will you?"

Luanne was quiet for a long time.

Hannah waited. She stood at the window, her fingertips on the glass, and prayed she was doing the right thing. For all her big talk, she was terrified that her mother was right and she was being stupid, again. And on a grander scale than before.

Ty wanted to give their marriage a shot. He wanted to give it—them—a chance.

I want another shot at a honeymoon. He'd been driving back down the hill, and she'd been trying her best not to sound as excited at the prospect as she was. Or maybe she was terrified. She still couldn't tell the difference. *Without any sneaking around or pretending this time.*

And yet also, apparently, without sex, she had replied dryly. *Yay?*

The look he'd given her was filled with a dark amusement she'd felt like heat and longing, everywhere. *You'll live. We'll get to know each other. We'll put in real time. Win/win.*

Hannah could certainly use a win.

Especially when it was Jack on the line this time.

"Jack is safe with me," her mother said at last, and if there was emotion there in her voice, she'd managed to smooth it out some. Hannah knew better than to mention it. "If you truly believe this is the way to build our boy the family he deserves, I support it."

It wasn't until they ended the call that she understood how important it was to her to have her mother's blessing this time. How very different that made her feel.

Like a grown woman making her own choices, not an adolescent rebelling against her mother's rules.

She looked around her room, making sure she'd packed up everything. Then she carried her bags down the stairs and tossed them into her pickup out back. She pulled around onto Main Street and came to a stop behind Ty. She watched as he gathered himself up, threw her a look she couldn't quite read—but found she could *feel* just fine— as he went to climb into his truck, and then started down the street toward the river.

Hannah followed him all the way out to Cold River Ranch.

By the time they made it down that bumpy dirt road, the late afternoon was inching into evening. Ty pulled his truck into the yard, and Hannah parked beside him.

She tried to ignore the butterflies in her belly that had gotten wilder with every mile, especially when she saw the ranch no longer looked deserted. There were a handful of other vehicles parked here and there around the yard. As she opened her door, she could hear the telltale signs of habitation all around her. Water running in the ranch house. Horses in the barn.

"I'm not sure this was a good idea," she said nervously, walking to meet Ty at the back of her truck. "Maybe you should have talked to your family first. Prepared them."

"What preparation would work in a situation like this?"

"I don't know. Any? What are you going to *say*?"

"I'm not planning to tell them that I can't remember you, if that's what you mean. I'm not getting into that."

The implications of that sunk in. Hannah scowled up at him.

"You're going to . . . what? Announce you've been married all this time, but I was somewhere else, and here I am? No explanation?"

He gazed back at her mildly enough, but that was an expression she did know. Pure, implacable steel dressed up in a seemingly easygoing package. Ty at his most maddening.

Hannah should have known he didn't plan to explain a thing.

"You do realize they're going to think that I abandoned you in your time of need. That I turned my back on you when you were broken and only showed up now because you're competing again next month. That I only want you for the glory."

"I don't care what they think." He studied her for a minute. "And they don't know I'm competing."

"What? Why else would you be training?"

"Ranch work is rodeo training all by itself, the rest looks like more physical therapy. And I don't make a habit out of sitting around explaining myself."

"Don't you suspect they might notice it when you disappear and then, magically, show up on television again?"

"I'll deal with that then."

"There are advertisements for your *one-night stand with destiny* in every rodeo magazine I've even glanced at these past few months. What makes you think they don't already know?"

"Great. I don't have to tell them myself if they already know."

That she wanted to scream felt good. Familiar in a

comfortable sort of way. Of course, she also just . . . wanted to scream.

"Ty. Come on. This approach isn't going to work. With your event or with me."

"I don't know what they're going to think about you, and I don't care," Ty said gruffly. "If you want to tell them where you've been for the past eighteen months, be my guest. I didn't think that was what you wanted."

"It isn't. Not yet."

"If you don't fill in the gaps, Hannah, people might do it for you. I can't help that. But what do you care what they think?" His shrug was expansive. "I don't. Like I said."

Hannah looked toward the ranch house, the butterflies inside her turning into something a lot less cute. And she didn't quite believe he was as nonchalant as he sounded.

"Come on now," Ty said, a lighter note in that drawl of his. "You're a rodeo queen. You must have handled all kinds of crowds all over the circuit. What are a few family dynamics next to that?"

It was all about weighing bad options, wasn't it? If Hannah wanted to be open about the fact that she and Ty were married while waiting to see if the relationship was a safe space for her child, then she couldn't complain about the stories people told to explain her absence from Ty's life until now.

Even though this really wasn't how she'd pictured meeting his family for the first time.

"Okay," she said, because she wasn't a coward. Not yet. "Fine. I'm ready if you are."

Ty nodded, a look of satisfaction and approval moving over his face. That lit a fuse in her, making her body hum.

Then his hand closed around hers, and that felt the way it always did. As if they could take on the world.

Or if not the world, a few relatives.

He led her into the ranch house, through the back door that fed directly into the kitchen, where the pregnant woman Hannah had seen in the coffeehouse was bustling around at the stove.

There was a very pretty younger girl with dark, glossy hair setting the table. A man who looked a lot like Ty was kicked back in a chair at the table. An older man, clearly also related to both men, stood in the arched doorway leading to the rest of the house, looking fresh from a shower.

Every single one of them stopped whatever they'd been doing. And stared.

They all looked at Ty, then at her. Then down to where their hands were clasped tight together.

No one spoke.

For what seemed to Hannah like approximately seven thousand years.

"You should have told me you were bringing a guest for dinner, Ty," the pregnant woman said, sounding perfectly pleasant. She exchanged a quick glance with the stern-looking man in the doorway, then nodded toward the girl at the table. "Becca, why don't you set another place?"

"This is Hannah," Ty said, sounding almost obnoxiously calm. As if he couldn't read the room. Or like he'd said moments ago, didn't care. But his hand was hard and warm around hers. And Hannah had decided to do this, come what may. "And she's not a guest. She's my wife."

11

Ty thought it went well, all things considered.

He didn't know how something like this was supposed to go. Given he had never come home with a woman before—much less a wife—he could only compare it to his memories of childhood. Always a dicey proposition.

As in most things, anything that wasn't a scene out of the *Life of Amos Everett* was a success in his book. By that measure, the whole evening went like a dream. There were no tears. No raised voices. There was no crockery smashed into smithereens on the kitchen floor and no further holes in the walls.

Ty counted it as a win.

When dinner was over, Abby shooed everyone out of her kitchen, and Ty walked Hannah across the yard to his bunkhouse cabin. Now *their* bunkhouse cabin, a shift that made his temples pulse at him.

"That was great," he said. Maybe too optimistically.

Beside him, Hannah made a scoffing sound. "Thank you for demonstrating, in case I'd somehow forgotten, that you are one hundred percent male."

"I don't know what that means."

When they reached his cabin, he opened the door and ushered her inside. It wasn't much. Two rooms and a bathroom. A basic kitchenette on one wall and a woodstove on another. Not a whole lot different from the trailer he'd lived in and taken from rodeo to rodeo for most of his life.

"It means that you're a man. Supernaturally indifferent to any and all awkwardness while every woman in the room cringes."

"Any time the table stays on all four of its legs, I count that as a victory," Ty said.

The cabin felt a lot smaller than it had this morning. This had been his idea, and yet now that Hannah was standing here, blond and blue-eyed and *his wife*, Ty wondered if he'd really thought this through. But too late now.

Talk about reckless. He cleared his throat. "I'll get your bags."

He pushed his way back outside. The sun was flirting with the mountains, casting the sky in shades of orange and red. The lights from the ranch house spilled out into the yard, buttery and bright, and it took Ty a moment to realize that he was . . . different.

Better, something in him whispered.

But it was something else. Something bigger. Hope, maybe, no matter how his head ached at him.

He pulled Hannah's bags out of her pickup, then started back toward the cabin. Where she was waiting for him. His heart kicked, and he still didn't know how he'd pulled away from her up on the hill. How he'd kept his hands to himself since.

How he was going to keep his word when she was going to be around him all the time now.

Because if he'd learned anything about this woman who

was his wife since she'd appeared in Cold River, it was that she was shaping up to be the death of him in tight jeans.

He ordered himself not to hurry back, and then wished he had when he saw Gray coming out of the barn, directly toward him so there was no pretending he didn't see him. Ty could feel the look his older brother leveled on him from ten feet away.

It was worse when Gray came closer.

He stopped when he was a foot or two away and then . . . stood there. The way he did sometimes, like he really was one of the mountains. Or possibly because he knew how intimidating his silence was.

Ty, naturally, was *irritated*. Not intimidated.

"A wife is a funny thing to forget to mention for almost eighteen months," Gray observed. Mildly. More to the night sky than to Ty.

Ty sighed. He set Hannah's bags down at his feet, not without a touch of theater. "If you have something to get off your chest, now's the time. Go for it."

"I'm not the one who has to get things off my chest, brother," Gray drawled. With an extra emphasis on *brother,* in case Ty had forgotten their family connection in the last twenty minutes. "I'm not the one who had a wife stashed away and failed to mention it. For over a year."

"She's not stashed away anymore." Ty grinned. "She's right across the yard. Brother."

They stared at each other, and Ty hated that this was the only man on earth whose opinion mattered to him. Especially because, unless he'd misinterpreted every interaction they'd ever had, Gray's opinion of him was fairly dim.

"You want to tell me what's going on with you?" Gray asked.

"Because we share now? Okay, then. Great. Let's dive right into this bonding thing we've never done." Ty let his grin widen. "There's nothing going on with me. Good talk."

Gray looked undeterred. Or maybe that was just his face. "Why didn't you tell anyone about her?"

"Who should I have told?" Ty eyed his brother. "Brady? Please. Dad? After the spectacular failure of every relationship he ever had? And Abby is a recent development. Before her, you didn't have anything good to say about the institution of marriage."

"Fair enough." That was too easy. "But it seems to me you had a lot of time to share the happy news. Particularly once you saw my new take on the institution."

"I guess it didn't come up," Ty said with a show of epic unconcern. "Not everybody can wake up one morning, go next door, and randomly decide to marry the first neighbor they find."

Gray laughed. Which was shocking, and even disappointing, because Ty had expected it to piss him off.

"Also fair," he said, because he was apparently on a mission to completely mess with Ty's head. "I'm not asking you to defend your marriage, Ty. It's your business. If she lives with you, if she doesn't, whatever. Entirely up to you."

"I sure appreciate the permission, big brother."

Gray laughed again. "It's not like you've been all that happy since you moved back. She lightens you up some. That's got to be a good thing."

"What does happy have to do with anything?" Ty asked.

Rougher than he'd intended. "Was that supposed to be the goal? Because I'm trying to stay alive and in one piece. That's it."

Gray's jaw worked. "Why does every conversation I try to have with you end up like a boxing match?"

"Oh, awesome. I can't wait to hear how I'm doing conversations wrong too."

Gray sighed. "What does that mean? I'm not talking about your conversational skills, Ty. I'm pointing out that everything with you is aggressive. Or drunk."

"You caught me. Blind drunk yet again."

But he should have known that giving into the edginess inside him was a recipe for disaster. His older brother's gaze narrowed on him. And no doubt saw too much.

"If you're not drunk, what? You're always this angry? All the time?" More of that too-narrow, too-intent focus. "And married, apparently?"

"I'm real sorry I didn't get the perfect gene, Gray," Ty drawled. "Maybe I should've worked harder at it when I was a kid. Then again, not everyone gets to grow up with Dad on one side and two messed-up brothers who can never live up to your example on the other. Only you."

"But sure. You're not drunk and you're not angry. You're great. Perfectly fine."

"It must be nice to storm around through a whole life, so sure of who you are and where you belong." Ty shoved a hand through his hair and had no idea why there was all that . . . *mess* in him. Clawing at him. "I'm happy for you. Truly."

Gray muttered something under his breath. "Maybe worry less about me. And Dad. Maybe—and I'm spit-balling here—try being *you*, Ty. Drunk, angry, married, lazy, I don't really care. But you need to pick one. Because all this constant switching around is giving me whiplash."

Then he headed off toward his house.

He didn't *storm* off, despite what Ty had said, because Gray Everett was a rock. Rocks didn't *storm*, even when they were furious.

It would be a lot easier if Ty could hate the guy. But he'd never managed that one, despite years of dedicated practice.

He stood there while the sky put on a show and shadows gathered all around him, wishing he could figure out a way to do what Gray had suggested. And pick one. Pick *him*.

But he still didn't know who that was.

The last time he'd lived here for any stretch of time, he'd been a kid. An unhappy kid. And he hated that he could be a grown man, spotty memory or not, and still feel that kid stuff tugging on him. The last thing he wanted to do was pick another fight with his brother. Either one of them. And yet.

He took a breath, then another, but he was having trouble regulating himself the way he normally could. If he'd been back in the chute at the rodeo, getting ready to do his thing, he'd have been so calm and cool, icicles could have formed on his shoulders. But it didn't work here. Not with Hannah and clearly not with the rest of his family.

He had no one to blame but himself. Because the trouble with living down to expectations was that those low expectations were all anyone ever had for him. Including him. And let those expectations sink low enough, and there was only one place to end up.

Drunk. Aggressive. Even the random acquisition of a wife—

It was the sort of thing Amos had been famous for.

Everything Ty did to be less like his father made him . . . more like him.

The only thing he had going for him was that his wife had come back, unlike Amos's wives and girlfriends. He needed to focus on that. He needed to make his marriage work, no matter what had happened that he couldn't remember.

He *would* make it work.

He was about to pick up Hannah's bags again when someone else walked out of the barn. Becca. He smiled at his favorite and only niece, and waited as she walked over to him.

"How's all the gardening going?" he asked.

"I'm working in the Flower Pot, not gardening," she said, for the millionth time. The eye roll was implied. Or it usually was. "It's the Trujillos' florist shop, not a greenhouse."

Tonight, Becca looked serious. She'd pulled her hair back into a ponytail, so she was all cheekbones and those big, dark eyes she'd gotten from her mother. Good thing everything else about her, like her good heart and her steady nature, she'd gotten from Gray.

Abby had dedicated herself to making Cristina something other than a dirty word around the ranch. She and Gray both worked hard to make sure Becca knew that there were no hard feelings, not anymore. That it didn't matter what Cristina had done, that people in town liked to shoot off their mouths, but everybody here—everybody who mattered, in other words—wished that Cristina was still around the way she should have been.

Ty figured that was their job. And it was probably good for Becca.

But he was Gray's brother, not his kid, and it turned out that his reaction to his former sister-in-law's extramarital activities was the same as it always had been. It was one grudge he still carried. He might not know how to do the brother thing. But he could carry the hate on Gray's behalf. And did.

He didn't need to share that with his niece.

"Congratulations on your wedding," Becca said, her voice oddly somber.

Ty tugged on her ponytail. "Thanks, peanut."

She pulled her ponytail out of reach and considered him a moment. "Are you and my dad fighting? Is that why you didn't invite us to your wedding?"

"No one can be in a fight with your dad, Becca, because your dad doesn't fight." Ty heard his own words and the irritating truth in them, and laughed. "And I got married a while back. It was a private ceremony. Nobody was there but me and Hannah."

"Hannah." Becca pronounced the name as if she had to test it out, yet still wasn't too sure about those two syllables. "Was the private ceremony her idea? She wears a lot of makeup."

Ty blinked. "Uh . . . the private ceremony was my idea."

Becca smiled sweetly at him, reminding him of the way she'd used to go around smiling as if, were she to stop, the world would collapse. "The one time I tried mascara, my dad told me it looked like I had a black eye."

Ty considered her for a moment. "Good thing Hannah knows how to use it properly, then."

Becca gave him an even wider, sunnier smile and a kiss on the cheek he didn't believe at all. And then left him as she made her way back to the house. Though unlike her father, she was definitely, if not *storming*, getting her stomp on.

Ty watched her slam into the house. He stood there for another minute or two, waiting to see if Brady would roll out to share his thoughts.

When he didn't, Ty thanked the heavens for small mercies, picked up Hannah's bags, and headed for his cabin.

Their cabin.

Inside, Hannah was sitting on the small couch in the main room, her phone to her ear. "I have to go," she said as she looked up and saw him at the door. She switched her phone off, but kept it clenched in her hand.

Ty stepped inside, shifting the bags to the floor as he closed the door behind him.

"That was my mother," Hannah said.

"I didn't ask."

"I'm telling you. It was my mother."

"Okay."

And it was one thing to make sweeping pronouncements about *working on a marriage*. But what did that mean? When most people talked about working on their marriage, as far as Ty knew—because he wasn't exactly anyone's idea of a marriage counselor—they did things like argue about who did more of what. They talked about taking more vacations. Spending more or less time with the kids, depending. They promised to have more sex.

None of those things applied to this situation, except the

last one—and Ty didn't want to think about sex. Because all he wanted to think about was sex. And all the many glorious ways he could indulge himself in Hannah.

"You're looking at me like I'm dessert," Hannah said from the couch. "But I'm pretty sure you decided that we're on a diet."

"You're the one who remembers our marriage," he said.

He moved over to the small fridge and pulled out a beer. He lifted another one in her direction as a query, waited for her to nod, then kicked the fridge closed. He retraced his steps—all three of them—handed it to her, and then sat on the couch himself. Unlike her, he didn't perch on the edge like something might bite him. He sat back, sprawled out, and told himself he was perfectly at his ease.

Slowly, inch by inch, she relaxed next to him.

"What do you remember us doing?" he asked. When she smirked, he laughed. "Besides that."

"There weren't a lot of activities open to us. Given it was secret and all."

"According to you, we spent quite a while not doing that while we were dating. We must have done something else. Right?"

"What do you imagine we did? We talked."

"I was afraid you were going to say that."

"Oh, right." Hannah rolled her eyes. "Because talking is only interesting when it's a path to getting into someone's pants. Otherwise it's to be avoided at all costs."

"Darlin', I can't remember getting in your pants. And I'm not bored." He considered her a moment or two. "But you've already had all these conversations. I haven't."

"We can have them again."

"If I'm honest, I've heard more than enough today about who I am," Ty said. "Why don't you switch it up and tell me who you are? With less mystery this time."

That seemed to throw her. She took her time taking a sip of her beer. "It's not a very interesting story."

"Tell it to me anyway."

"I was raised in a small town in Georgia. But you can probably figure that out from the accent."

He only waited, because that sounded a lot like a practiced line to throw out to keep strangers from asking anything deeper. Hannah blew out a breath and pulled her knees up beneath her on the couch next to him.

"I was raised by my mom and her sister Elizabeth, who we call Aunt Bit. I fell in love with horses when I was a kid, and I never figured out which I liked better, horses or books. I won my first Miss Rodeo Princess when I was fourteen at the county fair." She shrugged. "And that was that. I was hooked."

"Which part hooked you?"

When she wasn't talking about their relationship, Ty noticed, her face was open. The way it had been when she'd first walked into the Broken Wheel. There was none of that wariness. He liked it way too much.

"I loved the whole thing," she said, tipping her head back toward the ceiling as if she were looking at that video of her past that Ty wished was real, so he could watch it too. "I loved the rodeo. All the people coming together. All the animals, and the owners who were so proud and so careful with them. I loved how excited the little kids got when they rode sheep. And I was in awe of the barrel racers. They looked like superheroes."

"You didn't notice all the cowboys?" Ty shook his head at her. "And here I was sure that was the draw."

"I liked the cowboys well enough." Hannah wrinkled up her nose. "But I was captivated by the rodeo queens. They were like Disney Princesses, but they were real."

"And you liked them more than the barrel racers?"

"You could always see that the barrel racers were tough and strong, and they worked so hard," Hannah said slowly, as if she was working it out in her head as she spoke. "And the girls who did that in school were the ones who showed up in class smelling like the stables. It was only when they got on a horse that they made any sense, I guess. I felt like that too."

Ty tried to rub that pulsing thing out of his temple. It was better than trying to do something about how tight his chest felt.

Hannah was still staring off into her past. "The rodeo queens were like prom queens but all the time. They were so pretty, and they were always smiling, and they always looked perfect. They were nice to everybody, no matter what, and they made it look so easy. I was pretty awkward and very shy, and kids already made fun of me, but being a rodeo queen was the best of both worlds. You got the rodeo and the horses. But you also got to be pretty. And the kind of girl who, no matter what, people would love. Because everybody loves a rodeo queen. Don't they?"

There was something naked in that. Vulnerable, and Ty felt . . . hushed. Awed, maybe, that she would let him see it. His ribs ached.

"So, you won your first crown. And you never looked back."

"No, because it was even better than I'd imagined it would be. And a whole lot harder. At first, when I was only competing in local fairs and rodeos, Mama and Aunt Bit and I made my outfits ourselves. But when I kept winning, the outfits had to be better, and we couldn't afford it, so we had to start raising money. And nobody's going to give any money to shy, awkward girls who smell like the stables and look like they spent the day mucking out stalls. Even if they did." Her smile was soft. Real. "I found that the more I let the queen part of me take over my real life, the better my real life was."

"But you don't do it anymore."

The open, almost wistful expression on her face disappeared. "No."

"Didn't you tell me that your crown was tarnished?"

He knew she had. But now he was trying to piece together all the things she'd told him before he'd understood what was happening. And who she was.

She took her time looking at him, and when she did, the soft smile was gone. "What I like to focus on is that I'm the only girl who's ever won Miss Rodeo Forever two years running. That's an accomplishment any way you look at it. It doesn't matter what happened afterward."

"What happened?"

"What always happens?" Ty was pretty sure that was a rhetorical question. "Rumors start. And it doesn't matter if there's any truth to them or not, does it? When a cowboy is scandalous, it only adds to his character. To his legend. But there's no such thing as a scandalous, legendary rodeo queen. There's either the rodeo queen or the girl who lost her crown. The end."

"That doesn't seem fair."

Hannah laughed. "Of course it's not fair. But then, no one ever said it would be. And luckily, it turns out there really is life after the rodeo."

Ty remembered his beer and took a swig. "I'm not so sure about that."

"At least you get to go back," Hannah said quietly. "I assure you, no one has reached out to offer me the opportunity to reclaim my glory."

"It's going to be great," Ty said, because it was. Because it had to be. "I have no intention of going out broken. That was never the plan."

"How did you plan on going out, then?"

Ty considered her a moment. Then he took another pull from his beer.

"You've spent all these months here," Hannah said, pulling her knees up farther, so she was basically hugging them. He noticed she'd taken off her boots. And her toenails were painted a soft, pretty pink that made everything in him . . . hurt. "There are worse things than the ranch life."

"This is Gray's thing."

He said that so matter-of-factly. Dismissively, even.

"I swear a girl in a coffee shop told me your father left the ranch to all three of you," Hannah said. "Mind you, I know perfectly well that small-town games of Telephone often end up garbled."

"He did." Ty felt restless, but for once it wasn't because he couldn't remember something. This time it was because he did. "Some people are born to be ranchers. That's Gray. Since the day he was born, it's like half of him was already rooted out there in the land somewhere. Like he was part of it. He never had any doubt in his mind about what he was supposed to do."

"Just because he's good at it doesn't mean you can't be good at it too. It's a really big ranch."

"I'm not a rancher." Ty didn't want to sit there on the couch anymore. He stood, but that didn't exactly solve the problem. Because the cabin hadn't grown any. And then he was . . . standing there. "Believe me. I come from a long line of ranchers, and I know the type. That's not me."

"Okay. What is you?"

Ty moved over to the window, where the last of the light was taking its time surrendering to the dark. "My family has been right here for generations. You know that's like?"

"Yes," Hannah said. "I do. But my family doesn't actually get along."

Ty snorted. "And you think mine does?"

"I have my mom and my aunt, but that's it. There are other family members around, but they cut us off a long time ago."

"Everetts don't cut each other off," Ty told her, feeling the same edginess in him that had gotten the best of him out there by the barn when he'd been talking to Gray. The edginess that got the better of him too often here. "We all live here, no matter how ugly it gets, and take it out on each other. Generation after generation. The only thing that matters is the land. It's all we talk about. It's supposed to be in our bones, like marrow. We're supposed to live and die by what happens to every last blade of grass. And if you don't feel that way, believe me, no one stops and asks themselves if maybe you have another path, or passion, or whatever. Everetts have this land. Right here. Or nothing."

"But you left home when you were eighteen," Hannah said softly. "And you stayed away. You had an entire life and career in the rodeo."

"Because that's what I'm good at. The land is what Gray is good at. The rodeo didn't really make me popular with my family, Hannah."

"Granted, I don't know your brother at all, but if he didn't want you muscling in on his land, if it is his land, wouldn't he say so?" She sounded so reasonable.

"He can't," Ty said shortly, turning back to look at her.

Here in this tiny, tiny cabin.

"Are you sure? Because he didn't strike me as the kind of man who pays much attention to *can't*."

"Gray wants to keep the land because he's been work-ing it his whole life. Because that's what Everetts do. My brother Brady wants to sell. Because, like me, he left when he could and he never wanted to come back here. But Gray asked us to give it a year." He shook his head. "I prefer the rodeo, if I'm honest."

"But, Ty." Her voice was too imploring for his liking. Her expression too careful. "Let's say everything goes the way you want it to over the next few weeks. You get your eight seconds. You get a high score, and that's it. You've done it. You've had your comeback. What happens next?"

He stared at her.

"Because I meant what I said last night," she continued in the same voice. "You're not a young man anymore. That fall you took could have killed you, and no one really un-derstands why it didn't. The next one might actually fin-ish the job. Or put you in a wheelchair."

"That's a risk I take any time I step into the ring."

"Yes, but how much can your body take?" She lifted a hand, and he wondered what expression he had on his face. "I don't doubt for one second that you have the will to do anything. But you only have the one body. And you've kicked the crap out of it for over a decade."

"I'll figure it out."

"Ty—"

But he was done with this conversation. And he hadn't really thought this part through either.

"I have some things to do," he told her. Stiffly. "Out in the barn."

He didn't turn around to see if she could tell he was lying. Because he wasn't, not entirely. There was always something to do in the barn. "Make yourself at home."

He pushed his way back outside. Then stayed out there, walking great loops around the land he claimed had no hold on him but he still knew every inch of, over and over, until the lights went out in the cabin.

Then the joke was on him.

Because when he went inside, he found Hannah in bed. In *his* bed.

He'd agreed to do this. To be in this marriage. To make it work.

Which he was pretty sure meant that he needed to crawl up into that bed beside her, instead of sleeping on his couch. And then he had to lie there, surrounded by her scent, without doing anything about it.

Her hair was on his pillow. She was warm and soft. And she made the cutest sounds when she turned over and snuggled herself against him like she belonged there.

Ty lay back, staring at his ceiling while his body went

to war with itself, all that want and need making him greedy and hungry.

And out of luck.

Because it hadn't occurred to him that he was making himself a martyr.

A smart man would have kept sex on the table and slid into this bed to get his hands on the woman beside him. A wise man would have remembered that sex wasn't only a release, or an occasional weapon, it could be the glue that kept things together. It could take the place of these conversations that kept peeling back all his different layers and exposing him to entirely too much light.

But Ty had never been the smart one in the family. That was Brady. And he'd never been all that wise. That was Gray.

Ty had always been the reckless one.

So he lay there in his bed with a beautiful woman curled up next to him, and yet as out of reach as if he still had no idea she existed. He stared at his ceiling. He contemplated martyrdom. And that impossibly hot kiss up on the hill that was likely to haunt him forever.

He was pretty sure this had to be the most reckless, idiotic thing he'd ever done in his life.

But it was still better than being his father.

12

Hannah would have sworn up and down that there was no earthly way anything with Ty could possibly feel routine. He was too elemental. Too much, too electric, too . . . *Ty*.

But as the days slipped by, one week turning into the next—and that hollow, Jack-less place inside her blooming from an ache into a kind of agony—they built up a rhythm. Or a habit, anyway.

He might not have known the difference, but she did.

They had never had habits, before. Their rhythms had been stolen glances, hoarded nights, or whispered telephone conversations from two parts of the same crowded room. They had never had mornings. Maybe a glimpse of a sunrise here or there, but never one after the next.

Hannah discovered that no matter how much careful space she and Ty left between them on the big bed that took up most of the bedroom in this tiny house, they always ended up wrapped around each other before dawn.

That first morning, Ty's godawful alarm had jolted them both wide awake and into a confused rush of heat and touch, because Hannah was wrapped all around him.

And there was no pretending that both of them didn't feel both his response and hers.

He'd muttered something gruff about helping herself to any coffee she found and anything else that took her fancy. He'd been up, dressed, and out the door in under five minutes. But Hannah had stayed awake in the bed that grew less and less warm the longer he was out of it, unable to fall back asleep or keep all her tangled emotions from spilling down her cheeks, until the sun came up hours later.

Every morning it was the same thing. The shrill of the alarm, then the jolt of sleepy awareness. Until slowly, day after day, they stopped reacting like scalded cats. Hannah didn't gasp and fling herself away from him. Ty didn't mutter apologies. They woke up, tangled like a knot, and he rolled her off him. So gently it made her stomach flip over, every time. Then he eased himself out of the bed and headed out to handle his first round of chores.

They didn't talk about any of that.

There were a lot of things they didn't talk about. And unless Hannah wanted to start coming clean about all the things she was keeping hidden—particularly the baby boy she called every day after Ty left their bed, with his sweet laughter on their video calls and the babbling that sounded more and more like real words every day—she needed to find a way to be okay with that.

She told herself she was more than okay with it. This was an experiment. She was dipping her toe into intimacy with this man instead of flinging herself headlong into passion and pain. And more, she told herself piously, she was doing it as much for Jack as for herself.

The first morning, after she'd laid there wide awake and

filled with too many emotions—most of them unflattering and ugly—she'd rolled herself out of the bed, wondering if she smelled like him. She'd showered and tried her best to put her face together. Then she'd called back home, checked in with her baby, avoided her mother's questions, and cried when she hung up. She assured herself those particular tears were hormonal and biological.

And it was no one's business if she cried every time she hung up from a call home, that sharp stitch behind her ribs deeper and harder.

That initial morning she'd decided that since this was a working ranch and she was a woman who knew her way around a stable, she might as well go and see if she could make herself useful. She saw Gray and his brothers come back in from their first round of morning duties and headed over to the ranch house's kitchen herself.

The kitchen was warm and smelled like bacon, but in case she'd forgotten the rousing welcome she'd received the night before, there was a small, potent sort of silence when she walked in.

"I'm not too good at being idle," she said straight into the awkwardness, her rodeo queen smile on high. "I'd love it if y'all would put me to work."

There was more silence. It couldn't have been more than a few seconds, but to Hannah, it felt like a lifetime. Three sets of Everett brothers' eyes on her from around that big, scarred kitchen table, all of them varying takes on that same dark green. And Abby and Becca too.

A lesser woman, one who had never had to stand in front of huge crowds trying to look *delighted* to find herself a runner-up to a crown she'd worked her butt off for and wholly deserved to have won, might have crumpled. Hannah smiled broader. Brighter. She drifted farther into the kitchen as if she were unaware of the tension in the room, and leaned against the counter as if that were where she'd been heading all along. And not because it was a handy barrier between her and a silent table full of her in-laws.

"No shortage of work to do around a ranch," Gray said over his plate of scrambled eggs, and Hannah was fiercely glad she had so many years of practice keeping her smile in place. Because it was more than tempting to wilt in the face of Gray's stern gruffness.

"Of course!" Abby chimed in, sounding much friendlier than her husband. She had her hands on her belly as she spoke, and the smile she aimed Hannah's way was kind. "You may have noticed that I'm slightly pregnant."

"My mama took care to teach me never to ask another woman if she was pregnant," Hannah said, and she wasn't above playing up her drawl for effect. "Unless the baby was crowning and my assistance was needed for the delivery."

"Wise woman." Abby patted her big belly. "But the cat's out of the bag on this one. And you've arrived at the perfect time, because I'm only now getting around to admitting that I can't do all the things I'm used to doing."

"You have me," Becca interjected. The smile she aimed around the room, Hannah noticed with some amusement, was not kind. Or even remotely real. "We have everything handled."

"You'll have it even more handled with more help," Gray said in the same gruff tone, clearly ending the discussion.

Becca looked at her plate. Abby smiled encouragingly at Hannah.

Hannah had looked over at Ty, who had been supremely

unhelpful. All he'd done was grin and focus on his coffee, while next to him, his brother Brady eyed Hannah in a manner she could only describe as cool.

But then, Hannah had always thrived on challenge.

That morning set the order of things. Every day after that, Hannah made sure to turn up after the first round of chores were done, which was when Gray decided what needed to be done next and who needed to do it. Hannah stuck with Abby on the days she didn't work in town and with Becca when she wasn't off at her summer job. And they handled the things that cropped up in and around the ranch house and barn. From the stables and pens to the chickens and the ornery, entertaining goats. From canning projects in the kitchen to weeding the summer garden.

If it weren't for how much she missed Jack, all the time, Hannah might even have said that she was happy.

She liked the work. She always liked good, tough ranch or farm work. And it was better than what she'd been doing back home at the stables where she'd worked while she was in high school. Hannah still loved working with horses. What she liked a lot less was the sure knowledge that the local mothers didn't want their precious children around a woman of such loose morals and deserved disgrace as the fallen rodeo queen of Sweet Myrtle.

The Everetts might not have welcomed her with wide open arms and a parade, but they didn't treat her like the second coming of Jezebel either. It was almost refreshing.

Ty's family fascinated her. The brothers put on a great show of not getting along, but here they all were. No one had cut anyone off, the way her holier-than-thou grandparents had turned their backs on Luanne and therefore Hannah. Ty claimed he had no particular relationship with his brothers, but they worked the ranch every day. Together. And three meals a day, more or less, they gathered around the same table and ate. Also together.

For a family who claimed to be deeply dysfunctional and broken beyond repair—or maybe that was only Ty's take on it—they sure operated like they enjoyed each other's company.

Not an observation Ty enjoyed.

"Working toward a common goal isn't the same thing as having a happy family," he told her one night in their cozy little bunkhouse, where there was always too much conversation circling around the things they didn't actually want to talk about.

And too much sexual tension choking the life out of everything else.

Or maybe that was Hannah's problem. Since she knew what they were missing.

"That might be the actual definition of what a happy family is," she pointed out. "I think you'll find that every happy family you ever meet shares a few common goals."

"Maybe they do things differently in Georgia."

"In my part of Georgia, unhappy families don't sit around the dinner table every night having a pleasant conversation about their day. They tend to drink a lot. Throw down, get their redneck on. Engage in all manner of bad behavior."

"Give it time," Ty muttered.

"I can't really see your brother Gray tossing the kitchen table across the room." Hannah was in her usual place on the couch, because they were that familiar now. That intimate. She had a *place* on the couch. "It seems to me that you keep waiting for your father to rise up from the dead, walk into that house, and pick up where he left off."

Ty had stared at her for an uncomfortably long minute or two. Then he'd very quietly set aside the book he was reading and suggested they watch something on television, instead.

Because a reality show about wilderness escapades in Alaska was much better than searching questions and uncomfortable truths.

Hannah supposed she ought to have been outraged that Ty didn't want to spend every second having the same extraordinarily painful conversation about who they'd been, and what he couldn't remember. But she had never gotten to spend quiet nights at home with the man she'd married. Their time together had always been running out. They'd had to make every moment count, and they had. They'd never turned on a television. They'd never spent evenings sharing the same space, making occasional comments about the life they were both living. They'd never shared a life. They'd only ever shared a secret.

Maybe someday, if they got to have a someday this time, the thrill of that might wear off.

But not yet.

One afternoon, the three brothers came in from the fields for lunch, which Hannah was busy preparing while Abby put her feet up. Gray shouldered his way into the kitchen and grunted his approval at the sight of Abby taking it easy. Ty followed, giving Hannah one of his long, slow looks that made everything inside her flutter a bit. She took that as his form of approval too.

Brady, as usual, said nothing when he came in. And offered her only the barest thank you when she handed him his plate with the meal Abby had directed her to make. She wouldn't call him *rude*. But he wasn't exactly polite either.

But if Hannah couldn't handle any reaction that came her way, positive or negative and everything in between, she never would have made it through her first competition at the county fair. She served Abby, then brought her own plate to the table.

Conversation over lunch centered on the ranch and general livestock and equipment concerns, the way it always did. Gray and Abby were talking about another local family who were toying with the idea of setting up a kind of dude ranch operation.

"They're going ahead with a trial run before the fall weather starts," Abby said. "Jensen Kittredge was in the coffee shop yesterday talking about it."

"I don't begrudge a man who needs to feed his family and comes up with a creative way to do it," Gray said, shaking his head. "But the idea of clueless tourists running around *this* land makes my blood run cold."

"It's marketing," Brady said. "And it's smart. Everyone thinks they know what a dude ranch is, but if you asked a random person on the street of any city what happens every day on an actual, working ranch, they probably wouldn't have a clue."

"I'm not sure I'd want my land to be where city folks learned the error of their ways."

"Maybe you should consider it. It's not the worst idea in the world to use the ranch to do more than just—"

"Ranch?" Gray supplied. In that even, implacable tone of his. "I don't need the ranch to do more than what it already does, Brady."

"There's nothing wrong with innovation," Brady retorted.

"I agree." Gray pushed back from the table, but in the

same calm, measured way he did everything else. It gave the impression he had always been planning to stand up then. And that nothing Brady said or did could goad him into doing a thing. "Why don't you use your fancy education and all your great ideas to innovate what we already have? Instead of creating new enterprises because for some reason, you still believe that this life—my life—is beneath you."

"That's not what I said."

"And yet, that's what I heard. You talk a big game, Denver. You're always looking for ways to overhaul everything you see here, but never because you're trying to help me out. You want to help *you* out. And wanting to change the ranch to suit yourself isn't giving it a chance."

He left the room, and Abby looked around the table. She smiled, but she didn't apologize for Gray or try to smooth things over. Because she had her husband's back, of course. That felt like a big, bright revelation.

Abby awkwardly pushed herself up from the table and went after Gray. Leaving Hannah alone with the remaining two Everett brothers.

"It wouldn't *actually* kill him to listen for a change," Brady said darkly. "I know he acts like it would, but he'd survive it. In one piece, even."

Across from her, Ty was lounging back in his chair as if he'd never been so entertained in all his days. Worse still, he was grinning. Hannah frowned. Then shook her head at her husband.

Who ignored her completely.

"You can always ask Hannah for help," Ty said. With some of that studied geniality that had always gotten right up under Hannah's skin. She imagined it had a similar effect on his brother. "She's got herself a fancy degree. Just like you, college boy."

And then he laughed, because he found himself and the messes he stirred up so amusing.

Brady lifted his eyes from his plate. He considered his brother for a moment, then leveled a long look at Hannah. She could really only describe it as unfriendly.

Extremely unfriendly.

"Oh yeah?" Brady could not have sounded less interested or enthused if he tried. "Imagine that."

"Yes, sir," Hannah replied, smile firmly in place and enough drawl to choke a man out. "I got me a piece of paper from the University of Georgia that says I can call myself a Bachelor of Science and Arts. Go Dawgs."

"Brady here went off to the University of Denver," Ty supplied helpfully, still lounging there. "He liked it so much, he stayed down there in Denver until last fall. Brady has a lot of ideas to bring to the table. Gray resents this. And he would rather that Brady learned how to ranch from the ground up, the way he's been doing his whole life."

"Thanks a lot for the narration, Ty," Brady said, his voice tight. "And the zero support."

"I'm not taking a side. I'm explaining the situation to Hannah," Ty replied, sounding so profoundly unbothered that Hannah had to assume he was doing it to irritate his brother. It appeared to be working.

"I don't see why there has to be a choice between the two," Hannah said, trying to smooth things out.

It earned her one of those rare, real smiles from her husband. But all she got from her brother-in-law was another dark, cold glare.

After lunch, which Ty drew out because he was clearly

performing his lazy amiability *at* Brady, Ty went out to mess around with some or other engine that needed fixing before they headed back out into the fields.

Brady pulled out his laptop and typed away on it while Hannah got up and started on the dishes. Hannah hated doing dishes. She'd hated it when she was a kid. She'd hated it when she and Mama lived in that rattly old trailer they drove around from rodeo to rodeo. She plain hated washing dishes, but here she was, pitching in and doing her part and trying to be a good sport about it because that's what she would have done if this were real. If she and Ty had come home after they'd gotten married and there hadn't been all that time and Jack and the things they couldn't talk about because he couldn't remember.

Maybe that was why she focused on Brady instead. When he slapped his laptop shut, then stood from the table with that same closed-off expression he always wore around her, she hit him with the full wattage of her best smile.

"You don't like me much, do you?" she said, drying her hands off on a dish towel and leaning her hip against the counter as if this were nothing but a casual conversation.

Brady was the tallest of the three brothers. Like them, he had dark hair and those dark eyes that made a woman want to look closer, particularly when it turned out they were green. But where Gray was solid like a mountain and Ty was lazy like a cat about to pounce, Brady was . . . focused. There was power in him, but he usually kept it leashed. Buttoned down tight.

Hannah doubted very much his older brothers noticed that focus, but she sure did when it was aimed at her. And she could see a lot more of it than usual when he focused all his considerable attention on her.

"No," he said, his voice unequivocal. "I don't."

"I'm tickled we've finally gotten that out in the open," Hannah drawled. She folded her arms. "Are you going to tell me why? Or will it stay a mystery?"

Brady smiled, but it wasn't a lazy sort of smile, like the one Ty threw around sometimes. It wasn't polite, if disinterested, like Gray's.

Brady smiled like a man who knew exactly what he wanted and was used to getting it.

"I know who you are," he told her in the same even tone. "Ty likes to roll around here like he's invisible, but he's not. He likes to act as if the rodeo takes place in an alternate dimension, but it doesn't. What I'm trying to tell you is that I know what he's planning to do in a couple of weeks. Only Ty would think he could keep that a secret."

"Does everybody know?"

"As far as I can tell, only me. But you never can tell what Gray knows."

"So maybe Ty really can keep a secret."

Again, that sharp, impatient smile. It was a businessman's smile. Hannah had seen enough versions of it in her time charming stock contractors, town councilmen, mayors, and corporate or retail sponsors alike.

"He kept you a secret," Brady pointed out. "And it's hard not to notice that the timing of your touching return is suspicious."

"Oh, sugar, I know it is," Hannah said, smiling wider. "But there's not much I can do about that."

"I guess not." Brady moved forward until he was standing on the other side of the counter that divided the kitchen area from the eating area. He didn't seem unduly worried about the fact that he was facing off with her, right then and there. "But help me out here, Hannah. It doesn't take much digging to figure out that you were Miss Rodeo Forever, except you left last year before your reign was finished. Under a dark cloud, rumor has it."

"That's the trouble with a clear day," Hannah said softly. She didn't back down. "All it means is that the storm's coming."

"That's not an answer."

"I don't believe you asked me a question."

"I have to wonder about the character of an individual with that kind of history," Brady said, still with that masters-of-the-universe smile on his face. "And what kind of influence a person like that might have on my brother, who we can all agree isn't exactly handling this transitional time in his life too well."

Hannah smiled wider. She even batted her eyelashes. "I do wish you would hurry on up and accuse me of something."

"I want to know where you've been," Brady said, his voice not particularly hard. He was still smiling. But Hannah didn't mistake that for anything less than the threat it was. "My brother almost died. He was broken into pieces. He stayed in the hospital for a long time, and then he came home, without you. We didn't know you existed until you showed up the other night. So, where have you been? Because to the casual observer, it almost looks like you left the man when he was down and came back because he's on his way up again. Tell me I'm wrong."

Hannah studied him. "How much time did you spend by your brother's bedside, then?"

Brady's smile chilled by several degrees. Hannah's warmed in direct response.

"Both of my brothers have spent their lives dedicated to the thing they love," Brady told her, his gaze steady on hers. "One of them stayed here and the other went everywhere. But at the end of the day, they're both good, solid people. My family is filled with good, solid people these days. You already know this because you appeared out of nowhere and were welcomed in, no questions asked."

"This feels like a few questions. And less *welcome to the family*, more *you'll never be one of us*. Maybe I'm reading you wrong."

"My brother has already been hurt enough," Brady said, and this time, without that smile. "I don't want to see him hurt again."

There was a part of Hannah—a huge part of her—that felt scraped raw by this conversation. She wasn't the one who had wrecked their marriage, after all. She wasn't the one who'd wanted to leave Ty in the first place. The injustice of it about choked her.

But Brady wasn't one of the enduring challenges from her hometown. He wasn't being mean to her for fun. He was defending his brother. At the first hint of an opportunity, he had jumped right in to make sure that Hannah knew he had Ty's back.

This was the family that Ty found so dysfunctional.

In another circumstance, Hannah might have found Brady intimidating. Not that she let such things affect her, but she would have felt it. Today, she could only find it cute. Sweet, really. In that aggressive male way.

"Here's the thing, sugar," she told him, uncrossing her arms and tucking them in the pockets of her jeans. "I'm married to Ty. I'm afraid what that means is, I'm almost certainly going to hurt him again. Because people aren't perfect. And relationships are messy. But what I can promise you is that to the best of my ability, I will try not to do it on purpose."

She didn't know what Brady might have said to that because Gray came back in then. He lifted his chin a scant centimeter in the direction of the back door.

"Ready?" he asked Brady, in that same uncompromising way he did everything.

Hannah watched, fascinated all over again, as Brady . . . wrapped up all that power she'd seen in him. Then stuffed it down, out of sight.

Because here, he was the baby brother, not a man in his own right. That was what Gray and Ty saw—and it was all they saw. So that was who Brady was.

She was still puzzling over that when Abby came waddling back into the room, belly first.

"I'm sorry about that," Abby said. "I didn't grow up with any siblings, but Gray assures me it's normal for them to all storm around as if they hate each other all the time. Not the most pleasant thing to be around, I know."

"Ty swears up and down they have nothing in common, that they are a pageant of dysfunction, and yet all I see are three men who work all day, every day together." Hannah shrugged. "For the good of them all and this ranch. Almost as if they're actually more alike than not."

Abby's smile, always kind, tipped over into delighted. "Almost as if," she agreed.

Maybe it was the smile that worked on Hannah, because unlike Brady, Abby looked perfectly friendly.

"I'm an only child myself," Hannah told her. "Family dynamics are pretty much lost on me because there was only ever me and my mom. And my aunt, who as far as

I know has never argued with anyone. Which is saying something, since my mother could get into an argument in a sealed room. My aunt has been failing to take her bait all their lives."

"My grandparents raised me," Abby said. "My mother would sweep in every now and again to stir things up, but mostly it was me and my grandparents. And then me and Grandma after my grandfather passed. We didn't do much fighting."

"Who knew brothers were so . . . emotional?" Hannah lowered her voice like she was saying something deeply scandalous.

"*So* emotional," Abby agreed, laughing. "And then all the pretending that there's no emotion involved at all. It's exhausting."

"It's certainly very male."

Abby looked as if she was considering something, and then she reached over and put her hand on the counter near Hannah's. As if she'd considered touching her hand, but didn't want to cross that boundary.

"I have no idea if you'd even be interested in this," she said. Carefully. "But my two best friends decided that we need to go out to dinner to celebrate my last little while as a person who *can* go out to dinner, without a small human to tote around with me. They wanted to do it once a week. It's been more like every couple of weeks. But anyway, it's this Friday while Gray and the others will be running the cows up to into the hills to graze. And I'd love it if you'd come."

Hannah was so disarmed that she forgot to trot out her smile. "I wouldn't want to intrude."

"You can't intrude when I've invited you. And anyway, we're sisters now. Aren't we?" Abby's face looked as suddenly red as Hannah's felt. And about as nervous. "I would like to be. That's what I'm trying to say. And I'm sure that going out to dinner at one of our restaurants here can't possibly hold a candle to the sorts of things you're used to, but—"

"Thank you," Hannah said, simple and true.

Because she hadn't realized how desperately she'd wanted a sign of friendliness until this moment. One sign that she wasn't evil incarnate, or a walking disgrace, or even the liar she knew herself to be. She couldn't do anything about the knot in her belly and the near-overpowering ache that reminded her of the secret she was still keeping. The secret that she doubted very much Abby, this close to having her baby, would understand. Abby would hate her for keeping Jack a secret and keeping him from Ty. And for letting her try to fold Hannah into the family when Hannah was holding so much back. Hannah was fully aware of the damage she was doing.

But she couldn't help herself from accepting the first hint of friendship she'd been offered since she'd met Ty's family. From the woman who would have been her first and only sister, if this had all gone the way she'd hoped it would so long ago.

Hannah still didn't know why the lives she'd only ever imagined, these roads not taken, hurt her the way they did. Only that they did. And the hurt never quite faded.

It blended in with the expanding ache for her son, that punch of pain every time she breathed in, and became something else. Something almost debilitating.

Almost.

"I would love to, Abby," she said quietly, sealing her own fate. "More than you know."

13

Some of Ty's fondest memories of growing up on the ranch involved moving the cows to range in higher elevations every summer. To be distinguished from the less exciting tasks, like combing the hayfields for rocks that had to be removed before they messed up the haying equipment, learning how to act invisible when a part broke and ruined the whole day's plans, or hoping to do something cool out in the shop only to spend hours holding the treble light in exactly the right position that made arms tremble and backs ache. When his grandfather had been alive, Silas had led the cattle drives out into the hills and the land that was only accessible in the warmer weather.

Ty could remember all of it with the kind of detail he wished he had for those shadowy spaces still lurking in his memory. He remembered learning how to ride in slow diagonals to encourage the herd to move. He remembered the lessons on keeping pairs of cows and calves together, the hand signals, the debates about low-stress drives versus the use of dogs and hearty cursing that Amos always preferred. Mostly he remembered riding out behind Silas, the old man always straight in his saddle, no matter the ravages of time or gravity.

Silas had been the real deal. He'd never been one to start a fight, but he never ran from one either. He might not have understood his son, but he'd been the only person around who could influence him for the better. Amos had only gotten worse after his father's death.

Now, Ty rode out again, following Gray this time, as they led the herd to the last of the summer grass they'd enjoy before fall.

"Are you up for this?" Gray said after the ranch foreman and a number of the hands had set out to get things moving. Brady was already riding out ahead of them.

"Are you asking about my leg?" Ty eyed his older brother. "Because otherwise, I didn't realize there was an option to sit this out."

Gray looked like Ty's memories of their grandfather. Severe and unapproachable until you learned to look for the gleam in his eyes. "Do you need to take the honeymoon option?"

That was obviously a trick question. Ty had been the hitting the whiskey hard last fall, but he remembered pretty clearly that Gray's version of a honeymoon had been to stay the night in the hotel in town where he and Abby had been married. The one night. Then he'd been right back to work.

"I'm good," he said lazily. "I told you we got married a while back."

"So you did."

But there was no time for Ty to ask—or not ask— what that inflection in Gray's voice meant. There were stragglers to return to the herd. There were bawlers who needed to be reunited with their calves.

He remembered all the other times he'd taken this ride. The joy of the day on horseback, and the thrill of knowing he'd be sleeping out beneath the stars. He wished he could recall what he'd felt about Cold River Ranch back then. Had he intended to grow up and take part in the ranch operation? Had he figured he'd build himself a house on the acreage somewhere, so he could have his space but always be on hand to help shoulder the load of the family enterprise?

He wished he knew. Because if he could remember what he'd felt back then, it would help him make sense of what he felt now. Whether it was nostalgia or something else that was making him a whole lot more raw out here than he ought to have been.

He would prefer to be nostalgic. That was a lot better than the thing that hunched in him, day and night. It had claws and fangs. It kept him up late, woke him up early, and he would have said it was making his life a misery—except he wasn't miserable.

Ty was hung up on a woman. His wife, of all things.

And he had absolutely no idea what to do about it.

Luckily, a day spent handling the herd and all the usual cow nonsense didn't give him too much opportunity to brood about his problems. Better still, as he'd told Hannah, real life ranch work was the best training a man could have for the rodeo. He put the time to good use.

They set up camp out there in the hills, where there was nothing for miles around but pure, clean Colorado air and the brilliant Rocky Mountain night sky. The hands and the foreman had peeled off while there was still daylight to make the long ride back down to the ranch, leaving Ty and his brothers to make sure the herd had settled in before heading back the next day.

This wasn't the first of the drives they'd done this summer, and they had it down by now. Camp was easy enough to set up, since all three of them preferred a bedroll and the stars as a canopy rather than fussing around with any tents.

Gray had dryly asked Brady if he'd remembered to pack his tent the first time. Brady had blinked as if that were a real question. Then he'd responded with a rude gesture, not his words. Ty still laughed when he thought about it.

Tonight, Ty built the fire. Gray provided the ingredients for what Grandpa had always called Silas Stew—a random mix of whatever he'd brought with him that might have tasted strange at the dinner table back at the ranch house, but always tasted fantastic out here. Brady, surprisingly enough, was a decent camp cook, capable of making their version of Silas Stew even better than anything Ty remembered eating as a kid.

They sat around the fire in what Ty chose to interpret as companionable silence, listening to the cows complain in the distance, their horses muttering, and the wind high in the evergreens. There were no phones out here. No televisions. No trucks, no engines, nothing but man and beast in the wilderness the way it must have been for those first, hardy Everetts who'd crossed these mountains to find a new home.

Ty wasn't sure about the home part. But this felt a lot like heaven.

Gray handled the cleanup in his usual, efficient manner.

Ty lounged there beside the fire, watching the flames jump and crackle. He had a beer. His belly was full. He had a good night's sleep ahead of him and Trixie, his favorite horse, right there to make sure he got back to the ranch.

Life didn't get much more perfect. And instead of counting his blessings, he was missing Hannah.

He liked the way she slept, her forehead furrowed and her eyes squeezed tight like her dreams took fierce concentration. He loved it when she did herself up, but he also loved the glimpses he got of her at night or in the early morning when she hadn't had time to put her face on yet. When she was all sleepy blue eyes and the naked mouth it caused him physical pain not to taste. He liked waking up with the weight of her against him and often on top of him, all those soft curves pressed against him. Ty liked keeping her warm, and he liked the noises she made sometimes when she dreamed. If he listened closely, he was sure they were versions of that same slow drawl.

He was used to his own space and a big fan of his own company, so he'd expected it to be an adjustment with her there. The cabin was so small and the potential for getting and staying on top of each other's nerves was high. But the strangest thing was that he liked it.

He liked all of it. He liked looking across the table in the ranch house's kitchen to see her sitting there, eating with his family. He liked walking back to their bunkhouse in the dark, the way he always had, but with company. He liked talking to her, because he never knew what she would say. Or what she would very distinctly not say, and only gaze back at him instead. He liked that they'd gotten past the point where there always needed to be conversation, and sometimes they sat there in the evening with music on, reading, lost in their different worlds but together in this one.

Ty discovered she was as handy with a needle as he was, after all that time out on the road with a required costume every night. That she could work miracles with the laundry, getting stains out of absolutely anything if she put her mind to it, and had a lot of opinions about line drying versus electric dryers. She liked her coffee tooth-achingly sweet, her toast brown and crunchy, and had a great many opinions on the perfect piecrust and how best to achieve it. She didn't like to cook regular meals, though she could. She preferred what she called statement meals. Thanksgiving or Easter. Sunday dinner or a birthday.

You know me, sugar, she would drawl. *I like a show.*

Ty found himself fascinated by the sheer array of products she claimed she had to use each and every day or the sight of her might scare off small children. Nor was she the least bit ashamed of her stockpile.

It might take a village to raise a child, she told him one day when she found him gazing in astonishment at what was left of the counter space in the tiny bathroom they shared. *Think how many people and products it takes when that child is all grown up and needs to fight off the signs of age.*

Given she was all of twenty-five, she didn't have a whole lot to worry about there.

What Ty was learning, more each day, was that his wife intrigued him on pretty much every level. She was funny. She was smart. She really could hold a conversation on any given topic because she picked up a little bit of everything and carried it around with her like a very pretty encyclopedia.

All that and she was magic with horses, helped around the ranch, and was unfailingly sweet to his family, which wasn't something Ty could say for himself.

Basically, Hannah was the perfect woman.

It didn't surprise him in the least that he'd put a ring on it. What he still couldn't figure was what the hell he had done the night of his fall. Or why.

He kept worrying at those blank spots in his head, when a wiser man might have tried to enjoy what he had, whether he could remember how he got it or not.

Ty realized that he'd been off in his own world when he tuned back in to find Brady and Gray engaged in another one of their skirmishes.

"Diversification isn't losing focus," Brady was saying. Tensely. "It's making sure there's always something to focus on, no matter what happens."

"Seems to me I can focus on one thing better than five," Gray replied in that maddeningly calm way he had. Then his mouth curved. "But what do I know? I don't have a fancy college degree."

"But you sure have a chip on your shoulder about the whole thing."

Ty sighed, loud and dramatic, so they both looked at him.

"I did not bring enough alcohol to put up with all the squabbling," he drawled. "You two need to have a fistfight already. Just get it over with."

Gray let out a bark of laughter. "I'm not getting in a fistfight."

Brady looked like he'd be up for taking a swing or two.

"Brady," Ty said, with exaggerated patience. "You know that Gray is resistant to these ideas of yours. He's not going to magically stop resisting because you keep bringing them up." He looked at his older brother. "And you have hundreds of acres at your disposal. What would it hurt you to give him a few?"

"They're our acres," Brady said, his voice tight. "Not his. Ours."

Gray shook his head. "I don't want Cold River Ranch to turn into some hipster llama lavender hemp farm with a food truck selling handmade noodles and a pastel coffee cart."

Ty stared. "That's very specific."

"You should have told us last fall that you hate money, Gray," Brady said. "If I'd known that before you asked us for a year of our lives, I would have been better prepared."

"Gray doesn't hate money, Brady," Ty said, turning the same theatrically patient voice on him. "Our older brother sees himself as the last living link to legendary, historic cowboys like Grandpa. He wants to be a country song. And in fairness, there aren't a lot of country songs that focus on pastel coffee carts. Or llamas."

"Why are we talking about llamas?" Brady demanded. "I don't know anything about llamas. I don't want to know anything about llamas."

"Llamas spit," Gray offered. Helpfully.

"Gray," Ty began, like he was a schoolteacher. "You asked Brady and me to give the ranch a chance. That's what we're doing. But you're going to have to share your toys."

"I'm feeling a fistfight coming on every time you talk to me in that tone of voice," Gray said, still doing that thing that was maybe him grinning. Or maybe it was a trick of the firelight. Hard to tell.

"If you don't like me trying to make peace between the two of you, here's a solution," Ty said. "Quit going after each other every five seconds like a pair of pissy little terriers."

Both of his brothers stared at him, then, sizing him up in their own way.

"Since we're all out here sharing our feelings," Gray said, keeping that gaze of his on Ty. And there was definitely no curve to his mouth then. "Why don't you take this opportunity to state an opinion? On anything. We'll wait."

"I state my opinion constantly."

"No, Ty, you don't." Gray was lounging there on his bedroll, looking as relaxed as if he were kicked back on the big leather couch in his living room. "You talk a lot, sure. You make a lot of noise when you want. But what do you actually stand for? Brady wants to sell the ranch. I want to keep it. What do you want?"

"I want to stop arguing about it for thirty seconds. That seems like a good place to start."

"Do you?" Brady asked from the other side of fire. "Or do you like being in the middle? Always the tiebreaker. Always the final vote."

"Have we voted on the ranch before?" Ty asked with a laugh. "Because I don't remember it being my property before last fall. I've gotten pretty good at hauling my actual property around this country hitched to the back of my truck. I feel certain I would have noticed hundreds of acres back there when I tried to accelerate."

"A lot of noise," Gray said quietly, as if Ty was proving his point. "But never a hint as to what you think or feel about anything. Always the rodeo cowboy, putting on a show."

Ty didn't like the way adrenaline was spiking in him. Like there really was about to be a fight. And he might be the one throwing punches.

"I don't trust your wife," Brady said placidly. "See that? That's an opinion."

Ty's adrenaline did more than spike at that.

"You're welcome to your opinion, baby brother," Ty drawled, but he didn't do a very good job of sounding lazy and unbothered. "But that doesn't mean I intend to sit here and listen to it. You don't need to concern yourself with my wife."

"Where's she been for the last eighteen months?" Brady asked, undaunted. "What kind of wife leaves her husband to recover from life-threatening injuries in the hospital all by himself?"

"It's none of your business what my wife does or doesn't do."

"Funny you say that," Brady said, and he sounded almost cheerful. Or maybe that was a challenge. "Because that's pretty much what she said when I asked her directly."

Gray rubbed a hand over his face and muttered something that sounded a lot like a prayer for deliverance. But Ty was too busy trying to keep the back of his head from coming off to pay any closer attention.

"Are you out of your mind?" he asked Brady. "That's an actual question. Do you need medical attention? Because you're about to."

"I don't understand the secrecy," his younger brother said, with that obstinance Ty always forgot about. Because Brady was a tenacious little jackhole, or he wouldn't have made it down in the city. But Ty wasn't in the mood to applaud him.

More like pummel him.

"The big secret is, it's none of your business," Ty said, his jaw tight. "What do you care?"

"I didn't hear about your accident for months," Brady countered. "Why didn't you tell anyone?"

"It was televised," Ty retorted. "What was I supposed to do? Live stream my physical therapy sessions and text them to you?"

"Was Hannah there?" Brady asked. "Playing nurse for you?"

Ty rolled his eyes. Because it was that or start swinging.

Or tell the truth about his memory—but he couldn't do it. He couldn't admit that he'd very likely done something unforgivable that night, or why wouldn't Hannah tell him? And when he imagined *unforgivable*, there was only one face he saw.

His father's, twisted in rage, poison pouring out of his mouth.

It made Ty sick to imagine he'd ever treated Hannah like that. But how could he dismiss the very real possibility? Especially when of all of Amos's sons, Ty was the one who was most like him.

"I'm beginning to question how obsessed you are with my wife, Denver," Ty said darkly, because he needed to stop picturing things he couldn't change, if they'd actually happened. "Get a grip or get your own."

Brady looked horrified. "Yeah. Hard pass, thanks. I have enough family."

"And still," Gray said, lazily from where he sat, "I don't really know how you feel about a thing, Ty. You don't like Brady talking about Hannah. Is that your big stand? Privacy? Because I have to tell you, if you want private, you shouldn't be conducting your secret marriage in the middle of the family ranch."

"Dad visited me in the hospital," Ty said.

He threw that out there as a kind of life raft, or possibly a bomb, and it worked. Gray went still. Brady winced.

And for a blessed moment, there was quiet.

"I wouldn't have considered Dad the type for a hospital visit," Brady said, sounding dubious.

"It turns out he actually watched me on television." Ty eyed Brady. "Imagine that. That's how he knew where I was and what happened to me, by the way."

Gray only shook his head. As if he already knew where this was heading.

"I have to say I really can't picture Dad rushing off to be there for you in your time of need." Brady made a face. "Unless . . ."

Ty let that sit there. Then he got his rodeo cowboy on, as justly accused, and grinned nice and wide.

"Dad came to assess the extent of the damage," he told his brothers, not without a certain sense of relish. "He shared with me that he'd heard the doctors talking and the consensus was I was unlikely to walk again. He wanted to make real sure that I understood I had always been a disappointment to him. This, I knew. But it turned out that having a rodeo star as a son, while not quite moving me out of the disappointing column, was something he'd gotten used to. Enjoyed, even, especially when I did well and the folks down at Mary Jo's mentioned it when he stopped in for a bite on his way to get a part. What he couldn't abide was a cripple."

If Ty's goal had been to silence his brothers completely,

he'd succeeded beyond his wildest dreams. There was nothing but the crackle of the fire. The breeze all around, the stars above. Even the horses were quiet.

"I wasn't dependable like Gray. I wasn't smart like Brady. The only thing I had going for me, despite the fact I reminded him in every possible way of the worthless female he made me with, was the rodeo. Without that? His prediction was that I would—how did he put it—suckle off the teat of his land for the rest of my days. He'd told me a long time ago I didn't have what it took to stay on the ranch. No Everett blood in me, by his reckoning. He might not have had the science to back that up, but he was sure all the same."

Both of his brothers swore. Ty kept grinning.

"I hope you told him to get the hell out," Gray said gruffly.

"I told him I understood his concerns and as it happened, my plan was to walk no matter what the doctors said," Ty told them. "And then I commented on how strange it was that he was still tied up in knots about Mom when she never mentioned him at all."

Too late, Ty remembered there were minefields everywhere, and he'd gone ahead and set off about five.

Gray shook his head, but didn't say a word. Brady, on the other hand, scowled.

"You talk to Mom?"

Once again, Ty found himself in a space where it would have been awfully helpful to have access to his memories. Not only his memories, but all the feelings he was sure he must have had about these things before he'd been stomped.

He wished he'd watched his mouth. "I don't call her every day and ask her what outfit she picked out or what she bought at the store, if that's what you mean."

"Do you talk to Mom?" Brady demanded of Gray.

"No." Gray looked mystified. "She left. The end."

"It's actually not unreasonable to want to leave the ranch, you know," Ty pointed out. Because he couldn't help himself. "You only think it is because you're the only one who never tried."

"That or I have a sense of responsibility. And loyalty."

"To what?" Ty asked. "To Dad? Because you walk alone there."

"I want to circle back to how you've been talking to our mother," Brady said before Gray could reply to that, and he sounded different. Harder, maybe. "Because I didn't think that was something we were doing."

"I don't recall making a blood pact," Ty said witheringly. Which was true, he didn't. "But even if I had, I'm a grown man. I don't need my brothers' permission to make a phone call. If you want to talk to Mom, Brady, go right ahead."

"I don't want to talk to Mom." Gray sounded less mystified, more irritated. "Why would you? Do you remember that time she walked out on Dad and never came back—even though she'd left us with him?"

"Does Abby know your feelings on this?" Ty asked, keeping his voice deliberately mild. "Because seeking out the grandmother of her baby sounds like something that would be right up her alley."

"If Mom wants to play grandmother all of a sudden, great. I have no feelings about this." That Gray was rolling his eyes was clear in his voice. "Unlike the two of you, apparently, I've always had too much to do to worry about what I was missing."

"Right," Brady said, glaring across the fire. "Because whether or not someone wants a relationship with his mother has everything to do with how busy he is and nothing to do with, you know, basic human connection."

"You start singing 'Kumbaya,' Denver, and you're walking back to the ranch," Gray warned him. "Try me."

Ty rolled to his feet. He snagged his bedding with one hand and gave his brothers a small salute. "This is been great. Fun on a thousand levels. Let's never do it again. I'm going to go sleep . . ." He waved his arm toward the trees. "Over there."

"Why did you come back?"

Ty stopped walking. But Brady's question still hung there.

And he kept going. "You told Dad off, and I'm sure he didn't like that. It turns out you have a relationship with Mom. You don't seem to care one way or the other about Dad or any of the things he said to you. So why did you bother coming back for his funeral?"

This was his fault. Ty had wanted to steer the conversation away from his marriage. From Hannah. From Gray poking at him about whether he had an opinion or not when he'd worked hard his whole life to leave people smiling in his wake, not cursing his name, which was what happened when a man started throwing his opinions around.

He'd watched his father lose friends and make enemies his whole life. Every time he'd opened his mouth.

Ty should have known better.

"Your father dies, you come home," Gray said shortly. "It's not rocket science."

"I didn't come home to mourn him, Gray," Ty said, as much to the Rockies all around him as to his brothers. As if the dark could make the things he could actually feel less raw, somehow. As if it could wash away the ghosts and the blank spots and leave him whole. "I wanted to make sure that if he was dead, he'd stay dead."

He left his brothers with that and walked off into the dark.

Wishing he could really believe that Amos was well and truly dead and in that grave.

Instead of living on inside Ty, in all those shadowy places he couldn't reach. And all the terrible things he might have done that he couldn't remember, no matter how he tried.

14

Hannah regretted agreeing to go along on Abby's night out with her friends almost instantly.

"It's such a great idea that your friends want to have these dinners out before the baby comes," she said at lunch that week, on one of the days Abby wasn't working at the coffeehouse. Abby had roasted a couple of chickens the night before, and she and Becca were putting together chicken salad sandwiches while Hannah set out plates. "But I'm not sure that you need me tagging along, getting in the middle of all your history."

"It's *a lot* of history," Becca chimed in, smiling brightly.

Hannah smiled right back, because she had not been put on this earth to be outsmiled by a teenage girl who was clearly a tad over-possessive of her uncles.

"Don't be silly," Abby said, without appearing to pick up on the smile war happening all around her. "Both Hope and Rae are delighted you're coming. They can't wait to meet the girl who actually got Ty Everett to the altar. You're already something of a celebrity."

"Terrific," Hannah said weakly.

"Hope and Rae and Abby have all been friends since

they were babies," Becca said. Dripping with helpfulness and that ear-to-ear smile that didn't make it to her eyes. "When they get together, they tell stories about, like, third grade. It's so funny. It's like they have their own little world."

Hannah smiled at Abby and almost meant it. "I can't wait to see for myself."

Abby continued making chicken salad sandwiches with her usual quiet efficiency. Hannah wondered if she didn't notice that her teenage stepdaughter and her new sister-in-law were engaged in a silent battle of wills, or if she was wisely choosing to ignore it.

"Maybe I don't want to spend my life making meals for monosyllabic men, doing laundry, and seven thousand other domestic chores I would never do if left to my own devices," she found herself complaining to Ty the night before he left to move cattle.

"Then don't do it," he replied. Helpfully.

"I asked how I could pitch in, and apparently, that's how." She watched him balefully as he put aside the very few things he planned to take with him on his camping trip. "I hope you're enjoying your fresh, clean laundry. My wifely duties are complete."

He was standing on one side of the bed. Their bed. She was sitting on the other. And yet when he raised that dark gaze of his to hers, it was as if they were standing right on top of each other. Hannah felt herself flush. Her heart kicked at her wildly. It was suddenly very hard to catch her breath.

"The ranch runs fine whether you're here or not," he said distinctly. "What I mean is that anything you do to help is a gift. If you don't feel like giving that gift, don't."

She felt childish and out of sorts, then. It was no fun complaining if he was going to offer distressingly practical solutions she didn't actually want.

"I have to do something," Hannah said after a minute, tracing a pattern into the bedspread, in a deep burgundy that struck her as unnecessarily masculine. Unlike Ty himself, who was . . . perfectly masculine. "I've never been the type to sit around."

"What have you been doing for the past eighteen months?" he asked, lightly enough.

The way he always did.

Hannah looked up to find him watching her intently. "Not the laundry."

His mouth curved as he looked back down toward his bag.

Hannah had done more housework since she'd come to Cold River Ranch than she had before in her life. Because back home, Mama and Aunt Bit were involved in a lifelong competition that had begun in the room they'd shared as girls to see whose obsessive tendencies would win out. Hannah had been responsible only for her own area while she was growing up, and as she grew, the care and maintenance of her assorted rodeo costumes. When Jack came along, there was a lot more laundry, and a lot more washing of all the tiny delicate things he needed.

Jack.

God help her, but she was about at her limit. She needed to get home, to him. She missed him so much it came on sometimes like a fever, a flu. She even missed his laundry.

Here, the kind of labor required to keep the ranch running was far more daunting than a baby's laundry. There was the care of the land and the animals, which was what Gray and the paid hands and his brothers did. Then there was the care of everything else and whatever spilled over from the land and the animals. That was Abby's job. And since she'd been here, Hannah's.

"I appreciate that we're working on this marriage thing," she told Ty now. "But I feel like we're operating under some false pretenses here."

He eyed her. "I don't need a housewife, Hannah. Look at my house. It's tiny. You don't need to clean it. I know how to do my own laundry. We eat in the ranch house. It seems to me that a person with your background, a college degree and all your time doing the rodeo queen thing, can find something else she has to offer this place." He shrugged. "Open a school for rodeo queens yourself. Raise horses. Whatever you want."

"Is ranching your long-term plan?" she asked. "Because I'm pretty sure you said this was temporary. And I can wash dishes temporarily. Even temporary sandwiches I'm good at. It's a lifetime of making food for the men that I can't get my head around."

"You tell me," Ty replied. "Is this a lifetime? Do you trust me?"

That was a loaded question at the best of times. It was worse when they were on that bed the way they were now. The way they slept together—wrapped all around each other, nestling closer, snuggling in and holding on tight— became more of a problem every day.

And made her breathless every time she thought about it.

Or the secret she was keeping from him, which made her stomach twist in foreboding.

"Abby invited me out with her friends tomorrow night," she said instead of answering him.

Ty took his time working his hand over his jaw. "Okay."

"She's very nice. She doesn't have to include me. I appreciate the gesture."

"Abby's good people."

"I'm worried that while the gesture is really nice, in practice, it's going to be . . . awkward."

Another hit from that dark green gaze. "Then either go, or don't go, but don't be awkward."

"Thank you, that's very helpful."

"I don't know what you want me to say."

"No, no. You're right. Why am I asking you? You make it perfectly clear, every day in a thousand ways, that you don't care at all about a single one of your family relationships. Why should I?"

She regretted the words the moment they left her mouth. And more, that tone.

"It's real easy to pretend to care when you haven't decided if you're sticking around or not," Ty replied, his voice not all that lazy any longer. "Maybe you should think about that, Hannah."

Then he'd walked out of the bedroom, leaving her as breathless and foreboding and confused as ever.

And now it was Friday night. Her baby was going to sleep without her yet again, her husband was off camping with his brothers and still didn't remember her, and she didn't know what she was *doing*.

Hannah wanted—desperately—to back out of this certain-to-be-awkward evening, but she didn't feel she could. Instead, she'd given serious consideration to toning herself down. As a kind of penance, maybe. Not being overdressed and over made-up and trying to blend, for a change.

But that wasn't who she was.

She walked into the kitchen of the ranch house to meet Abby, then followed the sound of voices deeper inside. Abby and Becca were at the big, long table in the dining room Hannah had never seen used for a meal. She could see the remnants of several crafting projects spread over its gleaming surface, but Abby and Becca were currently working on something involving a sewing machine.

Something tricky, if their frowns were anything to go by.

Abby glanced up with a smile on her face, while Becca took an extra moment to arrange her features into something passably polite.

Abby looked the way she always did, all that simple, down-to-earth, girl-next-door prettiness, from her head to her toes. Hannah didn't know if it was pregnancy that put the color in her cheeks and the sparkle in her eyes, but she had the suspicion that the friendly smile was her actual personality. She didn't need to apply an entire bottle of mascara to achieve it, like some.

"Are you all going two-stepping?" Becca asked innocently. "At Dollywood?"

"Two-stepping?" Abby made a face. "I'm gigantically pregnant. Of course I'm not going two-stepping. And Dollywood is in Tennessee, last I checked."

Hannah smirked at the triumphant-looking teenager. "I believe Becca is making a reference to my rhinestone addiction." She held her hands out from her sides, fully aware that her jeans glittered. "Once a rodeo queen, always a rodeo queen. I'd wear my crown if I could get away with it."

"I would look ridiculous in a crown," Abby said, sounding wistful. "I never managed to get the queen thing down."

"It's amazing how quickly the queen thing comes to a person when they have a crown on their head," Hannah assured her. "It's like magic."

Becca looked like she was biting back all kinds of commentary on that, and Hannah almost felt sorry for her. And because she knew what it was like to be a teenage girl with absolutely no control over anything happening around her, she moved farther into the room to look at the dress they were trying to put together from a pattern.

She squinted.

"Maybe you have it backwards," she offered after a moment.

"We decided we were going to learn how to make our own dresses this year," Abby said chattily. She was disarming, and Hannah didn't get the feeling that she was doing it on purpose. It was who she was. Happy to talk to anyone, about anything. No megawatt smile required.

That was likely a lot easier when you exuded innate goodness from every pore. Hannah wouldn't know.

Because she could dress it up with as many rationalizations as she liked. The truth of the matter was, she was a born liar. Every point along the way where she could have chosen honesty, she'd gone in the other direction. It was easy to blame that on Ty. If he'd been a better man. If he'd lived up to his promises.

But he had amnesia. Hannah had no excuse.

She might as well be her own father, who Mama had

always taken great pains to make sure Hannah knew was a liar of the first degree.

Maybe it was genetic.

"Abby already knows how to sew," Becca said, sounding like she was making an effort. "I'm the one who doesn't know how. And I can't seem to learn either."

"I can teach you."

Hannah hadn't meant to say that. Especially when Becca looked at her with astonishment.

Abby was looking down at the mangled pattern before them. "Well, that's a relief. My grandmother taught me how to mend things because there isn't a single thing she can't do with her own two hands, but dressmaking is apparently a bridge too far."

She heaved herself up and onto her feet, sighing as she arched her back to take the weight of her belly. Then she excused herself to the bathroom, leaving Becca and Hannah alone.

"You obviously don't have to teach me how to sew. Or anything else," Becca said in a low voice, focusing much too intently on the sewing machine.

"I'm happy to teach you how to sew, sugar. It happens to be one of my few notable skills in this life."

Becca looked at all Hannah's bling, obviously dubious. "Okay."

"Move over," Hannah said. She slid into the chair Becca had vacated in front of the sewing machine and frowned down at the pattern. Then shook her head. "This dress won't suit you at all."

"I like the dress."

"I understand. It's cute. But it's not right for your figure."

The girl bristled visibly. "This really isn't a great idea—"

"Becca." Hannah kept her gaze steady. "You're tall, thin, and gorgeous. Your clothes should emphasize the length of your legs and the elegance of your height. This is a dress for a much shorter, much curvier girl. Watch."

The fabric before her was decent, so she quickly tossed together the kind of dress that would favor a girl shaped like Becca. It didn't take long. Maybe fifteen minutes, and when she pulled it out from the sewing machine and shook it, she realized that Abby had come to stand at the doorway.

"Here," Hannah said, handing the dress to Becca. "Don't take my word for it. Try it on."

"Go on," Abby encouraged her with a smile. Hannah was sure that was the only reason Becca actually took the dress into the other room.

"You did that so quickly!" Abby shook her head. "It once took me an entire semester in middle school to sew a skirt. And that was with instruction. I still got a C."

Hannah waved a hand. "One more skill you too could pick up if you spent your life traveling from rodeo to rodeo, constantly having to look fresh and fabulous no matter what horse stepped on you the night before."

Abby was laughing when Becca shuffled back in.

The dress did exactly what Hannah had hoped it would. It fell from one shoulder, wrapped around Becca's midsection, and then flowed to the other side, making her look taller. More elegant. And far more sophisticated than the sixteen-year-old on a ranch she was.

"That's possibly more drama than you're going for,"

Hannah allowed, after studying her. "I'm afraid my gauge has rhinestones all over it."

"Your father will hate it," Abby said with a small smile for Becca.

Becca laughed. "I *love* it."

Hannah's smile was less rodeo queen and more pleased, then. "I'm glad."

"Can you really show me how to do that?"

"Of course I can," Hannah said. "If that's what you'd like."

Becca smiled at her—a real smile, with a hint of shyness—before she ducked her head.

Abby was still talking about the dress on the drive into town.

"Becca is always going on about how she feels like a tomboy by default, but she doesn't know how to stop being one," she said. "And I'm no help, because I'm about the furthest thing from fancy there is. It's lucky that you're here now. Classing up the place."

Her earnestness made Hannah feel like a monster.

"It's only a dress," she protested.

Abby threw her a look as she navigated Gray's truck down into the town of Cold River. Which only made Hannah feel worse.

"Maybe to you," she said quietly. "It's different when you come into this world beautiful. You don't know how hard the rest of us have to work at it. Mostly, we give up, and decide we might as well concentrate on other things. Being helpful. Dependable. As practical as an appliance, even, which it turns out has its own perks."

Hannah's heart was throwing fits in her chest. "Wait. Are you the not-beautiful person in this conversation?"

"I'm the non-rodeo queen in this conversation."

"Abby. If I rolled out of bed looking as pretty as you do, I would throw out my curling iron and declare myself liberated from the tyranny of mascara forever." That was a terrible lie. Mascara was Hannah's first and truest love. But she was making a point. "This is you while you're pregnant, no less. And Becca—"

"Oh, I know. But she doesn't know she's beautiful. Can you believe it?"

Hannah blinked. "As a matter fact, yes. It appears to run in your family."

Abby laughed. "I'm sorry. I'm actually not digging for compliments. I find you . . ."

"Too much? Over the top? A hundred-dollar bill when a penny would do?"

"Intimidating," Abby said softly. "Not that I'm surprised Ty would marry the most beautiful girl he could find. He's not exactly hard on the eyes himself."

Hannah couldn't help but grin at that, though she tried to hide it.

"He's okay," she allowed.

And for a moment—a sweet, soft moment, while the summer evening gleamed around them and everything felt possible—she pretended she could really have this. That she hadn't wrecked it before she started. That this wasn't coming at the cost of the baby she missed so hard the ache made her dizzy. That she could have a sister-in-law, maybe also a friend. An extended family.

For a moment, just a moment, Hannah let herself imagine this was her real life.

15

Hannah and Abby parked outside one of the restaurants in town, set apart from the main stretch in a small field. It was done up to look like a barn, with reclaimed wood everywhere inside and a terrace out back that was strung with sparkling fairy lights. Abby smiled and waved at people as she led the way through the tables, taking Hannah to a table where two women waited.

One of them, Hannah was happily surprised to see, was the woman from the bookstore.

"I was wondering if you were *that* Hannah," Hope said as the introductions were made, with that same warm, delighted smile that made Hannah smile back as if they were already friends.

"She really was." The petite woman next to her, Rae, let out the kind of rich, infectious laugh that had people at nearby tables turning and smiling along. She was that potent. "She spent the last twenty minutes wondering, out loud, if a random woman she met one day in the bookstore—"

"And in Abby's coffeeshop," Hope interjected.

"—was, in fact, the famous Hannah who somehow got Ty Everett to propose marriage."

"Not only *propose* marriage," Hope said. "But actually make it to the altar."

She and Rae both eyed Hannah's left hand and the ring she wore. Hannah flushed despite herself.

"Maybe we could sit down," Abby suggested dryly. "And continue grilling Hannah while pretending to be civilized." She shook her head at Hannah. "I'm sorry. They're relentless. And yes, they're always like this."

"I would consider myself more insatiably curious than relentless," Hope argued.

Rae belted out another laugh. "I'm just nosy."

They all sat at the rustic wood table out there beneath the pretty lights, and Hannah braced herself for an inquisition. But none came. They were distracted by the appearance of the waiter and the chalkboard list of specials.

"You probably don't know how exciting this is," Abby said, from her place beside Hannah. "This is a new restaurant for Cold River. It only opened in May." She nodded toward the chalkboard. "And the owner clearly believes that Cold River is bursting at the seams with hipsters and tourists galore who want to spend all their money on fancy omelet entrées for dinner when most of the people around here have their own chickens."

"Summer restaurants always come in all optimistic," Rae agreed from across the table. "And then limp off sometime in mid-February. Winters are a whole thing here."

"It's a new town initiative," Hope said. "They're trying to lure in more wedding trade from Denver. The more they can make Cold River a four-season destination, the more restaurant choices we'll have."

They all ordered when the waiter came back, and then the three friends started talking, easily ranging from topics involving Cold River's restaurant scene to names for Abby's baby.

"I still don't know how you can handle not knowing what you're having," Rae said, shaking her head. "I would want to know immediately."

"You love Aunt Hope the best," Hope was murmuring directly to Abby's belly, reaching over the table to rest her hand on the bump. "*Aunt Hope.*"

"I'm going to know soon enough," Abby said cheerfully, swatting Hope's hand away.

Hannah felt as out of place as she'd worried she would, but, oddly, she didn't mind. If anything, it was an unexpected treat to be able to sit there, participate in the conversation as she chose, but otherwise not feel compelled to do anything at all but be present. She didn't have to perform. She didn't have to make anyone feel better. She wasn't the ambassador for anything anymore, but at home, she still acted the part.

She'd been so determined to keep her heartbreak to herself as much as she could in Sweet Myrtle. To prove to anyone who might be watching her—from her mother to the folks she'd gone to high school with to her disappointed donors—that she was fine. Good, even. That really, despite any rumors to the contrary, she'd *wanted* it all to be this way.

Hannah had worked so hard to always keep her head up, always remain calm and courteous. Even when uppity, jealous old classmates like that Heather Wardley questioned whether Hannah was moral enough to be around Heather's ill-mannered kids. To Hannah's face.

But that act wasn't required here. For one thing, Abby and her friends could carry on the conversation all on their own, whether Hannah participated or not. And for another, they knew nothing about her. They certainly didn't know the key bit of information that kept everyone in Sweet Myrtle so focused on her trajectory from rodeo to regret.

Maybe because of that, she let herself drift. She let herself tumble a bit, straight off into the kind of daydream that was nothing but dangerous. Hannah allowed herself to imagine what it would be like if this really was her life. If Jack were here in Cold River and home with Ty tonight, for example—an image that about made her start sobbing right there at the table.

What if she and Ty really did live here, tucked up together in that sweet little house, raising Jack together, the way it had been supposed to be? What if she got to have nights like this, filled with laughter, entertaining conversation, and women she strongly suspected she could be friends with? Real friends. The kind of friends who were thrilled about a pregnancy and celebrated it, instead of avoiding their friends' eyes in public or trying way too hard to act overly supportive when they clearly weren't.

"What if" will only wreck you, Mama had always told her.

Hannah knew better than to indulge in it. Especially here.

Because she was lying to everyone.

Abby was bighearted enough to welcome Hannah with open arms. And Hannah was greedy enough to let her do it, all the while knowing that there was a high probability she would be leaving, never to return.

But she couldn't help herself.

"So," Hope said when dessert came, spinning her spoon around and around in the puddle of fudge surrounding her giant slice of mud pie. "Ty Everett."

"That is his name, yes," Hannah said with a laugh. "And in case you didn't know, Ty isn't short for anything. It's not a nickname. Full cowboy, that one."

"I need you to tell me everything." Hope smiled, big and bright. "No detail is too small or too personal."

"The details might be too personal for *Hannah* though, Hope," Abby said, widening her eyes at her friend.

"Will we all be sharing personal details about our love lives?" Hannah asked, grinning. "Or only me?"

"Oh, no need," Hope said airily. "Let me catch you up. Abby married the love of her life who she had a humiliating crush on since birth while he didn't know she existed."

"I wouldn't call it *humiliating*," Abby objected.

Hope's expression suggested otherwise. "All's well that ends well." She pointed to herself. "Me, cursed to be single for the rest of my days." She nodded toward Rae. "Rae, on the other hand . . ."

Rae glared at Hope. "It's complicated."

"Rae got married very young," Abby said in aside to Hannah, though she didn't drop her voice. "It's better not to talk about it. Even when she brings it up."

"It's only complicated because his family and my family are constantly interacting," Rae said, rolling her eyes. "Otherwise it's boring."

"The Kittredges are another founding family in the area," Abby said. "A lot like the Everetts."

"Oh, like Amanda Kittredge?" Hannah smiled. "I met her in the coffeehouse."

"She's a cute kid," Rae said. If stiffly.

Hannah pictured Amanda blowing up Main Street.

"Is she a kid?" Hannah asked softly. "I thought she was around my age."

Everyone stared. Because, Hannah was sure, none of them had spent any time at all thinking about Amanda Kittredge's age. Not since they'd fixed her as a child in their heads years back.

"Now that you mention it, no," Abby said after a moment. "She is not a kid. She's in her twenties, which I know because she works for me."

"In my head, she will always be about nine," Rae said, and something moved over her face. "Wow."

"Yes, yes, we all grow up," Hope said impatiently. "Little Amanda Kittredge too. But Hannah. Tell us about Ty."

"Relentless," Abby mouthed at her.

Hannah sighed. "I don't know how to answer that, really."

"I had such a crush on him," Rae said with a sigh. "It was that first Christmas he came home after he ran off and joined the rodeo. Do you guys remember?"

"Yes," both Abby and Hope said at once. All three of them laughed.

"He swaggered into church on Christmas Eve, and we all lost our minds," Rae said. Dreamily. "And you married him."

Hannah grinned. "He still swaggers a lot."

"Well, he'd have to. Right? He's so . . ."

"Rae. Ty is Hannah's *husband*," Abby said reprovingly, shaking her head.

"What is it about those Everetts?" Hope asked. She hummed to herself. Happily. "What's in the water out there? You better watch it, Abby. You're going to give birth to one of them."

That diverted all the attention back to Abby and her baby. The three friends laughed and told stories and otherwise enjoyed themselves thoroughly.

While Hannah sat there, feeling like such a fraud. The kind of woman who would sit and have these conversations about a marriage that was built on lies and lost memories. And a baby she was still keeping hidden. The kind of woman who would let these genuinely kind and funny people treat her like one of them when she wasn't.

They would hate her when she was gone. And more if they discovered the extent of her lies. If they learned about Jack. They would sit around a table like this one, passing Abby's baby from arm to arm and loving on it while they dissected this entire evening. They would look for the clues that told the truth about who Hannah really was and how she'd kept the only information that mattered to herself.

The worst part was, unlike her so-called friends from the rodeo who hadn't waited for Hannah to leave before they started picking her apart, Hannah would deserve every single thing these people said about her.

She wasn't sure why, of all the things she was going to have to live with once this time with Ty was over, that notion stung her so deeply.

Almost as if she didn't want to leave, when she should. And soon.

That was the thought she took with her, after they all finished lingering over dessert and said their goodbyes out front. After she and Abby drove home together, Hannah taking the wheel so Abby could catnap on the way back, having clearly overextended herself.

"You can't tell Gray I passed out in the car on the way home," Abby said when she woke up as Hannah pulled into the dirt road that led to the ranch. "He's already so overprotective, it's ridiculous. He doesn't like me driving my car, which is old, but fine. He got a ridiculous satellite phone so I could reach him on the surface of the moon, if necessary."

"You're lucky," Hannah heard herself say, to her horror. Because her voice cracked. She cleared her throat. "Gray seems like the kind of overprotective dad any child would be lucky to have."

Unlike her child, who had no dad. Because Hannah had made certain of that.

Men always lie, Mama always said. *You can't trust them.*

Hannah knew that was right. She'd lived it. But Hannah was lying too. How would she feel if the situations were reversed?

She couldn't say she much liked her own answer to that.

The truck bounced down the dirt road, and Hannah was convinced that she'd somehow given it all away in that one sentence. That Abby somehow knew everything.

"Men who have a father like Amos have two choices," Abby said, very quietly, into the darkness. "They can follow his example. They can double down on all that cruelty and make sure they spend their lives making everyone around them miserable, the way he did. Or they can go in the opposite direction. And Gray and his brothers would rip out their own hearts before they would spend a single day behaving the way their father did."

Hannah wanted to believe that. How she wanted to believe that. But she knew better. And had to wonder if the problem wasn't Ty. If she was the one who brought the meanness out in him. Her own father had wanted nothing to do with her to such an extent that he'd signed away his parental rights before she was born. Both sets of her grandparents had turned their back on her.

Maybe there was a common denominator that she needed to look at more closely.

"Did you know Amos?" she asked instead. And then sighed. "I mean, of course you must have known him. You grew up here."

"My grandmother is a wise woman," Abby said in her same quiet, kind way. "And on the day Amos Everett died, she shook her head while she was puttering around the kitchen in my family's farmhouse, and she said that there is nothing sadder in this life than a person who is given every opportunity to make himself good, but chooses otherwise. Every time."

Abby was likely thinking about Amos Everett. Hannah was thinking about her own choices. Which was yet another clue that she was in no position to judge Ty on anything.

"I'm not sure any person is one thing or another," she said, when she could keep her voice even. "The sad truth is that most people are somewhere in the middle."

"Here's what I know about men," Abby said, turning to look at Hannah as she pulled the truck into the yard and parked it near the ranch house's back door. "And this is based my very scientific sample of one. But they take great pride in thinking they know what they want. Until you show them what they really want."

"If you happen to know it."

Hannah shouldn't have let that slip out. But it was too late.

"They probably won't thank you for it, at first," Abby said, as if she hadn't heard what Hannah had said. Much less the revealing way she'd said it. "But at the end of the day, all they really want—all anybody really wants—is someone who loves them. Don't we?"

Hannah couldn't help the scrape of a laugh that escaped her, then. "You make it sound simple. And it's not. Or maybe it was for you, but then again, maybe you got lucky."

Abby laughed. "Hope wasn't kidding when she said I had a crush on Gray for my entire life. Or that it was humiliating. I loved my husband a long, long time before he loved me. I married him thinking I could love him enough for both of us, and he didn't come around quickly. I'm not lucky. I'm stubborn." She reached over and patted Hannah on her leg, a gesture of solidarity. "And from what I know about you, you're just as stubborn. I've never met a man more adamant that marriage wasn't for him than Ty. But he married you, didn't he?"

Hannah wanted nothing more than to unload the whole, real story, but she didn't. She couldn't.

"He did," she whispered.

And she was the only one who knew how much he'd loved her, then. She was the only one who remembered.

Later, once she'd washed her face, braided her hair, and changed into the tank top and pajama bottoms she wore to sleep in the same bed as the husband she was sleeping with—but still not having sex with, because she clearly liked to torture herself—Hannah found herself sitting on the couch in the main room of the little cabin. In her *place*.

Mama had left a bunch of messages, none of them friendly.

We're coming up on two weeks, Hannah, she'd said in one of them, sounding as if she were in a wind tunnel. *There's trying to see if a marriage works, and then there's abandoning your child. Which is this?*

It was too late to call back home. Hannah had already called this morning, though Mama hadn't answered. Hannah had assumed she was expressing her displeasure. And she didn't want to raise her mother's suspicions any by checking in at such a strange time. After midnight back home was too conspicuous. She didn't want Luanne to know how fragile this all was.

Because she had everything she wanted. And yet nothing she wanted, at the same time.

Maybe she'd built a bridge with Becca tonight, but to what end? So the teenager could burn the dress in a fury if Hannah decided Ty didn't deserve to know about Jack, and disappeared?

Abby treated her like a sister. The sister Hannah had always wanted and had never found in the groups of friends she'd made either at college or on the circuit. She'd had too much studying to do in college. And there was always too much competing on the circuit, so as nice as it was to spend time with the only people who knew what queening was all about, there were always boundaries. Walls. Fake smiles with malice behind them.

For a time, she'd had Ty. She'd finally found her person. Her one. Until that had all exploded all around her.

And now . . .

God, what a mess she'd made of this.

If she told him now, he would hate her. If she didn't tell him, he would hate her anyway, because her time here was running out. She'd been away from Jack too long already.

No matter how long she sat there, worrying it through in her head, it all ended in the same place.

Ty was going to hate her. And his family and their friends here in Cold River were going to hate her too. All she was doing now was delaying the inevitable.

And the delaying only made her hate herself. More.

She rubbed at the place where her chest hurt the most, thinking back to that moment up there on the hill when she could have told him about Jack, but hadn't. When she'd still had the opportunity to give Ty all the information she had, instead of holding back the most important part.

Now, she'd waited too long.

Men always lie, that voice in her insisted.

But why was she clinging to that? When as far she could tell, the only person lying here was her.

She could leave right now. She could pack up and go, before Ty came back from his trip out into the wilderness with his brothers. She didn't expect him back until sometime tomorrow. Late, in all likelihood.

She could be out of the state by then, on her way home to her son.

But Hannah didn't move. She didn't leap to her feet, gather her things, and pack her bags.

The simple, sad, inescapable truth was that she didn't want to leave. Her mother had been right. Playing house had done absolutely nothing but make all of this worse. It had only hurt her more.

Because now Hannah knew.

The way she'd always wanted to know.

Take away the rodeo, take away the sneaking around, the secret they'd kept, and all the extraneous things that she'd always wanted, so desperately, to get rid of—and living with Ty was exactly as she'd imagined it would be. Even taking away sex helped, because it made everything very clear. There was nothing to confuse the reality.

There were moments of friction, of course, but the simple truth was that she liked him.

She liked spending time with him. She liked the things he had to say, and she loved that she could never predict what they might be. She liked the way he took up space, and how he never took up too much of it because he was always aware of her. She liked the little things he did for her without ever discussing it, like making sure to turn on the coffee pot when he headed out in the mornings so it would be ready when she got out of the shower.

Hannah liked living with him, sharing space, sharing a bed, sharing each and every one of those odd, small moments that taken together, threaded into one, made a life.

The life that she could live with him. The life she'd always wanted to live with him.

If she didn't have his baby.

Because that was still the kicker. He couldn't remember, but she could.

They had never talked about children. They had been too busy trying to keep their hands off each other, then exulting in the fact they no longer had to try so hard. Ty had always taken care of the birth control, and Hannah hadn't paid much attention when she kept missing periods because she'd never paid her cycle any mind. She hadn't had to.

Until she counted back and realized it had been too long,

When she'd told her still-new husband that she was over three months pregnant, she'd expected him to be surprised. She'd certainly been surprised. Maybe even terrified. But filled with an odd, encompassing joy too.

Because wasn't this the whole point?

But Ty hadn't been surprised. He'd been flat-out furious.

And this was the truth Hannah still didn't want to face. Ty might want to keep his vows to her. He might even fall in love with her again, if she stayed here.

But he was never going to magically transform into a man who wanted children, because he didn't.

That was what he'd told her—shouted at her, in a voice she'd never heard from him before—that terrible night before he'd marched out, gone into the ring, and failed to walk back out.

He'd been very clear.

He had never expected or wanted to get married, but he had made an exception for her. He'd fallen crazy in love and he'd done his best to adjust to that. He was *trying*, he'd told her, as if she was that hard to love.

But children were a step too far. A baby was the worst thing that could possibly happen to him.

I would rather be dead than become a piece of crap father like mine, Ty had told her.

Then, as far she could tell, he'd done his best to prove it.

16

Ty came home from the cattle drive with his brothers tired, cranky, and about full up on family. Particularly the kind of family that came with all these discussions he didn't want to have in the first place.

But after he'd tended to the horses, he found himself ridiculously excited to get to the cabin. Not because he was suddenly overwhelmed with that sense of belonging he'd never felt on this land, like every other person clinging to the various branches in the Everett family tree. But because he wanted to see Hannah.

Ty was growing more and more obsessed with the wife he hadn't known he had two weeks ago, and the funny part was how little that bothered him.

He threw open the front door, but she wasn't there in the main room of the bunkhouse. He checked in the bedroom to make sure, but Hannah wasn't there either. So, he bit back his impatience, cleaned himself up after his two days out on the trail, and rationalized that he couldn't expect her to be hanging around for some private time before yet another family dinner when he'd never told her that was what he wanted. It wasn't lost on him that these days, his version of private time involved sitting in a room in her company, instead of some of the far more entertaining ways he could think of to pass the time.

Nor had he forgotten that was all on him.

Maybe he'd taken his martyr act too far.

Ty went over to the big house to find dinner cooking, but no sign of Abby in the kitchen. Then again, his brother was obviously very happily married and could enjoy his wife's company any way and any time he pleased.

But he was taken back when he stepped into the dining room to find Hannah and Becca hunched over the dining room table. Something about the way the two of them sat there, their heads close together and all their attention focused on the fabric Becca was running through the sewing machine, killed him.

Ty couldn't really imagine what it was like to have a daughter. He'd never tried, as far as he knew, but it had to feel the way he did now, looking at a child he'd known since before she was born. Now too grown for his liking and paying close attention to his wife.

It was unbearable and it was perfect, all at the same time.

Hannah looked up as if she'd felt him standing there, and Ty would never tire of the look of her. That pretty face. Those eyes of hers, so blue it hurt, and yet so complicated at the same time. Tonight, she had her hair in separate, fat braids that framed her face. And he wanted to pick her up, wrap himself around her, and bury himself in her in every way he could imagine. And then a few more.

But instead, he smiled.

For a moment, while Becca was still focused on the sewing machine, Ty concentrated on his wife. And that electric, searing connection that stretched tight between them and held fast.

When Becca glanced up a few moments—or a lifetime—later, the sewing machine stopped. "Uncle Ty, how long have you been standing there? You scared me."

"My bad, peanut."

And he couldn't wipe that smile off his face. He went back into the kitchen and pulled a beer from the fridge. He was standing at the window, watching the dark creep in over the fields, when he felt Hannah come up beside him.

Ty was used to the ache of it by now, but that didn't make the kick of it any less bittersweet. It wasn't enough any longer to stand beside her. To get the scent of her in his nose, to feel her in his gut, and still stand apart, keeping his hands to himself. And this distance he didn't want anymore.

"How long have you been teaching Becca how to sew?" he asked, because he was an adult in his brother's kitchen, not an oversexed teenager who didn't know how to control himself. And wait.

"About twenty-four hours. This is the second lesson."

Ty liked that Hannah was standing close to him. He liked that it seemed unconscious, as if she was as drawn to him as he was to her. "Glad to see she's coming around to the idea of a new family member."

Hannah gazed up at him, her eyes sparkling. "Oh, you caught that?"

"My women are very protective," Ty drawled lazily. "They fight over me. It's a curse."

"She might even be fierce one day. But don't worry, I have it covered."

"I don't know. Ordinarily my money would be on Miss

Rodeo Forever, but a teenage girl?" He whistled. "That's a whole different level of machination."

"You forget that I used to be teenage girl myself." Hannah grinned at him, nice and cocky, the way he liked her. "Like I said. I have it covered."

Ty knew they had an agreement. There were rules, and he'd made them, but he couldn't seem to help himself tonight.

He reached over and got his hands on her face, holding her cheeks between his palms.

She melted against him as if she'd wanted the same thing all along.

"Hannah," he said, like her name was torn out of him. "Hannah, I . . ."

Her hands were on his chest, and he was sure they belonged there. Her body was arched into his, as if they really were puzzle pieces meant to be snapped together, just like this.

"Hannah—"

"Get a room," came Brady's disgruntled voice from behind them.

Ty took his time dropping his hands. Hannah's gaze searched his for a beat, then she turned away and busied herself with getting dinner on the table.

And Ty spent the rest of the evening trying very, very hard not to murder his little brother.

But everything was still highly charged. He felt like he was vibrating with need. Hunger, and not for the hearty food that Abby served up. Ty didn't care if it was memory or wishful thinking, because he wanted Hannah. He wanted all of her.

He was tired of only having part of her. Even if it had been by his own design and for the best of intentions.

But that wasn't the deal they'd made. He'd assured her he would wait for her trust, not his convenience.

He didn't say anything as they walked across the yard, side by side the way they always did. He didn't put his hands on her the way he longed to or turn her toward him again, no matter how many times he imagined doing exactly that. He set his teeth. He clenched his jaw.

Ty assured himself that somehow, he wouldn't die from this when they'd crawled into the same bed later.

Hannah seemed subdued. He wanted to ask her why, but he was afraid that if he opened his mouth, he would start begging. Not a great look.

Pull it together, he ordered himself.

She read her book for a while, then she excused herself to head off into the bedroom. Ty sat in the main room and told himself that he was made of stone. That he could handle anything without cracking or breaking his word. He listened to the water go on and there was a strange kind of peace in the fact he knew her routine. She took off her makeup, washed her face. Sometimes she did something else with her hair. She changed into her pajamas, then crawled into bed.

And he crawled in after her, then kept his hands to himself. Somehow.

There was silence from the other room, and then the sound of her feet scuffing against the floor.

Ty looked up to find Hannah standing in the doorway. She was wearing one of those tank tops she liked and he *really* liked, because it showed off her shoulders and made his tongue want to fall out of his mouth. And because it also hugged the rest of her, all those sweet curves he was doing his level best not to lose his mind over. Her pajama bottoms rode low on her hips, and he became unduly fascinated with the strip of smooth skin he could see between the hem of her tank top and the waistband of the pajama bottoms.

There was no denying it. He had it bad.

"You okay?" he asked. Gruffly.

"I'm terrific," she said, and he couldn't quite read that odd look on her face. "I like your family, Ty."

That was unexpected.

"They're okay," he said. Eventually.

"Your sister-in-law in particular. She might be one of the nicest, kindest people I've ever met."

"She's good people. I told you that."

"I like your brothers too. They both love you very much."

Ty shook his head, that weighted thing in him suddenly much too heavy again. "They're my brothers," he managed to say. "They're . . . annoying."

Hannah smiled, and there was a sweetness to it. But there was also a sadness that Ty couldn't understand. And didn't like. He focused on the sweet.

"I wanted to thank you for bringing me here. You didn't have to do that. I've truly enjoyed getting to know all of them." She studied him. "I never met any of them before. I guess they didn't come to watch you?"

"Gray met his first wife at a rodeo event," Ty said dryly. "He lost his appreciation for the sport after that."

"Even if they'd come to every event, it wouldn't have mattered, I guess. I couldn't have met them, then. It's been a gift to meet them now."

"Hannah. What's going on?"

She hugged herself. "It takes a lot of trust to bring someone, a stranger, into your home. I wanted you to know that I recognize that. I was in there taking off my makeup. And I realized that you're the only person I'm not related to by blood who's ever seen me without it on."

Ty waited, but she didn't say anything. She only looked at him expectantly. And then laughed when all he did was stare back at her.

"You don't even realize what I'm telling you."

"I like you in makeup," he told her. Carefully. "A lot. But you're also gorgeous without it. Basically, Hannah, you can't go wrong."

"Thank you," she said, still laughing. And the smile she flashed warmed him up, inside and out. "But Ty. What I'm trying to tell you is . . . *I trust you.*"

For a moment he didn't get it.

Then he did.

It was like flipping a switch. All that hunger, all that greed and longing, everything he'd been trying to put a leash on and hide away—it all stormed through him.

And slowly, intently, he rose to his feet.

"Say that again," he ordered her.

Hannah flushed, bright and red and so beautiful Ty wasn't sure he could keep his knees beneath him. But he managed it. Her eyes were locked to his, wide and blue, and filled with a new kind of heat now.

He felt a burst of satisfaction when she had to reach out to steady herself against the doorjamb.

"I trust you," she whispered. "With me. But I need to tell you—"

Ty started toward her, and she never finished her sentence. Her chest rose and fell. He could hear her breathing fast and it made his own speed up.

Ty made it across the room, but he didn't stop in the

doorway. He scooped her into his arms, tossing her over his shoulder as he headed straight for their bed.

The torture chamber where she had been all over him, and wrapped around him, and yet so out of reach for so long, he might be permanently cross-eyed.

She was laughing as he tossed her on the bed. And followed her straight down.

"You do not mess around," she said as he rolled over her, finally stretching out and getting that lush body of hers beneath him. Finally feeling her soft and warm all over the place he wanted her most.

"Baby, you have no idea," he told her.

Then he claimed her mouth with his.

Again.

At last.

Finally.

Hannah couldn't get close enough to him.

Everything was better than she remembered. He was hotter to the touch. His shoulders were wider, harder. The way he kissed her was a lightning heat, setting her on fire, making her melt and shudder and fight to take more. To take everything.

The ways she wanted this man almost scared her.

She had despaired over her response to him, in all those lonely months without him. But this felt like a sacrament.

This felt safe.

This felt like home.

He shifted, rolling them over so she was sprawled across him. And she couldn't touch enough of him. His arms. His chest. His wonder of an abdomen.

But he raised her up so she was sitting astride him, and he stared up at her for a long, shuddering beat of her heart. There was something possessive, dark and thrilling and blazing all over his beautiful face, and Hannah loved it. Exulted in it.

He looked like he couldn't believe this was real. Like he'd never get enough of her.

It made a kind of chill roll through her, though she wasn't cold.

Especially when he moved his hands from where they rested in the crease of her hips, sliding them up beneath her top.

"You are so beautiful," he muttered, half a curse and half a prayer.

Hannah was right there with him.

His hands were big and callused. They were a working man's hands, weathered and battered, and yet they were impossibly tender against her skin. He traced the line of her spine, and she could feel it everywhere. Where he touched her and all the places he hadn't gotten to yet.

She couldn't stop shuddering.

Ty had taught her how to do this, and Hannah wanted to do it with him. For him.

She reached down to find the hem of her tank top, then pulled it up and over her head, tossing it aside. He muttered something, and then his hands were there. He slid them over her belly, then tracked his way north until he filled his palms with her breasts.

Hannah arched into him, moaning at the contact. The friction. His hard, knowing hands right there where she was so sensitive.

He played with her, looking so intent that the heat of

it kindled into a fire and burned through her. She rocked herself against him, thrilling at the hard ridge of him, flush against the place she needed him most.

She almost cried out, he felt so good. So *right*.

She was close already. Closer every time his thumbs moved hypnotically over her nipples.

"Go on," he told her, a gruff, urgent command. Then he lifted his head, tilting her close and sucking one nipple deep into his mouth.

Hannah exploded.

It took her a good while to shudder back into herself, longer still to accept that this was real. That this was happening, again.

At last.

Ty rolled them over again, and it was suddenly a crime to her that he was still wearing his shirt. His jeans. She set herself to the task of removing them, laughing as he proved himself to be absolutely no help whatsoever.

He would rather touch her. Feel each and every part of her with his fingers, his palms. Taste her with his mouth. All over.

As if this were the first time.

Her heart kicked at her as she remembered that for him, it was.

And for once, the fact he couldn't remember her didn't fill her with pain. On the contrary, Hannah took it like the sweetest challenge.

She kicked her way out of the rest of her clothes, and then they were both naked, at last. Naked and together, touching everywhere, all the glorious differences between their bodies as much a joy to her now as they always had been. His hair-roughened legs next to her smooth ones.

The scrape of his jaw, the play of his muscles, where she was soft and rounded.

Each its own delight. Each thrilling and delicious in its own right.

She could remember their wedding night so clearly. The way Ty had laid her out like she was precious. A prize beyond comprehension. He had called her *wife*. And he had slowly, carefully, taught her where all that heat and longing between them had been leading all along.

Tonight, Hannah could do the same for him. She could teach him exactly how good it was between them. Maybe her body could remind him of the things her words couldn't reach.

Hannah devoted herself to the task as if she'd been born for it.

She moved over him like water, pulling out every trick she could. And not only because she wanted to make sure this was good for him, though she did. Desperately. But because she had missed him. She had missed this. He had taught her how to want and what to do with all of that need. Then he'd taken it away. And she had never really come to terms with any of it.

She laid a trail of fire down the center of his chest, picking her way across his scars, a living map of the life he had led. The amazing feats he had performed and then paid for with his own blood.

Each and every one of them made him who he was. Ty. Her husband.

The man she loved even now, when she understood at last that they weren't meant to be together. That she couldn't have him, not really. Not the way she wanted him.

She poured it all into each and every kiss.

Longing, regret. Loss. Love.

This was better than reading a book on a shared couch. This was better than careful conversation and too many stories, too many secrets. Because everything was better when Ty's hands were on her, one tangled in her hair, one with a hard grip on her bottom.

"My God," he groaned at one point when she'd made her way down to his feet, then moved back up again as if she wanted to anoint every single part of him with her love, one last time. "You know every single thing I like."

"Of course I do," she told him. She grinned up at him as she stopped there, where he was hardest. "You taught me."

Then she indulged herself by taking him deep into her mouth.

Ty let out a groan that rumbled in her like thunder. She slid her way down him once, then again, the taste of him making her shake and melt between her legs.

But then he was jackknifing up to sitting position and pulling her off him.

"You're killing me, baby," he managed to get out, sounding so rough it was like another, better caress. "You might actually kill me."

"That would not work for me at all," she said, breathless as he shifted her around on the bed. Getting her beneath him again.

"Hannah," he said, framing her face with his hands. She could feel the intensity of his gaze, bearing her down in the same marvelous way his chest was. "Hannah, I . . ."

But he didn't finish that sentence with words. He twisted his hips and surged deep inside of her.

Hard. Hot.

Home.

Then he moved.

And Hannah moved too, matching him and meeting him, building that beautiful, bright and shining bit of fire that was only theirs. It burned her. It exalted her. The way it always had.

Hannah felt whole again. She felt like herself again. Every glorious slide of his body deep into hers washed away another week of isolation, of shame.

She felt clean, new.

Ty dropped his head to her neck. He pressed open-mouth kisses along the line of her collarbone. And his hands were big and bossy, as he moved her where he wanted her to go, then showed her why he was right. Why she wanted it too.

Hannah locked her legs around him and surrendered herself to the beauty of it.

Sheer joy, passion, and need.

It was still better than anything else she'd ever known.

This was why she'd kept their secret. This was why she'd lied to her mother, lied to the Rodeo Forever Association, lied and lied and lied some more.

This had always been worth whatever it took to get here.

When a new wave started to break over her, sending her spinning off into an even wilder sensation than before, something else broke inside of her.

"I love you," she cried out. "I love you, I love you—"

Because she still did. Because she always would.

Ty followed after her, groaning out his release against her neck, so hard it might leave a mark.

She liked the idea of that.

It wasn't until she could breathe again that she realized he hadn't said he loved her back.

17

Of course he hadn't said he loved her.

Hannah was furious with herself for imagining he would. Or should.

He'd had a couple of weeks with her. A couple of weeks, a few days, and a story she'd told him. What had she expected?

But all the rationalizing in the world couldn't make her heart hurt any less.

Ty was sprawled out next to her in the bed, and Hannah knew that she could roll herself into his side. That he would hold her automatically. As if his body really did remember her in ways his mind could not. It would feel as comforting and right as it always had.

As he always did.

But there were tears pricking at the back of her eyes. And that kicked-in-the-gut feeling that only got worse, and heavier, by the second.

She rolled out of the bed and padded over to the bathroom. She went in and closed the door behind her, taking great care not to look at herself in the mirror over the sink. After a moment, a breath or two, she reached in and turned on the spray in the shower. Then she climbed in, letting the hot water beat down on her.

Hannah stood there for a long time, trying to lose herself in the heat and wet. Trying to let the water wash away any evidence of tears.

Or she hoped it did, anyway.

Her heart kept right on hurting, like a bruise behind her ribs. When her skin was pickled, she shut off the water. And took her time drying herself off, squeezing out her hair and throwing it into an easy braid on one side.

Another pair of pajama bottoms hung on the back of the bathroom door, so she climbed into them and pulled on the extra tank top she'd stashed there after her last laundry day.

Then, when she could put it off no longer, she opened the bathroom door.

Ty sat on the side of the bed, his elbows on his thighs. He'd pulled on his jeans, but nothing else, and Hannah was struck the way she always was by the beautiful lines of his hard body.

All those lean muscles. All that whipcord strength. Even if she weren't in love with him, she would have admired him. He was a work of art.

But she wanted a husband, not a piece of artwork.

"It's been a while," Ty said in a low voice, "but I'm pretty sure it's not a good thing if a woman throws herself out of bed and runs for the bathroom as soon as she possibly can."

Everything inside of Hannah wanted to roll with this. She wanted to smile. Make it all right. Let this keep going.

She wanted to tell him about Jack so desperately that

she could feel the words cluttering up the back of her throat. She wanted him to hold her while she did it, while she showed him all the pictures she had, right there on her phone. She wanted all of this to be okay.

But it wasn't.

"That's the problem," she said instead, her voice quiet. Too thick with what she wasn't saying. "All I am to you is a woman. I could be any woman."

His dark gaze hit hers. And held. "You're the woman with my name on a marriage certificate."

"It's nothing more than a piece of paper," Hannah heard herself say. She laughed, because she would have sworn a sentence like that would never come out of her mouth. But here she was again, doing things she'd been sure she never would. "Not to me. To me, it represents everything that happened before and after we got married. But to you? Any woman could have shown up here. Any woman could have told you a story. In the end, it's a piece of paper to you, that's all."

Ty looked stunned. He blinked and looked straight ahead for a moment, like he needed to orient himself. Hannah knew the feeling.

"What are you trying to say?" he asked.

That was an excellent question. But her heart hurt, and this was wrong. And not only because she was here under false pretenses, with a secret so big she shouldn't have been able to get out a word without tripping over it. That was bad enough.

This was all that and more.

"I love you," she said, and that hurt too. Especially when he got a different sort of look on his face. More . . . hunted. "And I know that you can't feel that, because you don't remember. I understand completely why you can't tell me you love me back. You've only known me for a couple of weeks."

"I don't know how I feel, Hannah. About anything." He stood up from the bed, but he didn't move closer to her. "It's like there's a thick glass wall between me and everything I remember. I don't feel anything. I haven't felt anything, if you want to know the truth, until you came along. I don't know what to call that. And it's not what you want from me, maybe. But it's not nothing."

"I believe you. I told you I trusted you, and I meant it. But don't you see why I can't do that? Why that's not enough?"

"I don't see." His jaw was hard now. "Because from over here, this sounds a lot like a breakup conversation. 'It's not you, Ty—it's me.' Is that what's happening?"

"It *is* me," she managed to get out. "I'm not . . . I can't be the kind of woman who sleeps with a man just because he's there. That's not who I am. I've slept with one man in my entire life, Ty. Only one. And I waited for him to marry me."

"I'm the same man," Ty gritted out. "And we're still married."

"You're not the same man." That hitch was in her voice again. And those tears were threatening the back of her eyes when she'd cried them all out in the shower, surely. "The man I married was in love with me. The ring he gave me was a symbol of that. And there are thousands of women out there who wouldn't bat an eye about those details, but I'm not one of them. I can't sleep with a man who doesn't love me. *I can't.*"

"How are you so sure I don't love you?" Ty demanded,

sounding far less in control than he had been a moment before. "I don't know that."

"It's not your fault." Hannah was hugging herself, holding herself together. Or trying. "This situation is such a mess. It's more complicated than you know. And I thought sex would make it better, make us closer, bring you back to me somehow—"

"Didn't it?" He moved, then, crossing the few feet between them and gripping her arms. "I don't know what experience you had here, but I'm pretty sure I found religion."

"I don't want to be your religion," she whispered. "I want to be your wife. But I'm not sure that's ever going to happen."

"Why not?" he demanded, close and low. "I spent two days away from you, and I hated it. I miss you when I know you're in the next room. I haven't thought about the rodeo, not really, since you showed up here. It's in two weeks and I don't care, and it was the only thing that kept me going for months. Until you showed up."

"I don't know which part of that is less healthy. But I'm pretty clear that it's not a marriage. Not really. And you would think so too if you knew—"

"I like you," he gritted, cutting her off. "I don't understand how it can be easy to live on top of each other like this, but it is. We make fantastic roommates, Hannah. And apparently, we're magic in bed. What else do you want? What else is there?"

"I told you." She wanted to push him away, but if she touched all that bare skin right there in front of her, the last thing she would do is push him anywhere. "All of that is playing games. The last time around, we had a lot of sex, but we never spent real time together. Now we've had some real time, but no sex."

"If you want to throw sex in the mix, I'm game."

Hannah shook her head. "I thought I could love you enough that it wouldn't matter that you couldn't remember me. But it does. This makes me feel like I'm cheating on my husband. That I'm betraying him by getting naked with this man who doesn't know me. And who definitely doesn't love me like he did."

Something darker crashed over Ty, then. Hannah watched it roll in like a thunderstorm.

"He loved you so much that you left him. And didn't come back, even though he was in the hospital. What kind of love was that?"

"I can't make it make sense, Ty, I can only tell you how I feel."

"Let me tell you how I feel. Like I have whiplash."

"I'm sorry about that too."

He let go of her and took a step back, raking his hair back with one hand.

"I don't need you to be sorry. But I can't smack myself on the side of the head and get my memory back. Believe me, I've tried." The look he shot her then felt like a punch. Hard and straight to the gut. "I don't understand why you came here, if not to give us another chance. And a chance takes more than a couple of weeks. Doesn't it?"

"I don't have a whole lot more time, Ty. I really don't."

"What are you talking about?" He shook his head. "For somebody who didn't want to have sex until she was married and in love, you sure seem to have jumped right past the 'til death do us' part of the deal."

She had to tell him. She'd put it off too long, and now

everything was even worse than before. Hannah knew why she'd made every decision along the way, and each one had made sense to her at the time. But she still didn't understand how she'd ended up here.

Rip it off like a Band-Aid, baby girl, she ordered herself, as if she were her own mother, standing right behind her with a militant look on her face. *Just get it done.*

"Ty." As if saying his name would lighten this blow. "I know you have a lot of feelings about your family."

"That's what I keep trying to tell you. You have a lot of feelings about my family. They have a lot of feelings about everything. I don't have any feelings." He moved a hand over his chest, that storm still holding him in its grip. "I'm not trying to indulge my inner cowboy here. I keep trying to tell you. *I don't feel a thing.* It's all . . . turned off."

This was exactly what she didn't want. Ty with no feelings, and her with his baby. How could this possibly end in any way that didn't hurt Jack? Hannah only wanted to protect her son. She would do anything to protect him. She had—she'd done this.

But she didn't know which path to take that would hurt him the least now.

"You keep saying that," she said, her fingers digging too hard into the flesh of her arms. "While everything you do is emotional. Maybe you don't know how to put your feelings into words. That's not exactly a surprise. That doesn't mean you don't feel things."

"Telling me how I feel isn't going to make my memory click back into place, Hannah. But it is guaranteed to piss me off."

She wanted to cry. Sob. "I'm not trying to piss you off."

Though she was about to do much worse than that.

"Are you sure? Because from where I'm standing, you seem to be grabbing at things to be mad about."

Say it, she shouted at herself. *It's never going to get easy. It's never going to feel right. Just* tell *the man.*

"You . . ." Hannah could feel herself begin to sweat. Her stomach churned. "I have to tell you . . ."

He was staring at her. Waiting, though he could have no idea about the bomb she was about to drop.

Hannah swallowed. She wished she could reach out and slap herself across the face, to snap out of whatever this was that held her in its grip.

She had made this bed. She might have done it with the best of intentions, but what did that matter? Everyone knew what kind of roads were best paved with good intentions. And where they led.

"Ty . . ." she started.

"If you're working up your nerve to tell me to get lost," he said, something dark glittering in that gaze of his, "you're wasting your breath. You and I made promises to each other. You sat in my truck and told me the story. This might not be a fairy tale, Hannah. It might not be working out the way you want it to. But I don't believe in giving up on things when they get hard. If I did, I never would have met you in the first place, because I would have slunk away the first time a bull threw me on my face."

This got worse by the second.

"That's not what I was trying to say. I have to tell you—"

But she didn't finish her sentence because a pair of headlights swept over the front of the bunkhouse, illuminating the room. That was weird enough, since last Hannah had checked, the whole Everett family was home for the evening. Of course, there were a thousand reasons that someone could have taken a ride out somewhere, from ranch business to Brady in search of a single man's social life. They'd been otherwise occupied for some time, after all. Maybe she hadn't heard one of the vehicles leave.

But in the next moment, a horn started blowing. Loud and long, and it didn't stop.

"What the hell . . . ?" Ty muttered.

He grabbed his shirt and shrugged into it as he moved out of the bedroom. He stamped into his boots and then headed outside. Hannah trailed along behind him, pulling on her own boots and grabbing one of his flannel shirts off the peg near the door to wrap around her. It got cold in these mountains at night, even in August.

There was a truck parked at a weird angle in the yard, right outside the ranch house. A quick glance around showed Hannah that the outside lights were all turned on and Brady was already standing in front of the truck. Abby and Becca were standing together in the ranch house's door, while Gray strode across the yard, the look on his face akin to another man's shotgun.

That was when Hannah realized she'd seen that truck before.

She told herself she was confused. She didn't know enough people in Colorado to go around identifying different pickups, but as she drew closer, her confusion spun out into something far more alarming.

Recognition.

Because once she got out of the glare of the headlights, she could see the woman standing in the open driver's door. She wore her hair the same as Hannah, in blond curls that tumbled down past her shoulders. She liked her jeans, she loved her boots, and she'd never met a concert

T-shirt she didn't covet. She bought them off the internet, and pretended it was as good as going. Tonight's featured Tim McGraw and Faith Hill in a spicy embrace.

But Hannah couldn't focus on Tim McGraw's forearm and hands. She couldn't breathe.

Especially when she saw the bundle the woman held in her arms.

"Mama . . ." Hannah whispered.

No one could possibly have heard her, but still, Luanne's gaze swung straight to her. And Hannah would have preferred to get hit with that truck, which she'd last seen in Aunt Bit's driveway. She felt the way her mother's gaze swept over her, taking in every detail. Ty's shirt, haphazardly thrown over what were clearly her pajamas. Her wet hair, and most damning of all, the fact she wasn't wearing a lick of makeup.

Hannah might as well have come out here with a sign, lit up in neon, telling all of Colorado what she and Ty had been up to tonight.

"Can I help you?" Gray demanded.

But Ty was looking from Luanne to Hannah and then back again. On the other side of the truck, Brady was doing the same.

"Well?" Mama said into the dark. Straight into the center of all that tension. Her eyes bored into Hannah, and Hannah knew that she'd never, ever back down. That wasn't what Luanne did. "Aren't you going to introduce me?"

Hannah's mouth was dry. Still, she opened it and tried to say something, only to find no sound came out.

Everyone was staring at her. And she couldn't summon up any of the tools she normally used. No smile. No drawl. Nothing.

That was when Jack began to cry.

Hannah's paralysis disappeared in a snap. She leaped forward, suddenly so greedy to get her hands on her baby that she forgot the situation she was in. It didn't matter. Not when he was crying. Not when he needed her.

She threw herself across the yard, pushing past Ty and Gray, her hands already out. Reaching. Desperate—

Hannah plucked Jack out of her mother's arms, already murmuring. Already saying his name and moving in to press kisses to the side of his face. The sweet baby smell of him rolled into her, soothing her. Just as her voice soothed him, because he stopped crying. His perfect lower lip trembled for a moment, and then he started to babble. He reached out and put his sticky, chubby hands on her face, right there on her mouth, and she couldn't help herself.

She smiled at him, big and wide, as if they didn't have an audience, arrayed behind her in worrying silence.

But they did.

Hannah met her mother's eyes over the top of Jack's head and the soft, dark hair he got from his daddy. She cradled him close and didn't react to the defiant challenge all over Luanne's face.

Then she turned around, slowly, and it was even worse than anything she could have imagined.

The outside lights were beaming and so were all the lights in the house, so she could clearly see Abby and Becca standing inside the back door. Brady had his hand on the hood of the truck and a scowl on his face. Gray was on the other side of the open driver's door. Ty had moved closer to Hannah, as if he was ready to protect her.

She would remember them lined up like that for the rest of her life. She could feel this scene branding itself on her heart. The family she'd almost had, but lost.

Right this minute.

Because she could already see understanding dawning.

"This is my mother," she said, dimly amazed that her voice was working again, now that it was too late.

She found Ty. She held his gaze even though it made her tremble. And she tried to pretend that they were alone while Jack made his noises and seized her braid, tugging on it as if it was a toy. *His* toy.

She understood, suddenly, why a heart could break and keep hurting. Why each and every piece ached the way it did.

Because she had never understood what it was to love, wholly and desperately and with her whole body and soul, until she'd met Ty. When he'd broken her heart, she'd been sure he'd kept all the pieces with him. Then she'd had Jack, and she'd understood her heart in a whole new way. That it was bigger and stronger and more fragile than she'd ever imagined. That it would forever live outside of her body, contained in a little boy who smelled sleepy and too warm and all hers, but wasn't hers at all. He was his.

Tonight, she had every love of her life standing there around her. Her mother, who she loved and despaired of, fought against and wanted so desperately to please. Ty, who she still loved, so hard and so deep there should be a different word for it, especially when it couldn't possibly work out between them. And Jack, her bright and shining joy, whose presence on this earth made her life make a different kind of sense than it ever had before. She wanted to cry, because it was hard, and worse, because she could never protect him from things like this.

Love and all the damage it did. All the ways it hurt.

And how pointless life would be without it.

Jack would grow up and learn all the ways there were to hurt himself. She would have to watch him do it. She would have to let him go.

Letting go, over and over again, was all love ever demanded of her. It was such a tiny thing, and it was the whole world, and Hannah was terrible at it. More than terrible. As this whole mess proved.

Ty was staring at her, frozen solid, a perfectly blank look on his face. She didn't need to hear the murmuring from behind him. She didn't need to feel her mother's impatience at her back.

She felt her own guilt just fine.

"And this is Jack," she said to Ty. As if they were alone and she'd done this the right way while she'd had the chance. If only she'd done this the right way . . . but she hadn't. "I was trying to tell you about him. He's your son."

18

Her words didn't make any sense.

Ty stared at Hannah, uncomprehending. Except something in him comprehended fine, because his pulse was rocketing around the way it did before he climbed on the back of a bull. His adrenaline was kicking, hard.

And he was still. Too still. The kind of still that kept him on bulls for eight crucial seconds. The kind of bone-deep stillness that kept him calm.

When he wasn't calm at all.

"He's ten months old," Hannah was saying, pure misery all over her face. Though he had to hand it to her, she sure was trying to keep her voice bright in all this darkness.

"Jack," he said, though he didn't sound like himself. His voice came from far, far away, lost somewhere in that stillness in him that wasn't real. And wouldn't last. "My son. Jack."

None of those words made sense.

"Ty . . ." Hannah whispered.

And she reached out to him.

That was what did it. Because she shifted the baby as

she reached out, and it was such an unconscious move. It spoke of long practice. Ten months of practice, if he could trust his hearing. Ten months of the life he'd made and hadn't known existed.

That pulse in his temples was more like an ice pick. Ty only realized that he'd stepped back—or staggered, really—when she dropped her hand.

"Okay," Gray was saying from behind him, at his sternest. "Show's over."

Ty was dimly aware of movement on his periphery. Of his family going back inside and taking the woman Ty had known immediately had to be Hannah's mother with them. He'd known who she had to be at a glance because she looked like she could be Hannah's sister. But she clearly *remembered* him, if that look she'd thrown his way was any indication.

He was aware of all that, but he couldn't look away from Hannah. And her baby.

His baby. His son.

Ty had never wanted a family. He could barely tolerate the one he had. And now he had a son. Had actually *had* a son for the better part of a year already.

He shook his head, but none of it went away, not even that pulsing pain in his temples. Hannah stood there, the baby on her hip, her eyes slicked bright with some combination of pain and a terrible longing. It caught at him.

It quaked through him.

"So in there . . ." He pointed in the general direction of the bunkhouse, but he couldn't bring himself to look away from her. "Right now. You were going to leave and . . . never tell me?"

"I came here for a divorce."

Her voice was rough, and maybe he only wanted to hear the note of guilt. But she also sounded . . . sure.

He could remember the day she'd arrived so clearly, in comparison to all the blank spots and missing pieces that he'd grown to accept was who he was, now. They'd stood out here in the dirt, surrounded by all of this land, the unendurable weight of it. And he'd seen a pretty girl with blue eyes that made the Colorado summer sky pale in comparison.

But Hannah had looked at him as if he was the enemy.

Because he had been.

"What happened that night?" he asked her, his voice low and furious.

Ty couldn't have said what he was furious about. Everything. Nothing. He only knew that the fury was everywhere. Dripping through him like whiskey and acid, burning hot everywhere it touched.

Hannah didn't ask him what night he meant. She took a deep, shuddering breath, and she held the baby closer to her, cradling his head.

Because she was comforting herself? Or because she wanted to protect him . . . from Ty?

How could he not know if he was a man or a monster?

You know, came an old voice from deep inside him, entirely too familiar. *You know what kind of piece of crap you are. Good-for-nothing punk.*

Amos might have died. Ty had attended the funeral completely sober, to make sure. But what good had the funeral done if the old man lived on inside him even now?

"I found out I was pregnant," Hannah said, her voice too thick. "And I told you. And you were not happy."

"'Not happy,'" Ty repeated. He ran a hand over his jaw,

but it didn't feel like his. *He* didn't feel like *him*. "Did you expect me to be happy? Had I turned into a man who wanted . . . this?"

"He's not a *this*." Hannah glared at him, and something in Ty turned over and made him queasy. Because she'd been cradling the baby for a reason, hadn't she? "He's a little boy. His name is Jack."

"Just tell me what happened, Hannah." Ty sounded old to his own ears. The kind of broken that settled in deep. "Make me understand why you would keep this secret all this time."

Her eyes were big and wide. She swallowed, hard. And Ty couldn't understand why he wanted nothing more than to pull her close to him and comfort her. Even now.

The urge made him . . . unsteady.

"You said a lot of things," Hannah told him, her pretty face solemn. "The major takeaway was that you couldn't be a father. That you never wanted to be a father. The only example you'd had of fatherhood was a monster and you would rather die than be that kind of father to a child of your own. And then you got hurt." She blew out a breath. "And maybe tonight, we can set aside the debate about whether or not you were more reckless out there than usual."

Reckless. That word again. His head pounded.

"Of course, I rushed to your side." Her face twisted. "What I mean is, I had to wait for hours and then sneak in early the next morning because I was still so worried that people would know about us. In case you thought you were the only one who acted regrettably."

"Regrettably," he echoed, and almost laughed.

What a prim word to describe the blackness in him. The desolation.

"And you already know what happened after that," she said.

Ty was spinning. Everything was spinning, and the earth was buckling, and he was getting so tired of all that seismic activity when he still couldn't remember the things he needed to know.

He couldn't remember, but he could certainly *feel*. Hannah might as well have stuck her hand into his chest and ripped his heart out. He tried to pull himself together, somehow, when he was more sure than he'd ever been before that he was nothing but a walking collection of broken parts.

Ty could feel the weight of expectation, there in the night between them. Around them. *In* them. Need and longing, pain and suffering, hope and fear.

In Hannah. In him. In both of them, when he couldn't get past the churning darkness that whispered to him in his father's voice.

Or the secrets she'd kept—for the baby's good. *His* baby.

This should have been impossible. Ty couldn't remember falling in love, no matter how drawn he was to this woman, but he accepted that could have happened. But he knew without a shred of doubt that he'd never intended to have children. He'd wanted the bitterness to end with him.

His head pounded.

"Let me see him," he said gruffly.

Hannah made a hitching sound, like a sob checked. She turned the baby around in her arms, so Ty was finally facing his own child.

His son.

The baby—*Jack,* he told himself—gazed back at him,

dark eyes big and his mouth open. He had dark hair that went wispy at the ends. He had *eyebrows*.

That struck Ty as miraculous.

"I'm sorry I didn't tell you the moment I saw you," Hannah said in a rush, and she sounded on the verge of sobbing. "All this time, I was sure that *of course* you remembered us. And didn't want any part of us. Of this. And I didn't want to subject Jack to that. To a father who didn't want him at all, not even for the odd weekend here and there. Because I know what that's like. I know exactly what that feels like, and I figured it was better to have no father than one who—"

"Can I hold him?"

Hannah stopped talking. She sucked in a breath, like it hurt. But her voice was quiet and solid when she spoke again. "Of course."

She held Jack out before her, and Ty took him, the way he'd taken hold of Becca a thousand times when she'd been a baby and he'd been home. He could have turned Jack into the crook of his arm, but he didn't.

Jack was solid. He kicked a few times, drooled, made a whole lot of noises that sounded like words, but weren't.

Ty held the baby up before him, eye to eye.

Man to man.

"Jack," he said, testing it out.

The baby's eyes opened wider, and for a moment, they simply stared at each other. Then Jack reached out with his plump hands and put them right on Ty's face.

Everything inside Ty shattered.

He remembered his father, years ago, cuffing him on the side of the head every time he fell off his horse until Ty learned how to ride like a dream to avoid it. *Fall off again and I'll give you something to cry about.* He couldn't have been more than six. He remembered getting older, and Amos swiping the schoolbooks out from in front of him while he tried to do his homework. Then hooting with derision and telling Ty there was no point. *You got looks, boy, but no brains.* He'd been nine.

He remembered his father in the chair beside his hospital bed, his hard-lined face screwed up with distaste while Ty lay there in pieces. *You screw up everything you touch, boy. This was the only thing you were any good at.*

Ty felt the darkness in him. The poison. It had been flowing steady his whole life, like the river out there, cutting through fields and keeping the land green. It filled him up. It made him who he was. A rodeo cowboy who never had a home. Only the circuit, on and on until it broke him for good, which it would. That was the promise the rodeo made to any man fool enough to follow it. And the poison was what kept him hidden behind a grin and a bottle.

It was what defined him. It made him the kind of man who spoke the way he had to Hannah. Who flipped out when he'd discovered he got his own wife pregnant.

That was the man he was.

He was glad he couldn't remember any of it. Or that it hadn't been any worse.

Because all this time, all along, he hadn't been *becoming* like Amos. He'd always been Amos. Ty was the drunk, forever and always. He didn't have to touch a drop of whiskey for both of his brothers to still treat him like he was rolling around half in a bottle of Johnnie Walker at any given moment.

Which could only mean he acted like a mean old drunk either way.

The only thing Ty had ever had going for him was that he'd kept his distance from anyone he could possibly hurt.

He couldn't remember why he'd imagined that he could overcome all of that for Hannah. Why he hadn't understood, deep inside of him, that all he would ever do was hurt her. Chase her away if she was lucky, ruin her if she stayed put.

Wasn't that why he'd stayed in touch with his mother all this time? She was no kind of parent to him, and his brothers were right—she'd abandoned them and never looked back. Ty didn't have any particular affection for her that he could recall.

Bettina was a cautionary tale.

Bettina was a monument to *what if*. She was what Ty would do to a woman because Amos had done it all to her.

How could Ty possibly have risked Hannah like that?

He brought Jack closer, liking the soft, warm weight of him. Liking the way he giggled, his whole face lighting up and his chubby legs kicking, as if laughter was a full-body experience.

Something in him shifted, sliding sideways.

But it only made him more resolved.

He turned back toward Hannah, holding Jack that much longer. That much closer. For one more moment.

"You have every right to be furious with me," Hannah began.

Ty passed Jack back to her, and on some level, was amazed how much that hurt him. She took the baby—*their* baby—automatically, settling him against her shoulder with that smooth ease that made everything in Ty hum. And hurt a whole lot more.

"He's beautiful," Ty told her, deep and matter-of-fact. "And so are you."

She let out a long breath. "Ty—"

"Hannah, listen to me very carefully." He didn't dare touch her. He wouldn't let go if he did. "You need to take him away from here and never come back."

"What?"

"You already know what you should do. Your instincts were right on. You need to take him back to Georgia and stay there." He shifted back, because he needed to put space between them. Or he would reach out to her again. "If you need money, I'm happy to give it to you. But I don't want to be a father. I can't be a father. Do you understand me?"

He didn't wait for her to answer him. He turned away, staggering as if he were drunk. Broken all over again.

But he'd hurt himself this time, instead of letting a bull do it.

Ty wasn't good for much. He could ride a horse. He could rope, ride bareback, and wrestle a steer. All that meant was that he was from generations of ranchers. He could outlast an ornery bull for less than ten seconds, more often than not. He was pretty sure that made him a lunatic. But that was it. That was his skill set, the end.

Just like his father, he had one skill. And he could drink through everything else.

The only other thing Ty could do was protect Hannah. From him. Whether she wanted him to or not.

Because he knew where the poison in him led.

So he left her there, standing with the child they'd made together in the yard, both of them flooded with the light from the house. He knew he would carry that image with him, burned deep.

And he walked out into the land.

The damned land.

Because he got it now. This was a particular kind of poison. And if a man tried to put it into his family, it would ruin lives. It would make a baby like Jack into a man like Ty, good for nothing and rotten to the core.

But these fields didn't care what kind of father he was. The mountains stood completely indifferent to what kind of husband he was.

He'd always thought he lacked the roots everyone else from the Longhorn Valley was so obsessed with. Especially in his family. But now he understood.

Gray was the exception, like Silas. Men who stayed, but didn't go bad. Most members of his extended family were like Brady, who'd gotten out. Ty was the rule. He was his father, straight through.

Everetts were like rocks. Like the mountains all around. They crushed anything they fell on, down into dust.

He didn't need to remember anything out here where the bones of his ancestors were part of the earth now. There was no need for ghosts down where the willow trees met the river, whispering stark and simple truths he should have heeded a long time ago. He didn't need to feel.

The land would take his blood. His sweat.

His fury.

The land would make him honest no matter what his inclination. It would take the rot in him and turn it green. Make it into food for trees, cattle, people. The cold, cruel river that swept down from the mountains, brimming with snow melt, had been telling him the truth about the family who lived here all his life.

Amos had been cruel. He'd focused on his women, his children, with deliberate intent to harm.

The river was indifferent. It would drown a man or quench his thirst so he could live, flood the fields or keep them fertile.

All Ty had to do was break the cycle.

It was too late for him.

But keep Jack away from here, away from a man who wanted to be indifferent but was far more likely to be cruel, and there was every possibility that he could be free of this.

Of the weight of all that cold stone and unbearable grief that Ty felt deep in his shattered, stitched-together bones, and expected he always would.

He couldn't give Hannah what she deserved. He couldn't be a father to his son.

But he could give them this.

19

Sweet Myrtle was exactly how Hannah had left it.

August melted along as stifling Georgia summers did. Humid and heavy, so that the air itself felt weighted.

Hannah felt pretty much the same way herself.

Every day that passed since that night on Cold River Ranch, the more it felt like it had all happened with a certain sense of inevitability. No matter how many times she relived it—walking outside, seeing her mother standing there in the wrong state, seeing Jack, then holding Jack as she turned to face Ty and what she'd done—

It had felt like a memory while it was happening.

Hannah was moving through her usual morning routine a week after that terrible scene. Nothing had changed. Everything was where she'd left it and worked the same way it always had. Her life was small here, but workable. Her mother and aunt helped with Jack. Mama had moved into the main part of the house when Jack was born, leaving the room out back for Hannah and the baby. It was the most natural thing in the world to live here in the place she'd grown up. It was easy. She knew all its rhythms.

Only now, she had no hope that things might change one day.

That Ty might have a change of heart. That he might appear at her door and say all the things she'd always dreamed he would. Apologies, love, all of it.

The thing about hope was that a person didn't realize how much it lived there in a life, threaded through all the little moments. Hannah had been so sure she'd given up on Ty that day in the hospital.

But she hadn't.

She'd held out hope, even though she might have lied to herself about that, across all those months.

And now that it was gone, she could see all the empty spaces where it had lived in her.

"You look so sad, sweetheart," Aunt Bit said when Hannah walked into the kitchen, a freshly changed Jack on her hip.

Hannah smiled automatically. "I wouldn't call myself sad."

She had no words for what she would call herself, so she didn't try. She put Jack down into his saucer so he could scoot around on the floor, slamming himself into walls in the kitchen. It never failed to make him shriek with delight. And as a bonus, it gave Hannah a moment to fix herself another cup of coffee.

Aunt Bit was sitting at the table, the daily paper spread open before her and a steaming mug of tea at her elbow. Mama was already long gone to open the doctor's office she managed.

It made Hannah feel deeply disloyal, not exactly a new sensation, that she liked the mornings when her mother wasn't here. Vibrating with all her tension and anxiety and focusing it all on Hannah.

You can be mad at me all you want, Luanne had said stoutly when it was all over, out there in the ranch's yard. Ty had walked off into the dark. Luanne had clearly been watching from the window because she came out straightaway, looking as if she was fully prepared to march Hannah straight back into that bunkhouse, pack up her things herself, and carry her out of there if necessary. *I did what needed doing. If he were going to rise to the occasion, he would have.*

What I need from you, Hannah had replied, in a voice she barely recognized with her baby held in the crook of her neck, *is for you to drop this subject. And never bring it up again.*

So far that had worked. They'd driven in a sad caravan all the way home, stopping a lot more often than Hannah had on the way out because they had Jack to consider. But Hannah had welcomed the miles. All that strange, suspended time between her past and her present.

She decided she was happy. All of her questions were answered. Now she could move forward.

She kept telling herself that, over and over, like a prayer.

"I've never seen your mother cry," Aunt Bit said now, in a lull between Jack's earsplitting squeals as he rammed himself into the cabinets.

Hannah dumped an extra dollop of the sweet creamer she loved into her coffee, despite the fact it had no nutritional value whatsoever and was almost certainly rotting her from the inside out. Then another big dollop, because who cared what was rotting her these days. It was better than all that emptiness where her hope had been.

"Mama doesn't cry," she said. She slid into her usual chair at the round, retro kitchen table that was nothing like the wide, scarred old door in the Everetts' ranch house. Nothing at all. She rubbed absently at her chest and told herself that sooner or later, even that would stop hurting. "She told me once she has no time for it."

"I don't know anyone who doesn't make the time for a good cry," Aunt Bit replied. "Except your mother. And I expect that's because she had to survive things she shouldn't have had to, at a young age, more or less on her own."

"Luckily, she had you. *We* had you."

Aunt Bit smiled. "I used to say I did her crying for her. But you know what it takes to stay that strong, don't you?"

"Never putting a wishbone where your backbone goes, like the poem," Hannah said, right on cue.

"Your mother never had the time to figure out that a wishbone and a backbone aren't necessarily mutually exclusive, and don't have to be mortal enemies forever," Aunt Bit said. "What I'm trying to say is that your mother is terrified that one slip, one stray tear, and she'll start crying so hard, she'll never stop. She'd have to cry for that fifteen-year-old girl who found herself in all that trouble. The sixteen-year-old girl who was abandoned by everyone who should have taken care of her. She'd have to cry for year after year of hardship, struggle, and the fact that she never had the choice to decide whether or not to be strong. She had to be, so she was."

"I know what Mama did for me," Hannah said softly.

Aunt Bit smoothed out the newspaper page before her. "I'm not telling you a story you already know to make you feel bad, Hannah. You're not your mother. If you want to be sad, you go right ahead and be sad. You don't have to hide it. And between you and me, you don't have to pretend that not feeling what you feel is a strength. We both know it's not."

Hannah mulled that over across the next few days. The weather didn't break. Her heart didn't heal. And she could see the beauty of her mother's take on these things. Because if only Hannah could stop *feeling*, she would be better. Happier, certainly.

One August afternoon, under a sky that had been threatening to storm for a day or so now but hadn't quite gotten around to it, Hannah drove home from her usual afternoon out at the stables. The last lesson had been canceled, so Hannah had spent the time catching up with her favorite horse, Marigold. She and Marigold had caught up on life, the world outside the rodeo, and ridden around the fields outside of town until Hannah's heart felt, if not healed, quieter.

So maybe she should have expected to find a strange car outside the house when she got home. And worse, when she climbed out of her pickup, the driver of that car got out too. *An Everett,* she knew in an instant, and her heart leapt—

But it was Brady.

Thunder rumbled overhead, and all through Hannah too.

"Let me guess," she drawled as Brady started up the drive toward her. "You came all this way to make sure I hurry up and start some divorce proceedings. Out of the goodness of your heart, no doubt. Because you love your brother that much."

Brady scowled at her as he came to a stop a few feet away from her. And he was the Brady she'd met in the ranch house kitchen that day. Big and powerful. Not the hapless younger brother at all.

"I don't know, Hannah," he threw at her. "The question is, do you love my brother?"

Hannah wanted to haul off and punch him. Run him over with her truck a few times. Instead, she smiled.

"Now, sugar, I can't believe you came all this way to question me about my romantic intentions."

"It's not your romantic intentions that interest me," Brady retorted. "It's my brother's fool head that he's set to crack wide open in yet another rodeo in three days."

Like Hannah didn't know that. Like she didn't have that particular date carved into her heart.

"He wants to reclaim his glory," she said. Airily. "I can't say as I blame him. If there were a way to reclaim my own, I expect that I'd be all over it."

"Would you?" Brady's scowl only deepened. "Because as far as I can tell, you're the one who walked away from your glory."

"If you mean Colorado, you were there. It wasn't me who walked away. And I'm not so sure I'd call any of that glorious, but I don't know your life."

"I'm not talking about Ty's response to the child you failed to tell him about."

"That's a real relief, given it's none of your business."

"I'm talking about you, Hannah. Miss Rodeo Forever two years running. I assumed you got kicked off the tour, but you didn't, did you?"

Hannah's stomach twisted up on itself. She glanced back over her shoulder, but there was no one in the house. Aunt Bit spent her Wednesday afternoons working in the county library. Mama had her early afternoon off from the doctor's office and decreed it her grandmother time with Jack. Meaning no one was coming to save Hannah from this conversation.

"I don't know why you're scraping up all that ancient history now. None of it matters."

"There were rumors, but that's all they were. If you'd really wanted to, you could have weathered them. You were set to turn over your crown to the next winner at the big pageant in May."

"I had no idea you were such a Miss Rodeo Forever fan."

"I'm trying to build a picture," Brady said. "That's all."

"I'm not sure what kind of picture that is, especially when it involves turning up on my doorstep," Hannah replied, her drawl thick and her tone light, even though she still wanted to *do* something. Preferably something unbecoming, yet unmistakable. "But I'm pretty sure you can carry right on doing whatever you're doing back in Colorado. Where you belong. I don't even understand how you found me."

"It lists your hometown next to your name on every single picture they have of you in the Miss Rodeo Forever archives."

"I'm surprised they haven't taken those down."

"It wasn't that hard to drive into town, ask at the first store I could find, and get directions right to your door. You're not exactly hidden away, Hannah."

"That's what I used to tell myself while I was waiting for your brother to wake up and remember he was married," Hannah retorted, then caught herself. She couldn't talk about Ty's memory. It wasn't her secret to tell. And her heart thumped at her, because she could pretend all she wanted that she was halfway to turning all her feelings off like her mother, but that was a lie. She was protecting that man even now. "And you're still not answering my question. What are you doing here, Brady?"

"That all depends on you," he replied. "You were more than happy to go toe-to-toe with me back on the ranch. I thought that meant you were a fighter. That you would fight for Ty. Fight me, if necessary. But then you walked away at the first sign of trouble. Maybe that's what you do."

"Sugar, your head is a muddle," Hannah said, playing up her drawl even more. Mostly so she really wouldn't punch him. "Am I a gold digger? After your brother for all that rodeo glitz and glamour? Or am I weak and easily scared, running away from trouble like a bunny rabbit? Which is it? You can't have it both ways."

"You tell me."

"The thing is, Brady, I don't have to tell you anything. I'm standing outside my house, minding my own business, right here in this life of mine that doesn't involve a single member of the Everett family."

"Except one," Brady said, his voice hardening. "My nephew. Ty's son. Who, in case this escaped your notice, has a stake in the land that's been in my family since the 1800s."

"Since when do you care about the land?" Hannah asked. "Or your family, for that matter?"

"I care more about my family than you or they will ever know," Brady gritted out at her, something moving over his face as he spoke. "And if this is a conversation you want to have, great. I welcome it. But you have to actually be in my brother's life to be in my face."

"Says the man who flew across the country to come get all up in mine."

"It's a simple question, Hannah. You're either in or you're out." His gaze was dark green like his brothers'—like

Jack's—and it pinned her where she stood. "You either love him or you don't."

Wishbones and backbones were all tangled up inside her, then, and mostly Hannah's own bones felt dangerously brittle. And it was impossible to talk about love and Ty without wanting to give in to the real storm that had nothing to do with the Georgia sky above them, and everything to do with that pain inside of her. That grief. She hardly knew what to call it anymore, because it was simply . . . life. Life without Ty.

Life without any hope he'd change his mind.

"Life isn't as uncomplicated as a quick question," she said after a thick, sweltering sort of moment. "No matter how much you wish it could be."

"He's going to get on that bull. There's every chance that this time, when he falls, he'll do even more damage than he already has." Brady shook his head, his jaw tight. "I've never known Ty to be all that happy-go-lucky unless he was drunk, but this Ty? The one you left? He's doing an excellent impression of the grim reaper."

That made her ache. And the ache made her mad.

"What can I possibly do about that?" she demanded. "You can't make someone love you, Brady. I know. I've tried."

"The only way you can be sure of something not working is if you stop trying."

"You shouldn't be here," she said after a moment. "Ty was pretty definitive. And I'm not that hard to find, as you proved. If he wanted me, he'd come find me."

"Maybe you've caught on by now that we didn't have the ideal childhood," Brady said, low and dark. "Our father spent a lot of time pitting all of us against each other. But Ty was in the middle. Always the people pleaser. Always a smile, a laugh, and the first one to convince you nothing upset him. He was real good at getting along."

"He's different on the inside," Hannah couldn't help but say.

"Aren't we all?" Brady shook his head, as if he couldn't believe he was here. Saying these things. That made two of them. "The thing about Ty is that he stopped fighting. When he was in high school, all he did was fight. With my father. With anyone who crossed his path. But the minute he joined the rodeo, he turned into the supposedly happy-go-lucky cowboy we know today. No more fighting. Winning, sure. But he stopped fighting what people thought about him. What he was supposed to be versus what he was. That's one of the reasons he drinks so much."

"He doesn't drink that much," Hannah said, because even now, she had to jump in there and try to defend him. "Maybe he doesn't bother fighting what people think about him because the people closest to him can't even see what's in front of their faces. When's last time you saw your brother drink whiskey?"

"I'm not going to argue about Ty's drinking."

"Because there's nothing to argue about. He likes a beer or two. That's it. Maybe you should ask yourself why he wants his family to keep seeing him as the family drunkard. I used to watch him do it at the dinner table. *At* you, as a matter of fact."

Brady considered her for a moment. "That's a rousing defense, Hannah. Almost like you care about the guy."

"He's the father of my child. My relationship with him, no matter how you'd like to boil it down to a single question, is always going to be complicated. What's uncomplicated are my feelings about you standing here in front of my house all up in my face. I don't want to argue with you. I don't want more Everett drama in my life."

"I understand that. But there's that rodeo stunt he's going to pull on Saturday."

"And . . . what? I should go stop him? Cheer him on? Get in his head when he needs to keep from cracking it wide open again? Why would I do any of that?"

Brady muttered something she didn't quite catch. Then reached into his back pocket and pulled out two envelopes. He separated them, one thin and one thick.

"You either love him or you don't," he said, his voice hard. Stark. "And what's the state of mind of a bull rider who has nothing left to lose? Who's not only sure he's doomed, but embraces it?"

He held out the envelopes, and Hannah took them, though she'd as soon pick up a pair of snakes.

"In one there's a plane ticket. It'll fly you out on Friday." Brady nodded his head toward the thicker envelope. "That's a legal document Ty asked me to have drawn up. It names Jack as his legal heir, lays out a financial settlement for you, and makes sure that Jack will get what he's entitled to no matter what happens to the ranch. Your divorce papers," he added, when she only stared back at him without comprehension. "Just like I assume you wanted."

Hannah stared at him, the envelopes like bricks in her hand. "Wait. He sent you here?"

"He did. And maybe you ought to ask yourself why he's all fired up to get his affairs in order, Hannah. Because I asked myself that question. And I can't say I much cared for the answer." Brady nodded at the envelopes she held. "Pick one."

Hannah stood there, her pulse too wild and her heart

too heavy, watching as the youngest Everett brother walked away, climbed into his rental car, and drove off.

She stood there while thunder rumbled overhead, but it was a pleasant melody next to the storm inside her.

She stood there and she stood there, as the summer afternoon got wetter and thicker all around her. She stood there until the first, fat drops of rain began to fall, and only then did she turn, blinking back the tears her mother wouldn't have let herself cry, and found her way into the house.

Then she got angry. She threw the plane ticket and the divorce papers into the top drawer of her dresser and told herself to forget about all of it. Forget about the Everett family. Forget about Ty. Forget about whatever he might or might not imagine he had to prove this weekend.

But she lay awake that night, replaying every word Brady had said to her.

She spent all of Thursday pretending she wasn't fuming. Pretending she was paying close attention to the usual ins and outs of a normal weekday here back home in this life of hers. But she couldn't get the things that Brady had said out of her head. Not only about Ty, but about her.

It had been a perfectly normal day. The thunderstorm on Wednesday had cleared the air for approximately twelve seconds, and it was good and humid again. Hannah put Jack down after dinner, then joined her mother and aunt out on the screened-in back porch to enjoy the August evening with the aid of the ceiling fan to move the air around.

Aunt Bit hummed as she knitted. Mama tapped away on her tablet. Hannah usually read a book, but her paperback lay unopened in her lap.

Instead, she found herself wondering if the real truth about a backbone was that it was made of wishes. The wishes that came true. The ones that didn't. Heartache and happiness, all fused together. That was what strength was.

Too far in one direction or the other, and the whole thing fell apart. As the last couple of years of her life proved.

Hannah was tired of falling apart.

"I'm going back to Colorado tomorrow," she announced, throwing that out there into the middle of a quiet evening when she hadn't planned to say a word. Or use that ticket.

There was silence. Aunt Bit stopped humming. Luanne stopped tapping.

"Baby girl," Luanne said after a moment, sounding weary, "I don't know how many times—"

"Why did you tell me to walk away from the rodeo?" Hannah asked her. "No one actually kicked me out. Buck Stapleton didn't pull me in front of the Rodeo Forever Association to answer to my great sin of being married and pregnant. He might have, in time. You know how seriously he takes his vision of the rodeo. But none of that had happened yet."

Luanne frowned. "It was only a matter of time before they came after you. Why stay and let them use you for target practice?"

"None of that had happened. You don't know that it would have."

"Of course it would have happened," Luanne said. "Because it always happens."

"Because it happened to you?" Hannah asked softly.

Luanne stiffened. "What happened to me has no bearing on this."

Hannah felt a great weight roll away from her, then. She even laughed, because she almost felt dizzy from the lack of it. So light and airy that if she didn't watch it, she might float up over the backyard, over the barbecue grill and Aunt Bit's vegetable garden, scrape the tops of the watchful oaks, and career off into nothing.

"What happened to you has bearing on all of this, Mama," she said softly, but not unkindly. "What happened to you is me."

"Don't you say that," Luanne said fiercely. "I wouldn't trade a second of it."

"I believe you," Hannah assured her. "But every single thing you've done, and I've let you do, since I told you I was pregnant was damage control for that teenage girl who had me all those years ago. I'm not you, Mama. Jack isn't me. And none of this has to be this way unless I let it."

"I don't know what that means. You know the ways of the world, Hannah. You can't trust a man. They lie, that's what they do. We're both living proof of that."

"Everybody lies," Hannah corrected her softly. "Most of us lie to ourselves first and foremost. I'm not sure that's a crime. I'm beginning to think that's just people."

Her mother shot to her feet. "I don't know what this is. If he wanted you, he would have claimed you. Right then and there when he could have in Colorado. Why would you go back for more?"

Hannah rose to face her mother. And she loved her. She could hardly begin to list all the ways she loved her. Luanne had given up everything for her, vowed she would do it again in a heartbeat, and Hannah never took that for granted. She never forgot.

But she couldn't keep living out her mother's same old cycle of bitterness. She didn't like where it ended up.

"Mama," she said, as gently as she could. With all the love in her heart. "I'm not you."

Luanne jerked as if Hannah had slapped her. "I'm perfectly aware that we are not the same person, Hannah Leigh."

"I'm not you, but more to the point, Ty isn't good old Brad Collingsworth, who wanted nothing to do with us. Ty married me. He loves me."

"And he sure showed that love, didn't he?" Luanne retorted. "You forget, Hannah. I watched him walk away from you. It looked pretty final to me."

"It doesn't matter what it looked like to you," Hannah said, as gently as she could, which was possibly not all that gently. "I shouldn't have left him. I should have walked right out after him. And do you know why I didn't?"

"Why would you chase after something when you already know how it ends?" Luanne asked, looking and sounding baffled.

"Because I always leave," Hannah said quietly, answering her own question. "I always leave before anyone can tell me to go. I always make sure that I don't let anyone really, truly hurt me. Sure, Ty said some terrible things to me in the hospital. But what kind of wife walks out and never returns? Never even checks in to see if maybe that was the pain medication talking? What kind of woman leaves her man like that?"

"He already left you. He already told you he didn't want you. Why would you set yourself up for more?"

"Because I love him," Hannah said, her gaze steady and strong on her mother's. "I'm in love with him, and it's not going to go away. It's not going to change. And I know he loves me too, as best he can. I am full up on all the ways he let me down. All the ways he disappointed me. But what about the way I abandoned him?"

"It's not the same."

"You're right. It's worse. Because I wasn't suffering from a head injury at the time."

"Hannah."

"I know you only want what's best for me." It was getting harder to keep her voice steady, but she made herself do it. "But Ty isn't a high school boy who told me lies at homecoming, got me pregnant, and then pretended none of it ever happened. He's a grown man. He's my husband. And a marriage can't work if there's all these ghosts of other people in the middle of it."

"What kind of marriage do you have?" Luanne sounded scornful, but Hannah reminded herself that she was always scared. "You snuck around while you were dating. You snuck around while you were first married. He told you to leave him and you had his baby in secret. Then you went back to him with more lies and without your baby. What kind of marriage is that?"

"My marriage," Hannah said distinctly. "And you don't get a vote."

That sat there, thick and sweaty like the Georgia night outside.

"I'm going back to Colorado tomorrow," Hannah said in the same tone. "I'm taking Jack with me. You can either support me or not. I'd like your support. I'd always like your support. I love you, Mama. But this is happening whether or not you approve."

She started toward the house, only then aware that she was shaking. Aunt Bit sat there with her knitting forgotten in her lap, but when Hannah caught her eye, she smiled.

"This is your pride talking," Luanne said, sounding . . . shaken. Angry. But Hannah couldn't help that.

Her mother had been angry as long as she'd known her. Hannah didn't have to be too. "You can't accept that you, Miss Rodeo Forever times two, who always kept her crown sparkling clean, don't get to have what you want. But I keep trying to tell you, baby girl. That's life."

"That's *your* life," Hannah replied, and she looked back at her mother, wishing that there was some other way to do this. "And you want it that way."

"Whether I want it that way or don't, it's reality."

"It's the reality that you choose," Hannah said, her voice as steady as her gaze. "Over and over and over again. The fact that you stay here when you could have left a lifetime ago. You want to be here, smack in the middle of the town where you know your parents will see you on the street. You want them to look at you. You wanted them to see me, growing up without them, happy. I suspect you even liked it when I came back home, because disaster or victory alike, you got to show them that we were fine. You like to stay right here in Sweet Myrtle where your continued existence is a big raised middle finger to everyone who ever looked down at you. It's spite, Mama. And I don't want to live my life out of spite."

If she'd hauled off and slapped her mother upside her head, Luanne couldn't possibly have looked more stricken.

But Hannah could only love her. She couldn't take care of her.

So, she turned around again, headed toward the house, and concentrated on a life built on better things than spite and painful history. Because she might not know what that looked like, exactly, but she knew where to go to start living hers.

20

Ty was more than ready to get back up on that ornery bull and finally do what he'd been training to do since the start of the year.

He had to get through one last family dinner first.

Ty would have happily avoided his brothers altogether, but Abby and Becca had suckerpunched him. They'd been lying in wait when he'd come back in from the fields this evening, glowing with good intentions and affection.

Ty didn't have the heart to tell them it was no use. It didn't matter how many members of his extended family packed into his bunkhouse. All he saw was the absence of Hannah.

"We made all your favorite things," Becca told him, in that bright, deliberate way she'd always used to talk. Back when she'd believed she was responsible for everything. She darted a glance at Abby. "Abby's grandmother's fried chicken, those sweet potatoes I know you love, and my cornbread. You always say I make the best cornbread."

"That's because you do, peanut."

Ty even managed to throw out a grin.

"We need to celebrate you before your next victory," Abby chimed in. And she'd smiled with nothing but kindness and understanding.

He didn't know how to tell her that didn't help.

"It might not be much of a victory," Ty said. "That bull wins more than he loses."

"The fact that you even want to get back on any bull, much less that one, is a victory as far as I'm concerned," Abby said matter-of-factly. "That's what we're celebrating."

There were worse things in life than subjecting himself to a meal made up entirely of his favorite foods. Ty ate. He drank and noticed Brady clocking the one beer he nursed with what struck him as entirely too much interest.

But he didn't care enough to ask.

"You're going to be amazing," Becca told him excitedly, after they'd all demolished one of Abby's pies. "And we're all going to come cheer you on."

Ty went cold at that. He looked over at Gray. "What? No. Your dad doesn't like the rodeo."

"Of course Gray loves the rodeo," Abby said placidly. Too placidly. "Because what reason would he have not to love it?"

Given that the reason had been Cristina, Ty figured Abby had suggested to her husband that he find a way to overcome his issues.

"I love the rodeo," Gray retorted, though his eyes gleamed when he looked at his wife. "It's a passion of mine."

"No one wants to miss your ride to glory, Ty," Brady said from beside him.

Something in Ty turned over at that, but he stamped

it back down. It didn't matter if they were there. It didn't matter if they weren't.

Nothing mattered. Wasn't that the point?

It was what he'd wanted.

"Terrific," he said. He pushed back from the table, doing his best to grin at Abby and Becca, lazy and at his ease, as always. "Thank you both for the victory meal. I sure do appreciate it."

It was a relief to push his way outside. To feel the dark and the land envelop him again.

Ashes to ashes. Dust to dust.

One way or another.

"Hey, jackhole," came Brady's voice. "If I could have a minute before you waft off into the darkness again?"

Because of course he couldn't let well enough alone. Ever.

"I don't have time for this," Ty said without turning back around. "I have to head out early tomorrow morning."

"What's your plan, exactly?"

Ty sighed. "Same plan as it always is, baby brother. Get on the bull. Stay on the bull. Jump off the bull when the buzzer sounds and try not to get trampled. The end. Bull riding is real simple."

"See that, Brady," came Gray's irritatingly mild drawl. "No need to worry. He might have busted himself up the last time around, but I'm sure it's fine that he figures he can reclaim his reputation on the business side of a pissed-off, two-thousand-pound bull. That's bound to end well."

Ty took his time turning back around. Once again, he was standing in the yard of the ranch house, forced into a conversation he didn't want to have. It was a good thing he'd come to terms with this land, because it sure seemed to insinuate itself into every part of his life. Hannah. Jack. His irritating brothers, standing shoulder to shoulder like a wall of *spare me*.

Behind them, the lights were on in the ranch house. Abby and Becca were still in the kitchen, either cleaning up or making something for the morning. Becca was talking animatedly, waving her hands in the air for emphasis. Abby kept looking up and laughing as she responded, one hand drifting to her belly.

All smiles. All love. All that family crap Ty knew, deep in his blackened soul, he would destroy if he got too close.

"What is this?" he asked, laughing at his brothers. Not nicely. "An intervention? For bull riding?"

"I was considering an intervention for your drinking," Brady said. "But then I watched you tonight. And you acted drunk the way you always do, but you didn't actually drink much. Why would anybody pretend to be drunk when they're not?"

"You're the one who needs me to be drunk, Brady." Ty didn't know where that came from, but he didn't take it back. "And you know me. Always happy to oblige."

"I don't really care if you're drunk at the dinner table," Gray said. "As long as you don't start flipping it, we're good. But what's fake drunk all about?"

"I never faked being drunk," Ty managed to say without shouting. He deserved a medal. "You decided I was drunk, and I didn't do anything to disabuse you of the notion. It's not the same thing."

"Ty," Brady said, in a very careful, extraordinarily placating tone of voice.

Speaking of jackholes.

"Just stop," Ty told him. "Whatever this is. I don't need

to talk. I don't want to talk. I have nothing to talk about."
He looked from Brady to Gray, then back again. "Okay?"

"I told you," Gray said, ostensibly to Brady, though
his gaze was steady on Ty. "He doesn't want to do anything but storm around, telling himself what a martyr he
is, when I'm pretty sure that's not the word most people
would use for a man who walks away from his own kid."

Ty lurched forward, something he hadn't known he was
holding tight snapping. And filling him with sheer, pure
fury, bright and hot.

"I didn't walk away from my kid," he threw at Gray.

Brady let out a laugh Ty found hostile. "You literally
turned around and walked off into the night."

"You have no idea what you're talking about." He shook
his head, but that didn't clear it. Nothing had in months.
And that pulsing ache was back. "I'm protecting him."

"From what?" Gray asked. "A father? He's not going to
thank you for that."

Ty fought to put all that fury back where it belonged,
deep inside him and locked up tight. "If we could go back
in time and have someone protect us from ours, I'd do it
in a heartbeat."

"Like Mom?" Brady asked mildly. And not for the
first time, Ty had to reassess his baby brother. Who didn't
sound anything like a baby then. "Who you've apparently
forgiven for leaving us with him."

Ty shook his head while the fury—and worse, the
sadness—that he'd locked away since the night everything
had fallen apart, again, roared through him. It made him
unsteady. It made him feel like someone else. "I haven't
forgiven anybody."

"And why would you?" But the way Gray was looking

at him, with a kind of grim understanding that boded only ill, made Ty more unsteady. "Start forgiving people and you might have to get around to forgiving yourself. And then what?"

"Why would I need to forgive myself?" Ty gritted out.

But Gray only shook his head. "I can't answer that."

Ty rubbed at his jaw, appalled to find his hand was shaking. Great. That was what every bull rider wanted most—a lack of control over his own body. "I really appreciate the two of you ganging up on me tonight. It's exactly the kind of Everett family send-off I should have been expecting. What a treat to relive ancient history."

"You're not Dad."

Brady threw that out like a bomb.

It exploded like one.

Everything shuddered to a stop. The world. Ty's heart.

When he'd been positive he'd gotten rid of that thing a long time ago.

"That's where you're wrong," he told Brady, biting off the words. "I had a chance to prove that I was nothing like him, and I failed it. Spectacularly."

"Oh yeah? What did you do?" Brady challenged him. "I assume you're talking about Hannah. Did you beat her up? Call her names? Treat her so badly she packed up and took off in the middle of the night?"

"Of course not." Ty's head was pounding. "But I can't really say that. I can't remember."

His confession didn't have the effect he was going for. Brady rolled his eyes. Gray looked . . . the way Gray always looked. Stern. Steady.

"Whiskey?" Brady asked.

"I wish it were whiskey," Ty threw at them. "A man who

drinks too much whiskey can always stop. But no. I can't remember what happened the night I got stomped." He pulled in a long, deep breath. "Or anything that happened for two years or so before that."

Both of his brothers were silent.

Brady blinked. "You mean . . . ?"

"You don't mean you can't remember something." Gray frowned. "You're talking about actual, medical memory loss."

"It's not unusual after an accident like mine," Ty said stiffly. "But there's no medical reason for me not being able to remember. The actual accident, sure. That's probably gone forever, and God bless. But the two years before that? My mind has taken it upon itself to basically erase my entire relationship with Hannah. Why would it do that?"

Both of his brothers stared back at him.

"I'll tell you," Ty said, because he didn't want them to throw out excuses when he knew the truth. "Because I don't want to remember what I said. What I did. Because I turned into Dad."

"You're not Dad," Brady said. Again.

And with more force this time.

"Even he knew I was." Something was cracking open inside of Ty. Huge and terrible. "He always knew. He could see himself in me."

"He could see himself everywhere he looked," Gray retorted. "Because the only thing he ever thought about was himself. Not because he was right."

"There is a poison in me," Ty told them, matter-of-factly. "There's no getting it out. You want to talk about the Everett family legacy? Well. It's a disease. And I have it."

There were too many stars. He could feel the mountains, brooding out there. Waiting. And the land. Always the land, stretching out so far it should have felt wide open, but Ty knew better now. It was a chokehold.

But he didn't mind anymore. He'd surrendered. He'd accepted what he couldn't change. Wasn't that supposed to be a good thing?

"You don't wake up one day and become Dad," Brady argued. "It's not a disease. There's no Dad virus. It's a choice he made, every single day of his life. That's not poison, Ty. That's a preference."

Gray's gaze was hard on Ty's. But in a way that made Ty want to meet it. Rise up to it, maybe. He didn't. He couldn't.

"If you don't want to be like Dad, it's real simple," Gray said. "Don't be like him."

"It's not that simple."

"It really is," Brady retorted. "Why are you letting dead men tell you who you are?"

Ty about staggered back at that one. But he held his ground. Somehow.

"I appreciate this," he told them, when he could speak. "I really do. Go Team Brothers. Now if you'll excuse me, I have to get my stuff together. Because I'm still leaving early in the morning, despite this charming conversation."

He turned and started across the yard.

"Ty." Gray's voice stopped him. But Ty didn't turn back around this time. "One way or another, you're going to get off that bull."

"That's the plan," Ty said. To the night as much as his brothers.

"And when you do, you're still going to be the man

who walked away from his own son," Gray said. A pitiless sucker punch.

"Thanks, Gray." Ty even grinned, though there was no one to see it. "I appreciate that."

"You'll be no different from Dad," Gray continued. "And not because you're poisoned. But because you're afraid."

Ty couldn't speak. He couldn't come up with a response to that, mostly because he couldn't argue the point. He shook his head and kept walking.

"When you decide to be like Dad, that's not his fault," Brady said, his voice following along no matter how Ty tried to get away from it. No matter how he tried to pretend he couldn't hear it. "He's dead. You choose to follow in his footsteps and that's all on you."

21

Hannah sauntered on into the rodeo like it was runway.

Her own, personal runway, to be more precise.

She'd outdone herself. Her dress boots were vintage and gleamed from beneath the perfect hem of her jeans. Her blinged-out western style shirt was tucked into a simple belt with a buckle that could blind a man at ten paces. Her earrings matched the bling on her neckline. She hadn't kitted herself out like she was heading into a competition with the rest of the girls in the queen's program. Hannah had dressed herself like she'd already won.

Because, of course, she had.

This particular rodeo's crown, in fact. Twice.

When she'd run off from the rodeo instead of waiting to be kicked out, she'd naturally taken her crowns with her. It was possible there were girls who would find it tacky to walk into a job arena they'd already left, wearing the uniform of their disgrace, but it turned out, Hannah wasn't one of them. She'd attached her glorious Miss Rodeo Forever crown to her black felt hat, bobby pinned her hat to her hair, and was prepared to fight anyone who tried to come for it.

Well. A rodeo queen didn't fight. Not with her hands, anyway.

Hannah smiled wider and adjusted Jack on her hip.

Not content to merely outdo herself, from crown to curls and all the way down to her favorite pair of boots, Hannah had made certain that Jack was all dolled up like a miniature cowboy. Just like his daddy.

And like every other rodeo she'd ever walked into, Hannah's nerves took her over while she was still outside. Her stomach twisted. Her heart rate soared. But the moment she walked toward the private competitors' entrance, she felt her usual cool settle down over her.

The wider she smiled, the calmer she got.

Tonight, she couldn't help but call that a blessing.

Because Ty might have come here to reclaim a slice of his former glory. But she was here to claim him. And her family. And while she was at it, the happy life she felt certain they both deserved.

She moved through the back corridors of the rodeo complex, smiling and waving at all the familiar faces, but not stopping. Members of the rodeo committee who did double takes. The stock contractors who still loved it when she called them *sugar.* The barrel-racing girls who always stuck together the same way the rodeo queens did, but actually smiled at her tonight. The bronc riders she knew by name and statistics, the steer wrestling partners, the flustered local livestock people . . . It was as if she were walking some kind of gauntlet.

But unlike when she'd been pregnant, alone, and afraid, Hannah was ready for this gauntlet tonight. She kept her head up high, the better to flash her crown. She kept her smile in place. And she defied anyone to look at the cute, chubby boy on her hip and not fall instantly and permanently in love.

"Why, Miss Hannah," came the deep, Texan drawl Hannah knew well. "I didn't expect we'd see you around here again."

Hannah had almost made it to the corridor that ran back to where the competitors were getting ready. She'd timed her arrival for after the opening and the anthem, hoping she'd avoid something like this. She could hear the announcer out in the ring and the crowd cheering and stamping their feet.

But there was no shrugging off Buck Stapleton. He was the president of the Rodeo Forever Association and prided himself on his hands-on approach to the running of his national rodeo, from the dirt to the queens' program to the bull riders' rankings and back again. He was also the individual most likely to be personally offended by the personal life choices of the girls he crowned queen.

Unlike other national rodeo queen reigns that stretched over the course of a calendar year, Miss Rodeo Forever won her crown in May, then spent the summer sharing the spotlight with her predecessor, before assuming her full title in the fall and carrying it on through to the end of the following summer. *Once a Miss Rodeo Forever, always a Miss Rodeo Forever,* Buck liked to say. *It's right there in the name.*

"I guess I'm nothing but a bad penny, Buck," Hannah replied now, settling Jack—who was thankfully still half asleep from the car ride—more firmly on her hip.

Both of them stood there smiling at each other, ear to ear.

Hannah had sauntered straight into a battle. Good thing she'd prepared herself for a war.

"Now, Hannah, I know you haven't been here in a while, and it looks like you have an excellent reason for that right there on your hip." Buck stopped in the middle of his chummy, fatherly performance to chuck Jack under the chin. Jack, already no fool, recoiled into a pout. "Isn't he a cutie? But you know that when you dropped all your commitments, we had to go ahead and crown another queen."

"I had heard that."

"The show must go on, darlin'. And it has. Now, what I can't figure is what you're doing backstage tonight, with that crown on your head."

"I did win the darn thing," Hannah replied, and the real contest, it turned out, was to see which one of them could get deeper into their drawl while simultaneously flashing a brighter smile. By her count, they were neck and neck. "In fact, as I recall, you put it right there on my head. Once a Miss Rodeo Forever, always a Miss Rodeo Forever, am I right?"

Buck let out his trademark booming laugh. Then he sobered. "Please don't tell me that you're here to cause trouble."

Hannah reached up with her free hand and expertly adjusted her crown, though it needed no adjustment. "That all depends on your definition of trouble."

"Now, Hannah," he began.

"I sure have enjoyed this chance to catch up with you," she replied, sweet enough to make her own teeth ache.

"You know the rules," he said apologetically. As if he didn't make all the rules himself.

"I'm not here to get into a catfight about a crown," Hannah said, with the rodeo queen laugh she'd perfected. Sparkly and airy. "But you are currently standing between a married woman and her husband. Is that where you want to be, Buck?"

"Married woman?" He sputtered. "When did you get married? Who did you marry?"

"That's the funny thing about rumors. They're so rarely true. Why don't you and I start one right now." She leaned in while Jack sucked on his fingers, his eyes big and dubious on Buck. "What would people say if they found out that you'd suddenly taken to barring family members from seeing each other before a show? When you have so long prided yourself on upholding the kind of family values that our audience holds dear?"

She tipped her head to one side and smiled sweetly. Buck, his own smile welded to his face to cover his shock, smiled right on back.

"I wouldn't dream of it," he said after a moment. He waved a hand to one side, giving her permission to pass him.

"Thank you so much," she drawled and carried on down the hallway.

"But Hannah," Buck called after her. "While I'm an understanding man, you did break your contract with me."

"I did," she replied, and then looked back over her shoulder. "But you didn't actually fire me from my position based on the rumors going around. What you did do was fill it without taking the appropriate steps, which I believe are laid out in that contract. A glance at the contract terms might make a girl ask herself, who really broke it?"

"I'd hate for this to get legal," Buck said sorrowfully,

which was maybe the funniest thing he'd ever said to her, given he was a lawyer himself.

"Why would we go and bring lawyers into this?" Hannah sighed. Theatrically. "I would love to have a private, personal chat with you about the damage that malicious rumors cause and how I felt I had no recourse than to do what was necessary to protect my family. And how brokenhearted I was that I couldn't ride out my reign. My *personal* feeling is that we should let bygones be bygones. But it's up to you."

They stood there a moment, smiling at each other, before Hannah swung around again and kept going. Battle down, war still to go.

She had every intention of winning that too.

A lot of the guys hung around in the same stretch of corridor as they got ready, out of view of the crowd. There was a lot of retaping of injuries. Shaking out aching muscles. Some men prayed. Others cursed.

But either way, Ty had always kept himself apart from the rest. Hannah sauntered on by the general dressing room, nodding at the men as she passed. She wasn't at all surprised to hear the chatter stop as she approached, then pick up as she passed, but she didn't care about that anymore.

She kept going, peeking into each room on her way. And then, as she knew she would, she found him.

Hannah stopped in the doorway, taking in a bare room with a fluorescent light, one shelf of boxes against the back wall. Ty stood in the middle, doing the stretches he always did before he pitted himself against a bull.

It was the same as every time she saw him. That jolt in her belly. The sense of the whole world screeching to a halt.

It never got old. If anything, her reaction to him was stronger now than it had been way back when.

She could have stood there for hours watching him move, lost in his own world, focused and determined. But Jack made a cooing noise, and the spell was broken.

Ty turned, and Hannah wasn't the least surprised when he scowled at her.

"What are you doing here?" he asked. In that hard, rough voice that made her heart jump around in her chest.

"Oh, you know," she said airily. "Righting wrongs. Saving my marriage. Even reclaiming some glory, as that appears to be the order of the night."

"Did my brothers send you?" he demanded, in a way that would have had her denying it even if they had. "Because I don't really care if any of you understand why I'm going to do this. I'm still going to do it."

"I have absolutely no doubt you will." She moved closer to him, and then, when Jack batted at her in excitement, she held him out. "Go on, take him. He's your son."

Ty looked as if he would rather cuddle up to the bull that was about to try to shake him to pieces. But he held out his hands and took his child, then tucked him into the crook of his strong, tough arm.

She couldn't help it. It made her feel giddy, looking at sweet, perfect Jack cuddled there in his daddy's arms. Especially since Ty was dressed to ride, in those black chaps, black vest, and his cowboy hat low. He looked like every girl's dream of a cowboy come to life. He had always been hers.

The sight of him with the baby they'd made was almost more than Hannah could take.

"I need to apologize to you," she said, with too much

emotion in her voice. Already. "I'm the one who can remember what sex was like between us. I should have anticipated that it would be intense."

His gaze was so dark it burned.

"I don't need you to apologize to me, Hannah."

"And you might be the experienced one, but the only experience I have is you. I should have expected it would all be . . . too much."

"You really don't need to apologize to me for sex," he said from between his teeth. "Or anything else."

She reached into her bag and pulled out the thick envelope Brady had delivered to her. "I also thought, since I planned to be in the neighborhood anyway, that I might as well return this to you."

"Good." He didn't look like it was good at all. She watched him swallow, long and hard. "It will be good to move forward."

"I agree completely." She tilted her head to one side. "I'm not signing it, Ty."

He stared at the envelope, then at her. "What do you mean?"

"I don't want to divorce you," she told him. "I'm in love with you, and nothing seems to change that. I don't think it's going to change. I think this is the deal. You and me. And Jack."

He scowled at her, but he was holding Jack in the crook of his arm, and adjusted his hold every time the little boy squirmed. It was hard to quail properly before the scowl when he was making her heart melt.

"Hannah. You can't be serious."

"Brace yourself, sugar, because I have more to apologize for."

She took advantage of the fact he was holding the baby and stepped forward to put her hands on him. There was a part of her that worried he might push her away. But he didn't.

"I should never have left you in that hospital," she told him fiercely, one hand over his heart. "Just like I should never have let you walk off into the night two weeks ago."

"I told you to leave me in the hospital." He looked like he was in pain. "And I told you to leave two weeks ago."

"You think I don't know what nonsense your father put in your head?" she asked, just as fiercely. "Because I do. You're not a monster, Ty. You never were."

"The stories you told me yourself suggest otherwise."

"You can't remember those stories."

"But you do."

"Ty. I understand. I was freaked out when I found out I was pregnant too." She shook her head, but kept her eyes locked to his. "You did the best you could, but I'm not at all surprised, now, that you reacted the way you did. I forgive you. And you know that's true because I hunted you down. I came and found you. When I could so easily have stayed away."

Something moved over his face, dark and terrible. It tore Hannah up inside. She wanted to take it away from him with her own hands, dig it out with her fingers and take it on herself if that would make it better.

But all Ty did was hand Jack to her. Carefully. As if the child he claimed he didn't want was more precious to him than anything else in the world.

"You're not going to change my mind by showing up here like this." But he sounded a lot like he was talking to himself, not her.

"Are you sure?" Hannah asked softly. "Because I'm in love with you. I'm not going to change my mind on that. The very least we can do is try being a family."

"That word," Ty said, his voice rough and raw. "*Family.* Do you know what that word means to me? Drunken rampages. A black eye for my eighteenth birthday present. The nasty, bitter old man who stood by my hospital bed and told me that he always knew I'd end up crawling back and letting the ranch support me, because that's the useless piece of crap I was."

Hannah wished Amos Everett were still alive, so she could go ahead and kill him herself.

"Family is also your brother Brady, who took me to task for my potential gold-digging ways. And then came all the way to Georgia to remind me that of the two of us, I remember how to love."

"Hannah . . ."

"Family is your brother Gray," she continued, as if she didn't hear him. "What would have happened to him and Becca if Gray never decided take a chance on the one thing he didn't believe in?"

"I can't do this." Ty's voice was so dark. She could see that darkness in him, and it made her want to cry. "You were right to be upset. I may never remember what happened between us. And something tells me that's a gift. Because as much as I might have loved you, it didn't prevent me from turning into my father at the first roadblock. You say you forgive that, but what happens when I do it to Jack? What happens when I treat him the way my father treated me?"

"You won't do that."

"I already did."

"You were upset," Hannah argued. "You're the one who's decided that you became the bogeyman, not me."

"Your reaction suggests pretty strongly that I did."

"My reaction tells you that you're not the only one standing in this marriage imperfect and flawed straight through."

"Some flaws and imperfections are worse than others. More dangerous."

"I was raised by my mother, who was never given any reason on earth to trust a man. And didn't. And still doesn't. And sure enough, she handed that right on down. I walked away from you at the first roadblock because I hoped that would save me from heartache. But it didn't." Hannah adjusted Jack on her hip. "Yes, you got angry. Upset. You raised your voice, yelled some. Said some things you probably would have regretted if you'd had time. All that makes you is a man."

"What that makes me is a man who can't control himself. A man like my father. A man who—"

"You weren't drunk. You weren't out of control. You were emotional," Hannah told him. "And I was yelling right back at you. I don't know when you decided I'm a shy, retiring, will-o'-the-wisp of a girl. But I'm not. We yelled *at each other*. It was not a high point in our marriage. But it shouldn't have been the end point either. And that's on me."

He slashed his hand through the air. "I can't take the risk."

"Life is risk, Ty. Love is risk. Everything that's worth anything in this life is risk. If it doesn't hurt, it doesn't matter. If it doesn't make you feel something, why would you bother doing it in the first place?"

"I can't be what you want," he said, simple and brutal. "There's a reason that my brain doesn't want me to remember what happened. Not any part of it. I don't know why you can't see that I'm offering you a lucky escape."

"I don't want an escape." She wanted to scream, but she was afraid it would tip over into the sob she could feel building inside of her. "What do you think marriage is? As far as I can tell, it's a collection of mistakes, strung together by hope and stubbornness. I know I've walked away, but I keep coming back. Isn't that the point? All we have to do is keep coming back."

"Hannah—"

"I love you," she said, and they weren't having sex now. This was no *heat of the moment* declaration. She said it solemnly. Starkly.

The effect on him was like a shattering. She watched it roll through him, over his face, making that big, strong body of his shudder. It made her own eyes damp.

"I don't believe you do," he said.

As if the words were torn out of him.

"You can believe it or not believe it. It doesn't make it any less true."

"Hannah . . ." Ty shook himself. "You don't know how much I wish I were another kind of man, but—"

"Then be another kind of man!" She threw that at him. "Let's say you're right and you're exactly like your father. So what? You choose how you act. Every moment, every day. It's your decision. Decide to be someone else, and you will be."

There was the sound of feet outside, and then a head poked around the door.

"Ty," the young man said, then stopped. He blinked at Hannah.

"Hi, Billy," she murmured. And she couldn't bring her smile online.

"They, uh, need you out there," Billy said nervously, his gaze darting from Hannah to Jack and back to Ty.

"I'm on my way," Ty growled.

Billy retreated.

"This is like déjà vu," Hannah said, and had to wipe at her eyes because she couldn't keep from leaking everywhere any longer. She didn't know why she was bothering to try. "But this time, Ty, I don't care if everybody in this building knows that we're not only married, we had this beautiful boy, and we have a beautiful future too."

"You have all those things," Ty said shortly. "I have eight seconds to get my name back and go out on top."

"And then what?" she demanded.

He was swiping his thick gloves off the floor, and he turned on her, then, his dark green eyes lit up with a kind of fire. "Why the hell does everybody keep asking me that?"

"You have eight seconds," she threw at him. "And then you have your life. What life do you want, Ty?"

He came toward her, then, a dark storm. A fury.

But she wasn't afraid.

And she knew he would never believe her, but she hadn't been afraid back then either. She'd been hurt. Scared, maybe, but of the situation. Not of him.

She had never been afraid of him. She loved him.

He came close, reaching out a hand to grip her by the shoulder. Firmly, but not painfully. Because he was the only person alive who thought he was anything like his father.

Between them, Jack laughed, as if this were all a game they were playing.

"I understand my life perfectly," he told her. "Half the men in my family are good seeds. Gray. My grandfather. Solid, dependable men. Decent, through and through. But the other half are like my father. Like me. And either way, whatever happens, the land swallows us up. Cattle don't care what kind of man you are. Not as long as you feed them. That's what I'm going to do with my life."

"Rage, rage against the dying of the cow?" she demanded, and maybe she was trying to be funny. Lighten things up.

Or maybe she wanted to slap him.

But it didn't matter either way.

"This can never happen," Ty told her with grave finality. "This—us—" And his fingers gripped her harder, reminding her how it had felt in the bunkhouse when he'd surged inside her, making them one. Making her his all over again, like they were new. "This never should have happened. This is wrong. It's all wrong."

That would have killed her eighteen months ago.

But Hannah was a different woman now.

Jack fussed and she shushed him, but her eyes were on Ty. She lifted up her hand to cover his, holding him in place.

"I need you to remember this," she told him, solemn like a vow. "This is us. This, right here. This is how we hurt each other. But then, this is also how we made this beautiful little boy. This is big and unwieldy, and it can feel terrible sometimes. It can also be magical. This is who we are. This is love, Ty. Life. And I don't care what you say to me, I'm not giving up on you. Not again."

"Ty!" came the voice in the hall. "You need to get out there!"

"I have to go."

He bit the words out as if they didn't make sense. As if they were too big.

"Eight seconds," Hannah said to him, her voice catching. Just a little. Just enough. "Eight seconds of glory, Ty. And then, if you want it, this. Your whole life. Right here waiting."

But he already looked broken as he swaggered away, off toward that destiny he wanted so badly.

No matter what he had to leave behind.

22

Everything narrowed to the corridor. The world shrunk down to his heartbeat and the sound of his boots on the floor.

Ty had showed up at the beginning of the night, walking out to dramatic lead music and tipping his hat to the crowd as the announcer hyped up the so-called showdown that would be taking place later.

Later was now.

He couldn't feel much from what he remembered of his life. He was missing those crucial two years. He'd lost Hannah in there somewhere. But what he knew, what he felt, what he was absolutely sure of was that he'd spent the last seven-plus months preparing for this moment.

Out in the ring, the crowd cheered as he made his way to the chute. He wished the stands were less full tonight. Or that the cameras weren't trained on Gray and Abby, sitting up there looking uncomfortable while the rodeo's favorite clown did a song and dance out in the middle of the ring to "We Are Family." The camera panned to Becca and Brady. Becca looked nervous. Brady glowered.

Family. That word. But Ty told himself he didn't feel anything.

He concentrated on the chute. The ornery bull waiting for him. His rope and his seat.

I love you, Hannah had said.

But he told himself he couldn't feel that either.

And anyway, he couldn't think about these things. Not now. The crowd was chanting his name. Tough Luck, solid and pissed beneath him, snorted and danced like the demon he was. Ty didn't remember the last time he'd done this, but he remembered the years and years he'd spent doing exactly this. Hundreds of bulls. In hundreds of places.

In eight second increments, if he was lucky.

The funny thing was, everyone thought he was after glory. Maybe he'd told himself that too.

But here, now, while the adrenaline sizzled through him and everyone waited for him to give the sign that he was ready, he knew it wasn't glory he was after.

It was that second chance.

He wouldn't get one with his father. He would never be the son Amos had wanted him to be. Maybe nobody could.

He'd had a second chance with Hannah. His wife. But she'd been lying to him the whole time, and there was a little boy in the mix, and he couldn't change the fact that he'd let her go off and have his baby on her own. It didn't matter what the extenuating circumstances were, he couldn't fix them.

But he could do this.

He gave the sign. The gate swung open.

And Tough Luck hurled himself out into the ring.

For a split second they were in the air, two thousand and then some pounds of flight, pure rage on the part of the bull, and an icy determination from Ty. He felt the shift, the way he always did. His body taking over and doing what it was best at, what it knew well. How to sit. How to grip the rope with one hand while his other stayed in the air. How to hold himself to avoid getting shaken right off.

Ty knew by now that his rides were always the best when he surrendered to it.

But Tough Luck's angry flight ended with a powerful wallop when they hit the ground.

Ty's temples lit up on impact with that same ice-pick headache.

And everything came flooding back.

"One second," the announcer shouted to the crowd.

Ty remembered that hot summer's day up in Bozeman. He remembered walking into the ring, dust on his shoes and sleepy from the previous night's carousing, on his way to do a spate of glad-handing with the sponsors. He'd looked up toward the stands, and there she was, trailing along with a pack of girls in the queens' program. He was aware of them, but all he saw was Hannah. Blue eyes, blond curls, and the sweetest curves he'd ever seen.

He'd looked at her, and it was like something walloped him on the back of the head. He'd felt his ears ringing. He'd felt his heart skip a beat.

He'd almost walked into the side of the ring.

She stared back at him like she'd never seen a man before. Then she looked away.

But it was too late.

It had happened that fast.

"Two seconds," the announcer cried, the crowd with him.

Ty remembered when he'd finally gotten her to go on their first date. How scared she'd been that night. Scared and exhilarated with it, sneaking out of that trailer she shared with her dragon of a mother and bolting across the dark to meet him.

She'd slid into his truck, laughing wild like a kid as she'd ducked down and let him drive them away from anyone who might recognize them. He hadn't even touched her then, and still she'd seared herself into him.

It was that laugh. And it was the way she listened to him as they sat together in a diner in the next county over. Really listened, and was never satisfied with his set, pat answers to anything.

Ty had spent his whole adult life hiding right there in plain sight. But he'd never been able to hide from Hannah.

"Three seconds!"

He'd turned into that man he couldn't conceive of bit by bit. Date by date. Every time they'd crossed paths, it had grown. Deepened.

Until what was inconceivable was life as he'd known it without her.

Ty remembered lying in the dark on one of their night picnics, the only way they got to spend more than a few moments at a time together. He'd been lit up, on fire, because she was lying next to him. Because their shoulders brushed.

He remembered wondering how it was possible he could feel *so much* from so little.

Sometimes he'd thought she was a witch. Sometimes he'd thought he was going crazy.

He'd told himself he had to end it, and fast, because he didn't know what was happening to him or where this could possibly go.

Hannah was everything he wasn't. Pure, sweet, innocent. Smart, tough, honest.

He should have run in the other direction.

But he never did.

"Four seconds! Halfway there!"

He remembered their first kiss. Down in the bowels of some arena, away from prying eyes. Hannah had said a prim hello the way she always did. Ty had grabbed her hand, the way he shouldn't have.

He'd held her against him, both of them panting because it hurt to want like that. It was like falling face-first onto a bed of knives, by choice.

But he kept choosing it.

They could both hear the cheers from the ring. But they were a secret, and they were all alone, and he kissed her for the first time there, fitting his mouth to hers so carefully.

Like she might break.

But instead, she surged against him, honey and fire, and demanded he teach her how to kiss him back. Without saying a word.

That was the trouble with Hannah. She was sweet like sugar, and then she was a tornado, and he had no control over either.

He'd pulled away, and both of them were out of breath. And laughing, because it was too much. Too big. He'd rested his forehead on hers.

You're going to kill me, baby, he'd muttered, wrestling himself back under control. *And right now, I don't think I'd mind.*

She tipped her face up and ran her fingers over his mouth, smiling her real smile when he pretended to bite at them.

Don't die, she'd told him. *I don't think I could do without you.*

"Five seconds, folks!"

Ty remembered.

He remembered the way they'd fought, which was hardly fighting at all by his measure. No violence. Just those tense, upsetting conversations about what they wanted out of life.

I can't be the kind of man you deserve, he'd told her, more than once.

Maybe I deserve to have the man I love, she'd replied. *Who loves me back.*

That had worked its way beneath his skin, because Ty didn't know how to do that. Any of that. He didn't know what love was.

All he knew was, he couldn't let her go.

It would be so easy for me to sleep with you, to throw you a bone and hope that would keep you, she told him on another night, this time in the back of his truck. They'd both been staring up at the stars, their hands linked after too much kissing had nearly wrecked them both.

Am I supposed to talk you out of that? he'd asked. Grumpily, because he was a grown man and this girl was going to break him. Had already broken him.

She'd turned over, propped herself up on her elbow, and regarded him. All solemn eyes and her mouth swollen from his.

Is that how you want me, Ty? she'd asked quietly. *Do you want* me, *or do you want the girl who would betray herself because that's easier than staying the course?*

"Six seconds!" the crowd cheered.

He remembered walking down what aisle there was in the chapel they'd found in Vegas. He remembered how bright her smile had been and how silly his had been in return.

He couldn't remember what the officiant had said or any of the vows he made in return.

Because all he could see was Hannah in the blue dress she'd brought for a dinner out that had turned into a wedding gown, all that love for him pouring out of her.

His wife. *His.*

Deep inside, he still had all those same shadows, all the same doubt, but there was something about Hannah that made him believe he could handle them.

He'd been determined he could handle them.

He'd carried her over the threshold of their hotel room, and he'd laid her down in the wide, soft bed.

And he'd made her his in every way he knew how.

He'd told her he loved her, over and over again. But he hadn't known how to tell her that she was the one who owned him, body and soul.

Or how much that had still scared him.

"Seven seconds!" The crowd was roaring. "Here we go—"

He remembered their fight that night, tucked away in a forgotten room in the back of a rodeo complex a lot like this one.

Pregnant? How the hell can you be pregnant?

Well, Ty, I'm no expert, but I imagine it came about in the usual way, she had drawled right back at him.

As she'd told him tonight, there had been no wilting.

She hadn't been cowering in a corner while he stormed at her and broke things.

On the contrary, she'd looked a lot like she might swing on him.

Maybe you forgot, but I was the virgin in this scenario, she'd thrown at him. *I thought you were taking care of the practicalities.*

I did take care of them. I don't understand how this happened.

If you take a peek around at the whole of the planet, I'm confident you'll find all kinds of people wandering around, miraculously alive because the practicalities don't always work.

This is a disaster, he'd shouted her.

That was when she'd cracked. But even then, she hadn't crumpled. She'd stood tall.

I don't know that I would call it a disaster, exactly, she'd said. *We're already married. Granted, that's a deep, dark secret, but I imagine it will come to light one way or another when I start showing. And of course, once that happens—*

This can't happen, Hannah.

This was always going to happen, she had said. Then she'd stared at him, her eyes getting bigger by the second. *Wasn't it?*

And he remembered.

He remembered everything.

What he'd said, which hadn't been kind or careful, but hadn't been cruel either.

More than that, he remembered what he'd felt.

Terrified.

From his head to his toes, absolutely terrified that no

matter his best intentions, he would end up doing to his own child what his father had done to him. What his father still did to him.

He couldn't bear it.

Ty had been kidding himself with Hannah. That was clear to him, then. He'd been playing with fire, and now they were both burned, and there'd be an innocent child in the middle of it.

How could he have been so thoughtless? So damned reckless, the way he'd been accused of being his whole life?

He remembered.

He'd stormed out of that room, not because he wanted to hurt her, but because he was terribly afraid he already had.

"*Eight seconds!*" the announcer bellowed.

The crowd cheered with him, and Ty was dimly aware that everyone was on their feet. He could feel the roar. He got a glimpse of the big screen all lit up and going wild with something like fireworks as his body did its thing.

And he remembered. Everything. Big, small. Not only that, he could *feel* everything that had been behind that glass. It all poured into him.

Love. Loss. Fear. Hunger and regret.

Faith, promises, and Hannah.

It all came back to Hannah.

Because Ty knew the darkness, inside and out. He'd left his father's house to get away from it. He'd done what he could to be nothing like the man who'd raised him, fearing all the while he was exactly the same.

But Hannah was a bright light.

He got his hand free, then took his dive, and he'd spent a lot of time worrying about how he'd do it this time. What if he froze up? What if he rolled the wrong way? Would the memory of what happened last time, stamped as it was on his body forever whether he recalled it directly or not, make him choke this time around?

But while Ty was aware of Tough Luck, all two thousand pissed-off and snorting pounds of him, he'd already stopped caring about him.

He hit the ground and rolled to his feet, and the cheering was so loud, he could feel it inside his bones. He could see people in the stands, up on their feet and chanting his name. All the glory he'd ever wanted and more, and Ty didn't care. It was all noise.

Until he found her, up there in the risers.

It was the same as it had been earlier this summer on the ranch.

It was the way it had been every other time, each and every one of which he could remember now.

The world stood still.

His ears rang.

His heart skipped a beat.

Because she was his lighthouse, beaming out all that brightness everywhere she turned, warning him away from the rocks—especially when the rocks were him.

He couldn't believe how close he'd come to losing her all over again.

The rodeo clown was making his way toward him, and the bullfighters were busy doing their thing, but Ty didn't care about any of them.

He headed straight for her, like his life depended on it.

Hannah had that smile welded to her face, serene and cool and all rodeo queen, and she held their baby in her arms.

And the closer Ty got, the less that smile stayed serene.

He vaulted up the side of the ring, tossed himself over, and stalked straight toward her. He jumped the wide stairs to get to her bench, the crowd parting around him like butter.

"You appear to be making a scene, cowboy," she drawled when he drew near.

He could see the tears on her cheeks, and he knew she'd cried when he'd gotten on that bull. Cried for eight seconds straight, unless he missed his guess. And sobbed when he'd rolled free at the end.

Now her eyes were suspiciously bright, but she wasn't crying.

She was the most beautiful thing he'd ever seen. Then and now. Always.

"I remember," he told her gruffly.

He didn't care that there was a crowd all around them. He didn't care who could hear them. If the cameras were on them. If they were breaking even more rules.

Ty didn't care about anything except making sure this woman, his wife, understood him. "Baby. I remember everything."

Jack wiggled in her arms, but Hannah's eyes filled with something like wonder. And hope. She reached over and lay her hand against his cheek, still wearing the ring he'd put back on her finger in Colorado.

"Welcome back," she whispered.

There were so many things Ty wanted to tell her. So many ways he wanted to show her that he'd finally woken up. Finally come back to himself. Finally found his way out of that dark, and all because she'd loved him straight through to the light.

But they were standing in the middle of a noisy arena. All the lights were on them, all those eyes and cell phones and wagging tongues.

And Ty remembered now, so he knew that too much of their relationship had been conducted in the shadows. So many lies. So many secrets. So many twists and tangles in what was the most beautiful and most simple thing he'd ever known.

He had a lifetime to tell her. He would.

Tonight, Ty had reclaimed his reputation and his glory in eight of the longest seconds of his life. He would give up the reputation and the glory in a heartbeat.

But he'd ride out those eight seconds a thousand more times if it brought him back to her. If it gave him back the love that had changed him.

He reached down and carefully took the baby from her arms, holding his son high against his shoulder.

"Hey there, little man," he said, looking into those solemn, dark green eyes that were a whole lot like his own. "I promise you, I'm never going to leave you again."

Jack squealed in delight.

Ty looked back down to the woman before him, who was no longer making any effort at all to keep her tears from flooding her face.

His beautiful Hannah, tough enough to take him on and smart enough to take her time. Sweet enough to wait him out. And tenacious enough to come back even after he told her to go.

He swept her up with his other arm, hauling her straight off the ground and up against him. She wrapped her arms around his shoulders, laughing a bit as she looked down at him.

"I never want to get so lost again," he told her, a gruff vow. "I never will."

"Ty," she whispered. "I'm always going to find you."

"You won't have to look," he promised her. "I'm always going to be right there beside you. I love you."

"I love you too," Hannah whispered.

Then he took her mouth, kissing her deep and hard, right there in front of the cheering crowd. Up there on the screen, where everyone could see them, and he made it good. Because he was so in love with this woman, he couldn't see straight, whether or not he was riding bulls. And because he wanted there to be no doubt in anyone's mind that she was his, he was hers, Jack was theirs, and this was how it was at the rodeo. And forever.

He kissed her and kissed her, out there in all that bright and beautiful light, because Hannah was the reason he could step out of the darkness at all. She was the reason he wasn't his father. She was the reason he could imagine hoping for something better.

Hannah was the reason. Every reason.

And Ty was never hiding her—or from her—again.

23

The second time Hannah married Ty, at the end of that same gold and bright August, they invited everyone they knew.

They said their vows beneath the shade of the big tree out behind that old barn where Ty had gotten that scar of his. Hannah wore a big white dress. They put Jack in boots and jeans and a freshly pressed cowboy shirt to match his daddy.

Mama and Aunt Bit walked Hannah down the aisle, one on each arm.

This time, when they said their vows, it was in front of both their families and the friends they'd made along the way. And when they were done, they got to celebrate. Without the bittersweet knowledge that they were going to have to hide afterward.

Abby, still pregnant and less okay with it two weeks after her due date and counting, had produced a handful of local musicians, which was how Hannah got to dance with her husband as the last of the sweet summer evening gave way toward a breathtaking Colorado night filled with stars. And all the potential of the life she planned to live with this man. Because God knew they'd fought hard enough for it.

"I love you," he told her as he held her in his arms. The way he kept telling her, as if he had to make up for the eighteen months where he'd forgotten.

Hannah couldn't say she minded.

"I love you too," she told him.

That would be enough. It was everything, all on its own, but there was already so much more.

Buck Stapleton had approached them after Ty's post-win romantic run to Hannah got national attention. He'd had a bigger and broader smile across his face than either one of them had ever seen, which was alarming. He'd wondered if they'd like to do some publicity appearances as a couple to bolster the rodeo's reputation—and capitalize on their pop of fame.

The king and queen of Rodeo Forever, Buck had boomed.

Hannah's initial response had been regrettably unladylike, if thankfully internal.

But she and Ty were rodeo people. They loved it and believed in it, or they wouldn't have given it their whole lives. The rodeo had been their family when their own had let them down. And no one had to tell Hannah that family could be complicated.

Why, Buck, she'd said, all smile and sparkle. *We'd love that.*

Though here, now, as she swayed in her husband's arms on the land his people had carved out of the wilderness, she knew that as much as it would be fun to do an appearance here or there, everything was different now. She didn't want to center her life around it. She had her man, at last. He remembered everything. And they had their own family now. Maybe she would do something with horses. Or wannabe rodeo queens.

Whatever she did, Jack deserved to grow up rooted in the legacy of this place—this Everett land—the way Ty had.

"You keep saying that," Ty said when she ranted something like that in his ear as they danced. "But those aren't really happy memories."

"There's no better magic trick than that," she said softly. "To take the bad memories of your own childhood and turn them into the best memories of your son's."

She tipped her face back and looked at him. "Isn't that the point of this whole life thing?"

Ty kissed her. A soft, public sort of kiss, laced with promise, that made them both smile.

"I promise you, Hannah Everett, that we are going to do whatever we can to make sure that when it comes down to it, there are always going to be more good memories than bad ones," he said. "I'm not going to give up on you again."

"There's no more giving up allowed," she whispered.

Luanne's response to all this had been a surprise. Hannah had called her the day after Ty's big victory at the rodeo, because she didn't have it in her to be estranged from her mother, no matter how mad or hurt she was. That wasn't who she was.

Still, she'd braced herself as she called, expecting the usual dose of her mother's patented acidity.

But to her surprise, Luanne had sounded . . . chastened.

Your Aunt Bit lost her temper with me after you left, Luanne had said.

Had she announced that dinosaurs had appeared on the streets of Sweet Myrtle, Hannah could not have been more shocked. She couldn't even quite imagine what it would look like if Aunt Bit lost her temper.

Hannah, her mother had said. *Baby girl. All I ever want is for you to be happy. I hope you believe that.*

Hannah had believed her.

She wasn't sure that her husband was entirely pleased that Luanne's next move had been to decide that she needed to relocate to Cold River because she'd gotten used to spending time with her grandson and was inclined to keep doing so. And more than that, because Hannah had been right. She didn't need to live her life *at* the citizens of Sweet Myrtle any longer. She didn't need to marinate one moment more in all that spite.

You mean she's going to live in town, Ty had said, sounding only faintly alarmed when Hannah told him the good news. *Not out on the ranch.*

She'd chosen her moment carefully, crawling over him on the couch in their tiny bunkhouse once Jack had gone down in the other room. She settled herself astride him, making him groan as his arms wrapped around her.

In town, Hannah had said, arching into him. *Definitely in town.*

Ty's hands moved into her hair, and he rolled himself against her, those dark green eyes of his glittering with need and love and forever.

Because I'm more than happy to take a few acres over by the river and build us a house. And I love you, Hannah. Madly. But if your mother thinks she's moving in with us, I'm prepared to live right here in this cabin for the rest of our natural lives.

She'd laughed down at him, looping her arms around his neck and sighing as he slid a hand up beneath her tank top. Then all the way down, to cup her bottom.

Mama and Aunt Bit are a package deal, she told him. *They'll find themselves a place to stay in town. Just think of all the extra babysitting. All the things we can do while my mother is there, watching the baby.*

Let's practice, Ty had suggested, reaching between them to find her slick, hot, and ready. Always ready.

And now, they danced.

Around and around, while their friends and neighbors— and neighbors that Hannah hoped would turn into friends, like Abby's marvelous grandmother, and Hope and Rae— were arrayed around them, celebrating. Gray and Abby were dancing after a fashion, laughing about *dancing this baby out.* The Kittredge family took up several tables on their own, and over Ty's shoulder, Hannah could see Amanda, looking beautiful and not at all twelve years old, in an animated conversation with Brady.

She wasn't ashamed to admit that she had used her seamstress skills shamelessly in an attempt to win Becca over again. The result was the gown she wore tonight, which had made Gray wince. A win, obviously. Becca looked sophisticated and beautiful, every father's worst nightmare.

She had even started smiling at Hannah again. Cautiously. But at least it wasn't that fake smile of hers.

She'll come around, Ty told her. *You don't understand what a triumph it is that she's acting like a teenager in the first place. Before Abby came around, she was like a robot. I know it might not feel like it to you, but this is better.*

The truth was, Hannah had been much more worried about getting herself back into Abby's good graces.

Though as it turned out, she didn't need to worry.

I understand, Abby had said when Hannah and Ty returned, and Hannah had come to her to apologize for . . . well, everything. Abby had rested her hands over her belly and smiled. *This baby isn't even born yet, and I would do absolutely anything to protect it. I don't blame you for doing what you thought you had to do, I promise.*

As surprising as that had been to Hannah, that appeared to be the end of it.

Brady had given her sharp nod at the next family dinner. Gray never acknowledged that there had ever been a situation to begin with.

And that was that.

That was family.

Ty dropped a kiss on her forehead now, and Hannah cuddled closer to him. She liked this land beneath her feet. This man's arms around her. Their baby nearby, being cared for by people she trusted. And nothing but their life ahead of them.

"I love that this time around, we can see the stars," she said in his ear. "I missed that in Vegas."

"Colorado, baby," Ty said, and the grin he gave her was all hers. "We've got sunlight in winter, all summer long, and all the starshine a body could take. Just stick with me."

Later that night, Ty laid her out on their bed and came inside her hard and sure, making them both groan with the sharp, sweet pleasure of it.

Jack was staying with his grandmother, which meant that they could take their time. There was no rush after this second wedding. They had no secrets to keep.

There was only this. Only them. Making memories instead of chasing lost ones.

Making promises instead of breaking them.

As they drifted off to sleep, they were tangled all around each other the way they always had been, no matter what they could or couldn't remember.

Their bodies always knew. Their hearts always knew.

Hannah put her hand over Ty's heart, and fell asleep like that, the way she intended to do all the days of her life.

After all, rodeo queens always got what they wanted.

One way or another.

Four thirty came the way it always did on the ranch, harsh and mean and *what is your life*.

But Ty couldn't be that upset about it today. Because his wife, properly recommitted and all, was curled up next to him. Sweet and warm, and this morning, he didn't mind if he made himself late. Because how was a man supposed to resist her when she was so sweet and flushed and adorable and all his?

Ty greeted the day the way a man should, and left her smiling and shaking in their bed.

He expected his brothers to ride him when he finally turned up in the barn. And they obliged him by rising to the occasion.

"You sure you got your memory back?" Gray asked, looking particularly stern. Until Ty looked closer and saw that gleam in his dark eyes. "Because that alarm was supposed to go off at 4:30, in case you forgot. Not 4:45, or whatever time you call this."

"It must be broken," Ty offered. He grinned. "I'll be sure to check it."

"You do that," Gray said, and rolled his eyes.

"He already did the checking," Brady chimed in as he walked by. "If that grin on his face is any indication."

"Keep your mind out of the gutter, Denver," Ty advised him.

After the morning rounds, as they were all headed back to the ranch kitchen to get another dose of coffee, and some breakfast, Ty paused.

The sun was dancing over the top of the mountains. He felt lighter than he ever had.

"I know we're not a family who really talks," he said. Squabble, sure. But actually talk? Not so much.

"No need to start, I hope," Gray said. But he stopped walking.

"I want to thank you," Ty said, sounding stiff because he *felt* all this. He felt everything. It was a gift and it was a curse, and he understood why weak men went to great lengths to numb themselves rather than face all that.

He'd been weak himself. For longer than he cared to contemplate.

But Ty had ridden bulls for most of his adult life. He'd been strong too. What were feelings but one more challenge—and this time, without the broken bones to go with it?

He looked at Brady, then Gray. They'd been raised by the weakest man he'd ever known. But they'd all come out of it strong, in their own ways.

"I didn't know how to be a father, and I still don't, but you're a good example," he said to Gray. "Thank you."

"The secret is, no one knows how to be a father," Gray said gruffly. "My general rule of thumb is: 'Don't be Dad.' It's served me well so far."

"'Don't be Dad' is pretty much my guiding principle in life," Ty replied.

"Amen," Brady agreed. "I'll make some T-shirts."

Ty looked at him next. "And thank you, Brady, for being a good brother. I'm not one myself, so I'm not sure I recognized it, but I do now."

Brady straightened. "Whatever our disagreements"— and he slid a look at Gray—"we're all we've got."

They weren't huggers, thank God. And they didn't shake hands, because that would be weird. They hadn't made any new agreement. This was overdue thanks, that was all. A spot of gratitude on a late summer morning. But they were all smiling, even Gray, as they started toward the ranch house again.

Brady went inside and cut toward his room. Gray followed, going straight to his wife. And Ty stayed where he was, looking through the window. Abby was sitting down while his Hannah moved around the kitchen, laying out plates while Jack played at her feet in his dangerous saucer.

Ty remembered what it had been like to look in on all that love and laughter and feel nothing inside him but the cold.

Now he had everything. He had his brothers. He had his wife and his son.

And the land that had waited him out.

That land was behind him and all around him, and he understood it now. Roots were what he made them. They couldn't choke him unless he let them. They could be gnarled and treacherous, or they could hold up huge trees to shelter the earth for years to come. It all depended on him.

Ty knew what he would choose. Hannah had showed him. Together, they would show Jack.

But right now, he took a deep breath as the sun came up, and he could smell the first hint of fall in the air as the new day dawned. He forgave himself for the darkness inside him, at last, because it had led him here. To love. To joy.

To a beautiful second chance at this rich, sweet life.

Ty had no intention of wasting a moment of it.

"Goodbye, Dad," he said to everything and nothing. The mountains and the sky. "You missed all the good stuff when you were here. You don't get to take any of it now you're gone."

Finally, Ty let the ghost of Amos go.

Then he walked through the back door of the ranch house, kissed his pretty wife, and picked up his perfect little boy, and together they headed straight on into all the gleaming bright tomorrows they could handle.

Hand in hand.